Winning Her Heart

Quills

First Published 2002
Second Australian Paperback Edition 2015
ISBN 9781488766763

First Published 2003
Second Australian Paperback Edition 2015
ISBN 9781488766763

Published by
An imprint of Harlequin Enterprises (Australia) Pty Ltd
Level 13
201 Elizabeth Street
SYDNEY NSW 2000
AUSTRALIA

® and ™ are trademarks owned and used by the trademark owner and/or its licensee. Trademarks marked with ® are registered in Australia and in other countries.

Printed and bound in Australia by Griffin Press

MIX
Paper from
responsible sources
FSC
www.fsc.org
FSC® C009448

CONTENTS

The
Earl's Prize

Prologue

꧁꧂

Joss—1792

My Lord and Lady Tallant had been quarrelling for the best part of two hours, which was an improvement in their relationship, according to the more cynical members of the servants' hall, for normally they barely exchanged a word. The words that were being exchanged now were less than civil. The Marquis's deep tones vibrated with sufficient anger to shatter the priceless vases on the drawing-room mantel-piece whilst his spouse responded in the shrill accents of one who was determined to break the glass in the fine gilt gesso mirror.

'You've never cared a fig for me, yet now I have the chance of true happiness you have not the generosity of spirit to let me go! Well, I won't stay with you! Never, never, never!'

'Cease this foolish prating, madam, and retire to your room until you can view matters in a more reasonable light. I have tolerated your tiresome infidelities for more years than I care to remember, but give you up to Massingham in this appallingly public manner I will not!'

The sound of breaking china greeted this assertion. The whole structure of the house seemed to shiver. The servants, going about their business via routes that took them close to the drawing-room door, shivered with it.

'I *want* you to divorce me, Bevill!'

'Pray do not be so absurd, madam. Now kindly withdraw.'

'I shall run away!'

'Foolishness! I will never permit it.'

'You are all bluster and no substance. You always were! I know you will not stand in my way.'

The drawing-room door was flung open and the Marchioness of Tallant flounced through in an explosion of silks and neroli perfume. She threw a challenge over her shoulder.

'I am going to pack my portmanteau—'

'Do so.' The Marquis sounded bored. 'It will keep you from making an even greater fool of yourself, at least for an hour or so.'

'Massingham will have a carriage waiting for me...'

'If he brings it closer than Oxford I shall have him horse-whipped from my estate.'

'Oh!'

The Marchioness gathered up the cherry-red silk of her skirts in one hand and ran up the staircase, her slippers pattering on the oaken treads, her petticoats foaming about her ankles. She scattered servants before her like corn in the wind. One of her golden curls had come loose from its elaborate coiffure and curled artlessly in the hollow of her throat. Her blue eyes were wild. She looked beautiful and abandoned.

'Out of my way! Where is Trencher? Send her to me at once!'

On the upper landing, beneath the three-light mullion window, a child was sitting. He was playing with a set of toy soldiers, lining them up, and laying out his battle plan with studied absorption. The light from the window lay across him in coloured bars of red, green and gold. The Marchioness almost tripped over him before she realised that he was there. She swooped down on him in a flurry of silk.

'Joscelyne! What are you doing here? Where is Mr Grayling?'

The boy shrugged. His amber eyes swept over her indifferently for a moment.

'I am sorry, I have no notion, Mama.'

The Marchioness suppressed a shudder. It was not the boy's fault that he looked so like the Marquis, but just at the moment it made her feel quite ill. Joss and his father shared the amber eyes of the Tallants, hair of the richest, darkest auburn, and a tawny complexion to match. They had features that were so pure and classical that the Marchioness had once imagined Bevill Tallant to be some Greek god, come to pluck her from her narrow existence and take her to some other, more exciting plane. But that had been nine years before, when she had not actually known her husband at all. Now she knew better, knew him to be a narrow-minded bigot who denied her even the smallest of pleasures with a self-satisfied smile. But never mind small pleasures now— the greatest pleasure she had found in the past months was waiting for her out there, somewhere beyond the lion gates and the double avenue of elms, waiting in a closed carriage to whisk her away from dreary England and her grey existence, dull as the weather. Clive Massingham. She shivered again, this time with anticipation.

It would mean losing her children. Her calculating blue gaze fell on Joscelyne once again as, head bent, he brought his cavalry into play. Such a strange child, with his self-absorption and his martial games. But he would barely notice her absence for she seldom saw him as it was, and soon he would be going away to school.

As for his sister upstairs in the nursery, that puling, puking child—she could never be quite sure who had fathered her but she knew that Bevill would do his duty by the girl. She had done hers by giving him an heir of undeniable Tallant blood. Juliana's parentage might be in doubt, but Bevill would never say so openly.

Dropping to her knees on the step below Joss, she looked her son in the eye. The bitter bile rose in her throat.

'I am going away now, Joss darling, but before I do I beg you to remember this piece of advice always. It is the best thing that I can do for you.'

She paused. The boy was looking at her now, unblinkingly, and it was quite uncanny. She put a hand on his arm and felt the tension in his body through the rich copper velvet of his sleeve.

'Never fall in love, my darling boy. Love is for fools and it will only make you unhappy. Do you understand me?'

There was a pause. The boy gave her back look for look. 'Yes, Mama.'

The Marchioness nodded. She got to her feet. 'I am going away for a space but I will see you soon. Be a good boy.'

'Of course, Mama.' There was something faintly amused in the boy's tone. The Marchioness frowned slightly. It felt odd, saying such things to the child, as though she were giving redundant advice. Joss had always seemed so self-contained.

'Goodbye then, darling.' She patted his cheek. At the top of the stairs she looked back, but Joss's head was already bent over his soldiers again. She sighed. Bevill would never let him join the army, not when he was the heir and there was no spare. Still, that would be none of her concern and already she was late for her rendezvous. She cast one last look at her son, absorbed in his play, and went to pack her cases.

An hour later, the Marchioness had dragged one portmanteau down the oaken stair and her maid, Trencher, had carried the remaining three downstairs, treading heavily on the discarded toy soldiers as she went. All the servants appeared to have vanished and the door of the drawing room remained obstinately closed.

The Marchioness stood in the middle of the white stone floor of the hall and looked around a little uncertainly. Even she could see the ridiculous side of knocking on the drawing-room door to announce to her husband that she was leaving him. After a few minutes, however, that was exactly what she did.

'Bevill, I am about to depart.'

The Marquis was sitting with his back to the door and did not even trouble to rise from his wing chair.

'Then go and be damned to you, madam. Is Massingham here for you? Send a footman to the gates and tell him to drive up to the house!'

'Are you then to let me go so easily after all?'

'Aye, madam.' The Marquis's voice was a low rumble. 'Be damned to you and to all women. Now, get you gone.'

Slightly baffled at her husband's *volte-face*, the Marchioness withdrew and sent Trencher to despatch a footman to the gates of Ashby Tallant. The carriage came, the baggage was loaded, and the Marchioness turned to take a final look at the walls of her prison.

Upstairs at the nursery window, a flash of white caught her eye. Little Lady Juliana Tallant was waving to her. The Marchioness waved back.

Downstairs in the drawing room the Marquis of Tallant replaced the brandy bottle on the small table beside him with a slightly unsteady hand. In the big stone bay window his son knelt on the cushioned seat and pressed his nose to the mullioned glass as he watched the carriage roll away in a cloud of summer dust. The Marquis had kept his son close by in case his errant wife had chosen to snatch the boy away with her. But he should have known better, the Marquis thought heavily. Lady Tallant would never wish to encumber herself and her lover with a seven-year-old boy, not even to spite her husband.

The Marquis stood up and walked over to the window embrasure, where he put a heavy hand on his son's shoulder. The boy seemed to wilt ever so slightly beneath the pressure. He turned his head slightly and his enigmatic amber eyes met those of the older man. Just for a moment, the Marquis thought that he saw an expression there that should never be seen on the face of a seven-year-old child. Just for a moment. But his mind was already cloudy with misery and bitterness and brandy and he dismissed the thought. Really, the Marquis thought, children would do better to avoid any facial expression whatsoever, just as they should be seen and not heard. It was better that way.

The Marquis leaned closer until he could whisper brandy fumes into the boy's ear. 'Listen to me, Joscelyne,' he said to his son and heir. 'Never trust a woman. D'ye hear me? They are perfidious creatures, right enough. Never trust 'em and never fall in love. It will only make you unhappy. Love is for fools, boy, you mark my words.'

In later life Joss Tallant, Earl of Tallant, was to say that he had only ever received one piece of advice that both his mother and his father agreed on and he had lived by it ever since.

Amy—1807

When the carriage came for her, Amy was already half-expecting it. Her mother's most recent letter, determinedly cheerful, had made her suspicious. At fourteen, Amy was adept at reading between the lines.

It had happened before, of course. Several times. There would be the rumble of carriage wheels on the cobbles outside, the muted hum of voices breaking into Amy's sleep, the flare of a light, the urgent hand shaking her awake. To-night it was just the same. When she opened her eyes she saw her mother's face, pale and resigned in the candlelight, and Miss Melville, the headmistress, her expression tight with disapproval.

'If only you could leave her with me a little longer, Lady Bainbridge! Amy is such a bright and promising pupil, but this constant disruption makes any progress quite hopeless…'

Amy dressed and packed her meagre possessions, and tiptoed away. There was no time for farewells. The other girls slept on, unaware and unconcerned, all but for Amanda Makepeace, who had the bed next to Amy's. Amanda rolled over, groaned as the pale light dazzled her eyes, then sat up.

'Amy, what is happening?'

'It is nothing, Amanda.' There was a lump in Amy's throat. 'I have to go. I do not suppose I will see you again...'

Amanda reached out of bed and hugged her tight. She had always mothered Amy, who was two years younger, and now she felt warm and familiar. Amy choked back a sob.

'Of course we shall meet again!' Amanda whispered. 'You'll see...'

For a long moment they hugged each other in silence, then Amy drew back.

'Goodbye, Amanda.'

She knew that she would not be coming back to Miss Melville's seminary and in a way she was glad. The embarrassment was so difficult to overcome. The last time that her parents had taken her away she had been gone a twelvemonth; when she had returned she had pretended that urgent family business had kept her from school. It was scant protection, but in a sense it was true. All the same, Amy had been aware of the sidelong glances and the giggles of the other girls. Miss Melville herself might be discreet, indeed, Amy suspected that her teacher was sympathetic, but the other pupils had family in the *ton*, family who gossiped and stirred scandal and knew all about her father, 'Guinea George' Bainbridge, a compulsive gambler who was perpetually financially embarrassed. There was no escaping the malicious talk and, even with Amanda to protect her, Amy had felt intensely vulnerable. Whilst outwardly she steeled herself against the sneers, inside she withdrew.

Amy had attended several seminaries for young ladies in her time. There had been two whole years at a school near Oxford, a time of relative stability when her father must have been on an extended winning streak. There had been the snatched months at Miss Melville's, a spell at a school

in Bath and almost a year in Hertford. Each time her parents
would send her to a different school where her family history
could be concealed, at least for a little while. Each time the
truth came out and the more spiteful pupils made her life a
misery with their sharp teasing. Each time Amy moved on,
she lost the few friends she had gained.

This time the journey back to London took just over an
hour, for Miss Melville's school was out at Strawberry Hill.
Amy, too sleepy and too disheartened to question her mother,
curled up in a corner of the carriage and dozed. She awoke
as the carriage jerked to a halt.

'Where are we, Mama? Mansfield Street?'

Lady Bainbridge did not reply at once. She made a business of collecting up her reticule and Amy's luggage. In the
pale dawn light her face looked deeply lined.

'No, my love. This is Whitechapel. We are…staying here
for a little while. A very little, until Papa is ready and we
can go to the country.'

'Whitechapel?' Amy flung open the door of the cab and
scrambled down. The hansom had come to rest in a narrow street between high buildings that seemed to scrape the
streaky dawn sky. It was cool, but the air was heavy with
the stench of rotting vegetables, alcohol and something else
more unsavoury still. Amy wrinkled up her nose. Splintered
barrels and crates littered the street and beside one of them
lay a man, deep asleep. An empty bottle lay beside his outstretched hand and a stream of liquid puddled on the cobbles
next to his prone body. A woman was sitting in a doorway
opposite, her dirty red skirts up about her knees and her filthy
bodice barely covering her bosom. She favoured them with
a long, slow stare.

'Mama!' Amy had become accustomed to the various in-
dignities that came upon them through her father's improv-
idence, but this seemed too much to believe. The distance
between Miss Melville's genteel classroom and this rookery
was too great for her to take it in so suddenly. She looked
beseechingly at Lady Bainbridge, but her mother had turned
away to pay the surly cab driver. He whipped up his horse
and left them standing in the middle of the street, Amy's
bags at their feet.

'Mama,' Amy said again, but this time it came out as a
whisper. Two gentlemen were turning the corner of the street
now, flashy and swaggering, no gentlemen at all, in fact. As
they saw Amy one nudged the other and they broke into a
run. With an exclamation, Lady Bainbridge picked up the
bags and whisked Amy through the door of a house whose
wooden signboard boasted the legend: 'Lodgings for Travellers'. She slammed the door behind them and Amy heard
the gentlemen run past, their feet thundering on the cobbles,
their fists beating on the boarded-up windows. Lady Bainbridge was visibly shaking.

The light was dim in the hallway, but the stench of tallow
and rot was all the worse. There were only two doors off
the corridor and Lady Bainbridge now opened one of these,
drawing Amy inside. The room was barely furnished, con-
taining nothing but a frowsy bed and a couple of broken-
down chairs. Lady Bainbridge's hands still shook as they
untied Amy's bonnet and helped her with her cloak.

'It is only for a little while, Amy, just a while. Papa will
be back soon, you know, and then we may go...'

Amy shivered, though the room was not cold. She took
her mother's hands in her own. Lady Bainbridge avoided
her gaze.

'Mama, how long have you been staying here?'

Lady Bainbridge shrugged her thin shoulders. Amy could see that her dress was stained and torn. 'A few days only. Soon we shall be gone again.'

'But where is Papa now?' Amy looked around, but the lodging house was silent. 'Why do we have to stay in this dreadful place, Mama?'

'It is only for a little while,' Lady Bainbridge repeated tonelessly. Her face looked grey. She drifted over to one of the chairs and folded herself into it.

'I do hope you are not hungry, my love. There is no food, you see, but it is only for a little while…'

The suggestion of food made Amy feel very hungry. She was a growing girl and her stomach was rumbling loudly, but at the same time she felt almost sick with fear that they should come to this. The house in Mansfield Street had been small and shabbily furnished, but at least it had been at the west end of town. Amy had no very clear idea of where she was now, but she knew that Whitechapel was no place for a lady. She took the chair opposite her mother and hunched herself up, against the hunger, against the fear.

'Is Richard to come with us to the country, Mama?' She asked. Matters might not be so bad if only her brother were with them.

Lady Bainbridge turned her faded blue eyes on her daughter. 'Why, of course not, my love! Richard is at Eton and must remain there. We could not interrupt his education…'

Amy sighed. She knew that Richard would have loved to have his education interrupted, whereas she—

There was a crash as the door of the lodging house was flung open. Loud footsteps echoed on the wooden boards

of the hall. Lady Bainbridge jumped up, one hand pressed
to her mouth.

'Oh! I wonder—'

The door burst open. A gentleman stood in the aperture,
a real gentleman, larger than life, with guinea-gold hair and
a gold embroidered waistcoat and high shirt points and a
higher colour. Amy leapt to her feet.

'Papa! Oh, Papa!'

His arms closed about her and swung her off the ground.
'There's my pet! Soon we'll be all right and tight, eh?'

He smelled of alcohol and familiar warmth. Amy burrowed close. 'Oh, Papa, I was so afraid! What has happened
to the house in Mansfield Street, and why must we go to the
country?'

'Guinea George' Bainbridge set her on her feet again. He
jingled the coins softly in his pocket. 'No need to fret, sweetheart! What say you we rent a nice house in Curzon Street
instead, and a coach and pair? And you will have a governess or go to whichever young ladies' seminary you choose—'

There was a sharp intake of breath from Lady Bainbridge.
The pink colour had come into her thin cheeks and a sparkle
into her pale blue eyes. She got to her feet and put her hand
tentatively on her husband's arm.

'George?' There was a note of entreaty in her voice and
Amy, swamped as she was with excitement and relief, still
heard it. She was attuned to such things by now. 'George,
you have won again? Oh, you *have* won again!'

Amy saw her father scoop his wife up to him and kiss her
hard. 'I have indeed! A new dress for you, my love—twenty
dresses if you will have them!'

Lady Bainbridge was laughing, crying and scolding all at
the same time. Amy watched her mother as she hung on Sir

George Bainbridge's arm, her eyes fixed on his face like a drowning woman. So it would not be today, or even tomorrow, that their ruin would finally catch up with them, but one day, perhaps...one day... Amy turned away. When I marry, she thought fiercely—*if I ever marry*—it will not be to a weak man, a gamester or a wastrel. I shall marry a man that I can love and respect, or I shall not marry at all. And I shall never gamble. They say that it is in the blood, but I will prove them wrong. Why, I should never even be tempted— not for a thousand pounds!

Chapter One

1814

The Marquis of Tallant did not believe in improving his
home—what had been good enough for his forebears needed
no enhancement from him—and therefore the drawing room
at Ashby Tallant was much the same as it had been twenty-
five years before. Today sunlight was pouring through the
diamond panes of the mullioned windows and its bright light
cruelly accentuated the bald patches on the blue velvet curtains and the threadbare rugs where the pattern had almost
worn away.

Joscelyne, Earl of Tallant, came into the room with an assured step, pausing only as it seemed empty. Then he smiled
a little grimly, for one of the wing chairs had its back turned
deliberately to the door.

'Good afternoon, sir.' He came forward to stand in front of
the fireplace, looking down at the man huddled in the chair.
'I believe you wished to see me?'

'I cannot say I wished to see you, Joss, but I certainly wanted to speak with you.' The Marquis's voice was harsh, a contrast to his son's light and drawling tones. He made a slight gesture and the sunlight flashed on the diamond ring on his finger, a larger version of the one nestling in the folds of his cravat.

'Sit down. You'll take a glass of something? Pull the bell, then.'

Joss complied, then took the chair opposite his father. The Marquis directed the footman to bring a bottle of canary.

'You are well, sir?' Joss enquired indifferently.

The Marquis shifted uncomfortably in his chair. The diamond flashed again as he grasped his stick a little tighter between gnarled fingers. His chin was sunk on his chest, but his eyes flashed sharply. 'I do well enough. Sorry to hear that, are you, boy? You'd be glad to see the back of me, I dare say!'

'Not at all, sir,' Joss said easily. He rose as the footman entered with the wine, and poured two glasses, handing one to the older man. He raised his own in salutation.

'To your continued good health, sir.'

A grunt was his only reply.

'Juliana sends you her best wishes, sir. She is well.'

'She takes after her mother,' the old man said sourly. 'No discretion. I've heard all the tales about her! I even heard that she is making a set for Clive Massingham, like her mother before her! As well that Myfleet is dead and gone and need not suffer the disgrace of his wife's infidelity.'

Joss shifted a little uncomfortably. 'I beg you not to disparage Juliana, sir. If Myfleet had lived there would have been no infidelity. Juliana was happy with him, and now, of course, she is not—'

'Happy, pah! You speak like a sentimental fool, Joss!

Which of us is happy? Are you?' The Marquis's chin sank down on his chest again, then rose, jutting aggressively. 'I hear all about you, my boy! Gambling dens, prize fights, running with Fleet, the worst rakehell in town! Once I had high hopes for you, before that disgraceful episode when you almost ruined the family with your gambling! Since then you have gone from bad to worse. Why, only last month I was obliged to pay off that blackguard Avery, who swore that you had debauched his daughter—'

'That was unfortunate,' Joss agreed smoothly.

'Aye, unfortunate that I had to part with a considerable sum to keep him quiet!'

'You should not have troubled.' Joss took a sip of his wine. 'I was scarce the first to debauch Angela Avery. Her father must be making a fortune!'

The Marquis flushed puce. 'Maidservants, landlords' daughters, virgins, widows and wives, they are all the same to you!'

'I beg you to be calm, sir.' Joss's drawl was even more pronounced. 'You are getting yourself in a taking over nothing. My exploits are nowhere near as dramatic as you have heard tell. Why, I am even known to attend the occasional tediously respectable ball! I fear your spies have overstated the case.'

The Marquis waved an impatient hand. 'Then it will not be difficult for you to fall in with my plans. I have decided I can tolerate no more of this wild behaviour. Scandal after scandal, dragging the family name into the gutter! You have brought it low—well, now you must redeem it!'

'You must be desperate indeed, sir, if you see me as the saviour of the family honour,' Joss said. 'In what way is this miracle to be achieved?'

'No need for your odious sarcasm, boy.' The Marquis

coughed a little and dabbed his handkerchief to his thin lips. He took a draught of the canary wine and sat back with a sigh.

'Needs must that you should marry, Joss. You are nine and twenty, after all, and we need an heir for Ashby Tallant. If you were to wed a charming, accomplished girl, settle here in the country and raise your brood, much of the past might be forgotten. What do you say, eh?'

'A conformable wife and a house in the country...' A mocking smile touched Joss Tallant's firm mouth. 'How deadly dull! No, I thank you, sir. The idea holds little appeal to me.'

'It was not a suggestion,' his father said, an echo of the Tallant arrogance in his tone, 'it was a command! You *will* marry creditably!'

Lines of amusement crinkled briefly at the corner of Joss's eyes. He rose languidly to his feet. 'As a gambling man, I would have to advise you that that is not a safe bet, sir.'

'Be damned to you, boy!' The Marquis grasped his stick and hauled himself to his feet, glaring at his son, his words spitting from his lips. 'You will do as I say! I shall disinherit you else—'

'I do not believe you able to do that, sir,' Joss said mildly.

'Be damned to the entail! I'll leave every last unsecured penny to your cousin Roger! You may have the estate but you'll not be able to keep it! I'll cut your allowance and see how you manage to gamble without that! Then you will need to marry—aye, and an heiress into the bargain!'

'Pray do not make yourself ill on my account, sir,' Joss murmured, putting a hand out to help his father. 'You know I shall go my own way.'

The Marquis subsided into his chair like a collapsing sack

of grain. 'Be damned to you,' he said again, but the venom had gone out of his words. 'You may marry the first female you see for all I care!'

'A whimsical idea, sir,' his son murmured. A gleam came into his amber eyes. 'Perhaps I may do precisely that. Your servant, sir.' He made an elegant bow, which received no acknowledgment, and went out into the hall. A manservant passed him his cloak, hat and gloves. There were no housemaids polishing the banisters, which was perhaps fortunate for Joss's matrimonial plans. He noted the absence and allowed himself a smile.

His curricle was brought around. It was a fresh May morning and before he ascended, Joss stood looking down the double avenue of elms and away across the parkland. The country. What a damnable place. He would return to town at once.

The journey back was uneventful. The first female he saw was the landlady of the hostelry where he stopped to change horses and partake of a pint of ale, but she was already spoken for and the landlord was built like the proverbial brick privy. On the whole, Joss was grateful. It had been an odd, quixotic notion, but he was prone to act on such ideas sometimes. It made life a little less tedious.

'Amy, dear,' Lady Bainbridge said gently, 'do extinguish the second candle. Two candles are quite unnecessary where one will do! Why, I am able to see to read by the light of a single candle so I am sure that you can see to sew just as well.'

Amy put down her knotting and leaned over to extinguish the candle that was on the chest beside her chair. A thick smell of wax and smoke filled the air, making her head ache a little. Her eyes ached also;

two candles in the parlour had been barely adequate to light her work and one would certainly not do, particularly as it was on the mantelpiece directly behind Lady Bainbridge's head. Her mother was holding her book up to the light and squinting at the page in a manner that Amy knew could not be good for her eyes, regardless of what she said. She was not entirely sure when Lady Bainbridge had become a miser but the habit was now deeply engrained.

· Amy folded her work up neatly and stowed it away in the wooden chest with the shuttle and thread. She had been adding a knotted fringe to an old shawl in the hope that it would make the garment look a little less worn. The thread was a deep ruby colour and her knots were rather pretty, like a string of red beads. Even so, Amy did not delude herself that she had done any more than make a tired old shawl look slightly less frumpish. She had not had any new clothes for several years and had been obliged to titivate her existing ones with lace and ribbon in an attempt to look presentable. The results were not always a success and in more modish company Amy knew she looked a fright. On the other hand, there were very few occasions on which she was required to look presentable, for she seldom went into society.

'I think I shall retire, Mama.' Amy stifled a yawn. The evening had been much like any other. She had taken dinner with Lady Bainbridge, picking over a meal of mutton stew that would have been barely adequate for one and certainly could not stretch to two. After that they had retired to the parlour, the house in Curzon Street being too small to boast a true drawing room, and Lady Bainbridge had read and Amy had sewed, like any other evening during the past two years since Sir George Bainbridge had died. They had not gone out and no one had called on them. Lady Bainbridge discouraged visitors, as she always felt obliged to offer them refreshment.

'Just as you wish, my love.' Lady Bainbridge frowned. 'There is a candle in the hall, is there not? Pray do not take it upstairs. You should be able to find your way up to your room perfectly well.'

Amy reflected that this was true, but only because she had become accustomed to navigating herself around the house in the dark.

'I shall wait up,' Lady Bainbridge said, with a little self-pitying sigh. 'It may be that your brother will be too tired to remember to lock the door securely when he retires and it would not do for someone to walk in off the street and steal anything.'

Amy thought it more likely that Richard's drinking rather than his tiredness would affect his memory. As for a thief randomly selecting the Bainbridge household, it seemed rather unlikely. She suspected that Lady Bainbridge's parsimony must be a by-word amongst the underworld, who knew they would find no pickings in the house in Curzon Street. Before his death, her father had pawned or sold every item of value that he possessed and it was common knowledge that they had no money. The house, let to them at a minimal rate by an old family friend and furnished in the style of thirty years before, was little more than a roof over their heads. At times during the past ten years they had not even been able to afford to maintain it. These days they had two female servants, a cook housekeeper and maid, and one male servant, Richard's valet, the inestimable Marten. They kept no carriage for they could no longer afford to do so. Lady Bainbridge had argued strenuously against the sale of the carriage the previous year, but Amy had pointed out that the horses were so thin from lack of food that they were likely to fall down in the street and make them a laughing-stock. This line of reasoning had so frightened Lady Bainbridge, who could not bear the censure of others, that she had finally acquiesced.

'I wish you would not stay up until Richard retires, Mama,' Amy said now, in her usual mild tone. 'You know that Marten will take care of him and make sure that all is secure. Besides, the gentlemen are likely to be at their play into the early hours. You will fall asleep in your chair, like as not, and wake up with a crick in your neck and your hair in disarray!'

Lady Bainbridge looked most alarmed. She still possessed the remnant of the beauty that had first captured George Bainbridge and she guarded it zealously. Yet everything about Lady Bainbridge was a little droopy, for she had wilted from the moment that she was widowed, and had never quite recovered. Faded brown ringlets fell about her shoulders from a lace cap that sagged a little. Her gown hung off her sparse figure and her mouth, once a perfect bow, turned down at the corners.

'Oh, I had not thought... If you put in that way, my love... Yet I cannot go up to bed, for I require my other book to help me sleep. This...' she waved the book in her hand '...is Mrs Kitty Cuthbertson's book and I use it to keep me awake. It is Mrs Edgeworth's book that I require for night time.'

Amy had long ago become accustomed to her mother's personal superstitions. Lady Bainbridge had her own set of beliefs to supplement the more generally accepted maxims of avoiding walking under ladders and refusing to let the maid turn the mattresses on a Friday. One of Lady Bainbridge's most steadfast convictions was that she had to approach her sleep with a particular routine: no looking over her shoulder as she ascended the stair, her slippers to be laid out pointing

away from the bed, a certain book to read before bedtime…
In these beliefs she was as unshakeable as a mountain.

Amy sighed. 'Where is Mrs Edgeworth's book now,
Mama?'

'Oh I do believe…' Lady Bainbridge patted her pockets
and the chair cushions ineffectually, 'I do believe I have left
it in the dining room. Quite unaccountable, I know, since
it should never leave my bedroom. Of all the unfortunate
things, that your brother should choose to entertain his cronies at home tonight!'

It was indeed unfortunate and it was also unusual. Sir
Richard Bainbridge was seldom at home, preferring to do
his gambling at White's or Boodle's. Amy could not remember the last time that her brother had invited his cronies to
the house in Curzon Street. It was neither large enough nor
grand enough to use for entertaining, but for a small gambling party it was suitably discreet.

'Why not send Patience into the dining room to find your
book?' Amy suggested. Patience was their maid of all work, a
terrifying puritan of a woman, who was as skilled as a lady's
maid as she was diligent with a duster. Patience's stock response to any situation was to disapprove of it. Amy's lip
twitched to imagine what she would make of a group of Richard's hard-gambling friends.

Lady Bainbridge brightened, then drooped a little.

'Oh, yes, what a good idea… Oh, I cannot! Patience has
sworn that she will not set foot in a room with Richard's
friends after one of them tried to pinch her in a…' Lady
Bainbridge looked embarrassed '…in an intimate manner.
She swore that she was obliged to box his ears and called
them all rogues and scoundrels!'

'It was a brave man to try,' Amy murmured, her mind

boggling a little at the thought of the hatchet-faced Patience receiving the amorous attentions of one of Richard's cronies. No doubt the man had been in his cups. 'Well, in that case send Marten in. I doubt that he will suffer such a fate!'

'No, indeed, but Marten has gone to visit his sister this evening and I do not believe he has yet returned.'

Amy bit her lip. 'This can scarce be an insuperable problem, Mama! Can you not read another volume instead?'

Lady Bainbridge looked cast down. 'Oh, no, my love, for you know that certain books are daytime reading and others are for the evening. The two cannot mix, I assure you.'

Amy stood up and picked up her shawl, wrapping it about her. 'Very well, I shall go to fetch your book. It will not take above a second.'

Lady Bainbridge gave a little squeak. 'Oh, Amy, my love, you cannot go in *there*! Why, the gentlemen are gambling—'

'I know, Mama.' Amy's expression hardened. 'I anticipate that they will be so engrossed in their play that they will not even notice me. I doubt that I shall suffer Patience's fate!'

'No, indeed,' Lady Bainbridge looked regretful, 'for no gentleman has ever shown *you* any partiality, Amy! But that is nothing to the purpose. It would be *quite* improper for you to enter a room full of gentlemen.'

'One of them is my brother, Mama,' Amy pointed out. 'Should anything untoward occur, I shall immediately call upon Richard's protection!'

She drew the shawl tight and stepped out into the hall. One candle burned here at the bottom of the stairs and threw long shadows. Amy saw her reflection in the pier glass and thought ruefully that she looked like one of the mummies she had seen at the Egyptology Exhibition the previous year. The shawl was huge, for she liked to have plenty of material

to wrap around her and keep the draughts out. The amount
of heating available to the Bainbridge household was directly
related to the amount of money that Richard gambled away,
so she was accustomed to the cold.

She could hear the sound of voices and masculine laughter coming from within the dining room as she approached
the door gingerly. As her mother had pointed out, it was utterly inappropriate for an unmarried lady to enter the room,
but Amy felt that the sight of her would be unlikely to in-
flame the passions of any of the drunken gamblers inside.
Most were such hardened gamesters that they would like as
not fail to notice her at all, and those who did see her would
dismiss her—as ever—as Richard's dowd of a sister. *Ton* society worshipped beauty and she possessed little.

She had always been a little brown dab of a girl and her
quietness had not helped. During her one and only London
Season, Amy had been so silent that some of the more unkind members of society had dubbed her the Simple *ton* and
after that there had been no more seasons for Amy and no
real suitors either.

She opened the dining-room door and peered in. The
scene inside was much as she had envisaged it. The room
was hot and smoky, from a combination of a roaring fire
and the twenty or so guttering candles that stood about the
table. There was no economy practised here. Presiding over
the bunch of drunken gamblers was her brother Richard, an
empty brandy bottle at his elbow, and a wooden bowl at his
side with a few rouleaus still in it. He was lounging in his
chair, his face flushed, the dice box grasped in his hand.

With one swift glance, Amy identified two of her brother's
cronies, though the other two men in the room were strangers
to her. Lord Humphrey Dainty was so drunk that he looked

in danger of sliding out of his seat. He was wearing a frieze coat inside out, and was sweating copiously in the overheated room. Amy thought that he was likely to fall over in a dead faint soon, his malady brought on by a combination of drink and heat. Mr Hallam, looking even more foolish than Lord Humphrey, was wearing a wide-brimmed straw hat adorned with more ribbons and flowers than Amy had decorating any of her bonnets. She shook her head slightly. She was accustomed to her mother's superstitions, but the foolish rituals that gamblers indulged in were another matter again. And Bertie Hallam never seemed to notice that his good-luck charms simply did not work.

Amy's gaze moved on. The other two men were strangers to her. One was fair, large and amiable-looking. He seemed slightly more sober than everyone else. As for the other man...

The draught from the dining-room door set the candle flames dancing and the man looked up just as Amy was studying him. His gaze fixed on her face. She felt a slight shock go through her, not just because his eyes were the most vivid amber colour that she had ever seen, but also because he was looking at her properly. Amy was accustomed to people looking through her or looking over her shoulder at someone prettier or more interesting. This man's gaze narrowed thoughtfully on her face and his brows rose a fraction. Amy pulled her shawl closer about her and tried to efface herself against the dining-room wallpaper.

At the same time, it was difficult not to stare. The man was older than Richard, Amy thought, twenty-nine or thirty, perhaps, to Richard's four and twenty. Long and lean, he appeared relaxed in his chair, his legs crossed at the ankles, his jacket discarded to reveal a pristine white shirt and a somewhat crumpled cravat. He was quite decidedly the most handsome man she had ever seen, with his tawny complexion and perfect, classical features. There was a huge pile of guineas and rouleaus at his side, in comparison to the others, who had barely any at all.

Then he smiled at her, and brushed back the lock of hair that had fallen across his brow, dark auburn hair, thick and straight. Amy frowned repressively. She hardly wanted to encourage gamblers to take the liberty of smiling at her.

Richard was pushing a new bottle of brandy across the green baize cloth. 'Fill up, Joss, fill up, Seb! You're way behind.' The bottle wavered and almost fell, and Richard looked up and saw his sister. He grinned. The candlelight gleamed on his guinea gold hair. His blue eyes danced.

"Pon rep, what are you doing here, sis? Come to check on my losses, have you? Blame Joss—he has the devil's own luck tonight.'

Amy tore her gaze away from the auburn-haired man, smiled politely and edged around the room. Lady Bainbridge had told her that she had left the novel on the window seat, but now the thick red curtains were closed and it was impossible to tell which of the four windows she had meant. Richard's guests were beginning to notice her now, which was most inconvenient. Lord Humphrey Dainty was lying with his head on his arm and was mumbling, 'Y'r servant, Miss Bainbridge, y'r servant, ma'am...' whilst Mr Hallam had jumped up and attempted a bow, almost overbalancing as the drink went straight to his head. Amy put out one hand and pushed him gently back into his chair. She had known Bertie Hallam since they had been children together and he had proposed to her once a year for the last seven years. She saw no need for either of them to stand on ceremony.

'Good evening, Miss Bainbridge. May I be of service in any way?'

The large, fair gentleman had left his seat on Richard's right and was bowing to her. He had a twinkle in his eye and Amy found herself warming to him. She did not wish to do so—her brother's friends, reprobates and wastrels to a man, had nothing to recommend them. Nevertheless, she found herself smiling back, very shyly.

'Thank you, sir. My mother believes that she has left a book down here and swears she cannot sleep without it—'

'There is a novel on the window seat behind you, Seb,' the auburn-haired man said lazily. 'I noticed it when we came in.'

He made no attempt to help in the search, merely sitting back in his chair and watching them with a faintly mocking smile in his eyes. Amy felt her skin prickle with a curious mixture of awareness and irritation. Despite the thickness and utter respectability of her dress and enveloping shawl, she felt very vulnerable. It was a relief when the large gentleman retrieved Lady Bainbridge's book from behind the red curtain, and presented it to her with another slight bow.

'I believe this must be what you seek, Miss Bainbridge. My compliments to Lady Bainbridge and I hope it helps her to sleep well.' He gave Amy another smile. 'Sebastian, Duke of Fleet, entirely at your service.'

The Duke of Fleet! Amy just managed to school her features to impassivity. So much for the gentleman's deceptive air of amiability. Richard was getting in very deep now, for Fleet and his cronies were inveterate gamblers with a reputation for fleecing innocents. Not that Richard could be considered an innocent, precisely. No son of the infamous gamester 'Guinea George' Bainbridge, who had been following his father's example since the age of eighteen, could be considered a complete amateur. Yet Amy knew her brother had not previously tangled with men like these. The Duke of Fleet and the Earl of Tallant ran with gamblers like Golden Ball and Scrope Davies. These men were dangerous. They would gamble thousands of guineas in one sitting and Richard could never sustain such losses.

Despite herself, Amy's gaze turned to the auburn-haired man. He was still watching her and she clutched the novel to her breast, feeling ridiculously self-conscious. If that was Sebastian Fleet, then this...

The man inclined his head. 'Joscelyne Tallant, at your service, Miss Bainbridge,' he said, quite as though he had read her mind. His voice was warm and smooth and it caused a little shiver to ripple along Amy's nerves. She had heard about Joss Tallant, heir to the Marquis of Tallant. Who had not? Gambling was said to be the least of his vices. Gambling and drinking and women, and other excesses that were only hinted at and never explained. As a young man, the Earl of Tallant had been exiled by his father for incurring monstrous gambling debts and almost ruining the family. Whilst abroad he had created another scandal by running off with the wife of his host and in the following five years his name had become a byword for scandal. The Duke of Fleet was still considered to be an excellent catch, redeemable by the love of a good woman, but no one ever suggested redeeming Joss Tallant. The matchmakers would shepherd their charges away with cries of alarm rather than push them forward for his notice.

Amy realised that the Earl was now looking her up and down with an insolent appraisal that made her heart jump uncomfortably. She was utterly unaccustomed to receiving such looks from a gentleman—generally they were reserved for the most attractive of females and Amy had considered them welcome to such calculated attentions. She twitched the material of her gown into place to cover her ankles. Her dress was a little short—she had had it for four years and she had grown an extra inch at the age of eighteen. She saw a smile touch the corner of Joss Tallant's handsome mouth as he noted the modest gesture.

Richard was shaking the dice box impatiently. 'Your call, my lord! Who'll play?'

'Pockets to let,' Lord Humphrey muttered, sliding quietly out of his chair. 'Tallant's taken m'fortune...'

'Not I,' Bertie Hallam said gloomily. 'Not a damned penny left, saving your presence, Miss Bainbridge!'

'Excuse me,' Amy murmured hastily. She smiled at Sebastian Fleet as he held the door open for her, steadfastly refused to spare the Earl of Tallant another glance, and slipped out into the welcome coolness of the hall.

Lady Bainbridge was hovering like a pale ghost at the foot of the stairs. 'Oh, Amy, my love, you were gone so long I wondered what had happened to you. Are you quite safe?'

'Oh, yes, Mama,' Amy said cheerfully, dismissing the memory of Joss Tallant from her mind. 'I have come to no harm at all!'

'Bertie Hallam did not propose to you?'

'No, Mama. Mr Hallam was too...busy.'

'A pity.' Lady Bainbridge sighed. 'It would have been one less mouth to feed.' She clutched Amy's arm. 'How many candles were there?'

'Oh, two or three,' Amy lied brightly. 'Nothing for you to worry about, Mama.'

'And the fire?'

'Yes, there was a small fire.'

'Why does Richard need a fire in May?' Lady Bainbridge mourned. 'It is *so* excessive!'

'Well, it is quite cool in the evenings, Mama.' Amy shivered in the draughty hall. 'Pray do not upset yourself. I am sure that he is making vast sums of money!'

Lady Bainbridge brightened. 'Oh, so you think so, my love? Indeed, he is just like his father! George was a prodigiously talented gambler, you know, and was forever buying me trinkets and treats on the proceeds of his winnings! Well, if that is the case we may all be easy. Now, did you find my book?'

Amy held the volume out to her. 'Here it is, Mama. It was on the window seat, just as you said.'

Lady Bainbridge peered at the book and then recoiled. 'Oh, but this is the book that Lady Ashworth left with me last week! Oh, no, I positively cannot read this now. It will not do at all.'

Amy took a deep breath, cursing the distraction that had led her to accept the book without checking its author. She took her mother's arm. 'Never mind, Mama. I will make you a cup of milk with nutmeg and cloves just as you like it. It will be warming and most efficacious, I promise you, and if that fails there is always the laudanum. I fear that nothing would induce me to set foot in that room again tonight!'

Later, when she could hear Lady Bainbridge snoring happily through the wall, Amy lay awake and listened to the roars of laughter floating up from the dining room. Trinkets and treats, indeed! It was extraordinary that her mother only remembered her husband's generosity and forgot the other, more painful, parts of being a gambler's wife. Amy had not forgotten what it was like to be a gambler's daughter. She would never forget, could never do so since she lived her life now in a genteel poverty that was a direct result of her father's excesses. Least of all could she forget the scandal and misery of two years before, when her father had taken his own life.

She turned her head against the pillow. Richard was like his father in so many ways, generous but feckless. It made her quite cross with him, but she was also very fond of her brother. He was too likeable for it to be otherwise. It was those others, she thought fiercely, the men of fortune such as Fleet and Tallant, whom she hated. They thought nothing of leading her brother out of his depth and robbing him blind. One day soon Richard would find himself in the same desperate straits that George Bainbridge had been in before him. Amy could not bear the thought, yet felt powerless to prevent the worst from happening. She lived constantly with the fear that history would repeat itself. More than anything she detested the likes of Sebastian Fleet and Joss Tallant for their careless confidence and callous disregard for others. Remembering the cool appraisal in Joss Tallant's eyes, Amy shifted uncomfortably in the bed. She hoped devoutly that Richard would not make a habit of inviting his gambling friends to Curzon Street. She had no wish to meet the Earl again.

Chapter Two

It was past five when Sir Richard's guests departed. The house was quiet. Marten, the valet, locked the door and helped his inebriated master up the stairs to bed. Richard was disposed to sing, for he had won two hundred guineas, but Marten successfully managed to dissuade him.

Outside it was a mild May night with the moon shrouded in cloud. The watch called the half-hour. Lord Humphrey Dainty and Bertie Hallam staggered away down the street, their arms about each other for mutual support.

'Youngsters going home to bed,' Joss Tallant drawled with a contemptuous smile, as he watched their shadows merge like a drunken spider. 'What about you, Seb? Can you stand the pace any better?'

The Duke of Fleet squared his shoulders. 'What did you have in mind, dear boy? Abbess Walsh?'

'I thought so.' Joss adjusted the set of his coat. 'I haven't seen the fair Harriet in a month. It seems time to make her re-acquaintance.'

Fleet fell into step beside him. 'It would be something to do, I suppose.'

Joss shot him a look. His friend's sheer indifference amused him, but then they were both cynical about life, albeit for different reasons. 'No more than that, Seb?'

'A pleasant enough interlude.' Fleet shrugged. 'It would lighten the load of these pockets as well. Damned if I ever met a man more talented at losing than Richard Bainbridge! Tonight was the first time I've ever seen him make a profit at the tables! One wonders how he manages to maintain any style at all.'

'Through the money-lending of Howard and Gibbs, so I believe,' Joss said drily. 'Richard apes his father, but he has none of Guinea George's flair and all his bad luck. That trifling sum he won tonight was more than he has scored in the rest of the year so far!'

Fleet laughed. 'His father was scarcely any more fortunate. George Bainbridge lived so far beyond his income that he was forever having to retreat to his house in Warwickshire whilst his creditors cooled off. Eventually he had to sell that too!'

'I remember that,' Joss said slowly. 'Was it not two or three years ago, when Miss Bainbridge had her come-out? Bainbridge lost all his money and shot himself. The family had to sell everything but for that small entailed estate in Oxfordshire and the Curzon Street house. Come to think of it, that doesn't belong to them anyway. Never saw Miss Bainbridge again until this very evening.'

'Funny little sparrow of a girl,' Fleet said. 'Shame she did not catch herself a husband in that first season of hers, but I'm not surprised she didn't take. Too quiet and drab. Confess my taste don't run to spinsterish virgins, though no doubt the Abbess might tout her as a novelty!'

A night coach clattered past.

'She was always very shy,' Joss said. He was surprised to feel a twinge of pity. Normally he never wasted any thought on the plain girls and Amy Bainbridge was decidedly plain. He had ascertained that earlier—and promptly dismissed her from his mind. 'They called her the—'

'Simple *ton!*' Fleet said, laughing. 'I remember! She never spoke and some thought her a lack-wit. Had a pretty little blonde friend, now I recall. Amanda something or other. I wonder what happened to her?'

'Amanda Makepeace. She married Frank Spry,' Joss said succinctly. 'He had property in Ireland, I believe.'

Fleet stared. 'Devil take it, Joss, you sound just like Debrett! Had no idea you had an encyclopaedic memory!'

'Why do you think I win so often?' Joss asked laconically. 'Truth is, I only remember because Juliana and Amanda Spry were in a way to being friends. I hear that Lady Spry is recently widowed and is back in London. Perhaps you should look her up, Seb! Taking little piece, as I recall!'

'So how is the fair Juliana?' Fleet asked with a grin. If ever there was a gamester who could outplay Joss Tallant it was his sister, Lady Juliana Myfleet.

'Oh, Ju is much the same as ever,' Joss drawled. 'High play, low company... Taken up with Clive Massingham, you know.'

Fleet drew his breath in sharply. 'That thought leaves an unpleasant taste in the mouth! Fellow's a wrong 'un, leaving aside the family connection!'

Joss shrugged uncomfortably. 'I agree, but there's damn all I can do about it! Juliana always goes her own way and, although she'll listen to me, I don't flatter myself I've got much influence. Not,' he added with a shade of bitterness, 'that I can play the moralist. To set myself up as such would be absurd. Saw my father yesterday,' he added. 'Thought the old man was about to wash his hands of both of us! It's a toss up as to which of us he disapproves of the most!'

Fleet chuckled. 'Threatened to disinherit you, did he?'

Joss shrugged again. Some residual respect stirred within him. 'Only natural, I suppose, when I fail to meet his expectations in so singular a manner! He wants me to marry and provide an heir. I can't say the idea appeals. Genteel females are all of a piece—insipid pattern-cards! Could marry an actress or some such, I suppose...'

'Or a harlot,' Fleet said slyly. 'The fair Harriet would grace any stately home!'

They had reached Covent Garden. Two ladies of the night, who were emerging from one of the stinking alleyways, regarded them with curiosity and a lascivious gleam.

'Rough,' Fleet said, shaking his head ruefully. 'Very rough indeed.'

In contrast, the entrance hall of Abbess Walsh's establishment was the epitome of tasteful opulence, the perfect fashionable bordello. The Abbess herself glided forward to greet them with a smile. She was a handsome, well-preserved woman of indeterminate age, who had a reputation for providing quality and novelty.

'Gentlemen...it is a pleasure to see you again.' She shepherded them up the marble and gilt staircase. 'Is there anything in particular that I can offer you tonight?'

'Something different, if you please, ma'am,' Fleet said, stifling a yawn. 'I may be fickle but I get so damnably bored...'

'Of course, your Grace...' The Abbess smiled faintly. She turned to Joss. 'My lord? Harriet has missed you...'

Joss's smile did not reach his eyes. He reflected cynically

that Miss Harriet Templeton's affections were for sale to the highest bidder and at the moment that privilege was his. Still, that suited him well enough. He had been very fond of his previous mistress, and when Marianne had told him that she had accepted a marriage proposal from another gentleman, Joss had found himself surprisingly chagrined.

He had had a certain regard for Marianne. Indeed, he might even have gone as far as to admit that he cared for her. They had been friends in an easy and undemanding manner, and though he had not been in love since his salad days, he had valued her company and missed her acutely. Fortunately there was no chance of such a situation developing with Harriet. Her affection was only as deep as his wallet and Joss was quite happy for the relationship to remain resolutely unemotional.

He strolled down the familiar corridor and went into the room at the end. Miss Templeton was sitting before her mirror, brushing her hair. At the sight of him, her fair, small-featured face lit with a dazzling smile. She dropped the brush with alacrity and sped forward, enveloping him in a sweetly scented embrace, her body pressed softly against his.

'Joss, darling…' she purred, 'I have been pining away for the sight of you…'

Her fingers were already at work undoing the buttons of his waistcoat. Joss shrugged himself out of his jacket and bent to kiss her.

'I have missed you too, my sweet. Shall we celebrate our reunion?'

He picked her up and tossed her on to the bed. Harriet giggled delightfully. She lay sprawled beside him as he pulled his boots off, her face alight with laughter and provocation. Her lace peignoir had come undone and there was little of the voluptuous figure beneath that was left to his imagination. Joss felt his body react but his mind stayed cold. Marry a harlot... For a moment he thought of Harriet gracing the corridors of Ashby Tallant as the new Marchioness, but the thought of marriage to anyone was anathema to him. Whenever he tried to imagine it he was left with the picture of two people hurling insults at each other from opposite ends of their great barn of a house. His mind shuddered away from the thought.

He lay back on the pillows as Harriet pulled him down beside her. For a split second he saw Amy Bainbridge's features superimposed on the painted, pretty face that lay beside him. The image gave him a sharp shock. Little Miss Bainbridge, so plain, so disapproving. In the time that he had been observing her he had seen her distaste for him clear in her eyes, had sensed her dislike, even though she had not addressed a single word to him.

No matter. He did not know what had even made him think of her, except that such transparent innocence was wholly at odds with his current surroundings. He had abandoned such innocence many years ago. It was not for him now. He gave himself up to Harriet's skilful hands and allowed his mind to slide away into darkness.

'It's a shambles, Miss Bainbridge! Sheer, wanton untidiness! However could a body be so disorderly? Your brother should confine his gambling to his club.' Patience's angular face quivered with disapproval. She brandished a kitchen knife at Amy. 'I've tried and tried to remove the wax and the stains but Lady Bainbridge doesn't like me to polish too hard. She says that it wears away the furniture!'

Looking around the dining room, Amy could see that

Patience had plenty of cause for complaint. Twenty candles had dripped their wax on to every available surface and there were dark rings on the polished wood of the table where the brandy bottle had slopped. There was a stale smell in the air. Amy moved over to the window and pulled the sash up hard, letting the fresh morning air into the room. The bright light made everything look so much more dilapidated. Amy sighed.

'Come, give me that knife, Patience. I will scrape the wax off the furniture if you polish it up afterwards. Why, there is almost enough to make a fresh candle out of the leftovers—'

'You sound just like your mama,' Patience said, but there was a hint of indulgence in her voice now. Her expression softened a little as she looked at Amy. 'Though you tell me, Miss Amy, what use it is you making fresh candles from old when your good-for-nothing brother will only melt them all over my table again!'

Amy winced. Patience took the old retainer's privileges to the very limit sometimes. She knew that Richard was not quite a universal favourite. Though petted by his mother and fawned upon by plenty of ladies for his good looks if not his fortune, he had singularly failed to melt Patience's stern heart. She herself could not approve of his gambling but she could also not help but care for him. It was Richard who had been with her through the dark days after her father's death, giving her the love and support that he needed from her in return.

'I know it is very bad of Richard to gamble as he does,' Amy said, trying to think of any mitigating circumstances that might pacify Patience, 'but he means no harm, and if he wins money at the tables then we may all benefit from it—'

'Humph!' Patience's snort made her feelings quite clear.

'The only benefit of Sir Richard's gambling goes to Sir Richard himself! Easy come and easy go, say I! And it's a crying shame, Miss Amy, when you scrimp and save to keep the household running and have nary a new dress from one year's end to the next.' She plied her duster with force. 'You could be quite a pretty little thing if only you were well turned out—'

Amy went off into a peal of laughter. 'Now there you are fair and far out, Patience! Did you not see me when I had my come-out? The best gowns that money could buy and I still looked a fright. Better to save the housekeeping for less of a lost cause!'

Patience put the duster down and came across to her. 'Those gowns did not suit you because they were too fussy. It was all your mama's doing! Look in the mirror, Miss Amy. What do you see?'

Amy peered obediently into the spotted glass. 'I see brown hair without a curl, a pale face and a figure as flat as a board. No potential there, Patience dear!'

'Strange,' Patience said in acid tones. 'I see beautiful fine hair, pretty blue eyes and a figure as neat and trim as you please. You may not be a diamond of the first water, Miss Amy, but you are a little pearl. You just need the right setting.'

Amy blinked at such an assessment from the unsentimental maid. 'Thank you, dear Patience. You are very kind to me—'

'Aye, and you don't believe a word I say!'

Amy did not reply. It was not that she did not believe Patience; more that she did not want to start to believe. With no money and no prospects it would be the height of folly to start dreaming of fine clothes and high society.

Patience picked up her duster again, dipped it into the pot and spread some polish over the nearest brandy stain. Amy leant over.

'Oh, what is that? It smells very sweet.'

'My own concoction,' Patience said, with grim satisfaction, 'so it costs next to nothing. Wax from the bees and lavender from the garden, with a drop of brandy to lift the stain. Nothing like brandy to lift brandy, I always say! A pity that gambling does not work to cure gambling!'

'I believe it is an obsession,' Amy said cautiously, shaking out the curtains to release the smell of smoke. 'Indeed, it seems that no warning example will persuade Richard to stop. Papa was just the same. They say that it is in the blood.'

'Stuff and nonsense!' Patience bent a stern look on her. 'You are the contradiction of that theory, Miss Amy! You do not gamble!'

'No, indeed, I detest it!' Amy shuddered. 'Yet I hear that there are as many great ladies in thrall to the tables as the men. Why, when I went into society they were for ever trying to tempt me to a game of whist or commerce. It was harmless, they said...' Her voice trailed away. There had been nothing harmless about her father's compulsion to gamble, nor its consequences for the rest of the family.

Patience shook her head. ''Twas a shame you did not take, Miss Amy. You could have had an establishment of your own by now.'

Amy prised a stubborn piece of wax off the table. 'I have the ordering of this house in all but name, and a fine challenge it is with Richard's spending and Mama's economies—'

The door opened and Lady Bainbridge came in. Amy quickly swept all the loose pieces of candle wax off the table and into her apron pocket before her mother could see how much waste there had been.

'Good morning, Mama. I hope that the hot milk procured you a good night's sleep?'

Lady Bainbridge cast a suspicious look around the room, taking in the one candlestick that Amy had left on the mantelpiece. Her gaze rested for a moment on Patience, who was polishing the table very gently.

'I slept quite well, I thank you, my love, and partook of a small breakfast. Now, I do believe Mrs Vestey may be coming to visit this morning. She made mention of it when I was last at the circulating library.' Lady Bainbridge subsided into a chair and waved one white hand languorously. 'Patience, when we have callers, please see to it that only tea and biscuits are served. Anything else will be quite unnecessary, and if we have the misfortune of Mrs Vestey bringing a friend with her, please ensure that there is but one biscuit each. Not cakes. Cakes are too rich and injurious to the digestion.'

'Yes, ma'am.' Patience knelt down and began to sweep out the grate.

'Do not throw those coals away!' Lady Bainbridge said sharply, pointing to some lumps amongst the ash. 'They may be re-used! Amy, dear...' she turned her faded blue eyes on her daughter '...I do believe we should go through the accounts again this afternoon and see where we may retrench. I am sure we will find plenty of opportunity.'

Amy sighed. They went through this particular pantomime at least once a month. 'I do believe, Mama, that it would be better to prevail on Richard to increase the housekeeping rather than try to cut back further. Why, he has an income of at least three thousand a year from Nettlecombe, even if it is the only property left to him!'

'Alas, that three thousand a year is nothing to a man of fashion,' Lady Bainbridge declaimed. 'Poor Richard, I am sure that he could scarce scrape by on twice that amount!'

'We manage to survive on a quarter of that sum,' Amy

pointed out. 'There are two of us and we do not repine.' She ignored the snort of disgust that emanated from the hearth, where Patience was still sweeping out the grate.

'Yes, my love, but we have no need of the items that Richard requires,' Lady Bainbridge observed, in kindly fashion. 'Why, he must have a curricle and horses, of course, and money to buy all the odds and ends that a gentleman needs! I do declare, you will be taking the very clothes from his back if you ask for more money! Your brother has a position to uphold in the world, after all—'

'Aye, and his sister has had no new gown for nigh on three years,' came a sepulchral voice from the hearth.

Lady Bainbridge frowned. 'That is enough, Patience! What need has Amy of new clothes? Now, if she were to go out in society it would be a different matter, but Amy has no ambitions for that, have you, my love?' She swept on without waiting for a reply. 'No, indeed, there is plenty of wear in all of Amy's dresses and if there is not she may always add a fringe here and a ruffle there.'

The doorbell pealed. Amy peeked out of the window. 'It is Mrs Vestey, Mama, and I do believe that she has brought Lady Amherst and Mrs Ponting with her.'

'Three of them! How vexing,' murmured her ladyship. 'Patience, I shall receive them in the parlour. Be sure to serve only three biscuits—I shall do without myself.'

Amy, left alone in the relative peace of the dining room, rearranged the good rosewood chairs about the table, moved her mother's armchair to cover a bare patch on the carpet and straightened the curtains. That was better. The room had lost the louche air of gaming that had hung about it and now looked shabby genteel, as indeed it was. As she was. Amy flicked another glance at her reflection. What good was it for Richard to present himself to the world as a gentleman of fortune when the entire *ton* knew that for the hollow sham it was? Once the Bainbridges had had a place in the world and were respected for it, but now Richard lived beyond his means, gambling away what little was left of his inheritance. He would never catch himself an heiress on good looks alone.

Amy closed the dining-room door quietly behind her and went to fetch her coat and bonnet. She had no wish to join Lady Bainbridge and her friends for a pot of tea with no biscuit, but she had plenty of errands to run that morning. There was a parcel of medicines to send to her former nurse, Mrs Benfleet, who lived in Windsor and had recently been ill. Amy wished that she could visit her, but the cost of the medicines meant that a journey was currently out of the question. Then there was the marketing to be done, for Lady Bainbridge entrusted no one but Amy with the purchase of fresh food in a city as ruinously expensive as London. Amy and her mother had had countless discussions about this, with Amy insisting that they could live far more frugally in the country and Lady Bainbridge adamant that Richard needed them to stay in London to look after him. Beneath the pretence, Amy knew that her mother was simply afraid that Richard's gambling would run out of hand without the restraining presence of his family and that they would retire to the country and be forgotten—and starve. It was only their constant presence in Curzon Street that reminded Richard that he had dependents.

Two hours later Amy had managed to stave off starvation for another few days through the judicious purchase of

Nicola Cornick

the cheapest fruit and vegetables that she could find. Lady Bainbridge had suggested that they could do without fruit but Amy had said that she had no wish to suffer from scurvy, like some of the navy's more unfortunate sailors. She had managed to find some good bargains in the market—cauliflowers which had outer leaves that were damaged but where the centres were quite fresh; potatoes with only the odd blemish, apples that were only a little fly-blown.

She was on her way back through Covent Garden when she caught sight of a familiar figure—familiar, at least, from the previous night. It was the Earl of Tallant, coming down the steps of a nearby house, adjusting his cuffs and the set of his jacket. The sun gleamed on the rich dark auburn of his hair. Amy froze. With his athletic build and energetic gait he looked like a sportsman rather than a man who had spent the first part of the night at the gaming tables and the second part... Amy felt a crimson blush spread up from her toes to the top of her head. She knew full well that the elegant frontages of these houses concealed the kind of den of iniquity that Richard and his friends were wont to patronise. She turned away hastily, for the last thing she wanted was to catch the Earl's eye. The thought of being obliged to greet him when he had just emerged from taking his pleasure in a bawdy-house almost paralysed her.

She took a blind step forward and the edge of her basket caught the side of a nearby cart, wrenching it from her hands and tipping its contents all over the cobbles. Apples rolled away into the gutter. Amy gave an exclamation and went down on her hands and knees. She could not afford to lose any of her precious food. She even crawled a little way under the cart to try to rescue two potatoes that had disappeared beneath the wheels, bumping her knee painfully in the process. When she emerged, her face was flushed and her hands were dirty and the last thing she wished was to peer out from beneath the wing of the cart to see the Earl of Tallant bending down and extending a hand to her.

'Miss Bainbridge? You appear to be in some difficulty, ma'am. Allow me to assist.'

He had placed one hand under her elbow and helped her to her feet before Amy could refuse. She blushed, stepped back from him and bumped herself on the cart, smoothed her dress down and found that she had managed to spread the soil from the potatoes on to her skirts. She saw Joss Tallant's gaze sweep over her, saw him smile and felt her blush get hotter.

'Thank you, my lord.'

'Have you injured yourself, Miss Bainbridge? I noticed that you winced a little when you stood up.'

Amy took a tentative step and tried not to wince again. 'No, I thank you. I am very well.' She bent to retrieve the basket and slipped the potatoes back inside it, hoping he had not noticed.

'May I escort you somewhere?' Joss Tallant enquired. 'Back to Curzon Street, perhaps?' He was leaning against the side of the cart now and showed no sign of leaving her.

'Oh, no, thank you!' Amy was horrified at the thought. Could the man not simply take himself off? Surely the last thing he would want to do was play the gallant for her. 'I am happy to walk and I am sure that you have other things to do.'

Against her will, her gaze drifted to the bland front door from which he had just emerged. She had no wish to dwell on what his other activities might be, but she found it strangely difficult to drag her mind—and her gaze—away. Despite herself, her inflamed imagination presented her with all sorts of images… And then she met Joss Tallant's gaze and realised that he had read her thoughts most accurately. He raised his eyebrows, a speculative look in his eyes.

Amy discovered that she could not blush any harder. Her whole body was already one burning mass. She looked hastily down at the cobbles, where an apple still lay against the kerb.

'I assure you,' Joss Tallant said, the twinkle still in his eye, 'that I am not engaged until later in the day, Miss Bainbridge. However if you do not wish to accept my escort, perhaps I could procure you a hack?'

'No, thank you,' Amy said again, very quickly. She could not afford to pay for a cab and did not wish to assume that he would do so for her. She grasped her basket tightly. 'I shall walk. Good day, sir.'

'Then you must permit me to walk with you in case you require any assistance,' Joss said, falling into step beside her, 'and please allow me to carry your basket. So many apples and potatoes—I hope they were not damaged?'

'It is quite unnecessary for you to accompany me,' Amy said, holding on to the basket as he took hold of the handle. 'Thank you for your consideration,' she added ungraciously, fearing she might sound too abrupt, 'but I have no need of your help.'

She tugged on the basket; Joss did not let go. She tugged again. He tightened his grip.

'Are we to play tug of war in the street, Miss Bainbridge?'

'This is ridiculous!' Amy let go of the basket and glared at him. 'You cannot possibly walk through the streets of London carrying a marketing basket, my lord—'

'I assure you, my reputation would suffer more were I

to permit a lady to carry her own shopping. That would be most ungallant in me.'

'You are absurd!' Amy cast him a furious sideways look. 'You have no need to put yourself to all this trouble! Indeed, I would that you did not!'

Joss merely shrugged, placed the basket over one arm and offered Amy the other, which she pointedly ignored. In this manner they made their way down Shaftesbury Avenue—mainly in silence, since Amy did not offer any remarks of her own and answered Joss's comments on the weather as shortly as possible. After a couple of awkward minutes she turned her head to look at him and saw that he was watching her with quizzical amusement. She turned her face sharply away.

Inside she was seething. The persistence of the man in the face of her obvious reluctance for his company was bad enough; she could not believe that he was really so obtuse not to realise that she wanted rid of him. Then to make her a laughing stock by insisting on carrying the basket as though he were a footman... She could see people staring and pointing and she wished she had accepted the offer of the hackney carriage.

'You are looking as though you wish me in Hades, Miss Bainbridge.'

Joss's words interrupted Amy's furious thoughts and she swallowed hard.

'It is simply that I do not understand your insistence on accompanying me, sir.' Amy forced herself to be civil. 'It is very good of you but quite unnecessary—'

'And quite unappreciated?'

'I do not appreciate having company forced upon me,' Amy agreed coldly.

'I see.' Joss seemed amused. 'Would that be my company in particular, Miss Bainbridge?'

Amy struggled with her annoyance. 'I am flattered by your notice, my lord—'

'I doubt that. You disapprove of me, do you not, Miss Bainbridge?'

Amy looked at him, startled. It was true, but she had not realised that she had made it so obvious. She felt a little ashamed that she had allowed her dislike to show. It was not that she cared whether or not she hurt his feelings, for surely such a hardened rakehell had none, but more that she knew it was bad manners.

'Well, I...' She met his sardonic gaze and raised her chin unconsciously. 'Yes, of course I disapprove of you.'

'It is obligatory for young ladies to do so,' Joss murmured. 'What are your reasons, Miss Bainbridge?'

'As you ask, my lord...' Amy took a deep breath. 'I do not approve of gaming and I deplore those who lead the young and impressionable astray.'

Joss gave a crack of laughter. 'Good God, surely you do not consider your brother young and impressionable? He could teach most hardened gamblers a thing or two!'

Amy set her jaw. 'Your attitude merely confirms my opinion, my lord. It is all very well for gentlemen such as yourself and the Duke of Fleet, who have the substance to support their obsession, to throw their fortune away as they please! It is another matter for you to encourage those who do not have the means to support their gambling!'

'Nobody forces your brother to gamble,' Joss said pleasantly. 'If he does not have the means to support the habit he should not play for such high stakes.'

Amy felt a rush of dislike for him that almost overwhelmed

her. 'I might have known that you would not understand! Or that you would deliberately choose to be obtuse—'

'My dear Miss Bainbridge,' Joss drawled, 'I understand perfectly. You are the one who does not understand. The truth is that if Fleet and I were not taking your brother's money you may be sure that he would be giving it to someone else. The gambling is his problem, not ours.'

Amy's fury was swelling inside her like a vast balloon. Her blue eyes flashed fire. 'You take advantage of his weakness, sir.'

Joss shrugged. 'Maybe.' He shot her a look and she was infuriated to see that he was still smiling. 'Your brother was doubly unlucky, was he not, Miss Bainbridge? For all his charm, it seems that you possess the strength of character that he lacks.'

Amy looked away. She was not about to agree with his criticisms of her brother, no matter how near the mark they were.

'We shall just have to agree to differ, my lord,' she said tightly, 'and perhaps we should refrain from further conversation until we reach Curzon Street.'

Joss raised his brows. 'Must we, Miss Bainbridge? We are only in Piccadilly and I always find that time passes so much more quickly when one keeps occupied! Perhaps we could talk of something innocuous, however, so that I need not incur your wrath any further.'

Amy was silent. She was not being deliberately stubborn but she was feeling so irritated that she could not think of a single inoffensive topic. After a second, Joss laughed. 'Oh, dear, is it that bad, Miss Bainbridge? And we have already discussed the weather...'

Amy looked at him. He was smiling at her and there was a warmth in his eyes that made her feel uncomfortable in an entirely different way. It was very confusing. She disliked him intensely, particularly for his callous dismissal of her plea about Richard, and yet she was aware of a thaw setting in around the edges of her mind. She deliberately froze it up again.

'We could raise the subject of the weather again,' she said coldly. 'After all, it is very sunny at the moment.'

Joss inclined his head. 'That is true. Though I do believe that if this heat continues we shall have a thunderstorm. Do you dislike thunderstorms, Miss Bainbridge?'

'Yes indeed, I dislike them intensely.' Amy looked around. 'I find the cold preferable to the heat. Too much sun can be very oppressive.'

'Yet too much snow can be most inconvenient.'

'I suppose so.' Amy stopped. 'Oh, look, we are almost at Curzon Street already.'

'How fortuitous. Though I do believe that the weather would have sustained us for several minutes more.' Joss put the basket down by the railings as they reached Number 3.

Amy hesitated. She did not wish to invite him in but civility demanded it. 'Would you care for any refreshment, my lord, following your exertions with that basket?'

Joss smiled. He took her hand. 'No, thank you. I have remembered one of those pressing engagements that you mentioned earlier, so I fear I must go. Thank you for your company, Miss Bainbridge. I hope that you will soon be better—I noticed that you were limping a little.'

'Oh...' Amy blushed self-consciously. 'It is nothing, my lord.' She tried to retrieve her hand. Joss appeared not to notice.

'I did think of carrying you,' he continued, 'but given the

fuss that you made over the basket I felt it would be inadvisable.'

'Very wise, my lord,' Amy said crossly, 'though I must thank you for your assistance, I suppose. Good day.'

Joss let her go at last and raised a casual hand in farewell. 'Goodbye, Miss Bainbridge. I am sure we shall meet again soon.'

Amy paused, one hand on the door. 'I doubt it, my lord.'

Joss grinned. 'You may depend upon it, Miss Bainbridge. You might even bet on it—if you were the gambling kind! It is inevitable when you are trying to avoid someone!'

He turned away and Amy watched, a little bemused, as he disappeared around the corner of Clarges Street. She hoped that he was wrong about them meeting again, although there was some truth in the fact that one often bumped into the very person one was trying to avoid, as though some kind of perverse fate was at play. She shrugged a little uncomfortably. There was something about the Earl of Tallant that she found entirely disconcerting and it would be better to forget all about him. They had nothing in common, not the least little thing.

Amy retrieved her basket and went into the cool of the hall. The parlour door was ajar.

'Is that you, Amy?' Lady Bainbridge called. 'Oh, dear, I have just partaken of luncheon and there was not sufficient for two. I was so hoping that you would not be back until later!'

'That is all right, Mama,' Amy said, stifling a sigh. She selected one of the bruised apples from the top of the basket. 'I will have this for my luncheon with some cheese and make the rest of the apples into a stew that will do us for the rest of the week.' She bent to kiss her mother's cheek. 'Is all well with you?'

'Yes, my dear,' Lady Bainbridge said, settling back in her chair. 'I have had a very pleasant morning. Lady Vestey stayed for far longer than she ought, though. I was hard pressed not to serve up another pot of tea.' She bent a look of enquiry on her daughter. 'Were you speaking with someone just now, my love? I thought that I heard a gentleman's voice.'

'No, Mama,' Amy said, avoiding Lady Bainbridge's eye. 'There was no one. No one at all.'

Lady Bainbridge slumped back in her chair. 'A pity. For I have not quite given up hope for you, you know, Amy. I am sure that there is a pleasant gentleman somewhere who wishes for a conformable wife. An older gentleman, perhaps, or a widower looking for a mother for his children...'

'It sounds a delightful prospect, Mama,' Amy said, reflecting how different from these imaginings was the Earl of Tallant. 'However, I fear I know no widowers or older gentlemen looking for a suitable wife. And I have no dowry, nor even my looks to recommend me...'

Lady Bainbridge patted her cheek. 'No, but you are a dear, sweet girl, Amy! We shall not look too high for you, though.'

'Any gentleman will need to look high,' Amy said with a smile, 'to see the shelf that I am on, Mama! Now, if you will excuse me, I shall eat my apple and cheese, and then I have some visits to make.'

'To the poor, I suppose!' Lady Bainbridge waved a languid hand. 'You are so good, Amy! That former landlady of ours, Mrs Wendover... You will persist in keeping in touch with her although you should not feel obliged, you know!'

'No, Mama,' Amy said, selecting the most battered-looking apple from her basket and biting into it, 'but at least I get a good piece of fruitcake when I am visiting in Whitechapel!'

Lady Bainbridge's eyes brightened. 'Then slip a piece into your bag for me, my love! You know I love a good fruitcake!'

Chapter Three

'I'm sure that Patience has beaten these rugs too hard,' Lady Bainbridge said that evening, peering at the carpet in the dining room by the light of one dim candle. 'The pattern is quite faded, you know. One can ruin a carpet with too much beating.'

'I imagine that the rugs are faded because they are old, Mama, not for any other reason,' Amy said. She pushed her apple stew listlessly about the bowl. Dinner had been as lacklustre as ever, but that was not the reason for her blue devils. She had been feeling restless ever since she had returned home from visiting Mrs Wendover and she was at a loss to explain why. The evening stretched ahead of her in the same pattern as every other evening for the previous two years; a book or sewing, a cup of hot milk if there was enough left and it had not curdled, and an early bed. For two years she had been quite satisfied with this routine, but tonight she felt as though she would explode.

A door slammed and Richard's voice echoed down the

corridor, then he breezed into the room with his customary flamboyance. Lady Bainbridge, who had been drooping over her bowl, brightened immediately.

'Richard, darling! Do you go to Lady Aston's ball tonight? Oh, you look so elegant!'

A dart of envy, as painful as it was unexpected, pierced Amy. She blinked a little. Ever since the disaster of her come-out she had sworn that she never wished to set foot in a fashionable ballroom again and, until tonight, she had never felt remotely like changing her mind. It seemed extraordinary that she could envy Richard the pleasure, yet now she was jealous. Amy examined her feelings carefully. Yes, she was envious of her brother's good looks, his elegant appearance and, more than anything, his invitation to Lady Aston's ball.

She looked at him. Tall, golden and good-looking in his evening dress, he reminded her so forcibly of their father that for a second her throat ached. Lady Bainbridge was still cooing over him and Amy told herself fairly that it was not surprising. If she saw George Bainbridge in Richard, how much more poignant must it be for their mother.

'Be sure to dance with Miss Loring,' Lady Bainbridge was saying. 'They say that she has fifty thousand pounds—'

'I do not suppose that Richard will see much of the ballroom, Mama,' Amy said. 'Surely it is the card room that will have his attention!'

Both Lady Bainbridge and Richard stopped talking and looked at her and Amy realised that the words had come out in a decidedly waspish tone. Fortunately Richard was so easy going that he never took offence. He gave her a speculative grin.

'You sound as though you're jealous, Amy! I thought you scorned the amusements of the *ton*!'

Amy pressed her napkin to her lips, then threw it down beside the rejected bowl of apples. 'I am sorry, Richard. I feel blue-devilled tonight! I am sure it will pass.'

'With a bit of judicious sewing, or perhaps a passage or two from an improving book?' Richard had never made a secret of the fact that his own interests and those of his sister were decidedly divergent. 'You would do better to come out with me! Play a hand of whist, dance the waltz!'

Lady Bainbridge started to object. 'Oh, not the waltz, Richard! It is a positively dangerous dance! And Amy cannot go without a chaperon, and certainly not to Lady Aston's. The place is a hotbed of immoral activity!'

'I hope so,' Richard said, grinning.

'Of which the most immoral is whist,' Amy said. 'That is even more dangerous than waltzing for it can be prodigiously expensive!'

Richard leant on the back of a chair and viewed his sister with his very blue eyes. 'I tell you what, Amy, you've been eating too much fruit. It gives one a sour disposition!'

Amy threw her napkin at him. Richard ducked. The chair creaked as he leant his weight against it.

'Children, children!' Lady Bainbridge expostulated. 'Richard, do not break that chair, we cannot afford to replace it!'

'Your pardon, Mama.' Richard retrieved the napkin and sat down. He turned back to Amy. 'Now here's the thing, Amy! I'll escort you to Lady Moon's ball next week—and you cannot say fairer than that, for it is the slowest thing to escort one's own sister—but only if you agree to play a hand of whist! You are for ever complaining about my gambling! Now it is time for you to understand what it is you are complaining about!'

'Lady Moon's ball,' Lady Bainbridge said thoughtfully.

'I am not perfectly sure that we may attend, Richard, for we cannot afford any new clothes—'

'A week is surely long enough to make over something old,' Richard said, brushing a thread off his immaculate evening jacket.

'True,' Lady Bainbridge said. 'It would be pleasant to have some different company and one may eat well enough for a week at a ball. What do you say, Amy?'

'Why not?' Amy said. She viewed her mother's thin figure and tried to imagine her storing enough food for a week, like a camel storing water.

'You might show a little more eagerness, my love,' Lady Bainbridge grumbled. 'It is nigh on twelve months since we attended a proper ball. It will be such a treat for you. Who knows—you may attract the interest of a gentleman...?' Her blue eyes appraised Amy thoughtfully, as did Richard, who had selected an apple from the bowl of fruit on the sideboard and was leaning against the table, chewing heartily. He shook his head.

'I think not, Mama. Amy is almost at her last prayers!'

'I believe you have a ball to attend,' Amy said frostily, watching as Richard straightened up and tossed his apple core carelessly into the fireplace. If only she had an ounce of that golden beauty, she thought suddenly. Then she would show them she was not on the shelf.

Richard bestowed a careless kiss on the top of her head, and a slightly more decorous one on his mother's cheek and strode out, whistling. The front door slammed behind him. Lady Bainbridge stood up and retrieved the fruit bowl.

'Remind Patience not to leave the fruit on display in future, Amy dear. Richard does not need to eat anything at home when he can eat at someone else's expense.'

'Yes, Mama,' Amy said. 'I believe Patience thought it might brighten the room, given that we never have any flowers.'

Lady Bainbridge shuddered. 'Flowers! Wanton extravagance! What use are flowers? One cannot even eat them!'

She disappeared through the door to the servant's hall.

Amy pushed away her bowl of cold fruit stew and got to her feet. Perhaps she might spend the evening helping Patience to polish the silver. That would prevent her from falling into a fit of the dismals. Action, not inaction, was the key. Genteel poverty could be hard, but it was not as desperate as the squalor she had seen in the Whitechapel stews. Even today, when she had visited Mrs Wendover, Amy had been struck afresh by the state of that widow's determined attempts to keep a spotlessly clean house amidst the filth around her. Amy repressed a grin. There were not many young ladies who could boast a stay in Whitechapel, but she had had that privilege twice, the second time when she had been sixteen and her father's finances had reached such a parlous state that there had been no alternative. At least now they could afford to keep a small house in the respectable part of town. Whitechapel had not been respectable but it had certainly been educational. She bent absent-mindedly to bank down the meagre fire, thinking of the time that she had spent there.

A scrap of paper was resting on the carpet beside the fireplace. Amy leant over and picked it up. It was a ticket for the national lottery. She knew that Richard, in common with a huge proportion of the populace, often gambled on the national lottery and on private lotteries as well when they were raising funds for various projects. As far as she knew he had never won a penny. It was just another wager, another way of throwing his money away, another gamble.

Amy smoothed out the crumpled ticket. The draw was dated for the following morning. Richard must have dropped the ticket from his pocket book without realising. She tucked it behind the clock, making a mental note to tell him in the morning. She might not approve of gambling, but some small, superstitious part of her mind prevented her from consigning the ticket to the fire. After all, it might, just might, win a prize. Smiling a little at her own credulity, Amy went off to polish the silver.

After breakfast the following day, Amy retrieved the lottery ticket from its place behind the clock and went out into the hall, intending to give it to Marten, Richard's valet, to hand back to his master. Fortuitously, Marten was just coming down the stairs with one of Richard's coats over his arm. He bowed. Marten never took the liberties that Patience did. He was always deferential.

'Good morning, Marten. Is my brother awake yet?' Amy enquired. Richard was prone to sleep very late on most mornings, especially when he had been playing into the early hours.

Marten sketched another bow. His expression was blander than cream. 'I fear that Sir Richard has not yet returned, ma'am. The ball went on long into the night, I believe.'

'I suppose he has a pressing engagement at the card tables.' Amy gave Marten a sharp look, which he returned with one of even greater impassivity.

'Indeed, ma'am, perhaps so.'

'Or perhaps he retired to another place for the night?' Amy was remembering the discreet house in Covent Garden from which Joss Tallant had emerged the previous day. Marten smiled politely.

'I could not possibly say, ma'am.'

Amy frowned a little. It was most unfortunate that her brother was absent the one time that she needed to see him. Since the lottery draw was taking place that very morning, it was urgent that she should hand the ticket over to him at once. She knew nothing of lotteries, but she did worry that one might have to claim the prize at the draw itself. It would be most galling for Richard if his were the winning numbers and yet he lost the prize because he had left his ticket behind.

Amy sighed. Her father had taught her how to calculate odds when she was a child and the odds against her brother's ticket being the winning one must be huge...oh, forty thousand to one, or some such figure. She knew it was silly even to imagine that he might win. Even so, she felt a certain responsibility to reunite him with his ticket, pointless though it was.

She put the ticket in her pocket, then took it out and looked at it again. It was such a tempting little scrap of paper. Amy felt something stir in her blood. Perhaps, just perhaps, this could be the key to thousands of pounds. No wonder that people prayed so earnestly to win and spent their very last shilling on the gamble. She smiled at the fanciful line her thoughts were taking. It was the first time that she had ever felt even the remotest temptation towards gambling, and the inclination was gone almost as swiftly as it had come.

Marten was still waiting, still deferential, to see how he might serve her. Amy held out the ticket.

'It is very urgent that this lottery ticket is delivered to Sir Richard, Marten,' she said. 'Do you have *any* notion where he might be this morning?'

The manservant shook his head. 'I regret that I do not, ma'am. Sir Richard made it plain last night that he did not intend to return until late morning, if then. He could be in any number of places, ma'am.'

Amy hesitated. 'Then do you know where the lottery draw takes place? I am sure he must be going there and I could meet with him...' Her voice trailed away and she felt herself blush. It was not that Marten had betrayed any surprise, for indeed his face was as impassive as ever. It was more that Amy felt that he *must* be surprised. She was hardly renowned for frequenting lottery draws any more than she was known for venturing into society.

'The lottery draw takes place at the Guildhall, ma'am,' Marten said calmly, quite as though Amy had only been enquiring after the weather. 'If you would like me to carry a message to Sir Richard—?'

'Yes, perhaps...' Amy wavered. It was simpler by far to send Marten. Except that it was a fine day and she wanted a walk, and, if truth were told, she also wanted a little excitement. Her low spirits of the previous evening had not quite dissipated and a lottery draw would be an interesting spectacle to watch.

'No, it is quite all right!' she said, making a sudden decision and feeling quite reckless. 'I shall go there myself! I have a letter to deliver in Holborn and it is a fine day for a walk.'

'Very well, ma'am,' Marten murmured. 'Pray do not hesitate to call me if I can be of service.'

He strode softly away and closed the door to the servants' quarters behind him. Amy was left in the hall. Before she could change her mind, she sped up the stairs, removed her apron and donned a pelisse and an old chip bonnet. She was still tying the ribbons beneath her chin as she hurried back down the stairs and out of the front door. This was decidedly more exciting than polishing the silver or discussing menus with Cook, and as it was some distance to the Guildhall she had better start at once. It would never do to be late and miss the draw.

Amy had not expected the crowd to be so great. By the time that she reached the Guildhall, the press of people in the building was intense and she could barely move.

She soon realised that the chances of finding her brother in such a throng were very small indeed. She had thoroughly underestimated the appeal of the lottery.

There was a stage at one end of the hall and she could see figures moving upon it, setting up some complicated mechanical contraption that she realised must be the lottery wheel. She could smell gin and sweat and cheap perfume emanating from the bodies that pressed against hers, and she had to swallow hard to prevent herself from retching. The heat was building now and with it an excitement that ebbed and flowed through the crowd like the waves on the seashore. Amy felt it too; it was a tingling in her stomach, a shiver along the nerves. It was intoxicating, like the wine she had occasionally drunk, or the thrill of something unexpected. Very little that was out of the ordinary ever happened in Amy's life, yet now she had a lottery ticket clutched tightly in her fingers and she felt as though anything could happen.

On her left side, Amy was pinned against a pillar by a fat woman with a large marketing basket. Several other people pressed against her back and a huge, red-faced gentleman in a straining, shiny waistcoat was squashed against her right-hand side. Since Amy was so tiny, she could not see over the heads of the people in front of her. After a few ineffectual

pleas to be allowed through the crowd, which probably nobody even heard since she was addressing some very broad
backs, she realised that she was very likely stuck fast until
the lottery draw was over. Richard might be standing a mere
twenty feet away, but if he was she had no way of knowing.
She began to regret her quest.

She turned her head and caught sight of a familiar figure
in the throng. Her heart skipped a beat. The Earl of Tallant
was standing over to her left, leaning casually against the
wall, engaged in conversation with a large gentleman whom
Amy recognised as the Duke of Fleet. She tried to shrink
away behind the broad back of the gentleman in the shiny
waistcoat. She had no wish for Fleet and Joss Tallant to notice her at a lottery draw of all places. She could not believe
that the Earl's point had been proved so quickly. She had
wished to avoid him, yet here he was. Some malign fate was
definitely in play.

Her involuntary movement caught Joss Tallant's eye and
she saw him focus on her, one eyebrow raised in cynical
amusement. Amy blushed. It was easy to read that look—
she remembered her protestations the last time they had met,
her declaration that she did not approve of gaming. Now he
had seen her here it was no wonder he had a sceptical view
of her claims. Amy felt vexed, her blush turning to one of
annoyance.

'Amy! Amy Bainbridge!'

It was not Sir Richard's masculine tones that accosted
Amy's ears but the higher-pitched tones of a young lady and
an excited one at that. Amy turned with difficulty, peered
around the large gentleman, and saw a lady of fashion, with
corn-gold hair and blue eyes in a beautiful oval face.

'Excuse me, if you please!' The lady fluttered her eyelashes at the fat man, who moved obligingly, stepping heavily on Amy's foot in the process. Amy and the other girl almost fell into each other's arms as the crowd pushed them together again.

'Amy Bainbridge!'

'Amanda Makepeace!'

'Good gracious, wherever have you been this year past?'

'I wondered what had happened to you!'

'What are you doing here?'

'I am up in London to stay with my aunt for a spell—'

They were both speaking at once, clutching at each other. Amy had last seen Amanda when the two of them had been doing the season three years before, Amanda as a young bride and Amy in her come-out year. Then George Bainbridge had lost all his money, Amy had retired to the country and Amanda's husband had carried her off to Ireland. The friends had kept in touch by letter, although Amanda was an erratic writer, and after she was widowed the letters had stopped altogether.

'I can scarce believe it!' Amanda said, her eyes shining. 'Amy Bainbridge—it is almost too good to be true! I lost your London address a little while ago and thought never to see you again! I should have known I might find you here. The world and his wife come to the lottery!'

'This is my first visit,' Amy said, looking shy. 'I had no notion it would be so busy! Oh, Amanda, it is lovely to see you again! You are looking well...' She eyed Amanda's sky-blue dress and porcelain pale face with envy. She felt hot and frumpish in her ancient sprigged muslin and she was sure that her face was flushed red. 'Where does your aunt live? You must come to tea so that we may talk properly—'

Those nearby turned to shush them, giving them glares and sharp glances.

'The draw is about to take place!' Amanda whispered in Amy's ear. 'We must have a coze later, but for now we must not miss the numbers. Oh, I declare it is *so* exciting!' She fumbled in her reticule to retrieve her ticket. 'I play the lottery every time I am up in Town, which is not that often, of course, but the rest of the time I *dream* about what I would do were I to win! I am quite comfortably circumstanced these days—enough to live in the country anyway—but who would turn away the chance of up to thirty thousand pounds? Thirty thousand, Amy! Lud, it is a fortune!'

Amy felt a little faint. She had had no idea that the lottery prize could be so huge. Yet no doubt Richard could run through thirty thousand pounds in one sitting at White's. Fortunes were relative.

The two wheels were starting to turn now and the crowd was starting to roar. Amy craned to see what was happening. Two boys were up on the stage, drawing numbers from the two wheels.

'Bluecoat boys,' Amanda whispered. 'One picks the number of the winning tickets from the left-hand wheel and the other chooses the amount of the prize from the right.' She was positively dancing with excitement. 'Wait, what number was that? Number two thousand five hundred and eighty-eight wins—what? Twenty thousand pounds?'

'Thirty thousand,' the fat man said, screwing up his own ticket in disgust and looking as though he would spit on the floor were it not for the presence of the ladies. 'One winner takes all today, madam. Thirty thousand pounds.'

'Not I,' Amanda said regretfully, stuffing her ticket back

in her reticule. 'Hey day! I must wait another few months, I suppose, for my chance of fortune. Amy... Amy?'

Amy barely heard the excited sound of voices roaring in her ears, for in her hand was a small, crumpled lottery ticket with the numbers two, five, eight and eight on it. She stared until the figures blurred before her eyes.

'I believe that there must be some mistake,' she said faintly.

Amanda squinted at the ticket, then grabbed her arm. 'Amy!' she exclaimed softly. 'You have won thirty thousand pounds!' She threw a sharp look over her shoulder as the crowd jostled them. Everyone was starting to move towards the door now, ripping up their tickets, chattering with good humour or sometimes with bad. Amy saw one man throw his ticket down and jump on it in disgust.

'Put your ticket in your reticule,' Amanda whispered in her ear, 'and do not give any sign that you have won. That would be most dangerous!'

Amy obeyed as though in a dream and obediently allowed Amanda to take her arm and steer her towards the exit. The words *thirty thousand pounds* hammered in her brain. The momentum of the crowd carried her along. All about her was noise and colour, whirling through her head until she thought she might faint. It was with the greatest relief that she felt the fresh air on her face and allowed Amanda to help her on to the steps outside, past ragged groups of people all discussing the draw and the identity of the person who might have won.

'It could have been me,' she heard one woman say regretfully to another, as she ground her ticket beneath her heel. She drew a dirty baby closer to her breast. 'I need food for Emily now that Jack is gone—'

Amy jerked convulsively and Amanda bent closer to her ear. 'Do not listen, Amy! If I know you, you'll be giving your ticket away and the shirt off your back. All the world needs money—why, by the look of you, you could do with a deal of it yourself!'

Amy suddenly remembered just why she could not give the money away even if she wanted. It did not belong to her. It was Richard's ticket and Richard's prize. The thirty thousand pounds belonged to her brother and she would have to hand it over as soon as she saw him. She felt a breathless mixture of relief and rebellion, relief that the decision was out of her hands and rebellion at the thought of wasting a fortune. She knew that Richard would gamble every penny away as surely as the sun rose in the morning. If only the money were hers... There were so many things that she could do with thirty thousand pounds. Amy felt a sudden and entirely natural rush of disappointment. There was no point in thinking what she might do with such a fortune. It was not her money. She would not see a penny of it. For a second her hand clenched on the reticule with its precious cargo and then she relaxed again. It was unfair—*life* was unfair, but there was nothing that she could do about it. She would not be spending the money on herself and she certainly could not use it to do good for others. She had best disabuse herself of any such thoughts at once, before she was tempted.

'Come along, Amy,' Amanda whispered urgently. 'We must get you home safely. It would never do for anyone to realise that you hold the winning ticket! Why, you would be kidnapped before you could go a step!'

Chapter Four

The air outside the Guildhall was fresh and cool and reviving. As her head cleared, Amy realised that she was not sure what happened next and hung back, drawing Amanda into the shelter of the portico.

'I am not perfectly sure what to do,' she murmured. 'Do I not have to go up to claim the prize?'

'No, no.' Amanda cast her an amused look. 'I forgot that you said you had not played the lottery before, Amy. Is this really your first time?'

'Of course it is,' Amy said. She felt confused. No doubt she would wake in her narrow bed in Curzon Street at any moment. 'This is not even my own lottery ticket, you know, Amanda—'

Amanda was not really listening. She was too excited. 'Lud, and you won the prize at the first go! In order to claim the money you need to attend one of the lottery offices. They will pay your winnings. Or, better still, send your man of business. You would likely need a platoon of soldiers to guard you against robbery were you to go yourself! Now, where is your carriage? We need to get you safely home before someone realises who you are and kidnaps you or murders you for your ticket!'

Amy shuddered, clutching her reticule to her. 'Amanda, tell me that you are in jest! I have no carriage and I walked here from Curzon Street.'

Amanda stopped and looked at her, concern replacing the amusement in her eyes. 'Here's a to-do! No carriage! What are we to do now?'

'I was hoping to find Richard here, you see, and thought that he might escort me home.' Amy was prevaricating, thinking that this was scarcely the time to start explaining to her old friend that she did not have the means to run a carriage. She looked around frantically but there was no friendly face in the crowd. People were drifting away now, tearing up their tickets. The pieces fluttered in the breeze.

'We cannot take a hack,' Amanda was saying with a frown. 'Why, you might be down an alleyway and despatched to heaven before one could say lottery!'

Amy gave a little moan. 'I shall give away the ticket before anything ill befalls me—'

'That you shall not!' There was a martial light in Amanda's eyes. 'You need this money, Amy. This simply requires a little thought—'

'Lady Spry, Miss Bainbridge, I thought that I recognised you. May I be of service?'

Amy turned and almost dropped her reticule with the precious ticket in it. The Duke of Fleet had drawn up beside them in his phaeton and now handed the reins to his groom and jumped down beside them. He looked large, genial and, in some respects at least, the answer to their prayers. Amy smiled and curtsied, but though he bowed in reply, she had the strangest feeling that he had not really seen her. The explanation was not far to seek. Fleet's gaze was fixed on Amanda's charming countenance. He looked utterly smitten. Amy suddenly remembered the balls during her come-out season, where Amanda had been like a little golden honey pot around which all the gentlemen buzzed. Amanda had not been spoiled by the attention; she had laughed at her admirers with good humour, treated them all with equal favour but had never done anything to upset Frank Spry, who seemed pleased that his new wife was so sought after. Now, however, Amy was surprised to see that the Duke's chivalry was not warmly received. Indeed Amanda was looking most uncomfortable, her face flushed, her head turned a little away so that the brim of her bonnet shielded her from the gentleman's gaze.

'Thank you, your Grace, but I am sure we shall fare quite well on our own—'

'Miss Bainbridge will vouch for me, I am sure,' Sebastian Fleet said, with another slight bow in Amy's direction. 'I am a friend of her brother and very willing to offer my escort back to Curzon Street if that is what you wish.'

Amy was torn. On the one hand, she barely knew the Duke and what she did know of him scarcely disposed her to be friendly towards him, for was he not a gambler and a wastrel, the very type of man she deplored? On the other hand, they were in a slightly delicate situation and Fleet was a friend of her brother and could surely be relied upon to provide a safe escort...

'I am sure we may safely accept the Duke's offer, Amanda,' Amy said, a little reluctantly. She wondered if her friend was concerned in case the Duke was one of the thieves and kidnappers she had just been mentioning. Surely not. She could not believe that Fleet, for all his faults, would stoop to criminality to fund his gambling. Amanda's reservations must be based on some other concern—the Duke's womanising, perhaps.

She turned to him hopefully. 'I do not suppose, your Grace, that Richard is with you? I have been searching for him this hour past...'

Fleet shook his head. 'I fear not, Miss Bainbridge. Joss Tallant is with me, however, and will be very glad to take you up whilst I escort Lady Spry.'

A strange prickling sensation on the back of her neck prompted Amy to turn her head. The Earl of Tallant was walking towards them. He was immaculately dressed in a black coat, buff pantaloons and black top boots with a high polish. He looked elegantly austere, as though his attire was in direct contradiction to the extravagance of his reputation. As he saw Amy turn towards him, he smiled in quizzical amusement, allowing his gaze to travel over her thoughtfully. His appraisal was as deliberate as it had been the night they had met and Amy found it both curious and disconcerting. She was assailed by a strange breathlessness, which she would have liked to have attributed to the excitement of winning a fortune. Honesty compelled her to admit, however, that it probably had a different cause. There was no doubt that Joss Tallant's company was enough to fluster any young lady, but she did not intend to succumb.

'Joss, my boy,' the Duke drawled as the Earl joined them, 'I was just pledging you to escort Miss Bainbridge back to Curzon Street. I am taking Lady Spry up with me.'

The Earl bowed. 'Thank you, Sebastian. I am, of course, delighted, Miss Bainbridge...'

Amy had always been sensitive to slights—her upbringing and her come-out had made it inevitable. Now she fancied that she heard a note of resigned amusement in Joss's voice and at the same time she thought she recognised the expression in his eyes. It was the one she knew from the faces of all the young men who had approached Amanda for a dance, found she was already engaged, and realised that good manners obliged them to dance with her friend instead when they had no wish to do so. She felt herself blush.

'There is no need to inconvenience yourself, my lord. I am persuaded that we shall soon find my brother—'

Amanda, who had been uncharacteristically silent to this point, added her own protestations. 'Oh, indeed, we may manage very well on our own...'

The Earl flashed Fleet a look of amusement. 'Your fabled charm appears to have failed signally here, Seb! Miss Bainbridge...' he smiled at Amy '...I fear that your brother is not at the Guildhall. He told me last night that he had an appointment at the Cocoa Tree this morning. Lady Spry—' he bowed to Amanda '—I can assure you that Sebastian is the most harmless of fellows and that you are quite safe in his company! I'll have my horses brought around...'

There seemed to be little choice and, indeed, Amy was glad on balance to have the escort. The thought of walking alone through the streets of London with a ticket worth thirty thousand pounds in her reticule was enough to make her blood run cold and, even if it was Richard's money rather than her own, she had a responsibility to get it home safely. Already she was starting to think of ways in which she might influence her brother to part with a little for the benefit of the family, before he gambled the rest away. He was generous—she was sure that he could be persuaded to give her a thousand pounds to make the Curzon Street house more comfortable. They could supplement their diet with some beef, perhaps, and even—Amy felt quite excited—buy a new outfit or two for the autumn.

She stole a look at Joss Tallant as he helped her up into the phaeton. There was something reassuring about a bodyguard even if he did not know that he was performing such a function, although the Earl of Tallant was probably not the man that one would freely choose as a bodyguard— quite the reverse, in fact, if all the rumours were true. Although she was an innocent in the ways of the world, Amy had heard enough of Joss's exploits to know that his company was damaging to a lady's reputation. Further, she had heard that he would damage more than a mere reputation if he so chose. She remembered Lady Bainbridge telling her of a shocking occasion on which the Duke of Fleet and the Earl of Tallant had held up Lord Gibson's coach for a wager and whilst Fleet had relieved the occupants of their money and jewellery, Joss Tallant had relieved Lady Gibson of her virtue. It had been a long time ago but, as far as Amy was concerned, it epitomised the other reason that Joss Tallant was quite beyond the pale—apart from being a wastrel, of course. Really, Amy thought candidly, as she made herself comfortable on the phaeton's seat, the man had nothing to recommend him. His entire life was one big waste of time.

Amy glanced at him again from beneath her lashes. To be fair, Joss Tallant was prodigiously good looking and he was also quite charming, both of which qualities would help in his career of seduction. But she also felt that she was quite safe with him. She had never met any gentleman who had been intent on damaging *her* reputation. She was simply not the sort of girl who attracted amorous overtures from a man.

On that thought Amy relaxed, looked at the view and enjoyed the rare pleasure of being driven. Richard seldom took her up in his curricle these days and she had occasionally taken a drive in the Park with a gentleman during her season, but not very often. This was different. Joss Tallant was a whip of enviable skill and he made the driving seem very easy, which Amy suspected it was not. They had emerged from the Guildhall Yard now and were picking their way through the crowded streets. The noise and crush was enough to make the highly bred team of greys jib, but Joss controlled them with ease. Amy was impressed, although she resolved to keep quiet whilst her companion undertook the difficult task of navigating through the crowds.

'I am surprised to find you at the lottery draw, Miss Bainbridge,' Joss said, when he was able to take his attention from the team for a moment. 'When we spoke yesterday I formed the strong opinion that you disapproved of gambling.'

Amy glanced at him. He was smiling at her in what seemed an entirely genuine manner. She gave him a slight smile of her own in return. She might not like the man, or trust him, more to the point, but he was doing her a service and she could at least be polite.

'Oh, well, I do disapprove of gambling in the general run of things, but I thought to meet Richard at the draw, only it appears that we had a misunderstanding. He had a ticket for the lottery but he left it behind and I was bringing it for him. I would not have attended otherwise.'

'I see.' Joss's amber gaze flicked over her face thoughtfully, making her intensely aware of his scrutiny. 'What did you think of it?'

'The draw?' Amy raised her brows. 'I had not expected it to be so popular. I can understand the appeal of it, I suppose.

For most people, winning thirty thousand pounds would change their lives completely. It is a tempting thought.'

'But a dangerous one?'

'Oh, yes.' Amy remembered the excitement that her seized her in the Guildhall as the tension built before the draw. 'It is addictive and costly. If you do not have the money to support your obsession, yet you buy tickets time and time again in the hope of winning—'

'You could end up ruined and in the street,' Joss finished for her.

Amy turned her face away. 'That can happen whatever the form of gambling.' The memory of her father's wilful squandering of the family's fortune was still as fresh in her mind as when it had occurred and she had to swallow hard and push the memory away.

Joss took his hand from the reins and touched hers, so lightly, Amy wondered whether she had imagined it.

'Forgive me, Miss Bainbridge. I see it is a painful subject for you and I should not have raised it.'

Amy met his gaze. They looked at each other for what seemed a long moment, and then she shook her head slowly.

'You are too generous, my lord, letting me off so easily. If I hold strong opinions, then I feel I must defend them and not hide behind convention.'

She saw the smile creep into Joss's eyes like sunlight on water and strangely it made her shiver.

'That is very honest of you, Miss Bainbridge. I admire that.'

Amy shrugged, a little embarrassed. 'I know that I must sound like a reformer at times! In mitigation I can only plead that I have seen the ruinous effects of gambling at first hand

and therefore feel at liberty to view it as a most pernicious disease!'

'That is, of course, your privilege, Miss Bainbridge,' Joss said, smiling. 'I can only argue in defence that it gives a lot of us a great deal of pleasure!'

'Including my brother. I believe that we had this conversation yesterday, my lord. I do not think it wise that we should pursue it since we evidently hold such differing views.'

Joss inclined his head. 'We shall not speak of it if that is your wish, Miss Bainbridge, but I confess that one thing puzzles me. I have thought much on this since our discussion yesterday. How comes it that your brother is so ardent a gambler and you are the utter opposite? Such a freak of nature requires explanation!'

Amy was surprised into a laugh. 'Oh! Well, there was my father's example, I suppose. Richard takes after him. They say that gambling breeds gambling.'

'Yet you did not follow your father's example. In your case it bred an utter distaste for the sport!'

'It is not a sport, my lord,' Amy said severely. 'I consider sport to be something requiring more physical effort than the throwing of a dice!'

Despite herself, she could not help running her eye over him and could not deny that he was in infinitely better shape than a man deserved to be who spent all his time at the gaming tables or in bawdy houses. Then she saw the amusement in his eyes and felt herself blush scarlet.

'What is it, Miss Bainbridge? Do I not look suitably dissipated to fit your image of a wastrel?'

'Oh!' Amy was mortified. Not only had he caught her staring, but he was uncannily good at reading her thoughts. 'I beg your pardon—'

'Do not. I would rather have your brand of honesty than the artifice of most conversation!' Joss smiled. 'Tell me, Miss Bainbridge, have you ever dared to play yourself?' He flicked her a mocking glance. 'A hand of whist? A game of vingt-et-un, perhaps? You might find that you actually enjoyed yourself!'

'You make it sound quite tempting and the height of decadence, sir,' Amy said, a dimple appearing in her cheek as she smiled back. She was struggling against feeling in charity with him and was finding it surprisingly difficult. The man's charm was almost tangible and she was not so naïve that she did not realise he was turning it deliberately on her. The only thing left to wonder at was why he was bothering to do so. It could hardly mean anything.

'I have played cards, of course, but never for money. How could I when I have no fortune—' She broke off, remembering the fortune that she carried with her now. Thirty thousand pounds. It was a huge sum of money and the thought of it made her feel quite faint.

'A lack of fortune seems to be no hindrance to most gamblers,' Joss drawled. 'They play upon nothing but a promise.'

'Your words describe Richard to the life,' Amy said, a little sadly. 'Which is why, my lord, I have no wish to fall into the same trap myself. Two gamblers in the Bainbridge family would be two too many.'

They turned into the Aldwych. The horses' hooves rang on the cobbles. The light breeze stung Amy's cheeks to a pretty pink.

'Do you really believe that gambling runs in families?' Joss asked, watching her with interest. 'Is that why you are not inclined to try it? Are you afraid to step onto the slippery slope yourself, Miss Bainbridge, for fear of very ruin? It is a piquant thought!'

Amy blushed. 'I have no fear of being led astray, my lord,' she said, with a very direct look. 'If you are speaking of gambling, I think that it is an excuse to see it as an inherited tendency. One does not fall heir to it, like so much gold or a parcel of land! It is no more than a weakness indulged in by people with too much time on their hands and not enough direction!' She shot him a look that was slightly ashamed, saw that he was smiling quizzically and let her breath out on a long sigh. 'I beg your pardon, my lord. I had no wish to sound so opinionated, but in my defence I should add that you did provoke me.'

'I did indeed,' Joss murmured. For a second Amy could have sworn that she saw a flash of admiration in his eyes. It seemed unlikely, however, and after a moment his gaze was fixed on the road once again. 'I had no idea, Miss Bainbridge, that the result of my provocation would be so stimulating. You have stronger mettle than you show.'

Amy looked away, staring with determination at the familiar sights of Pall Mall. It was curious but true that conversing with Joss Tallant did have a strange attraction that she had never experienced before. Never in her life would she have imagined that she could have so interesting a discussion with a man with whom she had nothing in common. And therein lay the rub. Joss Tallant inhabited a society that might be parallel to her own but was in all particulars utterly different. She did not belong to the world of society balls, dashing rakes and inveterate gamblers. She had neither the means nor the inclination. She did not even like Joss's pursuits; she despised them. The whole thing was ridiculous.

Amy sighed. Soon they would be in Piccadilly and then

home, and she knew she would not see Joss Tallant again. She would give Richard his lottery ticket and the good news of his win and then she would watch him gamble it all away to line the pockets of men such as Joss and the Duke of Fleet.

The Duke's phaeton was ahead of them as they drove down Piccadilly and Amy could see that the Duke was speaking to Amanda, and that her friend's animated face was turned up to his as she smiled and replied. Evidently Amanda's reserve had melted under the onslaught of Fleet's charm. Amy had thought on that first night that these men were dangerous but now she was beginning to see just how perilous they could be, with their careless charm and polished address. Her head was screwed on with practicality and commonsense, but she could feel it turning even so.

Amy cast a sideways look at Joss's face. He was concentrating on the driving, for they had reached a place where the road narrowed and a brewery dray was drawn up ahead whilst the carter rolled barrels of ale across the street. Joss's dark brows were drawn together slightly in concentration and the amber eyes were narrowed, but there was still a hint of a smile about that firm mouth. The sight of it did strange things to Amy's equilibrium.

Joss turned his head and smiled at her and her heart performed a sudden and erratic leap. Amy was immediately cross with herself. She did not even like the man and had previously been thinking of him in terms of direst disapproval, yet now—just because he had smiled at her—she was in a fair way to forgiving him for being a scoundrel. It was not good enough.

'It is an unusual female who can forbear to talk all the time, Miss Bainbridge,' Joss said easily as the phaeton regained the clear road, 'but then I am beginning to think that you are…quite unusual.'

Amy's heart fluttered again and she quelled it ruthlessly. 'Oh, I was only concerned that I should not distract you from your driving,' she said airily. 'For though I have heard tell that you are a prodigious whip, my lord, it seems that these carriages are somewhat dangerous and I had no wish to be overturned in the gutter.'

Joss burst out laughing. 'Upon my word, Miss Bainbridge, you have a way of depressing a fellow's pretensions! I'll have you know that I have never overturned a phaeton in my life!'

Amy smiled sweetly. 'There could always be a first time, my lord!'

'For everything, so they say.' Suddenly there was a disturbing light in Joss's eyes and Amy felt herself go hot all over, without knowing quite why. She looked away.

'Logically that must be so,' she said crisply. 'I cannot let your observation pass, however, my lord! It seems to me that you must have a low opinion of females. I assure you that some of us are quiet by nature, though we are all different, of course.'

Joss grimaced. 'I feel suitably reproved, Miss Bainbridge.'

'So I should hope!' Amy frowned. 'I have the strangest feeling, my lord, that you do not view the female sex in any very positive light—'

'Ah, now you are quite mistaken, Miss Bainbridge.' Joss's drawl was pronounced. 'I have a very high opinion of females and their *attributes*!'

Amy blushed but persisted. 'I did not mean like that—'

'Like what, precisely?'

Amy glared at him. 'Now you are deliberately teasing me when you know quite well what I mean! I am sure that there are ladies that you admire in a particular way…' She caught the amusement in his eye and subsided. 'Very well. We shall end the conversation there!'

'Pray do not! I am vastly enjoying myself.'

Amy sighed. 'You know perfectly well what I meant!'

'As a matter of fact, I do.' Joss grinned at her. 'You, Miss Bainbridge, have fallen into the trap of making assumptions. You suppose that my only interest in women is…' He caught her eye and smiled. 'Is of an amorous nature. On the little that you know of me, you have decided that I am a gambler and a rake, with no virtues to counteract my vices! You are as guilty of making generalisations as I am!'

Amy blinked. Put like that, she could see the justice of his remark. 'Very well!' she said with spirit. 'What good qualities can you offer in mitigation for the bad?'

Joss laughed. 'Why, none at all! In my case it is quite true. But you see, Miss Bainbridge—' the twinkle in his eye became more pronounced '—I do not see anything wrong in my behaviour. I make no judgements about right and wrong. I do not have your certainty!'

Amy felt confused. 'But gambling is wrong, just as theft is wrong—' She broke off, remembering the ragged children in Whitechapel who had been punished for stealing a loaf of bread to survive. 'That is, theft is wrong but sometimes there may be reasons to excuse it. But gambling is always wrong and there are no excuses!'

Joss's lips twitched. 'Very well, Miss Bainbridge. I concede. You would make a fine judge!'

Amy felt hot and frustrated. She had never previously thought that her ideas were inflexible and now that she examined her views she was still convinced of their rightness.

The only thing that worried her slightly was that no one had challenged her before. It was an entirely new experience.

The press of traffic had brought them to a temporary standstill, which was not what Amy wanted. She wanted to be home very quickly and to put an end to this disturbing conversation. It was not to be, however, so she searched around for a lighter tone.

'Speaking of gambling, my lord—'

'Yes, Miss Bainbridge?'

'I confess that there is one thing about it that has always puzzled me. Perhaps you could explain to me, my lord, what pleasure there is in losing? It seems to me that some people take almost as much joy in the one as the other. As such an ardent gamester yourself, perhaps you could enlighten me?'

Joss laughed. 'That is a very interesting question but not one that I can answer! Did no one ever tell you that I never lose, Miss Bainbridge?'

Amy stared at him. 'Truly? You are funning me! The odds against winning all the time must be immense.'

Joss laughed again. 'I see that you know plenty about betting, Miss Bainbridge! What would you say are the odds against winning the lottery?'

Amy's gaze narrowed thoughtfully. Lady Bainbridge had once told her that most men did not like females of a mathematical bent but she had thought it was one of the most foolish things she had ever heard.

'I would calculate…about forty thousand to one?'

'Very good. Apparently it is about thirty-five thousand to one. You must have a keen mind for arithmetic—or an inbred talent for weighing the odds. Perhaps your family would make more money if your brother gave up gambling and you took it up in his place? I am sorry to have to say it, but his talent appears to be for losing!'

Amy pursed her lips. 'I have observed it myself. Perhaps I should address my question to Richard, then, rather than yourself?'

Joss inclined his head. 'As to that, I think I can explain. It is the game that is the thing, Miss Bainbridge. The excitement is in the challenge of play. It matters not one whit whether one wins or loses—to play is all!'

Amy shook her head. 'I am sorry—that makes no sense at all.'

Joss grinned. 'Perhaps not, to one of your practical disposition. Can you imagine, Miss Bainbridge, the excitement of waiting on the roll of the dice? The pure chance of it? In hazard, for example, you know that all rests on the one throw. You might lose or you might win all. Just as in the lottery your ticket may come up and you might be…oh, thirty thousand pounds the richer! You see—' his gaze had sharpened on her and Amy felt a shiver go through her '—you do feel it! No one is immune from that excitement.'

Amy shivered again, sharply. Whatever she said, she did understand the lure. For a moment she too had been swept up in the excitement of playing and winning, until she had remembered that she was winning the lottery on someone else's behalf. That had brought her swiftly down to earth.

'Did you have a lottery ticket for today's draw, Miss Bainbridge?'

The question took Amy off guard and she jumped, blushing. For some reason she did not wish to admit to Joss that she was in possession of the winning ticket. It seemed too much like hypocrisy after her words earlier. She paused, frowning. Surely his opinion of her should not matter in the slightest…

'I…yes…no…certainly not! I would never buy a ticket! I only went to the Guildhall to meet Richard—' She broke off, flustered. Joss was watching her with interest, which only served to fluster her all the more.

'I see. Yes, I remember you saying you were taking Richard's ticket for him. Yet suppose that you had…found…a ticket of your own, Miss Bainbridge. What would you have done then?'

Amy flushed scarlet. 'I have no notion, sir. The matter does not arise.'

She stopped, a little shocked that she had been less than truthful with him. It seemed absurd to be so guarded because once she had given the ticket to Richard and told him the good news of his win he would surely share his good fortune with his friends. No doubt he would share it literally, in fact, by gambling all the money away to them. There was no real reason why she could not tell Joss that Richard's ticket had won the thirty thousand pounds, except… Except that she felt a curious protectiveness about the money and the win. God help her, she was already starting to think of it as *her* money.

Amy grimaced. She had to cure herself of that delusion before it led her further astray. Any moment now she would be asking herself whether she really had to tell Richard at all. She could arrange for the family's man of business, Churchward, to collect the prize. He was very discreet and would tell no one if she asked him. Then she could use the money for various good causes—in small portions, of course, so as not to arouse suspicion. There were hundreds of people more worthy than her brother, people who deserved her help. Mrs Wendover, for example, bringing up four small children in that slum in Whitechapel, and Mrs Benfleet, the nurse, suffering her ill health uncomplainingly out at Windsor… Amy's heart did a huge lurch. It was so tempting, but, of course, it was theft; had she not just said that theft was wrong—although there were sometimes mitigating circumstances.

'Stop!' Amy had not realised that she had spoken aloud, desperate to halt her wayward train of thought before it tempted her any further. Joss was looking startled.

'I beg your pardon, Miss Bainbridge. Is there some problem?'

'No,' Amy said, screwing her eyes up tightly in mortification. 'I was merely thinking of the lottery and did not realise that I had spoken aloud.'

'I see. Was it the thought of all that dreadful gambling that distressed you, or the heady temptation of it all?' Joss's voice dropped to a soft murmur. 'It is so terribly tempting, is it not? So seductive...'

Amy opened her eyes and stared at him. The Earl of Tallant was a very perceptive man, which somehow seemed quite wrong, given his reputation. He was also a very dangerous man. Once again she felt that stirring of excitement that had rippled through her body when he had spoken of the lure of gambling. It was not simply a question of enticing innocents to part with their money. The temptation was inside everyone. It was subtle, wicked. She looked at Joss accusingly.

'I do believe that you are a very wicked person, my lord, to speak so persuasively of something that is so bad...'

Joss laughed. 'You are correct, Miss Bainbridge. There is no end to my wickedness!'

They were back in Curzon Street at last. Amy gave a little, unconscious sigh, suddenly uncertain whether she was glad or sorry to be back home. Whilst she felt a certain relief to be back on familiar ground, she also felt disappointed.

'Thank you very much, my lord. It was very kind of you to escort me back.'

'Not at all, Miss Bainbridge.' Joss Tallant inclined his head. 'I have enjoyed your company.'

They drew to a halt outside Number 3. Fleet was already helping Amanda down from his phaeton. Amy thought that her friend looked flushed and slightly ruffled, as though she was torn between enjoyment and disapproval. Amy knew just how she felt.

Before she was quite prepared, Joss took her hand and swung her down from the phaeton to the ground, his arm hard about her waist. For a second her palm rested against his chest and she could have sworn, fancifully, that she felt the beat of his heart. It was all over swiftly, yet Amy was left with an impression of strength and power and felt a curious, quivering awareness through her whole body. She did not feel quite steady as Joss set her on her feet and let go of her, very gently.

'Good day, Miss Bainbridge. Lady Spry…'

Fleet was directing the grooms to take the phaetons away. Both he and Joss gave the ladies a punctilious bow, before striding off in the direction of St James.

'So that is that, then,' Amy said, feeling curiously flat and finding it difficult to tear her gaze away from Joss's retreating figure. 'What a very odd day this is! Would you care to come in for a cup of tea, Amanda, and we may have that chat we promised ourselves?'

Amy was amused to see that Amanda's gaze was riveted on the Duke of Fleet and that she had to repeat her question before she was heard.

'Amanda? Amanda, are you feeling quite the thing?'

'Oh, yes!' Amanda said, her blue eyes shining. She turned

away and focussed on Amy's face. 'I beg your pardon, I was woolgathering. A cup of tea would be most delightful, Amy!' She cast a look over her shoulder. Joss and Sebastian Fleet had just turned the corner into Clarges Street.

'I wonder… They say that he is the most dreadful rake and I know I should avoid him, but—' She broke off and gave a tiny shrug. 'Ah, well. The Duke has invited me to accompany him to a ball next week and I am not at all sure I should accept!'

'But do you think you will go?' Amy enquired, opening the door and ushering her friend inside. 'You may be more accustomed to such society than I am, Amanda, but I find the company of rakes and gamblers a little too exciting for my tastes!'

'Oh, I live quite retired now and a Duke is far above my touch,' Amanda said, her blue eyes twinkling. 'When we were first introduced I was determined to be cool to him, for Fleet is most unsuitable! All the same, he was vastly agreeable to me, Amy, and I think I may accept his invitation.'

'Did he flirt with you just now?'

'Oh yes, of course!' Amanda giggled. 'That was part of the fun of the journey!'

'I cannot flirt,' Amy said, a little regretfully, as she took her cloak off and helped Amanda with hers. 'I do not know how to do it. I am too shy, I suppose.'

Amanda looked at her thoughtfully. 'I'll allow that you have always seemed reserved on the surface, Amy—with gentlemen, at least, but I would not say that you are shy, precisely. You have a sharp wit when you choose to exercise it! Besides, think how your family have relied upon you to keep matters together since your father's death. You should be proud of that, I think!'

Amy looked self-conscious. 'You are kind to me, Amanda! You always were when we were at school together. But there is no denying it—I did not take at my come-out and I have no means to attract the gentlemen.' A frown wrinkled her forehead. 'Not that I am entirely sure I would wish to do so...'

Amanda smiled. 'If you wish to learn to flirt, it is surely a skill I could teach you!'

'No, thank you.' Amy viewed her reflection, sparrow brown, in the hall mirror for a moment. 'I think not. I do not look the part.'

'It is but a matter of dress and presentation.' Amanda had moved to stand at her shoulder. 'You have good taste, Amy, and with a few new clothes you will look the very thing. Now that you have the money, there is no difficulty.'

Amy clutched convulsively at her reticule. This was the moment to put her friend to rights about the lottery win, before there were any more misunderstandings. Before she was tempted once again to keep the money for herself.

'Amanda,' she began, 'the money is not—'

The parlour door opened.

'Lady Bainbridge!' Amanda turned with a rustle of silks and perfume. 'How charming to see you again, ma'am.' Before Amy could gesture her to silence, she had burst out, 'You will not believe the most wonderful news—Amy has won the lottery!'

Chapter Five

Joss Tallant cast aside the *Morning Chronicle* and reached for his glass of claret. On the sofa opposite him slumbered the Duke of Fleet, sleeping off the previous night's excesses, his large bulk shaken every so often by a sonorous snore. Fleet had declared that the lottery draw had taken the last of his strength. The Club was quiet and almost empty. Only the occasional rattle of the dice box and rustle of a newspaper disturbed the early afternoon peace.

Joss had given up temporarily on the affairs of the nation, for he had been amused and surprised to find his thoughts veering towards something rather more close to home. Miss Amy Bainbridge, to be precise. Miss Bainbridge, who had proved to be no pattern-card female, who had roundly condemned gambling and who had, he suspected, stolen his winning lottery ticket.

Perhaps stolen was putting it a little strongly, Joss reflected, with a grimace. He took another sip of the wine and sat back, considering. Certainly he could not blame Miss

Bainbridge for his own carelessness in losing his ticket in the first place. Until the draw had taken place he had not even been aware that it was lost, but as soon as he realised that it was gone, he had traced his actions back to the dining room at 3 Curzon Street and the gambling session two nights before. How simple to drop a small piece of paper and not to notice! How easy for Miss Bainbridge to come along in the morning, pick it up, go to the lottery draw and find herself the winner—of thirty thousand pounds!

He could be wrong, of course, but he had a gambler's instinct that he was on the right track and there were various clues to help him. First, there had been Miss Bainbridge's excessive attachment to her reticule. Every so often she would glance down at it to make sure that it was still there. She had been clutching the bag as though it were a lifeline—or as though it contained something very precious.

Then there was the fact that she had looked very dazed and confused when he had first come up to her outside the Guildhall. Joss had had that effect on any number of females, but on this occasion he was not vain enough to ascribe Miss Bainbridge's condition to his charm. No, indeed, she had looked like someone who had won a huge sum of money but could not quite believe it. Or someone who knew they had won a huge sum of money by means that were not quite proper...

Later on, he had deliberately asked her if she had obtained a ticket for the draw and she had stammered and blushed with a look of absolute guilt. He had asked her what she would do if she had found a ticket and she had turned scarlet. She was no natural conspirator, but she was certainly hiding something.

Joss swallowed another mouthful of claret and gazed

thoughtfully into space. He had a good memory for figures and he could recall the exact number on his lottery ticket. Two thousand, five hundred and eighty-eight, winning thirty thousand pounds. He did not need the thirty thousand pounds from a financial point of view, although it would still have been welcome, but his sense of fair play told him that money was rightfully his.

So what should he do? Joss smiled faintly. He could ask Miss Bainbridge directly, of course, or he could mention to Richard that he had dropped a lottery ticket in his dining room and see what kind of response that elicited. Those were by far the most sensible, the most prosaic courses of action. He could even dismiss the whole matter from his mind, given that thirty thousand pounds was a mere drop in the ocean of the restored Tallant fortune. However, such a sensible course was also a trifle dull and he detested the ordinary. So, instead, he could watch Miss Amy Bainbridge for signs of sudden prosperity—see when a modish gown from Bond Street's finest couturier replaced the dress of faded lavender.

His lips twisted cynically. Miss Bainbridge was undoubtedly an unusual woman. He had actually enjoyed her company, which in itself was rather startling. It had been a novelty for him to hold a conversation with a woman who employed no arts to attract him and in whom he had not the slightest romantic interest. She was not conventional; he had suspected it when he had first met her in Covent Garden. Their recent conversation in the phaeton, which had started predictably enough, had soon veered off in an unexpected direction. Joss had been intrigued. Instead of the ordinary conversational gambits that he had intended to employ to pass the journey, he had allowed himself to enter into a genuine debate, a debate that had been decidedly stimulating. Nor was little Miss

Bainbridge as reserved as he had at first imagined. No, indeed, there was a core of strength beneath that quiet exterior.

Was it a core of strength that had permitted her to deliberately appropriate someone else's property and use it for her own financial gain? Joss could not be sure. On the one hand, she had struck him as thoroughly honest, but the requisitioning of his lottery ticket for her own ends did suggest an adaptable attitude towards morality. Joss raised his glass in a mocking tribute to the absent lady. There was no doubt that Miss Bainbridge was a decidedly unusual woman. It would be no hardship to study her a little. No, indeed, no hardship at all.

'I am not sure that a lottery win is respectable,' Lady Bainbridge said thoughtfully. 'We must make sure that no one knows the truth of it. Cits and nabobs are disreputable enough, but a win on the lottery is quite beyond the pale!'

It was early afternoon and Amy, Amanda and Lady Bainbridge were ensconced in the parlour with a pot of tea and chocolate biscuits in celebration of the occasion. Lady Bainbridge had insisted on celebrating, even when Amy had finally managed to make both her friend and her mother stop talking for long enough for her to explain that the lottery ticket belonged to Richard. They had both looked disappointed for a moment and then Lady Bainbridge had ventured the opinion that it need not matter and had immediately gone back to the fascinating topic of what to do with the money.

'No, it is not at all respectable,' Amanda was agreeing with a laugh, 'but you must own, Lady Bainbridge, that it is vastly exciting to be in possession of thirty thousand pounds.'

Lady Bainbridge nodded with more animation than Amanda had seen in her in years. 'Well, of course. It is not *tonnish* to win money, of course, especially not for a woman. In fact, it is quite scandalous! And no amount of cash makes one truly acceptable to society. That need not matter in Amy's case, however! We shall simply put about a story that she has inherited a fortune! No one need know where it has really come from!'

Amy frowned slightly. She was a little puzzled at the direction the conversation was taking, for it seemed that Lady Bainbridge was wilfully misunderstanding the situation. She sat forward on her chair.

'But, Mama, I thought that you understood? We cannot spend any of the money. The ticket must belong to Richard. I did not buy it and I found it in the dining room!'

Lady Bainbridge looked slightly shifty. 'I do not recall that your brother mentioned buying a lottery ticket, my love. Ten to one you will find it was not his! Maybe it blew in from the street—'

'Or a bird dropped it down the chimney!' Amanda finished eagerly.

Amy looked at them suspiciously, and then the penny dropped. 'Oh, I see! You do not wish it to be Richard's ticket! Mama, how could you?'

Lady Bainbridge drooped. 'I know it is dreadfully dishonest, my love, but your brother has an income of his own whilst you have nothing, and besides, he would only gamble it away...'

Since this was exactly what Amy had thought from the first moment, she could not really dispute it. She pulled a face. 'I know that is so, Mama, but we cannot pretend that it is mine—'

'Oh, why not?' Lady Bainbridge looked anguished. 'You

could say that you found it in the street, or that it was stuck
to the doorstep! Any number of excuses could do!'

Amy put her teacup down and moved across to the window seat. 'Mama, I am as concerned as you yourself that
Richard will gamble the whole fortune away—'

'Then why give it to him?' Lady Bainbridge twisted her
hands together. 'Oh, Amy, we would be able to live so much
more comfortably—refurnish the house and buy a few more
candles…' She wavered to a halt at the look on Amy's face.
'Must you be so tiresomely virtuous about this? Why not give
Richard half, if your conscience troubles you? Even fifteen
thousand pounds would be something.'

'Make it twenty thousand,' Amanda advised. 'That way
Amy might have the chance of an advantageous marriage.'

'Wait! Wait!' Amy besought. 'I have no wish to marry,
certainly not to a man who is only interested in me for my
fortune! Amanda, you must remember all those dreadful
men we met during our come-out! Why, half of them had
no conversation, and the other half had conversation that
consisted of talking about nothing except themselves. It was
dreadfully boring.'

Amanda was nodding sagely. 'I know, Amy, but you may
find that matters will be very different now.'

'A man can make himself extremely agreeable for the sake
of thirty thousand pounds,' Lady Bainbridge added.

Amy frowned. 'I do not wish a man to make himself agreeable for my money, I wish him to do so because he likes me
for myself! Oh, this is ridiculous! I do not wish to go into
society and I do not wish to marry and the whole thing is
speculative anyway since I have not won the money—'

'My dear Amy!' her mother said, in the tones of one addressing a simpleton. 'Surely you do not expect us to continue living retired now that we have come into money?'

'Why, yes!' Amy said. 'Even were the money mine, I have no wish to go out into society!'

Amanda and Lady Bainbridge exchanged a look. 'My love,' Lady Bainbridge said carefully, putting down her teacup with solid emphasis, 'I believe you must have misunderstood our situation. We do not live retired because we wish to do so. We live retired because it is cheaper!'

'Yes, Mama.' Amy fidgeted a little uncomfortably. 'I understand that, but I prefer to live quietly. The balls and entertainments of the *ton* do not appeal to me.'

Lady Bainbridge blinked. 'How can you know that, my love, when you had only one season and that was so tragically foreshortened by your father's death? You will find that society is an entirely different matter when you are courted as an heiress.'

Amanda was nodding enthusiastically. 'Oh, yes, Amy! Lady Bainbridge is in the right of it, you know!'

Amy felt as though she was struggling in a quicksand. Both her mother and Amanda had glossed over the issue of the rightful ownership of the lottery fortune and had moved on to Amy's prospects with breathtaking speed. She drew breath to argue, but before she could say anything else, the door opened and Richard Bainbridge strolled in, home at last. He bent to give Lady Bainbridge a dutiful kiss, then straightened up, grinned at Amy and gave Amanda an elegant bow and an admiring glance.

'Lady Spry, is it not? Your servant, ma'am. Mama, is there a cup for me?'

'Of course, dearest!' Lady Bainbridge rang the bell. 'Richard, you will not believe! The most extraordinary good luck—'

'Please, Mama!' Amy said quickly, leaping in before her mother entangled them all in a web of untruths. 'Richard, did you have a lottery ticket for the draw today?'

Richard looked confused. 'Why do you ask, Amy? No, I did not. I was going to buy one but I never got around to it.' He took a chocolate biscuit and bit into it. 'How delicious. Are we celebrating?'

'Yes!' Lady Bainbridge seized the moment. 'Richard, your sister has won thirty thousand pounds on the lottery! Is it not fine? We have just been making a few plans...'

'A moment, Mama!' Amy said desperately. She swung round on her brother. 'Richard, are you certain that you did not have a ticket?'

'Of course I'm certain!' Richard looked quizzical. 'As for you, buying tickets on the sly... I can only congratulate you!'

Amy blushed. 'Oh, but I did not—'

Lady Bainbridge cleared her throat meaningfully. 'Amy means that she did not expect to win, Richard.'

'Mama!' Amy glared.

'I should go,' Amanda said, getting reluctantly to her feet. 'I am sure that you must have a million and one things to discuss *en famille!* Dear Amy—' she swooped on her friend with a scented kiss '—you have no idea how much I envy you your good fortune! I trust we shall be able to meet up again soon.'

Amy grasped her sleeve. 'Oh, but we have not had chance to exchange our news! Please come to see me tomorrow.'

'Of course,' Amanda said, with an enchanting smile. She dropped a curtsy to Lady Bainbridge. 'Good day, ma'am.'

'Richard, go to procure Lady Spry a hack,' Lady Bainbridge said authoritatively as her son, nothing loath, escorted Amanda from the room. 'Such a pretty child,' she added, as the door closed behind them. 'It is a shame that her fortune is no more than ordinary, for Richard really needs to marry an heiress.'

'Mama,' Amy said, 'I had no notion that your thoughts ran along so mercenary a route! You have quite shocked me today.'

Lady Bainbridge opened her eyes wide. 'My dear Amy, I am only trying to do the best for my children and if I have not seemed to put myself out before it is because we did not have the fortune to do the thing in style!' She smiled contentedly. 'But now all that is changed, of course. It is high time that Richard was wed and an heiress will be just the thing for him. As for you, now you have a fortune of your own it will be monstrous easy to see you settled! I think we shall invent an elderly spinster aunt from whom you have inherited. Yes, indeed, old Aunt Bessie from Kent, lived quite retired for many years, but devoted to you, my love, and surprisingly rich...'

'Mama!' Amy said again, horrified at her mother's duplicity.

'Well?' Lady Bainbridge looked defiant. 'You heard your brother, my love. The ticket is not his!'

The door opened again as Richard came back into the room. 'What a charming girl your friend is, Amy. 'Tis a pity she has no fortune, for then she would be more engaging still!' He sat down and swung a careless leg over the arm of his chair. 'Is there any cake, Mama? Surely we can run to that now that Amy is so rich?' He grinned at his sister. 'Can you lend me a couple of thousand guineas, just to tide me over? There's a game on at the Cocoa Tree tonight...'

Amy made a despairing gesture. 'Richard, it is not as simple as that—'

'Too soon?' Her brother looked disappointed. 'I dare say

you have not had chance to claim the money yet? I'll go for you if you give me the ticket, or better still, send Church-ward! Time the poor chap had some pleasant business to un-dertake for this family!'

'Exactly what I thought,' Lady Bainbridge nodded and smiled. 'Churchward will see to it, Amy. He can make a few sound investments for you, my love, and then we will have the rest to spend. You need a couple of new dresses, but not too many,' she added hastily. 'We must still be careful to make sure the money is not wasted!'

Amy blinked hard. Matters were moving very quickly and she felt as though she could not quite catch up. The lottery ticket in the dining room had not been Richard's after all... Whilst her mother rattled on, she tried to think. If Richard had not been the owner of the ticket she had found in the dining room then it must have belonged to one of his cro-nies who had been playing hazard two nights ago, to Bertie Hallam or Humphrey Dainty, or the Duke of Fleet...or Joss Tallant. She suddenly went cold all over. She had appropri-ated a lottery ticket that belonged to someone else...

Richard got up to hold the door as Patience came in with a laden tray. 'Excellent! More tea and fresh biscuits! Do we have any cake, Patience?'

Patience looked outraged. 'Cake? I should think not, Sir Richard. Pure extravagance!'

'We are celebrating, Patience,' Lady Bainbridge said hast-ily. 'Amy has inherited a sum of money—'

'I'm sure I wish you very happy, miss,' Patience said, her stern face almost cracking into a smile. 'Perhaps there will be some money to spend on you now!'

She swished out with a righteous rustle of black crepe.

Richard winked at her and Amy felt herself blush hard.

The tales were already being spun; the story was already running out of control. Soon it would be halfway around London. She had to put a stop to this once and for all.

'Mama! Richard!' she said, so sharply that Lady Bainbridge jumped and spilt her tea. 'You do not understand. I have been trying to explain to you this age that the lottery ticket does not belong to me! I found it!'

There was a short silence. Richard and Lady Bainbridge looked at each other and then back at Amy.

'So?' Lady Bainbridge said, as though expecting more. 'That merely makes you twice as lucky, my love!'

'No!' Amy frowned fiercely. 'It makes it imperative that I find the rightful owner.' She swung round on her brother. 'I found it in the dining room. I thought that it must be yours, Richard, for it was lying beside your chair.'

Richard's face was a picture. 'In our dining room! Well, perhaps I did buy one after all—'

'No, you did not!' Amy got to her feet and paced restlessly across the room. 'You said earlier that you had not got around to buying one. Do not try to gammon me! It must belong to one of your cronies—to Bertie, or Humphrey Dainty, or the Duke of Fleet, or…or the Earl of Tallant.' Her voice wavered a little on the last name.

Lady Bainbridge was looking bewildered. She started to pull her delicate lace handkerchief through her fingers. 'I do not understand! Surely you are not suggesting that the *money* belongs to someone else, Amy?'

'It must do, Mama!' Amy swung round on her. 'I have been trying to get that point across to you this half-hour past! The ticket is not mine and it is not Richard's! The servants do not gamble and I do not suppose that you had a lottery ticket in your possession?'

'No, indeed.' Lady Bainbridge sagged a little. 'Though if I had known that I should win thirty thousand pounds I would most certainly have procured one!'

Amy frowned a little. 'We digress, Mama! The ticket *must* belong to one of Richard's friends and we should give it back!'

'Oh, no!' Lady Bainbridge moaned softly. 'All that money. I cannot bear it!'

Richard had his head in his hands. He looked up, his eyes bright with hope. 'It cannot belong to either Bertie or Humphrey, for they were both with me at the Cocoa Tree this morning and neither of them made mention of the lottery draw. Seb and Joss, I do not know. I could ask them, I suppose...' He looked most unhappy at the thought.

'The Earl of Tallant drove Amy back from the Guildhall and the Duke of Fleet escorted Amanda Spry,' Lady Bainbridge said eagerly. 'Surely they would have said something if either of them had dropped a ticket here that night?'

'I am sure they would.' Richard stood up and stretched. 'So really we need not regard it.'

Amy looked at her relatives wrathfully. 'Really and truly I cannot believe what I am hearing! You both think that we should just forget that the money belongs to someone else?'

Richard flushed and Lady Bainbridge looked defiant in a genteel manner.

'If it was Joss or Seb who had found the ticket and won the money, they would keep it for themselves,' Richard argued hotly. 'They need not know that it was you who found it! Besides, they are both rich and do not need the money as we do. Winner takes all!'

'Oh, yes,' Lady Bainbridge said quickly, 'I am sure that must be true, Amy dearest! We are far more deserving.'

Amy shook her head. 'It is immoral, Mama—'

'So is gambling,' Richard said, with a quick grin, 'yet you are the one holding the winning lottery ticket, sis.'

'I went to the draw to try to find you!' Amy snapped, her patience at an end. 'I thought the money was yours—'

'Then give it to me if it salves your conscience!' Richard reached for her reticule.

'Oh, no, you don't!' Amy grabbed at it. 'I shall hand this over to no one but Mr Churchward and I shall ask him to hold the money safely until I have discovered the real winner. Now, I am going to lie down. My head aches and I need to decide what to do.'

'All this excitement is so fatiguing,' Lady Bainbridge agreed. She exchanged a significant look with her son. 'I feel sure that when you are rested, Amy dear, you will see that it is well nigh impossible to find the rightful owner of that ticket now. Why, if you asked a gentleman if he had dropped a lottery ticket in our dining room, I dare say he would be bound to say yes out of sheer curiosity! You could end up handing the money over to a complete fraud, and one who is a gambler and a wastrel into the bargain!'

'In which case,' Richard said mockingly as he held the door for her, 'you might as well have done and give it to me now, sis! I fulfil all those criteria!'

Amy was burning with indignation as she made her way up the narrow stairs to her tiny bedroom. She clenched her reticule so hard that the beaded workings scored her fingers. To find that her relatives had such a dubious view of morality and one that did not in the least accord with her own was quite a shock. She thought them too worldly and no doubt they thought her a principled fool, but she knew she had to discover the true owner of the thirty thousand pounds. Since

Richard seemed unlikely to help her, she would just have to do it herself. She would have to speak to Bertie Hallam and Humphrey Dainty and she would have to seek out the Duke of Fleet and Joss Tallant. She felt quite shaky at the thought, but she knew it had to be done.

Sitting down on her bed, Amy pressed her fingers to her aching temples and tried to think straight. She could hardly go to visit any of the gentlemen privately if she had a care for her own reputation. What she needed was a social event at which she might casually approach them all and sort the matter out with the minimum of fuss. She frowned. The difficulty was that they so seldom received invitations these days. *Ton* society had practically forgotten that they existed, for although Richard had the entree to any number of events, his mother and sister lived quite retired.

Amy lay down on the bed and closed her eyes. After a moment she sat up, placed the reticule beneath her pillow and lay down again. It was not that she did not trust her mother and brother precisely, but until she could speak to Mr Churchward she simply would not feel safe.

She remembered the single invitation card on the mantelpiece in the dining room. Lady Moon's ball was in four days and Richard had already agreed to escort them. Assuming that the other gentlemen were present, she could speak with them and ascertain the identity of the mystery winner. Amy started to relax. Her headache receded a little. Yes, she could see a strategy now. Soon all would be well.

It was not the sound of someone creeping into her room to steal the reticule that roused Amy later that night, but a rather loud crash outside the house, followed by the sound of the front door opening, hushed voices and something being dragged across the floor. Amy climbed out of bed, lit her candle and trod silently to the top of the stair. Down in the hall, Richard was sitting on the floor, his head lolling against the wainscot, his face a pale, waxy green in the candlelight. Marten was kneeling beside him on the carpet and Joss Tallant was just closing the door.

'You will never get him upstairs on your own,' Amy heard him say. 'It was all I could do to get him into the carriage. Let me give you a hand, man—'

'Oh!' Amy's candle wavered and some hot wax fell on her hand, and the men in the hall looked up and saw her standing there. A look of dismay passed quickly over Marten's normally impassive face, but Amy was focussing on Joss Tallant and saw that he looked thoroughly exasperated to see her.

'Miss Bainbridge.' He gave her a punctilious bow. 'Might I suggest that you return to your bed, ma'am? There is nothing you need do here—'

Ignoring him completely, Amy ran down the stairs and knelt at Marten's side. Richard groaned and rolled his head against the panelling but he did not open his eyes.

'Marten, is my brother ill?' Amy touched Richard's forehead gently but recoiled at the cold sweat beneath her fingers. 'Ugh! I believe he must be suffering an ague—'

'Sir Richard is jug-bitten, miss,' the valet said unhappily. 'Nothing for you to worry about, as Lord Tallant says. If you would like to go back upstairs, I will take care of Sir Richard.'

Amy frowned. She got slowly to her feet, vaguely aware that Joss Tallant had helped her up with a somewhat weary chivalry. 'Jug-bitten, Marten? You mean that he is drunk? But he must have taken far too much…he looks so ill! Does this happen often?'

She saw a hint of a smile touch Joss Tallant's mouth and

turned on him swiftly. 'You need not look so superior, my lord! I am perfectly aware that *gentlemen*—' she invested the word with a heavy sarcasm '—drink far too much sometimes, but this...' she gestured to Richard's prone form '...this is beyond anything! I had no notion...'

'I will take Sir Richard upstairs,' Marten murmured, suiting actions to words by slinging Richard over his shoulder as though he were a lightweight. 'Thank you, my lord...'

Amy, belatedly realising that Joss Tallant must have brought Richard home, looked at him a little uncertainly. 'I suppose that I should also thank you, my lord...'

Joss favoured her with a slight smile. 'Pray do not if you find it sticks in your throat, Miss Bainbridge! Now, may I urge you to retire? It is past three.'

Glancing at the long-case clock, Amy realised that this was true. 'I suppose that you were all drinking and gambling heavily tonight? You and Fleet and Humphrey Dainty—'

'Do I seem foxed to you?' Joss sounded irritated. 'Miss Bainbridge, it is bad enough you blaming me for your brother's gambling, but I will not take responsibility for his drinking as well! Why, I could have left him to the mercies of the Club servants, but instead I thought to bring him home. I almost wish that I had not bothered!'

Amy sighed. 'Did Richard lose very heavily tonight, my lord? Generally he only drinks himself insensible when his losses are great...'

'He did not lose to me,' Joss said drily. 'Any questions about tonight should be addressed to your brother, and not to me.' He pulled on his gloves and moved towards the door. 'Good night, Miss Bainbridge—'

'Oh, but—' Amy started forward, determined that he

should not escape without telling her more of what had happened. 'I want to talk to you—'

Joss turned and looked at her. His amber gaze, mocking now and not in the least deferential, drifted over her with thoughtful appraisal. His gaze lingered on her unbound hair like a caress, slid down the length of her whole body, pausing briefly on the curve of her breast beneath her nightgown, and came to rest on her bare feet.

'Do you really?' he said slowly.

Amy abruptly forgot what she had been about to ask him. She felt as though she was rooted to the spot, vulnerable and shockingly aware. Then there was a thud from above as Marten deposited Richard on his bed, and Amy jumped, blushed scarlet and glared at Joss.

'You have very pretty feet,' he said, with a grin. 'Goodnight, Miss Bainbridge.'

Chapter Six

'Oh, Amy, I am so glad we were able to come tonight!' Amanda clasped her friend's arm with all the excitement of a child. 'It is years since I have been to Vauxhall. How prodigiously exciting it all is!'

They were strolling down one of Vauxhall's gravel walks towards the central square, where they were to take supper in one of the boxes and to hear a concert of Mr Handel's music. Amanda had professed herself disappointed that they had missed the jugglers and acrobats who had been performing the previous night, but Amy thought that the gardens, with their lamplit grottoes and groves, were exciting enough.

She smiled. 'It all looks very pretty, does it not? I do not think that I have been here since the year Papa died...'

Her voice faded away and Amanda gave her arm a sympathetic squeeze. 'Your mother seems to be enjoying herself,' she whispered. 'She is looking most animated.'

Amy watched with amusement as her mother nodded regally to one of her acquaintances in passing.

'There is something of the stately dowager about her this evening,' she agreed. 'I do believe that now we are to go out into society, she feels she has regained her place in the world.'

'And all because of your winnings,' Amanda said, with a sly, teasing look. 'I knew that you would come round to the idea of re-entering the *ton*—and of spending the money on yourself! You look very fine tonight. You see what I mean about clothes making the woman!'

Amy smiled and thanked her. She had no intention of telling Amanda that she still intended to find the rightful owner of the thirty thousand pounds. After all, there were aspects of what Amanda had said that she could not deny. She had spent some of the money on herself—and she had enjoyed it. She liked her new clothes and liked even more the sensation of looking elegant. She cast a glance at Amanda, who was wearing a raspberry pink silk dress cut daringly low. Amanda was truly beautiful, Amy thought, with a little repressed sigh of envy. Her hair gleamed corn-gold and her blue eyes were bright with excitement, and all the gentlemen were staring. Amy knew that she would never stop the carriages in Hyde Park, but still, she was looking better than she had done for years and that gave her a confidence she had previously lacked.

Amy stroked the cream sarsnet gown, with its bodice of emerald green and matching cream scarf. The sleeves of the dress were slashed for the color to show though and she had a green velvet ribbon holding her curls in place. Amy had ruthlessly refused to have any of the blonde lace that her mother had insisted should adorn the dress. Now that she could finally choose exactly what she wanted, she had no intention of being dressed up like the Christmas capon.

The lace had not been the only area of disagreement when

the sarsnet dress had been purchased. At first Amy had been loath to spend any of the lottery money, until Lady Bainbridge had stated, not unreasonably, that she could not go to *ton* events in one of her four-year-old gowns. In the end, Amy had reluctantly accompanied her mother and Amanda to Bond Street, where she had agreed to buy two evening gowns. She had utterly refused all the other underclothes, day dresses, evening dresses, slippers, hats and shawls that her mother had accumulated hopefully whilst she had been trying on the sarsnet dress. They had left Madame Louise's shop somewhat out of sorts, with Lady Bainbridge muttering under her breath about Amy's lack of family loyalty and misplaced principles. Amy had been obliged to treat her mother to an ice cream at Gunter's in order to restore her spirits. So now the lottery money was already a little diminished but Amy was certain that Mr Churchward would be able to help her find enough to make good the loss when she came to hand the winnings over.

A gentleman passed them, ogling the girls through his quizzing-glass. Amy blushed and looked away. Amanda giggled.

'It is Mr Quarles, Stanton's heir. Do you remember him from your come-out, Amy? He seemed to admire you, as I recall!'

Amy shuddered. 'I remember. He was very full of his own importance.'

The gentleman had turned for a second look.

'And he still admires you,' Amanda commented. 'He is still watching you! No, don't look!'

Amy tried not to turn and stare. For some reason, being told not to look made her itch to do so, even though she was indifferent to Mr Quarles's admiration. In an effort to look the other way, she scanned the supper boxes in the nearest colonnade. And forgot about Mr Quarles entirely.

The Earl of Tallant was leaning against the balustrade of the nearest box. Behind him, a number of ladies and gentlemen were partaking of a chicken-and-ham supper and there was much laughter and banter coming from the group. Joss Tallant's gaze met Amy's and he bowed slightly, and Amy looked away, annoyed at having been caught staring. Then, utterly unable to resist this time, she glanced back. To her horror, the Earl had left the box and was walking towards them across the floor. Amy shrank back.

She had not seen the Earl since their most improper exchange in the hallway at Curzon Street at three in the morning, yet when she had been buying the cream sarsnet dress, Amy had found herself wondering whether Joss would admire her in it. The thought had made her very cross with herself, for the answer was almost certainly no. It was only her feet that had excited his admiration, after all, and he should never have seen them in the first place.

'Lord Tallant is coming over!' Amanda said excitedly and superfluously. 'Oh, I wonder if the Duke of Fleet will join us? I am not sure who the others are in his party, except that I think the lady in green is his sister and I do believe that the lady in the frumpish purple gown is Lady Parrish.' She leaned closer to Amy's ear. 'It is the most monstrous scandal, you know. Lord Parrish is the most terrible rake,' Amanda whispered happily, 'just like Fleet and Joss Tallant. I pity his poor bride! They have only been married two months!'

Amy's gaze moved on to Lord Parrish. He was very dark and wicked-looking in a thoroughly piratical manner. No doubt the ladies were swooning for him.

She grimaced. 'Thoroughly bad company!'

'And good evening to you too, Miss Bainbridge!'

Exactly on cue, Joss Tallant came to a halt before them. Amy, realising that he had heard Amanda's last remark and her own rejoinder, sought to efface herself behind a group of statuary. Joss bowed to Lady Bainbridge and Amanda, then took Amy's hand in his, drawing her a little to one side. Hard as she tried, Amy could not avoid a glance down at her feet, clad tonight in delicate slippers to match her dress. Joss saw the glance and smiled.

The Duke of Fleet had come over now to speak with Amanda and his sister was exchanging polite commonplaces with Lady Bainbridge, who looked delighted to be noticed.

'How pleasant to see you again, Miss Bainbridge,' Joss Tallant said, in his lazy drawl. He relinquished her hand with studied slowness. 'I appreciate that it must be a trial for you to acknowledge such dangerous acquaintances as myself and Fleet, and I admire your fortitude!'

'I do not believe that there is any likelihood of my being overset by the experience, my lord,' Amy said coolly. 'We will not be keeping you from your party for long, I am sure.'

Joss smiled faintly. 'If you wished to keep me from my companions I should be delighted, Miss Bainbridge! They are at daggers' drawn and it is most tiring! May I tempt you to a stroll down the *Dark Walk* instead?'

Amy gave him a very straight look. 'No, my lord, you may not.'

'A pity.' Joss's speculative expression made her face burn. He considered the cream-coloured gown and ribbons, and put out one gloved hand to touch the matching scarf lightly.

'You look very pretty tonight, Miss Bainbridge. And I believe I must congratulate you—I have heard rumours that you have come into a fortune.'

Amy flicked the scarf out of his fingers. Despite the lightness of his words there was a very different expression in his eyes. It looked oddly like anger—or disappointment—and the set of his mouth was grim for a moment. Then he saw her watching him and relaxed.

'It is only a temporary fortune,' she said swiftly, wondering as she spoke why on earth she felt the need to justify herself to him. It was strange, but with Joss she always seemed to say more than she intended. Perhaps it was because he made her self-conscious and so she chattered to cover her discomfort. Whatever the cause, there was an uncomfortable awareness fizzing through her blood.

'A temporary fortune?' Joss raised his brows. 'How original! Does it turn to dust and ashes at midnight?'

'Pray do not be ridiculous, sir,' Amy said, trying not to laugh. 'The fortune itself is not temporary, merely my tenure of it! I am looking after it for someone...'

She stopped, wishing that she had said nothing. This was awkward, for although she knew she might have to speak to Joss about the ownership of the lottery money at some point, this was hardly the time or place to eliminate him from her enquiries.

'And you have been spending some of it for them, by the looks of things,' Joss said drily, his gaze skimming her gown again. 'Indeed, how could you resist?'

Amy frowned a little. Given her previous misgivings about spending the money, this touched a nerve. 'I do not know what business it is of yours,' she said, a little sharply.

Joss took her hand again and held on when she tried to pull it from his grip. 'I beg your pardon. It is none of my business indeed. Indulge my curiosity, Miss Bainbridge...

Nicola Cornick

Why did you purchase a beautiful new outfit and yet wear it with darned gloves?'

His thumb was smoothing the top of her glove as he spoke, the soft, repeated caress sending a tingle through her blood. Amy's eyes jerked up to meet his, then she broke the contact equally swiftly. She felt very hot and bothered for such a cool evening.

'They are only tiny darns. I could not discard a pair of gloves for so trivial a reason—'

'But you could have bought new ones—'

'Extravagance!' Amy said. 'As I told you, the money is not mine.' She would have sounded like Lady Bainbridge deploring wastefulness were it not for the fact that Joss's touch was undermining her composure and her voice came out with a husky edge. She knew he had heard it too; she saw his gaze sharpen on her with all the predatory intent of a man who knew exactly the effect he could have on a woman. Their eyes locked, his bright and hard with an emotion that took her breath. Amy gave a little gasp as a shiver went through her. He felt it; she saw a slight smile touch his mouth as he held her gaze very deliberately with his.

'Amy!' Lady Bainbridge's fluting tones brought her straight out of the dream. 'Here is Mr Quarles asking to escort you to supper. Excuse me, my lord...' She looked at Joss meaningfully, evidently hoping he would take himself off and leave the field clear for a genuine suitor.

Joss released Amy's hand gently. 'Then I shall relinquish you, Miss Bainbridge, but I shall hope to see you again soon.'

He gave her a bow, acknowledged the hovering Mr Quarles with the very slightest inclination of the head, and fell into step beside Fleet as they strolled back to their box. Amy let her breath out on a long sigh as she felt her body relax slightly. The blood was still singing through her veins and she felt shaken.

'What a shame that the gentlemen are already engaged for supper,' Lady Bainbridge said, clearly torn between enjoying the exalted company and disapproving of the gentlemen's reputations. Quarles offered Amy his arm as they moved off to find their own box.

'I do not believe that you should cultivate the company of such gentlemen, madam,' he said, in the querulous, reedy voice that Amy remembered. 'Tallant has an unsavoury reputation and Fleet is little better. Sadly unsteady, ma'am, sadly unsteady!'

Lady Bainbridge looked crushed and Amy thought that she heard Richard smother a guffaw. No doubt Mr Quarles was correct and she should prefer his steady presence to the more mercurial charm of the Earl of Tallant. Unfortunately, some perverse part of her, the part that could still feel the echo of Joss's touch, persisted in thinking that the Earl was more exciting company. Not that that meant she would seek him out. Indeed, that would be a very foolish course. Joss was experienced and she was not, and Amy's common sense told her that his attentions to her could have no real substance. It was a sophisticated game of flirtation that she had no intention of playing.

The following afternoon, a footman delivered a pair of beautifully embroidered gloves that fitted her without a wrinkle. There was no card, but Amy knew perfectly well where they had come from and she spent plenty of time thinking about it whilst she helped Patience to polish the windows. Common sense was all very well, she thought with a sigh, but the attentions of a rake were more exhilarating, even when she should know better.

* * *

'Dear Sir Humphrey, please try to remember!' Amy said. 'It was only a week ago!'

It was the night of Lady Moon's ball and Amy's campaign to find the owner of the lottery ticket had begun in earnest. She had quizzed Bertie Hallam when he had called in Curzon Street that afternoon, and had been downcast to find that the ticket was not his. She had wanted it to belong to Bertie for it would have been so much more comfortable not to have had to speak to the others, particularly to Fleet and Joss Tallant. Unfortunately, this was precisely what she had to do.

Seeing a chance shortly after supper, she had lured Sir Humphrey Dainty out on to the terrace and had put the same question to him, only to discover that the absent-minded baronet simply could not remember.

'Last week... Let me see...' Sir Humphrey's gaze darted away from Amy's face and fixed rather desperately on the door of the card room. His body was tense as though he was going to dart off in the same direction. 'Now, I might have had a lottery ticket... Or was that the private lottery to fund the Foundling Hospital? Yes, I do believe it was!' He brightened. 'I won two hundred and thirty pounds and doubled it at play the same night! What luck, eh?'

Amy tried not to drum her fingers impatiently on the stone balcony. She knew that Sir Humphrey had always had the most appalling memory. A neighbour of the Bainbridge family in Warwickshire, he had been perfectly suited to the life of country squire until a substantial inheritance had transformed him into an ardent gamester and transported him to the depths of London's gambling clubs. The inheritance was long gone, but Sir Humphrey found himself unable to break away and return to the country.

'Yes, Sir Humphrey,' she said, struggling to erase the impatience from her tone, 'but what about the most recent draw? Last week—'

'Oh, no,' Sir Humphrey said decisively, 'I did not have a ticket for that. I was playing hazard with your brother at the Cocoa Tree, Miss Bainbridge.'

Amy began to realise that as long as they could measure time and place by Sir Humphrey's gambling, they would stay on approximately the right track.

'You are sure, Sir Humphrey, for this is very important. You might not have dropped a ticket when you came to play in Curzon Street a sennight ago?'

'No, indeed,' Sir Humphrey said again, fidgeting as though an invisible string was drawing him towards the card room, 'for my pockets were to let that night. If I had had a lottery ticket I could have used it as a stake! So it follows I cannot have had one. There! I knew I should remember in the end.'

There was a certain logic to this explanation, Amy felt. It did not help her to find the missing lottery winner, but at least it eliminated the second of the four possibilities. As she watched Sir Humphrey make his impatient way back to the whist table she was tolerably certain that he was not the one. Two down and two to go. She had left the two most difficult until last, hoping that the mystery would be solved by then.

Amy sighed and walked slowly back through the long windows and into the ballroom. The long drapes stirred in the evening breeze. Inside the room the lights blazed and it was considerably hotter. A cotillion was in progress; Amy watched Amanda twirling in the arms of the Duke of Fleet. Her heart missed a beat at the thought of quizzing him about the lottery ticket, but she felt even more nervous at the thought of approaching the Earl of Tallant.

Amy accepted a glass of lemonade from a passing footman and stood in the shadow of the doorway, watching the
ball. It was much the same as any ball she had attended during her come-out and she was certainly not overwhelmed
with partners. She was wearing her other new purchase, a
dress in jonquil silk. It had scarcely made the gentlemen sit
up and notice her, but one or two had been kind enough to
favour her with a dance and a little conversation. She had
also had a chat with Anne Parrish, whom she had first seen
on the night of the visit to Vauxhall. Amy felt a certain affinity with Lady Parrish; they were both outsiders in the *ton*,
although surely Lady Parrish's situation was far worse than
hers, with the *on dit* going the rounds that Adam Parrish had
never wanted to marry her and was dancing attendance on
every lightskirt in town.

Across the ballroom, Lady Bainbridge was seated in a
knot of chaperons, chatting nineteen to the dozen. The ostrich feathers in her turban waved gently. After a moment
she turned and gave Amy a significant look. Mrs Vestey,
Lady Amherst and Mrs Ponting all followed her gaze. Their
mouths formed perfectly round, excited 'ooohs.' Amy rather
suspected that she could guess the conversation, in which a
certain fictitious Aunt Bessie was likely to figure. Her mother
seemed utterly incapable of accepting that Amy was giving
the money away, which made the discovery of the rightful owner of the thirty thousand pounds even more urgent.
Amy placed her empty lemonade glass on the windowsill
and turned to find the Duke of Fleet at her elbow.

'Would you care to dance, Miss Bainbridge?' Fleet was
smiling down at her. Amy's heart skipped a beat, but not because the Duke was so handsome and so charming and so
utterly above her touch. She knew she was obliged to cross-

question him about the lottery ticket. She had been dreading the moment and now there was no escape.

They exchanged a few of the usual commonplaces about the ball as they took their place in the set of country dances, then Amy plunged straight in.

'We were most grateful for your escort home from the Guildhall last week, your Grace,' she murmured.

'I was glad to be of service,' Fleet replied, with a smile and an eloquent glance in the direction of Amanda, who was further down the set. 'I understand that you are an old school friend of Lady Spry, Miss Bainbridge? It must be pleasant for you both to have met up again.'

Amy reflected that it did not take a great deal of intellect to see which way the conversation would tend if the Duke had his way. It reminded her of her come-out season, when she had spent a vast amount of time chatting to Amanda's hopeful admirers about her friend's many charms. Without exception the men who had sought her out had done so to get closer to Amanda, just as the Duke was doing now. Unfortunately, she could not afford to indulge the Duke of Fleet on this occasion. She had a far more pressing matter to investigate.

'Yes, of course, it is delightful to see Amanda again!' she said brightly. 'We are the greatest of friends. So tell me— were you attending the lottery draw at the Guildhall because you had a ticket of your own, your Grace?'

Fleet smiled down at her, his expression a little puzzled. 'Yes, I was. I buy a ticket quite often. Miss Bainbridge, do you know if Lady Spry is to stay in Town for long? She would not vouchsafe her plans to me!'

Amy covered her irritation with a patient smile. If he could be persistent, so could she. 'I am not certain what Amanda plans to do, your Grace. Perhaps you should apply directly to her for the information. Did your lottery ticket win anything?'

'Unfortunately not.' Amy could tell now that Fleet was definitely puzzled at her determination to pursue the subject. She knew she could not persist much further, for he was not a stupid man and might guess the reason that she was asking. It was difficult because she had to be absolutely certain—without giving away the fact that she was looking for the rightful owner of thirty thousand pounds.

'But you are quite sure you did not win?' she persevered. 'You had your ticket with you?'

'I had it with me and unfortunately it did not win,' Fleet repeated. 'What is this sudden interest in my gambling habits, Miss Bainbridge? One might imagine—'

Fortunately the dance obliged them to step apart at that moment and did not bring them together again for quite a while. When they finally met up again the dance was coming to an end. There was a quizzical twinkle in the Duke's eye as he bowed to her and he showed no signs of wanting to relinquish her company.

'Thank you for the dance, Miss Bainbridge. Now, as for your interest in my lottery ticket—'

'Oh, that was just idle curiosity on my part,' Amy said, looking around for the chance of escape. She was not engaged for the next and could not immediately perceive a means to extricate herself.

'I see.' Fleet's smile was rueful. 'I confess that the subject interests me—'

'Oh, I fear it does not interest me!' Amy said with blatant untruth, hiding a yawn behind her fan. 'You must know that I detest gambling, your Grace—'

'I had heard as much,' Fleet murmured, 'which only makes your persistence on the topic all the more remarkable, Miss Bainbridge. However, if the subject bores you suddenly, I suppose I must let the matter go, for it would never do to vex a lady.'

Amy felt the relief wash over her. Thank goodness for the Duke's good manners! Now all she had to do was to find a means of escape. Fleet had escorted her back to her rout chair but showed no signs of departing. Indeed, he was watching her with a mixture of curiosity and amusement. Amy felt flustered. She did not think that the Duke was interested in her for herself—after all, he had made his admiration for Amanda more than plain—but she knew she had piqued his curiosity with her unsubtle tactics on the dance floor. She was sure he would raise the topic of the lottery again in a moment so she fanned herself and commented that it was very hot and prayed for deliverance. It arrived, but not quite in the form that she had hoped.

'I see Joss Tallant is coming over, no doubt with the intention of asking you to dance,' Fleet murmured. 'You are honoured, Miss Bainbridge! Joss never singles out any young ladies for his attention!'

Amy's heart, which had just settled down to a steady beat, leapt into her throat again at his words. She turned her head and watched the Earl of Tallant as he came towards her across the room. She felt hot and shivery at the same time and found herself unable to pull her gaze away from him. It felt strange—she had not seen Joss for a couple of days, but he had seldom been far from her thoughts.

Nor was she the only one disturbed at Joss's approach. The débutantes were scattering from before his path with a kind of enjoyable alarm. They need not have worried; Amy saw that he paid them not the slightest attention as he cut his way through the throng to her side.

'Good evening, Joss.' Fleet was looking amused as he looked from one to the other. 'I assume you have come to wrest Miss Bainbridge from me?'

Joss bowed. 'Good evening, Sebastian. Your servant, Miss Bainbridge. Would you care to dance?'

Fleet, obviously anticipating her acquiescence, smiled and wandered off. Amy would dearly have liked to cry off, but she knew that she had to speak to Joss. All the other candidates had fallen by the wayside and he alone must be the owner of the lottery ticket and the thirty-thousand-pound fortune. She had to tell him so. Besides, she had not yet thanked him for the gift of the gloves, improper as it was.

Beyond Joss's shoulder she could see that her mother had broken off her conversation with the other chaperons, who were all watching with their mouths forming the same round, excited 'ooohs' as previously, though this time no doubt for a vastly different reason. She put her hand on Joss's proffered arm.

'Thank you, Lord Tallant. I shall be delighted.'

They moved towards the dance floor.

'Thank you for the gift of the gloves,' Amy said, a little shyly. 'They are very pretty.'

'I did not like to think of you wearing darned gloves,' Joss said abruptly. He glanced down at her hand, where it rested on his sleeve. 'I see that you do not wear them tonight. Did you not like them?'

'Oh, yes.' Amy darted a look at him. 'It was just that I did not think that it would be quite proper.'

Joss smiled. For a second his hand covered hers. 'It would not be, although there are many things more improper. If you like them, Miss Bainbridge, be damned to convention and wear them!'

It was only as they took their places on the floor that Amy realised that the orchestra was striking up for a waltz. She moved gingerly into Joss's arms, not daring to look up into his face. The waltz was new since her come-out and, although she knew the steps, she had seldom danced it in public. The last time, she recalled, had been with an elderly General who had stepped on her feet several times and had utterly failed to make her feel as though she was lighter than air. Dancing with Joss was easy in one sense and difficult in another. Until that moment Amy had never experienced such an acute physical awareness in her whole life, and the feeling was overwhelming. She did not know whether to pull away from Joss in maidenly withdrawal, or relax into what promised to be a sinfully sensual experience.

Joss solved the problem for her by drawing her closer to him. Her cheek brushed his shoulder and for a second she was certain that his lips had touched her hair, and she had to close her eyes to compose herself whilst her feet moved with the mechanical perfection the waltz demanded. Inside she felt hot and vulnerable and somehow astounded at what was happening to her.

'We seem to have managed to scandalise the entire ball-room simply by dancing together, Miss Bainbridge.' Joss's voice was low and edged with amusement. 'I am sorry to have made you the focus of all eyes—unless you wished to be, of course.'

Amy glanced round and realised the truth of his words. Everyone was staring, the fans were fluttering, the débutantes whispering. Lady Bainbridge was so red in the face that Amy feared she might have a fit, and somehow the united horror of the crowd served to steady her for their outrage seemed so ridiculous. She looked up into Joss's face.

'I cannot see why there is such a fuss,' she said. 'We are but dancing, my lord.'

'True.' A whimsical smile touch Joss's mouth. 'Perhaps I should enlighten you, Miss Bainbridge. Firstly there is the fact that I seldom dance with débutantes, and when I do most people assume I am intending to seduce them.'

Amy raised her brows. 'Then we need have no fear, for I am not a débutante.'

She heard him laugh. 'Perhaps I should have phrased myself a little differently for the sake of clarity, if not propriety. How can I put this? Miss Bainbridge...' he slanted a look down at her '...if I dance with *any* lady, the world assumes I am intending seduction.'

Amy smiled. 'How extraordinary. That would be so exhausting for you, my lord. Can it possibly be true?'

'No,' Joss said ruefully, 'but gossip seldom takes account of the truth, Miss Bainbridge.'

'All the same, the gossip must have started somewhere, my lord.'

'Ah, now there you have me.' Joss smiled. 'There is always some truth in rumour, I suppose. Are you sure you feel quite safe with me, Miss Bainbridge?'

'Because the waltz is licentious and dangerous?' Amy enquired.

'Or because I am myself.'

Amy opened her eyes wide. 'I do not fear for my safety in a crowded ballroom, sir.'

'Very sensible. But you disappoint me, Miss Bainbridge. How is my rakish reputation to be maintained if you steadfastly refuse to believe in it?'

'No doubt you will think of a way, my lord,' Amy responded. 'Besides, though you may fail to frighten *me*, there are a dozen young ladies in our vicinity who are only too willing to be terrified of you!'

'You reassure me. However, when I wish to lose my dishonourable repute I shall come to see you. I am persuaded that it will melt away beneath such blistering common sense!'

They had completed one circuit of the floor and Amy was presented, once again, with her mother's disapproving frown. It was extraordinary, quite as though she expected the Earl of Tallant to seduce her daughter there and then on the dance floor. Amy, reflecting on the foolishness of this, repressed a little regretful sigh.

'So what was the second reason, my lord? You said *firstly* we were scandalising everyone because of your reputation as a rake. So, secondly?'

'Secondly, it will not have escaped the notice of anyone in the ballroom that I am enjoying your company, Miss Bainbridge.' There was a strange expression on Joss's face for a fleeting moment. 'I doubt that anyone here will remember a like occasion.'

Amy felt a warmth steal through her. It was impossible not to feel flattered even if she was not sure of his sincerity. 'Then I am honoured, my lord.'

A smile quirked Joss's lips. 'Cut line, Miss Bainbridge! I doubt you are! What is your opinion of me—a gambler and a wastrel…?'

'And a rake, of course.'

'I am obliged to you for reminding me. So you cannot be honoured by my attentions, given that you have a low opinion of all of those activities.'

Amy smiled back. 'I was only trying to be kind.'

'That is certainly a novelty for me.' Joss inclined his head. 'Let us change the subject before my esteem suffers any further blows. It is pleasant to see you out in society again, Miss Bainbridge. I thought that you lived quite retired these days?'

'Generally I do, my lord,' Amy returned, 'but Lady Spry is up in London for a short while and persuaded me that I would enjoy the ball. I confess it is quite entertaining.'

'Did you then expect that it would not be?'

'Oh, no, not precisely.' Amy hesitated. 'I do not have happy memories of my début, my lord, for I was very shy and did not take.'

'I remember.' Joss gave her a searching look. 'You barely spoke a word. So what has happened to you in between, Miss Bainbridge?'

Amy looked up at him, startled. 'Why, nothing. Whatever do you mean, my lord?'

'Well, you are not shy now. What happened to change that?'

Amy was taken aback. It was true that she had engaged in conversation with Joss very easily once the initial shock of being in his arms had faded. Their repartee had been light and amusing, and as such was far different from the laboured conversations she was accustomed to holding with her partners. But that was just... She struggled a little, because the truth was that it was only with Joss that she felt at such ease. She felt able to express her views and opinions openly and found him interesting to converse with. And that particular fact was not one she wished to examine too closely.

'I am still a reserved character, my lord—'

'I say fustian to that, ma'am! How can you possibly say

so? You have had no difficulty in expressing your views to me from the moment we met.'

'But that was because—' Amy stopped dead. She had almost said, 'That was because I had no wish to attract you,' but managed to prevent herself just in time. One of the things that had hampered her during her season was her mother's fervent insistence that she find a suitable man to marry. Amy had tried because she too was desperate to find a way out of the violent swings of fortune that composed life in the Bainbridge household. She wanted to live in calmer waters. So she had viewed each young man she met as a potential suitor but had found them all lacking one way or another. There was no common ground;

they did not appear interested in talking to her and seemed disappointed that she was so plain. Her mother harried her and nagged her to become suitably established but it was all in vain—Amy could not attract any offers.

Yet when she had met the Earl of Tallant she had disapproved of him so thoroughly that it had seemed irrelevant to view him in the light of a potential suitor. She had not even tried and thus had managed to speak to him perfectly normally. Now, thinking about it, she could not repress a gurgle of laughter at so outrageous an idea as Joss courting her.

Joss was watching her, his eyebrows lifted questioningly.

'Really, Miss Bainbridge, are you not to explain yourself? That was because...what?'

'Oh, I beg your pardon.' Amy smiled at him. 'You are quite right, my lord. I have been most outspoken in expressing my views to you.'

'I thought that we had agreed that already. I was interested in the reason why.'

'Oh...' Amy cudgelled her brain to come up with a suitable explanation. Could she say that speaking to him was like talking to an elder brother? No, that would not wash. It was far more interesting than conversing with Richard. What about telling him that she felt comfortable with him? That was not precisely true either. His company was too stimulating for that.

The thought brought her up sharply. Stimulating—Joss Tallant. The gamester and womaniser. The man she disapproved of so thoroughly, who was leading Richard astray with his excessive gambling. Her smile faded. How was it possible that she could distrust Joss and yet enjoy his company so much? It was as mysterious as it was disturbing.

'I believe that I may have acquired more town bronze since then, my lord, that is all,' she said.

'Enough indeed to be able to produce a convincing excuse when you need one,' Joss observed drily. 'You are to be congratulated, Miss Bainbridge.'

He bowed to her and escorted her round the floor, but they did not speak again and it was as though some constraint had fallen between them. Amy had totally forgotten that she was intending to quiz Joss about his lottery ticket and it was only when Lord Anston approached her for the next dance, neatly cutting out Mr Cavendish, who had been advancing from the left, that she remembered that there was business unfinished between them. It was too late, however; Lord Anston was triumphantly claiming her hand and Joss walked off with negligent elegance in the direction of the card room.

After that there seemed to be a queue of gentlemen suddenly eager to make her acquaintance. Amy could not believe that dancing with Joss Tallant had brought her into fashion and darkly suspected that it must be her mother's hints of a fortune that had made her so sought after. Whatever the case, it was after supper that Bertie Hallam finally caught up with her to demand a dance. After they had finished he took her arm in a surprisingly masterful grip and steered her towards the candlelit conservatory. Amy, suspecting that Bertie was about to make one of his regular proposals, tried to deflect him.

'Oh, is not Lady Alice Broughton over there? I am sure you said that you admired her, Bertie. Why do you not ask her to dance?'

Bertie was not to be deflected.

'Now see here, Amy,' he said, when they were seated on a bench beneath the sparkling fairy lanterns, 'I've decided that really you must marry me. It's not right that you should spend your days fetching and carrying for Lady Bainbridge, reading and sewing and...' Bertie wrinkled up his face, evidently trying to imagine what else Amy might do with her time '...and other things,' he finished, a little lamely. 'You are not as young as you were and it's time you had your own establishment.' He took her hands in his. 'I know you're accustomed to refusing me and I know you disapprove of my gambling, but dash it, Amy, you ought to accept my proposal!'

Amy sighed. Over the years she had grown accustomed to receiving an offer of marriage from Bertie Hallam. The habit had started when he was six and she was five, and he had shown a dogged devotion ever since. It was quite dark in the conservatory, but by the faint light of the coloured lanterns she could see that he was looking at her with a hopeful expression on his lugubrious face.

'Dearest Bertie,' she said gently, 'it is very kind of you to ask me but I fear that the answer is still no.'

She had just finished speaking when she became aware that they were not alone in the shadowy conservatory. The shadows moved and shifted and then a tall figure was standing beside the bench and a cool voice said,

'I do apologise for my intrusion, Miss Bainbridge. I had merely come to ask you to spare me another dance. I had no notion that I was interrupting at such a delicate moment. Pray excuse me. Your servant, Hallam.'

The Earl of Tallant. Amy recognised the voice, with its undercurrent of amusement, and felt the colour burn her face that he had found her in such a situation. Bertie got to his feet with what Amy recognised was an attempt to match the Earl's own sangfroid. He failed miserably, for his demeanour was stiff and his good-humoured tone a little forced. Amy recognised his discomfort and felt a rush of sympathy for him—and a burning annoyance with Joss Tallant for being cool and amused and so nonchalant; everything that Bertie was not. Then she felt irritated with herself, for she was the one who had rejected Bertie's proposal of marriage and it was hardly fair to take out her guilt and bad temper on someone else.

'Servant, Tallant,' Bertie said heartily. 'Amy, do you wish to go back into the ballroom?'

Amy knew that that was the proper course of action, but she had suddenly remembered that she had to ask Joss about the lottery ticket and that this would probably be her only opportunity. The field had narrowed—to one. There was only Joss left, and for some reason she felt very nervous about asking him. She would just have to get the matter over with quickly.

'You go on without me, Bertie,' she said quickly. 'There is something that I wish to ask Lord Tallant.'

Bertie hesitated, clearly struck by the impropriety of this. 'Amy, I really do not think that I should leave you here—'

'I shall only be a moment,' Amy said. Clearly her erstwhile suitor had now reverted to acting as an elder brother. Whilst she felt more comfortable with Bertie in that role, she did not wish him to exercise a fraternal interest just now. She turned towards Joss, leaving Bertie standing open-mouthed and startled. 'Lord Tallant, would you walk with me a little, if you please?'

'With great pleasure, Miss Bainbridge.' Joss Tallant fell into step beside her and gave her a searching look.

'What a surprising young lady you are turning out to me, Miss Bainbridge! Seeking out my company in such a way is most singular!'

His sleeve brushed against hers. Amy repressed a shiver.

'I know it,' she said a little uncertainly. 'It may seem a little odd...'

'It does,' Joss agreed pleasantly, 'not to mention bold and surprisingly out of character, Miss Bainbridge! You are surely aware that to ask a gentleman to walk with you through a dark and deserted conservatory could be interpreted in rather a dubious light?'

'That would depend on the gentleman, I dare say,' Amy said.

'Very probably.' Joss slanted a look down at her and Amy could tell that he was smiling. 'Some would take it as an invitation, Miss Bainbridge.'

'But you would not make that mistake, would you, my lord?'

'We have already discussed that, have we not, Miss Bainbridge? You are quite aware of my reputation.'

'I am,' Amy said crisply, 'and I am certain that I am in no danger.'

It was true. Despite his rake's reputation and the fact that they were alone together, Amy had the strangest feeling that they understood one another. How they had reached such a rapport was curious and she might even have imagined it, yet she felt entirely safe with him.

'You are intrepid indeed, Miss Bainbridge.' Joss laughed 'So, having dismissed that issue, we may talk. What is it that you wished to ask me?'

Amy cleared her throat. 'I have asked the same question of several different gentlemen including Mr Hallam—'

'How intriguing.' Joss turned suddenly, taking Amy's hands in his. His touch was warm. 'So, will it necessitate the same actions as your conversation with Mr Hallam?'

Amy snatched her hands away. She wished she was seated so that she might make assurance doubly sure by sitting on them.

'Of course not! How absurd you are! Mr Hallam was holding my hands because—' She stopped, cross with herself. It was none of Joss Tallant's business what she had been talking about with Bertie. 'Well, that is nothing to the purpose anyway—'

'He was holding your hands because he was making you an offer,' Joss said. The undertone of mockery in his drawling voice made Amy's annoyance worse. 'I am sorry for interrupting you at such a deucedly awkward moment. I hope it did not ruin matters for you.'

'Of course not! Mr Hallam proposes to me every year and I fear it has become something of a habit with him,' Amy said. 'Not that it is any business of yours, sir.'

'It is not, but satisfy my curiosity further. Did you refuse him?'

Amy was glad of the darkness that covered her blushes. 'You are impertinent, sir—'

'I am. Did you refuse him?'

'Yes, I did.' Amy spoke in a rush. 'I do not love him.'

There was a short silence. 'I suppose you require the grand passion to persuade you into matrimony, or at least the appearance of it?' The mockery was still in Joss's voice and Amy prickled with annoyance. 'You disappoint me, Miss Bainbridge. Most young ladies are tiresomely sentimental, but I had thought that you might be different.'

'I certainly require to have more than mere liking for the gentleman I marry,' Amy said sharply, 'if you consider that sentimentality! However, I do believe that you do my sex little justice, sir. At least half of us are prepared to marry for money and position alone!'

Joss laughed again, this time with genuine humour. 'This kitten has very sharp claws! I am relieved that I need not repine, Miss Bainbridge. Somewhere there will be a lady prepared to overlook my faults and marry me for my money alone.'

'I was not aware that your lordship wished to marry,' Amy said. The thought gave her a strange feeling inside. 'Your behaviour does not suggest it. You are a self-confessed rake, after all.'

'So?' Joss laughed. 'I have yet to learn that that is a bar to marriage.'

'And you are evidently a cynic too! It seems a shame to embark on matrimony with such an attitude.'

'Ah, so we are to talk morality now, as we spoke of gambling before? How stimulating!'

'No, I do not wish to debate morality with you, my lord,' Amy said. 'There are plenty of reform societies for you to visit if that is your wish.'

She sighed. Debating with him was like wrestling a slippery fish, only much more enjoyable than fishing. Seldom were her wits tested to this extent in her daily conversations with Richard or Lady Bainbridge. It felt exciting, as though she was straying into deep waters. Part of her wanted to go with the tide and the other part, the sensible part, held back.

'Thank you.' Joss inclined his head. 'I am obliged to you for pointing that out although I feel that a conversation with you might have been more enjoyable, Miss Bainbridge. Crossing wits with you is peculiarly interesting.'

'Thank you,' Amy said briskly. 'We seem to have drifted quite a distance from the topic in hand, my lord. I had a question for you, if you recall. It was simply this. Did you have a lottery ticket for the draw last week?'

There was a pause, and then Joss bowed slightly. 'No, Miss Bainbridge. I did not have a ticket. Why do you ask?'

'Oh, no reason,' Amy said airily. She felt both relieved and disappointed at the same time. 'I was merely curious—'

'About my gambling habits? They are extreme, I am afraid. But of course you know that—and deplore it. But I should call time on you for that Banbury tale, Miss Bainbridge. There must be a better reason for your question than simple curiosity.'

Amy pressed her hands together. The Duke of Fleet had not persisted in questioning her, but she had had a feeling from the first that Joss Tallant would not be quite so amenable. And now she had a greater problem. Since the ticket did not belong to any of Richard's gambling cronies, nor was it clear who else might claim it, what was she to do? She frowned slightly, thinking aloud.

'I found a lottery ticket in the dining room at Curzon Street, my lord, and it won the prize last week. I have been trying to reunite the money with its rightful owner, but I cannot seem to find him.'

Joss raised his brows. His tone was incredulous. 'You found a winning lottery ticket and you wish to give the money away? Miss Bainbridge, you astound me!'

Amy threw him a look that was part ashamed, part challenging. 'Why so?'

'Come, you must know the reason! Firstly, I am amazed that you would tell me such a thing and, secondly, I cannot believe that you would give the money away! It beggars belief!'

Amy gave an angry sigh. 'Why must everyone make me feel as though I am doing wrong rather than doing right? All I am trying to do is to see that the rightful owner is given the money!'

Joss laughed. 'Who is everyone?'

'Oh, you and Lady Spry, my mother and Richard! It is the most shocking thing, my lord! All the world would keep the winnings for themselves and cannot understand why I believe I must give them back!'

'Your honesty will be making people uncomfortable, I believe,' Joss said slowly. 'Not one man in ten—and I include women as well—would do as you are doing, Miss Bainbridge, and they will not like you for it.'

Amy frowned. 'Surely there would be plenty of people who would not keep what is not rightfully theirs? I cannot believe the world so venal as you describe it, my lord!'

'Believe it, my dear Miss Bainbridge. I fear you are naïve!'

'Well, there is no need to patronise me!' Amy said crossly. 'Just because you would do differently yourself.'

'Ah, yes, of course—so I would.' There was an odd note in Joss's voice. 'Yet still I may be helpful, perhaps. Have you interrogated all the servants to check on their gaming habits? Perhaps one of them would admit to it—for thirty thousand pounds?'

'None of the servants play the lottery and the ticket belongs to none of Richard's guests, nor to me or to Mama or Richard himself. Amanda—Lady Spry—wondered if it had been blown in off the street, perhaps, or been dropped down the chimney by a bird.'

'How imaginative of Lady Spry—and how convenient.' Joss smiled. 'It would undoubtedly be simpler to accept her views.'

Amanda frowned again. 'Well, I cannot see what else I can do now!'

'Forget the matter and spend the money on yourself would be my advice. Or give it to Richard so that I may win it all from him!'

'Certainly not!' Amy gave him a repressive look. 'If I must keep it, my lord, I shall use it to do good.'

Joss sighed. 'Must you? How tiresome. Can you not allow yourself to be corrupted by the possession of it?'

'No, indeed. How absurd you are!' Amy sobered. 'There is just one small matter...'

'Yes?'

'I wonder—would you not tell anyone about my winnings? I have no intention of going about in society very much and will give the money to good causes, but I could not bear if it was rumoured that I was the lottery heiress, or some such ridiculous soubriquet.'

'Of course.' Joss's hand covered her own for a brief second on his sleeve. 'There is just one thing, Miss Bainbridge...'

'Yes?' Amy found her voice a little unsteady. That brief touch had lit something inside her and she moved back a step. 'What is it?'

'Did you tell anyone else the reason for your enquiries? I mean, did you tell Hallam, or Dainty—or Fleet?'

'No.' Amy hesitated. 'I was trying to be discreet and did not wish anyone else to know.'

'Then why tell me?'

There was a silence. Amy felt tense. She did not wish to answer the question, did not even know the answer. She had known Bertie Hallam for years and trusted him as a brother, yet it was not to Bertie that she had confided the truth but to Joss Tallant.

'I am not entirely sure,' she said uncertainly.

The silence stretched, taut as a drum.

'Yet you trust me with this information?'

'I...yes.' Amy had a sinking feeling in her stomach. She remembered what Lady Bainbridge had said about the scandal that would ensue if it became known that she had gained a fortune through winning the lottery. She had put herself in Joss's hands now.

'Well, your secret is safe, I promise. No doubt you will wish to avoid all those fortune-hunting adventurers who will want to capture your hand, heart and money,' Joss said, and the lightness of his tone eased Amy's tension. 'I fear you may be a little late, however. Your mother has already boasted— most discreetly, of course—of your good fortune. Only she has been suggesting that it is a bequest from an elderly relative, so I understand...'

Amy gave a little moan. 'I thought so! I asked Mama to keep quiet!'

'Impossible!' Joss tucked her hand comfortingly through his arm. 'It would be too much for maternal flesh and blood to keep silent. Lady Bainbridge told Mrs Vestey, who told Lady Bestable, who told half the company here tonight. It is the latest *on-dit*! Now, come and dance, Miss Bainbridge. You will find that life as an heiress is not so bad after all.'

Chapter Seven

Joss Tallant relinquished Miss Amy Bainbridge to the eager arms of Viscount Truscote and strolled over to the long terrace windows for a drink and some fresh air. The heat in the ballroom was becoming oppressive and he had no further desire to dance. Perhaps it was time to leave the genteel entertainments of Lady Moon's ball for less salubrious surroundings. A picture of Harriet Templeton came into his mind, but for some reason it seemed unappetising. Joss shrugged philosophically. No doubt Harriet would regain her appeal soon, but if not he could always find another mistress.

He replaced his empty glass of wine with a full one and stood watching the dancers. Amy was waltzing with Truscote, moving daintily and with grace. She might be small, but she was perfectly proportioned and danced divinely. She was looking up into Truscote's face with a confiding smile and it seemed she was enjoying the Viscount's company no matter what she had asserted before about finding little to entertain her at balls and parties. Joss felt a shaft of irritation pierce him. He put his wine glass down with a slap that showed scant regard for the delicate crystal. It was definitely time to move on. He felt bored and blue-devilled and had a fancy to drown the evening in brandy.

He could not be certain what it was that had prompted him to disclaim ownership of the lottery ticket. When Amy had first spoken, he had felt relieved to discover that his suspicions about her honesty had been groundless. This was so strange a reaction that it had held him silent for a few moments, for surely he should not have cared either way? He had dismissed the thought as she had carried on talking and had become intrigued by her attempts to find the rightful owner, charmed even by her determination to do the right thing. He had been less flattered by her instinctive assumption that he, along with everyone else, would have kept the money for himself. But then there was no reason for her to have a good opinion of him. And there was certainly no good reason why he should care if she did or if she did not.

'You seem to have played Pygmalion rather successfully this evening, Joss.' The Duke of Fleet had paused beside his friend and was also looking in Amy's direction.

'Miss Bainbridge is much in demand,' Fleet continued. 'Why put yourself to the trouble to bring such a plain girl into fashion?'

Joss met his friend's bland expression with a stony one of his own. He knew perfectly well what Fleet was up to and he was not about to give him the satisfaction of rising to provocation.

'I scarce think that my attentions will enhance Miss Bainbridge's reputation, Seb. The reverse is probably true.'

Fleet looked quizzical. 'Then why inflict your company on her if you think it will bring her into disrepute, old chap?'

Joss shrugged. 'I wanted to talk to her.'

'Was it worth it?'

'Decidedly.' Joss tried to crush the irritation that Fleet's conversation was engendering, but was only partially successful. 'Miss Bainbridge is not in the common way, which is good, for the common way bores me.'

Fleet frowned a little. 'Do you have no concern for her reputation?'

Joss shrugged again. 'No one comes to any harm waltzing with me in a crowded ballroom and any chaperon who believes otherwise has too vivid an imagination.'

'As long as you are not putting ideas into Miss Bainbridge's head with your attentions. It would be a pity to disappoint her. Unless...' Fleet paused. 'You did say that your father was suggesting matrimony?'

Joss laughed, although somewhere in the recesses of his mind the idea took root with surprising firmness. He tried to dislodge it. 'My father was suggesting progressive farming methods last week! His suggestions need not concern me, I am glad to say.'

Fleet shook his head. 'You're a cold fish, Joss. Fancy some Haymarket ware to warm you up?'

'Not tonight. I fancy a warm brandy bottle and a game of hazard at White's.'

Fleet nodded. 'I'll join you. It is better sport than this.'

Joss gave him a mocking look. 'Has Lady Spry lost her charm, Seb?'

'Not really, but she's too damned proper for me.' Fleet sighed. 'A widow with no inclination towards dalliance. My cursed luck!'

Joss clapped him on the shoulder. 'To White's?'

'Why not? If you have no desire to dance with the mousy Miss Bainbridge again.'

Joss had turned away but now he stopped, finding that he could not let that one pass. He felt so angry that he had to take a deep breath before he spoke. So Seb had found his mark. Damn him.

'I have not the least desire in the world to dance with Miss Bainbridge again,' he said coolly, after a moment. 'But as one who is at least a gentleman by title, I have to tell you, Seb, that Miss Bainbridge is *not* mousy.'

He turned on his heel and walked off. Fleet watched him go, a self-satisfied smile on his lips.

'A result at last,' he murmured. 'Joss, m'boy, this is going to be interesting.'

'I am so glad that your mama permitted me to be your chaperon tonight,' Amanda Spry said, as the new Bainbridge coach took them the short distance from Curzon Street to Portman Square, 'although I am sorry that she has the migraine. It is only a small party, not a ball, but I am sure that there will be many eligible gentlemen there tonight.'

Amy fidgeted nervously. She was aware that Lady Bainbridge had been swayed by this piece of information into letting Amanda take a role to which she was surely unsuited. Amy did not consider that she needed a chaperon, being one and twenty, but since she was obliged to have one it seemed silly that that person should be Amanda, who was twice as impetuous as she.

Amy stroked the pale blue silk of her new evening gown. She had chosen it because it matched her eyes exactly, and brought out the golden lights in her brown hair. She had stood before the mirror in her bedroom and had reflected that she actually looked quite pretty for once—but that was before she had seen Amanda, ethereal in apricot satin with a matching bandeau adorned with soft white feathers.

The carriage drew up outside the door. Amanda had told her that Mrs Wren was a widow of great respectability who gave marvellously entertaining parties. However, Amy was not long inside the house before she realised that Mrs Wren's parties were not the sorts of affair at which any débutantes would be present. The hostess set the tone in a clinging dress with a plunging décolletage that displayed to advantage a diamond necklace that Amy considered to be frankly vulgar. Mrs Wren's rooms were full of ladies and gentlemen chatting loudly and with a freeness of manner that was startling. The wine was flowing very copiously indeed and there was no lemonade. Even when the musical entertainment started the guests did not bother to lower their voices and Amy was irritated that the excellent singer was quite drowned out by conversation.

Amanda was soon dragged away from Amy's side to play a hand of whist and Amy took refuge behind a pillar where she sipped her glass of wine and wished that she had stayed at home. She had seen Richard across the room but her brother seemed disinclined to come and talk to her when he had a dashing blonde lady hanging on his every word. Amy, feeling shy and uncomfortable, resolved that she would not stay another minute. The party was threatening to turn into something rather less respectable, and at lightning speed. Yet even as she turned towards the door she was stopped in her tracks.

'Leaving so soon, ma'am? Why not come and have a li'l chat with me?'

Someone put their hand on her arm and Amy turned,

repressing a shudder as the gentleman leaned closer and breathed stale wine fumes in her face. She could tell from the gleam in his eyes that he was drunk, but not sufficiently to be incapable. She backed away.

'Don't be coy,' the gentleman leered. 'You're a taking little piece! We should become better acquainted...'

'Thank you, sir, but I am waiting for someone,' Amy said, hoping that her desperation did not show in her voice. With the pillar behind her and the drunkard in front, her options seemed decidedly limited.

'Waiting for me, in fact,' a voice said briskly. Joss Tallant took Amy's arm and drew her close to his side. 'I do apologise for my shocking tardiness, my dear. Baverstock, you need not trouble the lady with your company any longer.'

The Earl of Baverstock muttered something and sidled away, and Joss drew Amy's hand through his arm and steered her towards a quiet alcove where they sat down.

'Of all the places where I might have expected to find you, Miss Bainbridge...' Joss said ruefully.

'I know!' Amy felt a little shaken. 'I believe that I was misled about the sophistication of the evening.'

'There is nothing very sophisticated about this crowd,' Joss said dismissively, looking around, 'but I take your meaning, Miss Bainbridge! Perhaps you should go home?'

Amy craned her neck for a glimpse of Amanda. 'I came here with Lady Spry. I do not suppose that I should simply abandon her.'

Joss laughed. 'Surely it is the other way about? Is she not intended to be your chaperon?'

'Yes, but...' Amy sought to excuse her friend '...it is not as though I need her protection.'

Joss raised his brows. 'Indeed? Were you enjoying Baverstock's attentions?'

Amy flushed. 'That was different, and, no, of course I was not! I am sorry, my lord—I should have thanked you for rescuing me.'

'It was a pleasure.' Joss gave her a slow smile. 'I have some sympathy with Baverstock, however, for you do indeed look most attractive this evening, Miss Bainbridge.'

Amy almost gaped. 'Come now, my lord! Not even my mother would allow that I looked more than tolerable! In such company—' She gestured at the painted ladies milling about them.

'You mistake your charm.' Joss stretched, giving her an assessing look that made her blink. 'In such a company as this it is precisely because you look fresh and innocent rather than jaded that you stand out, Miss Bainbridge. As for your mother, perhaps she should have spent more time telling you how charming you look, so that you would not lack the confidence to believe it!'

Amy looked at him in shocked silence. There had been an undercurrent in his voice that she did not understand. Their eyes met and then Joss sighed.

'I beg your pardon. I should not have said that about Lady Bainbridge.'

'No, but...' Amy was confused. 'I understand that you were only trying to make me feel better—'

'No!' Joss spoke so sharply that Amy jumped. 'That was *not* what I was doing, Miss Bainbridge! Why can you not believe me sincere?'

'I am sorry.' Amy was even more confused now. He sounded exasperated, but beneath that she sensed a hurt that she did not understand. Surely the Earl of Tallant could not care about her good opinion? And why should it matter to him that she believe that he admired her?

She stared at him, her eyes narrowing thoughtfully. 'My lord—'

'I will go and find Lady Spry for you, Miss Bainbridge,' Joss said, interrupting abruptly. 'It is not in the least suitable that you should remain here any longer.'

Puzzled, Amy watched as he disappeared into the card room, to emerge an impressively short time later with Amanda. Amy wondered if he had summarily removed her in the middle of a rubber of whist.

It seemed so, but when Amanda reached her side, she was not the least inclined to leave the party.

'Amy,' she wheedled, 'I know that you wish to go home, but I would just like to play another hand. Please! And we need a fourth to make up the numbers, just for this rubber. Oh, please say that you will play!'

Amy groaned. She had no wish to disoblige her dearest friend, but playing whist, even for a nominal sum, was not her idea of fun. The evening was not far advanced but the behaviour was licentious, she was too hot and wanted to go home. She gave Amanda a look of exasperation. 'Mandy, you know I never play! Why not ask Lady Bestable if she will join you? She is a bosom bow of Mama's and I know she loves whist.'

'Lady Bestable is already playing,' Amanda said. 'We need someone else. Please, Amy...' Amanda put on her most beseeching expression. 'I know that you dislike to gamble, but there is no harm in this! We are not playing for more than pennies! And you were always lucky at cards. You know you were!'

'That is beside the point,' Amy said. She could feel herself weakening and tried to strengthen her resolve. Amanda had always been deplorably persuasive, even in their schooldays. She had always managed to persuade Amy to some scrape against her better judgement. And now Amy felt like a kill-joy, denying her friend some innocent entertainment. Perhaps she was making too much of her dislike of gambling, especially when it was a harmless game for a risible sum. Everyone gambled, after all. Perhaps, as Richard had implied, she was taking it all too seriously.

Amanda had taken her arm now and was propelling her towards the card room. It was even hotter in here. The curtains were drawn, blocking out both the darkness and any breath of wind that might have cooled the room but might also have scattered the cards. The air was thick with concentration and tension. Servants moved soundlessly between the tables, plying the gamblers with drink. Amy watched and found her stomach curling with the apprehension of memory. She could see her father's face, flushed and excited as he checked his cards, and she had to repress a shudder.

'Amanda, I don't think I want to do this...' she began, but it was too late to pull out without embarrassing her friend. Amanda was dragging her over to a table in the corner, where two ladies were already sitting. One was Lady Bestable and the other was a lady who looked vaguely familiar, although Amy could not place her. She had dark auburn hair, elaborately dressed, green eyes and a bored, lazy expression.

'Lady Juliana Myfleet,' Amanda said, performing the introductions, 'may I introduce Miss Bainbridge? Amy, Lady Juliana and I are friends from my come-out. The two of you have not met before?'

Lady Juliana shook her head. Her eyes were bright as they surveyed Amy from top to toe.

'So you are the little puritan who does not care to wager?' she murmured. 'How piquant that Amanda persuaded you to join us. Are we to play for pennies?'

Amanda blushed and Amy shot her a reproachful look.

'Amanda said that you needed a fourth to make up a game,' she said stiffly. 'However, if you are to play for high stakes I wish you would excuse me, ma'am—'

'No need, my dear, I do but tease.' Lady Juliana smiled her feline smile and cut the deck. 'This is a practice run for me. I shall do my serious gambling in a little while. Shall we start?'

Amy had played little in the last few years, but although she was out of practice she quickly remembered the mechanics of the game. She was partnering Amanda, who was a reckless rather than a skilful player and who often overplayed her hand. For all Lady Juliana's assurances, it was soon clear that she took the game extremely seriously and it was no surprise when she and Lady Bestable ran out easy winners. Amy, feeling that she had met her obligation to Amanda, was about to make her excuses and leave when a footman delivered a note to her friend and Amanda slipped away from the table with a word of apology. Mrs Wren immediately took her place. Their hostess wore a sharp, acquisitive expression. Her fingers, tapping the deck of cards, betrayed the tension of the dedicated gambler. Amy suddenly felt as innocent as a country girl in a brothel.

'Juliana, darling, we must have a game of vingt-et-un!' Mrs Wren exclaimed. 'Positively we must! I have been waiting all evening to play!'

'Very well, Emma,' Lady Juliana said, nothing loath. Her malicious gaze rested on Amy briefly. 'Lady Bestable, Miss Bainbridge—will you play?'

Vingt-et-un was the only game that Amy actually liked.

It had been the first that she had learned, for her father had taught her as a child and had explained that it would be a useful way for her to learn to calculate. Amy had soon learned that each of the cards had a different value and that she had to get her hand to add up to twenty-one. Later she realised that her father's justification that the game helped her reckon figures better was nothing more than an excuse, but by then she was very good at mathematics so perhaps there had been some truth in his assertion. For that reason she thought she probably retained a small, nostalgic regard for the game. All the same, it was not enough to keep her at the table.

'No, I thank you. I have played enough for one evening.'

Mrs Wren pulled a face. 'Just like your dear papa, Miss Bainbridge! They always said that he did not have the temperament for the game. He proved it in the end, did he not?'

Amy felt a hot spurt of anger. She knew that Emma Wren was only trying to provoke her and on most occasions she would have allowed the insult to go over her head. Tonight she found she could not. Perhaps it was the memories that crowded in on her, or perhaps it was simply her dislike of Mrs Wren, but she found that she did not wish to retreat ignominiously.

'I do not believe that I am much like my papa,' she said coolly, looking Mrs Wren in the eye. 'Perhaps I shall play this one game...'

It soon became apparent that the ladies were now playing for high stakes. Lady Juliana suggested an initial bet of ten guineas and proceeded to win the first game very quickly. This encouraged her to double the stake on the second. She was well in the grip of gambling fever by now, sitting forward, eyes a-glitter as she pounced on her hand of cards. Once again she beat the others to twenty-one, with Mrs Wren barely managing to conceal her hostility when she could only muster a total of nineteen points from her cards. Amy, for all her proficiency at the game, came in a poor third.

'You have the very devil's luck, Ju,' Emma was complaining. 'Damned if I can see why the Tallant family should be so prodigious good at cards! Give the rest of us a chance!'

Amy jumped at her words. She had had no idea of a connection between Lady Juliana and the Earl of Tallant, and she told herself that it made little difference, except to point out that she had vastly underestimated the level of skill and passion of her opponents. These were no middle-aged ladies playing patience to pass the long evenings. These were gamesters as dedicated as their male counterparts and as reckless. She had only herself to blame if she felt out of her depth. She should have followed her first instinct and kept well away.

Mrs Wren's spiteful gaze turned towards her again.

'I suppose one should not wholly dismiss you as a card player, Miss Bainbridge, since like Juliana you come from a gambling dynasty! Only your brother is not so lucky as Juliana's, is he? Nor so rich!'

Lady Juliana laughed. 'Let Miss Bainbridge be, Emma! She has not had so much practice as I have!'

'Another round?' Mrs Wren said eagerly. 'Let us make it the best of three.'

Amy hesitated. She cast a look at Lady Bestable, feeling in some way that her age must make that matron the safest of her companions, but her ladyship's eyes were riveted on the cards like a dog with a juicy bone.

'Let us make it an elimination!' Lady Bestable said. 'Double the stake—sixty guineas!'

Amy started to rise from her seat, then sat down again. She had sixty guineas and more, much more now that she possessed a fortune of thirty thousand pounds. But she certainly did not want to gamble her fortune away. She felt no thrill in the cards, only nervousness in the pit of her stomach and a strange, trapped feeling that seemed to be growing with each hand. The darkened card room and the eager thrill her companions took in the proceedings was horribly familiar. In her mind's eye she could see all those images that she had striven so hard to repress—she was a small child again, peering around the door of the library to watch her father and his cronies at play; she was a schoolgirl being driven away from the latest establishment when the money ran out; she was back in Whitechapel…

'I think little Miss Bainbridge does not wish to play,' Lady Juliana put in, in her sly drawl. 'Can you not take the heat, Miss Bainbridge?'

'Or perhaps she cannot…afford…to play?' Mrs Wren said, with deliberate innuendo. 'Although I do hear marvellous things about your prospects, Miss Bainbridge! Can you not share some of your fortune with us?'

Amy looked at her and reflected that she had seldom disliked anyone as much as she detested Emma Wren. It was neither noble, nor indeed, very mature in her to wish to humiliate her hostess, but the fighting spirit was suddenly there.

'I shall play,' she said, 'but I do not believe that I shall be sharing my fortune, ma'am.'

Lady Bestable cackled. 'That's the spirit, my dear!' She dealt the cards, her little eyes flashing with cupidity. Amy felt as though the ladies were already feeling the weight of her gold in their pocket and her resolve hardened, banishing the fear. She would show them that a Bainbridge could play and win!

It was Lady Bestable who was eliminated in the first, low-

scoring round. Amy managed a score of fifteen, with Mrs
Wren achieving eighteen and Lady Juliana sulking because
she had only seventeen in her hand. Amy remembered her
father saying that cards made a man disputatious and reflected that that was true of women as well. Lady Juliana
looked as though she would like to knife Mrs Wren were
only a weapon to hand.

Their game was attracting some attention now as word
went round that they were playing an elimination and that
the stakes were doubling each time. Some of the gentlemen
drifted across from the faro table to watch. Richard was there,
and a tall, fair man with a too-knowing expression, whom
Amy had seen previously paying lavish attention to Lady
Juliana. She felt acutely self-conscious. The stakes doubled
again from sixty to one hundred and twenty guineas. Amy
felt a little faint as she played her cards. She could not quite
believe what she was doing and she wished she had been
eliminated instead of Lady Bestable, who was sitting like a
malignant toad at the side of the table and clearly resented
the fact that she was no longer in the game.

A slight gasp went up from the crowd when Mrs Wren was
eliminated in the second round. Mrs Wren herself did not
look as though she could quite believe it. For a second Amy
thought she was going to tear her cards across, but after a
moment she controlled herself and gave Amy a sharp smile.

'A dark horse indeed, Miss Bainbridge! But you have not
won yet.'

Richard nudged the fair man in the ribs. 'Always knew
Amy had it in her! Gambling's in the blood, don't you think,
Massingham?'

The fair-haired man laughed. 'In the Bainbridge blood for
certain, Richard! But my money is still on Lady Juliana!'

Someone went into the outer room and fetched a ledger. To Amy's shock, she realised that they were taking bets now on the outcome of the game, on whether she or Lady Juliana would win. The most outrageous sums were being mentioned. She heard Richard wager a hundred guineas that she would triumph, and her nerve almost failed her on the spot.

Lady Juliana sat across the table from Amy, her green eyes glittering with excitement. 'Double or quits, Miss Bainbridge! The bet is two hundred and forty guineas. Will you accept?'

Richard was lounging against the doorframe, his face alight with a gambler's excitement. Amy met his eyes. She felt a little sick and her hands shook slightly. She could not believe what she was doing. The crowd pressed closer about the table.

Amy cleared her throat. 'I will play.'

Lady Juliana gave a crow of laughter. 'Oh, how we underestimated you, Miss Bainbridge! Let's play, then!'

Though, down to two players the game took much longer. Amy, keeping cards and discarding, was conscious of nothing but the flickering candlelight, the circle of avid watchers, and the frown between Lady Juliana's eyes as she faced her across the table. There was a buzz in her blood that was like excitement and wine; a part of her wanted desperately to escape but another part, the stronger, wanted equally desperately to win. The heat in the room seemed stifling and unreal—Amy told herself that none of it mattered; that soon it would be over like the dream it seemed to be.

'I do believe that Miss Bainbridge has won,' one of the gentlemen murmured as Amy, a little blindly, put her cards down on the table at the end of the game. 'A perfect vingt-et-un. Twenty-one precisely, Lady Juliana, unless you can match it?'

Amy's vision cleared. Lady Juliana was looking furious, a black frown between her brows. 'I have a twenty but not a twenty-one. Damnation! I cannot believe it.' She threw her cards down and they scattered like leaves in the wind. 'Do you care to play again, Miss Bainbridge—winner takes all?'

'No, thank you,' Amy said. Her mouth felt parched and she had a headache behind her eyes. The excitement had melted away as swiftly as it had come. 'I shall not play further.'

Lady Juliana's eyes narrowed. 'That is your right, of course, since the elimination is at an end. Alas, I cannot pay my debt immediately, Miss Bainbridge. You will take a promissory note?'

Amy knew the rules well enough not to decline. 'Of course.'

Lady Juliana's face broke into a sudden smile. 'Oh, no, I have a better idea! I will settle my debt of honour, Miss Bainbridge—by offering my brother in return!'

The crowd had started to break up, drawn back to their own tables and the promise of play, but they stopped at this new twist. A ragged laugh ran around the room.

'Good try, Juliana!' Massingham said humorously. 'Tallant is hardly yours to sell, though, is he?'

Lady Juliana's feline smile broadened. 'Oh, I do not know, Clive. If Captain Gramond can sell his sister in a game of faro, why can I not use Joss as my stake? He might be persuaded to help me...for one reason or another. You, there!' She turned imperiously to a footman. 'Fetch Lord Tallant! We shall see if he will come to my aid!'

Amy felt herself turn hot all over. Everyone was laughing and waiting to see the outcome of Lady Juliana's extraordinary suggestion. Amy closed her eyes and prayed fervently that Joss had already left the ball. She could not imagine facing him in this situation, and as for Lady Juliana's offer—well, that was quite ridiculous.

'I do not accept your stake,' she said, a little desperately. 'It was not what we originally agreed.'

Lady Juliana raised her eyebrows mockingly. 'Alas, my brother is not acceptable to Miss Bainbridge! Now, what shall we do?'

Mrs Wren leaned forward. 'Your brother is acceptable to me, Juliana!' she said with a meaningful smile. 'Miss Bainbridge—' she turned to Amy '—I will buy up your debt for three hundred guineas if you will turn Lady Juliana's offer over to me!'

Someone guffawed. 'Is Tallant worth that much, Emma?'

Mrs Wren flashed a wicked smile. 'That and more, so I hear!'

Amy felt her blush deepen. This was all getting far too complicated. When she had accepted Amanda's plea to play a hand of whist it had only been to oblige her friend, and now she had got herself into the most frightful fix. She had never intended to play for so long, or for such high stakes and she was starting to feel quite shocked at the gambling passion that had gripped her, albeit briefly. Besides, where had Amanda gone? It was dreadful of her to desert her like this! There was not a single friendly face in the room—even Richard seemed utterly unable to understand her distress—and the louche atmosphere was making Amy deeply uncomfortable. Massingham had paused to drop a kiss on Lady Juliana's pouting lips and Amy looked hastily away.

Richard came across and crouched down by Amy's chair. 'I think you must accept the stake or pass to Mrs Wren, Amy,' he said. 'It is a debt of honour after all and you cannot really refuse. Though it all depends on what Joss has to say to it, of course—'

'On what I have to say about what?'

A whisper ran round the room like the wind through corn. Amy turned in her seat. The Earl of Tallant had just come in, accompanied by the Duke of Fleet. She could see that Joss already had his coat on, as though he had been on the point of leaving when Lady Juliana's message had reached him. Amy wished with her whole heart that he had been less tardy. For a second her eyes met his and she saw a flash of some emotion there—surprise, perhaps, followed by a strange tug of empathy—before she dropped her gaze from his. Her heart was beating a swift tattoo.

'Joss, darling...' Lady Juliana stretched out an elegant hand '...the most dreary thing! I have just lost to Miss Bainbridge and do not have the means to meet my debt at the moment. I know that you could settle it for me, but then I thought that perhaps it would be more entertaining to use you to pay the wager instead. You must be worth at least two hundred and forty guineas—'

'They charge more in Covent Garden,' someone in the crowd put in.

'So if I promise you to Miss Bainbridge for a week,' Lady Juliana finished sweetly, 'would you do that for me to help me settle my debt? Please, Joss dearest...'

Amy, shifting uncomfortably in her chair, thought that Joss looked utterly unmoved by the plea. She held her breath, waiting for him to refuse. She was desperate to be out of there. The raffish atmosphere, the insinuations of the crowd, made her deeply unhappy.

'What does Miss Bainbridge have to say about this?' Joss

asked. His amber gaze fastened on Amy and her heart missed a beat. His expression was unreadable.

'Miss Bainbridge doesn't want to take my stake,' Lady Juliana said with a mournful sigh. 'She finds you unacceptable, Joss.'

Joss inclined his head. Amy saw the flash of amusement in his eyes, the cynical twist to his lips before his customary impassivity returned.

'I see.'

'I find you more than acceptable, Joss,' Mrs Wren purred. 'I have already offered to buy up Lady Juliana's debt.'

Amy saw Joss's eyes narrow on her. She could read a definite challenge in them now. 'Thank you, Emma,' he said, his gaze never leaving Amy's face, 'but Miss Bainbridge has the prior claim. I regret, ma'am—' his bow to Amy was immaculate '—that you cannot decline my sister's offer. As it is a debt of honour you would give offence in the refusal...'

The chatter in the room died to silence.

'Debt of honour. Absolutely,' Richard Bainbridge said. 'You *are* honouring Lady Juliana's pledge then, Joss?'

'Absolutely,' Joss repeated, still refusing to take his gaze from Amy. She felt as though she was burning beneath it. 'It is my pleasure.'

Richard turned to his sister. 'Amy, I do not believe that you can refuse...'

Amy looked from him to Joss Tallant and back again. 'I see. Lady Juliana, your offer is accepted.'

Lady Juliana gave a crow of triumph. There were catcalls and lewd jokes that made Amy's cheeks burn.

'That little girl will learn enough in a week to fit her for Abbess Walsh's whorehouse!' she heard Juliana say to Clive Massingham in an undertone.

She stumbled to her feet, shaking Joss off when he put one hand on her arm to steady her. Her eyes were bright with unshed tears. She had gambled and won, and in the process she had betrayed her principles and made a fool of herself into the bargain. As for Joss... Amy cast him one searing glance as she hurried from the room. If she had made a fool of herself, he had connived at it. She would not forgive her own folly and she certainly would not forgive him.

Amy was barely in the carriage before she turned on her brother and all her pent-up feelings from the gambling session came pouring forth.

'How you could have let me do such a thing, Richard! I must have been mad! It was quite dreadful! Oh! For you to stand by when Lady Juliana made that monstrous wager—'

Richard raised a placatory hand. 'Amy, I don't know why you are making such a fuss! Juliana Myfleet was only joking and Joss decided to call her bluff. I have no doubt that you will have the money tomorrow rather than Joss himself.'

'Well, if that is the Earl of Tallant's idea of a joke, I do not want to be the butt of it.' Amy shivered and drew her cloak closer. 'Your friends and their exploits are too sophisticated for me, Richard!'

'You may be right,' Richard said unexpectedly. 'You should never have been playing cards with Lady Juliana, Amy, not an unmarried girl like you! Now if you were married of course, it would be different—'

'Which just goes to show how foolish society can be,' Amy said crossly. 'If I was married it would not make a jot of difference.'

'Except that you would have understood more of the jokes,' Richard said.

'I would still have no wish to gamble,' Amy said mulishly. 'It was the most dreadful experience.'

Richard shrugged. 'No one forced you to do it, Amy! Could've knocked me down with a feather when I saw you at the table! After all your high-flown sentiments...'

Amy shuddered. She felt sick and empty now, to think of what she had done. 'Richard, do not! I cannot bear it! It was so foolish of me—I wanted to show that odious Mrs Wren that she could not slight Papa and expect me to accept it so meekly! So I gave in to an impulse to play—' She broke off.

'And found that gambling fever can lurk in the blood of even the most innocent!' Richard finished, with a grin. 'And to think that I believed you were only there to oblige Amanda Spry!'

'I was originally!' Amy frowned. 'And that is another thing. Amanda vanished into thin air and left me to my fate! Oh, of all the miserable things for a friend to do.'

Richard shook his head. 'Seems to me that you are trying to blame everyone but yourself!' he said acutely. 'Besides, you won! I confess that I do not understand you, Amy—'

'Nor I you.' Amy huddled back against the seat. 'What a dreadful evening. I cannot understand how anyone can enjoy gaming. It makes me feel sick in the stomach.'

'Maybe you feel sick because you are shocked that you enjoyed yourself,' Richard said, with the same uncomfortable percipience. 'And before you deny it, Amy, think a little! Even if you did not enjoy the game itself, you liked administering a set-down to Mrs Wren. You enjoyed the winning!'

Amy did not contradict him. She stared out at the darkened streets. 'What a disastrous evening. And now I apparently have the Earl of Tallant for a week into the bargain, and I have no idea what to do with him!'

Chapter Eight

The morning following the ball was another glorious May day, but Amy awoke with a headache and a feeling that there was something very wrong. She rolled over in bed, opened her eyes, and immediately remembered her win at cards the previous night. A mixture of disbelief and guilt hit her hard, tempered by a very faint, stubborn pride. It was lowering to find that she had compromised her principles, that she was not immune to the lure of gambling. On the other hand she had no intention of playing again and so should just put the matter behind her. Except...except that there was the problem of the payment of the wager...

Amy got up and dressed slowly, going downstairs to breakfast late and alone. Lady Bainbridge had not risen and was no doubt still recovering from her migraine. Richard had mentioned going to White's the previous night and had probably not returned. It was bright and warm in the dining room, but Amy's spirits did not reflect the day. If Joss chose to come in person to pay the debt... But he would not. Amy was sure that Richard had been right and that she would receive the money that morning and that would be the end to it. She devoutly hoped that she was right.

Amy stirred some curd into her stewed apple and reflected that she must make sure that the household budget was increased immediately so that they actually had something appetising to eat for breakfast. That would mean supplementing their income from the thirty thousand pounds, of course, but since no one had claimed the money...

She stared at her reflection in the spoon's uneven surface. She had always been intrigued as to why it appeared upside down. Not that she would look much better the right way up. If she was about to spend her lottery winnings, then it could be argued that the most needy cause was still her appearance. She had bought several dresses now but she was aware that what she really needed was an entirely new wardrobe. Yet her heart was not in it. Looking good in the way that Amanda always did, for example, seemed unconscionably time-consuming. It was also expensive and she had already spent what seemed like an inordinate amount of money on the new carriage. What she really wanted to do was to give serious thought to her charitable causes. There were so many deserving cases.

Amy wrinkled up her nose as she tried to think of them. Climbing boys and street women and the people who had been rescued from drowning in the Thames and orphans and widows... Really, thirty thousand pounds was nothing when confronted with such a need for charity. She did not know where to start.

Feeling slightly better at the thought of some benevolent activity, Amy got to her feet. She had almost reached the dining room door when it opened and Patience, her face as disapproving as the sole of an old boot, stuck her head around.

'The Earl of Tallant is here to see you, Miss Amy. I have put him in the parlour. He says his business is most urgent.'

Amy jumped. Until now she had just about managed to keep at bay any thought of the outrageous wager that Lady Juliana had made. Now, however, she was forced to confront it and the prospect was not pleasant. She realised that she had been hoping that Joss would not honour the bet. The thought of seeing him again, and in such circumstances, was painful to her.

Her footsteps were slow as she crossed the tiny hall to the parlour door. She tried to console herself by thinking that Joss had only come to pay the money and explain that it was all a joke. She paused outside the door and brushed her old cambric dress down with a defiant gesture. She would take the money, of course—she could not really refuse a debt of honour—and then she would send him away with a flea in his ear for making her the object of a joke between himself and his sister. They might think that it was funny. She did not.

Nevertheless, she felt more than a little apprehensive as she opened the parlour door. Joss was standing by the window and the pristine austerity of his black coat and buff pantaloons made the small room seem even shabbier to Amy's eyes. This made her want to dislike him all the more but in this she failed miserably. He looked as elegant as ever—elegant enough to make her pulse race. She cleared her throat.

'Good morning, Lord Tallant.'

Joss bowed. 'Good morning, Miss Bainbridge. I apologise if I have disturbed you by arriving at this hour, but I did not wish to seem tardy.'

Amy frowned slightly. 'It is very early to call, but I assume… That is…' She realised she was making rather a hash of this and started again, somewhat bluntly.

'Have you come to settle Lady Juliana's debt, my lord?'

Joss smiled. 'Certainly I have, Miss Bainbridge. Did you think I would renege?'

Amy looked away from the mockery in his eyes. 'Oh, no, indeed. Of course not!'

'Good. For here I am at your service, Miss Bainbridge.' Joss bowed again. 'So, what are you going to do with me?'

Amy sat down rather quickly in one of the armchairs. 'Oh, but surely… I thought that you meant simply to pay? You cannot intend…to honour your sister's bet by…um…pledging yourself to my company for an entire week?'

Joss frowned. 'Certainly I intend it. You cannot know much about me, Miss Bainbridge, if you think I would fail to honour such a debt.'

'It was not your integrity I was questioning, but the nature of the payment,' Amy said, rubbing her hand across her forehead. The headache, lurking during breakfast, had returned with a vengeance. 'It seems so much easier to pay the two hundred guineas and have done with it.'

'May I?' Joss indicated the other chair and sat down. 'Well, of course it would be easier to pay, but I confess to a certain curiosity to spend a week in your company, Miss Bainbridge.' His gaze dwelt on her indignant face and he smiled a little. 'It might prove rather more amusing than merely handing over the money.'

'I am not an entertainment!' Amy said sharply. 'Nor do I consider this joke to be remotely amusing, my lord!' She fidgeted crossly with the frayed material on the arm of the chair, unravelling it even more. 'The next time that you and your sister design such a trick I beg that you will find an alternative dupe. I have no desire to provide you with diversion! Upon my word, you must be very bored to indulge in such behaviour!'

Joss laughed. 'I assure you this is no diversion, Miss Bainbridge, nor did Juliana and I design it for our amusement. She lost a bet to you. I am here to pay her debt because I wish to do so. That is all.'

Amy looked at him defiantly. 'Then you may go away again, my lord! The bet is cancelled. You do but waste your time here.'

Joss sat back in his chair. 'That seems a shame, Miss Bainbridge. Do you have no wish to spend a week in my company?'

'Certainly not!' Amy glared at him. The emotions inside her—a tumble of dread, nervousness and an edgy excitement—were not to be discussed with him. 'You are the last man I would wish—' She broke off, aware that she was about to be unpardonably rude. She took a deep breath. 'This is a foolish nonsense. I thank you for honouring your sister's pledge, my lord, but now I must ask you to go.'

Joss showed little sign of doing so. 'I am disappointed that I am not acceptable to you as a companion, Miss Bainbridge. In order to help me improve, perhaps you could give me a little advice. What is it about me that is particularly... inappropriate?'

Amy looked at him suspiciously. She was certain that this was just another way for him to amuse himself at her expense.

'I cannot believe you in earnest, my lord, but as you have asked... We have no interests in common and I am sure we should be bored with each other's company within an hour!'

Joss glanced at the clock. 'Let us put that to the test, Miss

Bainbridge. If in an hour's time you find me tedious beyond bearing, then I shall go without further complaint. What do you say?'

Amy looked a little shamefaced. 'You make me sound very ungracious,' she said. 'All that I meant was that I feared we should have little to talk about.'

'Let us see, then.' Joss settled back. 'What do you imagine my interests to be, Miss Bainbridge?' He eyed her telltale blush with amusement. 'Dear me, are they all so shocking?'

'Yes…no!' Amy was thrown into confusion. 'I do not know, my lord.'

'But you must know, for you made a judgement that we had nothing in common. Take gambling, for instance, which I know you consider my chief pursuit. You were gambling last night, or we would not be sitting here. Therefore it must be something that we have in common.'

Amy looked at him. 'I thought you seemed a little surprised when you saw me in the card room.'

'I was. On the basis of our previous conversations I should say it was the last place that I would have expected to find you.'

Amy felt a little confused. 'Oh, I was only gambling last night because…' She hesitated. 'Amanda persuaded me to play a hand of whist and then Lady Juliana suggested vingt-et-un…' She met his gaze a little defiantly. 'I have to confess to all the wrong motives, I fear, my lord. Mrs Wren provoked me and I let my anger overcome my scruples. I was once quite good at vingt-et-un, you see, and I wanted to show her…' She hung her head. 'It does not reflect well on me, I know!'

Joss looked amused. 'You played for revenge, Miss Bainbridge? I would never have thought it of you!' He gave her a quizzical look. 'And did you get drawn in by the lure of the

game? You did, didn't you! Admit it! The excitement of the
cards is a fever in the blood—'

'I most certainly did not!' Amy said virtuously and un-
truthfully.

'So, how comes it that you were playing for doubling
stakes, Miss Bainbridge?'

Amy bit her lip. 'I am not entirely sure,' she said. 'Someone suggested it and then I found myself swept along with
the game... I kept imagining that I would be out in the next
round, you see, but I had some luck and ended up winning.'

'Just like a country squire who finds himself winning at
White's for the first time,' Joss said drily. 'Did it not go to
your head, Miss Bainbridge? Were you not tempted to carry
on playing and see where your beginner's luck might take
you?'

'No, indeed,' Amy said feelingly, 'for I soon felt quite sick
at the thought of what I was doing! That must be where I differ from the likes of Sir Humphrey, I suppose. I have no urge
to try my luck further.' She looked him straight in the eye.
'Yet I do understand how an innocent might be lured into
thinking that they might win and win...or, if they lose, that
they only need gamble again to recoup their losses. There
are always unscrupulous people leading them on.'

Joss shifted in his chair. 'Is that aimed at me, Miss Bainbridge?'

Amy shrugged. 'If the cap fits, my lord...'

'Well, it does not. It was your brother who put Sir Humphrey up for membership of White's, for example. You may
acquit me of deliberately leading any man into gambling just
so that I may fleece him. I am not so unscrupulous.'

Their gazes met and held, Joss's challenging, Amy's very
straight. After a moment she said, 'I accept what you say,

my lord, but at the very least it confirms that this is a topic which we do not have in common.'

'On the contrary, we may not see eye to eye but we have been enjoying a stimulating discussion for the past fifteen minutes! One need not always agree on a subject, you know. Sometimes it is more interesting not to do so!'

Amy smiled. 'I will concede that, but it does not make it a common interest.'

'True. So what else is there?'

Amy blushed. 'I do not know.'

Joss eyed her closely. 'Ah, I see that you are remembering I told you I was a rake and you are thinking that it must keep me quite occupied! That, alas, is probably not a topic for further discussion between us, at least not yet.'

Amy blushed crossly. 'I did not need you to tell me! Everyone speaks of it.'

Joss stretched. 'Now that *is* an interesting topic. Reputations. Why should we believe that everything we are told is true? That is tantamount to believing gossip!'

Amy frowned. 'In this case it is presumably true since you confirmed it yourself!'

'Yes, of course. But the wider discussion would be interesting. I am told that Miss Bainbridge is a reserved lady with scarcely a word to say for herself, yet I have found that manifestly untrue. You appreciate my example?'

'Of course,' Amy said, trying not to feel even the tiniest bit flattered by his words. 'This is nothing to the purpose, my lord. We were trying to establish that we had nothing in common.'

'You were trying to do that, I was not. I was looking for common ground. What else do you know of me?'

'You are a noted whip.'

'And do you enjoy driving?'

'Yes,' Amy said, incurably truthful, but feeling the ground opening up at her feet as she saw where this was going, 'although I have little opportunity.'

'Capital! Then I may take you driving in the park. That will wile away a few hours.'

'A few hours of what?'

'A few hours of our week together. But the time is not yet up. Are you bored, yet?'

'No,' Amy admitted, feeling the trap yawning wider, 'but...'

'But? Do you have some other objection to my company?'

'No...' Amy was struggling. She did indeed object, but she could not tell him why. It was not that she disliked Joss's company—the reverse was true, though she was at a loss to explain why. He should have been exactly the sort of man she disliked and despised, but oddly she found herself drawn to him. It made her most uncomfortable and it was the last thing that she wished to admit to him.

'I am encouraged that we have found at least one thing in common,' Joss continued. 'Perhaps we should make a list of all the activities we might indulge in together?'

Amy stared. 'A list?'

'You are familiar with the concept?'

'Yes, of course...' Amy made countless lists to help her manage her household duties.

'Or perhaps you feel there will not be sufficient items to put on the list?'

'It is not that.' Amy looked at him in reluctant fascination. 'It is simply that I cannot imagine you as a list maker, my lord. The idea seems absurd.'

'Why so? I assure you it is most useful. How could I possibly remember otherwise which gambling den to visit in which order, or which young lady I am reputed to have seduced?'

'Now you are funning me,' Amy said, shamefaced, 'and it is too bad of you.' She got up and went over to her walnut bureau, extracting her writing box. 'Very well, let us start.'

Half an hour later, Amy had ordered a pot of tea and cake for them and they had still not finished. The time had elapsed because the list was by no means without controversy.

'Driving in the park, or possibly riding,' she read out. 'Balls, parties, soirées and other social events.' She put the paper down. 'I am still not certain whether I wish to accept your escort to these events, my lord. Quite apart from my dislike of balls, there is the talk that would be consequent upon such action—'

'My dear Miss Bainbridge...' Joss made a slight gesture '...I thought that we had agreed that neither of us paid any regard to that sort of gossip?'

'Yes, but Mama will have a fit if I accept your escort to a ball!' Amy could not help giggling. 'Oh dear, it is not funny! Whilst I have no time for gossip, it is foolish to be careless of one's reputation!'

'Agreed, but we shall be behaving with perfect propriety.' Joss fixed her with a look. 'At the very least, agree to attending Lady Carteret's ball with me tomorrow night. Then, if you do not enjoy it, we shall attend no others.'

'Oh, very well.' Amy sighed and consulted her list again. 'Attend the exhibition at the Royal Academy. I confess that might be of interest. Attend the meeting of the Bettering Society.' She cast Joss a doubtful look. 'I cannot believe you will find that enjoyable, my lord.'

'Ah, but think how improving it will be for me, Miss Bainbridge!'

Amy frowned. 'I do wish you would not jest all the time. It is not for me to try to improve you.'

'Yet you currently *disapprove* of me.'

'Yes, well…you are dreadfully bad, but that is your choice.'

Joss grinned. 'How delightful you are, Miss Bainbridge! There will be no Spanish coin from you!'

Amy frowned. 'Coin! Oh, that reminds me! I have yet to decide what to do with my lottery winnings. I was puzzling over it when you arrived, my lord. There are so many good causes that I can scarce think which to address first. It is most perplexing. Perhaps *that* is a topic on which you might help me?'

Joss raised an eyebrow. 'You have decided to keep your winnings, then?'

'Well, as I cannot find the rightful owner of the lottery money, all I can think of is to give it away. Yet it is not that simple. I wish to weigh up the rival merits of the different charities and see which is most needy, but…' Amy wrinkled her nose up '…I do not have sufficient information.'

'Perhaps the Bettering Society might be the place to start? Or the Royal Humane Society? There must be plenty of people there who could advise you. Wait until after the meeting tomorrow. I am certain that we shall find you a good cause.'

Amy looked at him dubiously. 'Do you really intend to accompany me, my lord?'

'Yes, I do.' Joss smiled encouragingly. 'I know you will probably be ashamed to be seen with me, Miss Bainbridge, but please consider it an act of charity!'

Amy gave him a reproachful look. 'I asked you not to tease! Do you not think you will be hopelessly bored?'

'Not at all. I am certain that I will learn something new. Which reminds me—' Joss checked the clock '—are you bored now, Miss Bainbridge? We have been talking for almost two hours and we did agree that I would relieve you of my presence if you found it tedious.'

Amy avoided his gaze. 'I must confess… I am not bored, precisely…' She looked up to see Joss smiling at her in a way that made her feel very warm inside. She picked up her list and read an item almost at random.

'Attend a masquerade at Vauxhall Gardens—I do believe that you have added that one when I was not looking, my lord! How dreadfully improper!'

Joss twitched the list from her fingers. 'I admit it. I added it and it is quite improper but who knows you may find that you would like to attend? In fact, it may be that this week will be an education for both of us, Miss Bainbridge!'

'So what happened next?' Amanda enquired. She drew her friend's arm through her own as they strolled along the path in St James's Park. It was late afternoon and they had been shopping in Bond Street with Lady Bainbridge. Lady Bainbridge had declared herself fatigued by all the excitement and had gone home, but Amy and Amanda had wished to see how the preparations for the Regent's victory fête were progressing.

Amy giggled. 'After that I told him that I did not require his attendance for the rest of today as I would be going shopping with you and Mama. Do you know, Amanda, Lord Tallant even offered to accompany me to Bond Street, saying that he was quite an expert on the subject of female dress! Can you imagine the fuss that that would have caused?'

'I can,' Amanda said drily, 'and I do believe Lord Tallant told nothing but the truth. He is indeed a connoisseur of female charms!'

Amy blushed self-consciously. 'Oh, I know! I realise that he is the most dreadful rake! But our activities this week are going to be quite blameless, Amanda. Why, Lord Tallant is escorting me to a concert by the Charity Children of Westminster tonight. Mama and Richard will be there as well, so it is all quite innocent!'

Amanda raised her brows. 'Lord Tallant at a charity concert? Good God!'

'Yes, indeed, and tomorrow we go to a lecture at the Royal Humane Society! I have it in mind to give them a large donation from my winnings. So you see, Amanda, there is nothing scandalous about what we are doing!'

'Only the giving away of large sums of money,' Amanda said feelingly. 'That is quite disgraceful, Amy!'

Amy blushed. Although she had made up her mind to give most of the money to charities and she was quite determined to go through with it, the combined disappointment and disapproval of her family and Amanda was difficult to bear. Only Joss Tallant had not condemned her decision.

'You are aware that people will talk anyway if they see Lord Tallant dancing attendance on you?' Amanda was saying now, with a speculative glance at Amy's face. 'He never pays attention to any respectable female unless he wishes to seduce her! People will be saying that he has ruined you through this so-called debt of honour.'

Amy had already thought of this and some imp of obstinacy had refused to let it spoil her plans. Now that she had been persuaded to accept Joss's company, she was not going to be so poor-spirited as to be put off by a little gossip.

'I dare say people will talk scandal. There will be little for them to talk about, however, and what little there is will not be interesting. Oh, look—is that not a Chinese temple that they are building over there? The Prince's creations always have a grand design!'

They fell to discussing the victory celebrations.

'I did not tell you before,' Amanda said, 'but one of the reasons I came up from the country was to see all the victory festivities! I was last up in town in April for the visit of King Louis XVIII—I was in Piccadilly when the procession drove past, you know!' Her face fell a little. 'It was a sad disappointment, for the King is old and lame and the crowds were quite uninterested! I glimpsed the Duchess of Oldenburg as well, you know—she is a terrible fright and they say that the Regent and she took an instant dislike to each other!'

Amy herself read the newspapers when Richard took them, and so was quite aware of the visit to London of a whole bevy of princes and generals following the victory of the Allies in Europe. Unlike Amanda, however, she was quite indifferent to the phalanx of visitors. She knew that the Bainbridges were too unfashionable to receive invitations to any of the Prince Regent's private celebratory entertainments and had no wish to be crushed by the crowds who would wait for up to a whole day simply to see the famous pass by.

'I am quite beside myself at the prospect of seeing the King of Prussia,' Amanda continued. 'Czar Alexander will be visiting next month as well and he is reputed a vastly handsome man! I wonder if the Duke of Fleet could procure me an invitation to one of the Regent's dinners? He is an intimate of the Prince, after all. It is such a shame that half the fashionable world seems to have gone to Paris!'

Amy smoothed down her gloves. They were new and had flowers embroidered on the back and were really very pretty. She was beginning to feel almost part of the fashionable world herself. The Bond Street purchases, lavish as they had been, had not made a huge dent in the thirty thousand pounds. Amy reassured herself that there was still plenty left for her chosen charities.

''Tis a shame my aunt does not own a house along the Czar's procession route for I heard tell that people were asking fifty guineas to rent a window along the way!' Amanda said. 'Still, we may admire the preparations for the fête, I suppose! Look over there, Amy—they are building a Chinese bridge across the lake and a pergola and all manner of follies! The Prince is mad about Oriental fashions, you know, and so very extravagant, but I imagine it will be a magnificent party!'

Amy followed Amanda's pointing finger in the direction of the preparations, but rather than concentrating on the progress of the Prince's building work, her attention was caught by four gentlemen who were strolling towards them. She stiffened.

'Amanda, look! It is Richard—and the Duke of Fleet and the Earl of Tallant and Lord Parrish! Now what are we going to do?'

Amanda drew her breath in sharply. 'Oh dear, I do so hate having to cut anyone of my acquaintance dead! And especially your brother, my dear, let alone the Duke of Fleet. This is most delicate...'

It was not the gentlemen themselves who were the problem but the fact that each had his arm entwined about the waist of a personable young female. Amy stared—and felt herself blush. A strange feeling swept over her and a lump seemed to wedge itself in her chest, hard and hot and painful, as she watched Joss Tallant with his mistress.

'Ladybirds!' she said, in a stifled voice. 'Mama would have forty fits if she knew Richard was parading his *chère amie* in the park in the afternoon!'

'Lucky that Lady Bainbridge did not choose to walk with us this afternoon,' Amanda said, ever practical. 'A female's nothing but a fool if she expects men to be other than the way they are!' For a second there was a hint of bitterness in her tone that made Amy glance at her curiously, but then it was gone, leaving Amy wondering. She had thought Amanda's marriage had not been happy. Perhaps the late Lord Spry, whom Amy had met only once or twice, had been another such, who paraded his conquests with scant regard for his wife.

Her gaze was drawn back to the lady on Joss Tallant's arm and she gave a little, unconscious sigh. So this was how the Earl of Tallant spent his time when he was not attending upon her! Suddenly her lavender gown did not feel so stylish and Amy herself felt decidedly cross-grained. She and Joss had spent such a pleasant morning discussing their plans for the week, yet now he had obviously returned to his preferred entertainments. Amy, who had been at a loss to understand why he would wish to spend any time with her at charity lectures and visits, felt strangely humiliated. Her envious eyes took in every detail of the fashionable impure who graced Joss's arm. She struggled hard to overcome her ill temper, but was only partially successful.

'The…er…ladies are prodigiously pretty, are they not, Amanda? One can see the attraction!'

'The one with the Earl is Harriet Templeton,' Amanda said, lowering her parasol to conceal the fact that she was watching. 'She used to be an opera dancer, by all accounts, and now she has a part share in a very exclusive club in

Covent Garden! But that is enough of this salacious gossip! Your Mama would be disgusted with me, discussing such matters with an unmarried lady!'

'I am no débutante,' Amy said, trying to sound cool, 'and I think I may stand the shock of knowing that such ladies exist! The question is—what are we to do?' The group was still strolling towards them and suddenly Amy felt a little panicky. Was she to ignore her own brother because of the company he kept? She had no idea how to deal with the situation. Yet it was on Joss Tallant rather than Richard that her gaze was still fixed and when Joss turned his head and looked at her, as though drawn by her scrutiny, she did not look away, and neither did he.

Amy was not sure what she had been expecting—that Joss would deliberately turn away to spare her embarrassment perhaps, or even that he might appear slightly abashed to have been caught in such a situation. Instead, he held her gaze with a steady regard that contained just the slightest hint of amusement and more than a little challenge. Amy's chin came up and she gave him back look for look. She saw his smile deepen and the hot, angry feeling inside her welled up and threatened to spill over. Then she turned away, finding it quite easy to cut him dead after all.

Amanda took her arm and led her down a little path off to the left, and in a moment the danger was past and the gentlemen and their ladies, laughing and chattering, had passed on by. Amy was shocked and a little breathless to find that she was trembling.

'Whatever was that all that about, Amy?' For once Amanda's voice had lost its light tone. 'I hope you are not developing a *tendre* for the Earl of Tallant! I was worried about it as soon as I heard about this foolish debt! Lud, he is the last man on earth for an innocent miss to tangle with!'

'I assure you that there is no such danger,' Amy protested, trying to quell her shaking. 'I barely know the man and what I do know of him does not dispose me to like him!'

'Gracious, what has liking to do with anything? One can look once and…' Amanda shrugged airily. 'What I cannot understand is that *he* was staring at *you*!' Her gaze skimmed her friend thoughtfully and Amy could not help but laugh.

'I know! You are wondering what a man like the Earl of Tallant, with the beautiful Miss Templeton hanging on his arm, could possibly see in me!' she said, with a hint of bitterness. 'Well, Amanda, I beg you not to trouble yourself. I am persuaded that you are making too much of this. The Earl has no romantic interest in me and I…do not think of him in that way at all!'

Her friend looked unconvinced. 'Yet you will be much in his company during this week—'

'And the rest of the time he will be following his own inclinations,' Amy said lightly, 'as we have just seen.' She took a deep breath to steady herself. It seemed ridiculous, but seeing Joss Tallant like that had, just for a second, felt like a betrayal. Amy had enjoyed his company that morning but now she felt disappointed and resentful. She knew it was ridiculous, for she had no claim to him, but it felt suspiciously as though she was about to cry. It felt loweringly as though she was jealous…

She stole a look at Amanda's face. Her friend did not seem much happier to have witnessed the Duke of Fleet with his *chère amie*. She gave Amanda's arm a little shake.

'Shall we take some tea at the rotunda? I have had quite enough of gawping at the sights for one day!'

Amanda smiled a little sadly. 'A good idea, Amy. There is nothing so reviving to the spirits as a hot cup of tea!'

Chapter Nine

'**D**id you enjoy the lecture, Miss Bainbridge?' Joss asked, as he tooled his curricle through the park the following afternoon. It was a cooler day, grey with a chilly edge to the breeze, so the crowds were fewer and Amy had been obliged to wrap up warmly in her new pelisse. They had been to a lecture given by Dr Thomas Hardiment, a notable fundraiser, at the Royal Humane Society and afterwards Amy had resolved to donate a large sum for the funding of the Society's work. She intended to speak to Mr Churchward about it the following morning. She sighed. There was something very worthy about charitable giving, of course, but the lecture had been dry and a little depressing.

'I am sure that Dr Hardiment does a marvellous job,' she said now, in answer to Joss's question, 'but for my part I found his lecture a little tedious. All those graphic descriptions of resuscitation, for example! Perhaps the fault is in me for being so squeamish, but I did not care to know the detail.'

'The good doctor is certainly fond of his subject,' Joss said with a grin, 'but I fear that not everyone has your delicacy, Miss Bainbridge. I do believe that there are plenty of people who relish the grisly details of illness and death!'

'The same people who would enjoy a public hanging, I suppose,' Amy said ruefully. 'Oh, I dare say I am too nice in my opinions and the Society does a great deal of good work.' She turned to look at him. 'I do hope, my lord, that you do not feel you are suffering from an excess of charity? Remember that it was your idea to accompany me!'

Joss shot her a grin. 'My dear Miss Bainbridge, I beg you not to concern yourself! I found the Westminster Orphans' School concert to be most entertaining last night! Some of the children could sing very sweetly; as for that angelic child who played the harp—I am persuaded that the orphanage would not give her up even if twenty people offered her a good home, for she is far too talented for them to lose!'

Amy frowned at him. 'Upon my word, you are a dreadful cynic, sir!'

'You know that I am right. Charity is a business as much as any other.'

Amy looked troubled. 'I do not like to think of it in that way, my lord. There is no question that the likes of Dr Hardiment do a most useful job—'

'Oh, indeed, I would not dispute that. But it is also their task to raise funds and promote their work. There is no harm in it. Someone needs to persuade the idle rich to part with their money to help the deserving poor!'

Amy frowned all the harder. In some ways she hated to hear Joss speak like this and yet there was an uncomfortable truth somewhere in what he was saying.

'Do you think, then, that a great many people make donations to salve their consciences?' she asked.

'Assuredly. It makes them feel as though they are doing some good.' Joss turned and looked at her. 'They *are* doing good, Miss Bainbridge. So everyone wins.'

'Yet it feels more satisfying to actually do something to help, does it not?' Amy sighed. 'Something active, I mean.'

Joss smiled at her. 'Which is why you pay visits to the old and sick as well as giving so generously to the work of the Society. You are a positive paragon, Miss Bainbridge!'

'Oh, do stop teasing!' Amy looked at him. 'I suppose that you do nothing useful with your time, my lord?'

'You suppose correctly. Nothing other than entertaining myself. That seems useful enough to me.'

Amy shut her lips in a tight line. It was at moments like this that Joss irritated her almost beyond reason for she was certain that the flippant exterior hid something deeper. She had been willing him to tell her that she was wrong and to recite a whole list of the useful causes in which he was involved. Yet she knew that he would not. Joss had always been quite open about his selfish lifestyle and just because in some irrational way she wanted him to be a better person, it did not make him so.

'Would you like to hear about my activities, Miss Bainbridge?' Joss was saying now. 'I drink and play cards excessively, I read the newspapers, attend the races, go to balls and routs, visit my friends, drive in the park and, of course, do other unmentionable things as well! That is my idea of gainful employment!'

Amy refused to reply. She knew he was trying to provoke her and she was well aware of his unmentionable activities. The incident in the park the previous afternoon had remained unspoken between them, as though it had never happened. When Joss had arrived in Curzon Street to accompany the

Bainbridges to the charity concert Amy had been careful not to enquire into his afternoon's activities, but the memory of Harriet Templeton hanging on his arm still made her feel sore and scratchy.

'I assume, then, that you did not enjoy the lecture,' she said crossly. 'Perhaps Dr Hardiment's words left you quite cold?'

'It is the manner of these philanthropists that offends me, rather than their message,' Joss said, with a lopsided smile. 'I fear that their paternalistic attitudes remind me rather too strongly of my father. They always appear to think that they know what is best for everyone.'

Despite herself, Amy's attention was caught. It was the first time that Joss had ever referred to his family. 'Is the Marquis very dictatorial? He never comes up to London, does he?'

'No, never. He prefers the country. And to disapprove of me from a distance, of course. It is the way with fathers, I suppose.'

'Dear me.' Amy tucked back the tendrils of hair that were being tugged from her bonnet by the wind. 'No doubt you give him plenty of which to disapprove.'

'I do. As does Juliana. It is difficult to know which of us is more of a disappointment to him.'

There was no hint of expression in Joss's voice but for some reason Amy was sure that he was more upset than he showed. She looked at him thoughtfully. 'Does that not... distress you?'

'To be estranged from my father?' Joss flashed her a smile. 'Not really. He cannot disinherit me. He could cut off my allowance, I suppose, but that would reflect badly on the family honour...'

'I was thinking along personal rather than mercenary

lines,' Amy persisted. For all Joss's flippancy, there was some other feeling there. 'Would you not prefer that there should be some affection between the two of you?'

Joss raised a cynical eyebrow. 'My dear Miss Bainbridge, what an extraordinary idea! I believe that there was once some affection between my parents and look where that got them!'

'I see.' Amy thought that she understood. She remembered that the Marchioness of Tallant had decamped many years ago with one of her lovers, leaving her children behind in the care of their unbending father. 'Is your mother still alive?'

'I believe so. I have not heard otherwise.' Joss's tone was careless. 'She has lived in Italy these twenty years past and I lost count of the string of her lovers. Meanwhile, my father and I only speak when he wishes to upbraid me or to try to persuade me into marriage.'

'That sounds melancholy. Have you no wish to oblige him?'

Joss shot her a look. 'Not in that, no. A love match is out of the question and to marry for convenience seems equally empty to me, although I expect I shall bring myself to the point one day.'

Amy shivered in the spiteful little breeze. It seemed a very grey day indeed. 'I remember you telling me before that you thought romantic love to be sentimental. Just because your parents were unhappy does not mean—' She broke off, unhappily aware that she was in no position to preach. She had no experience to draw on. Her father had undoubtedly made her mother unhappy, but in a different way, yet, despite that, the love between Sir George and Lady Bainbridge had never been in question.

'I agree that it would be foolish of me to dismiss the idea

out of hand simply because my parents were unhappy.' Joss had slowed the horses and his voice slowed as well. 'I am not so shallow, Miss Bainbridge, for all that I might seem so. Even so, you cannot be surprised that it might make a man wary. To me, the idea of finding happiness in marriage seems as remote as flying to the stars. Yet I am not so much of a cynic to deny that others have found it. Even my sister at one time seemed exceptionally happy with her husband...'

Amy wrinkled up her face. His words were bleak but he was right—they lacked his customary ring of cynicism. He did not deny the existence of love, only doubted that he would find it. That seemed sadder in a way.

'Do you know, Miss Bainbridge,' Joss said slowly, 'my parents both gave me the same piece of advice on the same day? It was the day my mother left and I remember it well, for all that I was only seven years old. My father told me that love was for fools. My mother said the same. I suppose I took it to heart.' He looked at Amy and she saw that there was a strange, dazed look in his eyes before he blinked and it was gone. 'Good God,' he said in tones of deep disgust, 'I cannot believe I have become so mawkish! I never told anyone that before. It must be all these charitable thoughts that have unmanned me!'

They drove for a little in silence.

'Did you never wish to marry, Miss Bainbridge?' Joss's voice was his own again, cool and a little hard. 'It is surely the ultimate aim of every young lady?'

'Of most, I suppose,' Amy conceded. A dimple touched her cheek as she smiled. 'Unfortunately no one has asked me, my lord—apart from Mr Hallam, of course! But, yes, when I was younger I wanted to marry. I was quite desperate to find a husband! I thought that would give me a settled home.'

'Your father's changing fortunes must have been most disturbing,' Joss said. His voice had softened a little. 'I can see that a quieter existence might prove attractive.'

'Oh, yes! I was mortified that I had moved about so often, you see. Governesses never stayed for long—we could not afford them—and I went to so many seminaries for young ladies that I do believe I could write a guidebook! My education was somewhat neglected as a result and I did not have the chance to learn all the ladylike accomplishments. I never learned to play the piano, for example, as I had nowhere to practice. So when I failed to attach a husband I was convinced that this must be the reason!'

Joss laughed. 'If you ascribed it to a lack of discernment on the part of the gentlemen, Miss Bainbridge, you would be closer to the truth.'

Amy smiled. 'Thank you. That is a very pretty compliment, sir. However, it does not matter now, for I am a lady of independent means and have achieved the security I craved! To my mind that is much better!'

'There might be other reasons for marriage,' Joss observed, after a moment. 'The society, the companionship, the shared interests. It is sometimes lonely being on one's own.'

'That may be true,' Amy said, 'though it surprises me to hear you say so, my lord!'

They had reached Curzon Street and now Joss helped Amy to alight, swinging her down from the phaeton in a manner that never failed to take her breath away.

'I will see you tonight at Lady Carteret's ball, Miss Bainbridge, but what do we do tomorrow?'

Amy hesitated. She had planned to go to Whitechapel the following day, to take a hamper of food and children's clothes to Mrs Wendover and to visit the School for Ragged

Children. She had already decided that it would not do to ask Joss to escort her. That would entail an explanation of her connection with the Wendover family; besides, it was one thing to accept a gentleman's escort to the Royal Humane Society and quite another to drive to Whitechapel alone with him. She tried to imagine Joss leaving his elegant phaeton outside Mrs Wendover's lodging house and was almost betrayed into a giggle. It would be minus its wheels in five minutes—unless, of course, Joss bribed an entire gang of street children to guard it.

'I am not sure,' she said, hastily composing her face. 'I do believe that I shall visit a friend in the morning, and perhaps we could go to the Royal Academy in the afternoon?'

'That sounds most pleasant,' Joss said, taking her hand. His perceptive gaze scanned her face. 'I do believe though that you are keeping something from me, Miss Bainbridge! Who is this mysterious friend that you do not wish me to meet?'

'Oh...' Amy felt herself blushing and pulled her hand away. 'It is...an old school friend who lives in reduced circumstances, my lord. I would not wish to overwhelm her with too many visitors!'

'Very thoughtful of you! It is not that you are ashamed of me, reprobate that I am?'

Amy stared. 'What an absurd idea, my lord! It is simply... I only thought...' She hesitated on the brink of disclosure. It would be the utmost folly to confide the truth in Joss, for he could not be anything other than shocked to know that she had once lived in a lodging house in a Whitechapel rookery. She turned away.

'As I said, my lord, my friend has very limited means and I would not wish her to feel obliged to entertain us.'

Joss pressed a kiss on her hand before letting it go. 'I can tell when you are being sparing with the truth, Miss Bainbridge, but no matter! I will look forward to seeing you later.'

He stood watching as Amy went in at the door. Bond Street and a little lottery money had wrought quite a change. Her saucy blue straw bonnet matched the elegant pelisse and fitted her neat figure to perfection. Beneath the hat her hair was brown and glossy, feathering her cheeks in wind-blown tendrils. She looked thoroughly enchanting. As she reached the door, she turned and gave him a very sweet smile and for some reason Joss felt as though a hand had squeezed his heart. It left him feeling slightly breathless.

He gave the horses the office to move off. It had been an interesting afternoon and he looked forward to seeing Amy again that night at Lady Carteret's ball. It was refreshing to speak with her for she had decided opinions and was not afraid to voice them to him. He smiled to himself a little ruefully. Perhaps that was what led him to play devil's advocate with her sometimes—it was interesting to provoke her to discussion. She was so utterly unlike any other lady of his acquaintance.

That reminded him of Harriet Templeton. When he had left her bed that morning she had been quite sulky at the thought of not seeing him for the entire day. It had cost him the promise of a pearl necklace and a trip to Vauxhall to buy back a smile, and it all seemed damnably like too much hard work. He knew that he was tiring of her—the signs were unmistakable and had been for a while. Yet for some reason he was reluctant to end their association just yet, as if the thought of ridding himself of Harriet would leave him too exposed. He remembered Fleet's suggestion that he should marry Harriet to scorn his father. She would look magnificent in the

Tallant diamonds, but the thought of her as Marchioness of Tallant was otherwise repugnant to him.

Marriage… Joss frowned. He could scarcely believe that he had told Amy the tale of his parents' separation and far less that he had mentioned their advice to him. He had thought such childhood memories were long forgotten. Yet perhaps they did remain to colour one's judgement. Certainly Amy had been most affected by George Bainbridge's fecklessness. But now the spectre of genteel poverty was banished and she had all the security she needed. Perhaps, now that she was an heiress as well, she would attract a suitor who pleased her.

The warm feeling that Joss had experienced whilst thinking of Amy vanished abruptly at the thought of a suitor who might catch her interest. The idea certainly did not please him. He could not imagine that any future husband of Amy's would countenance for a moment the continuation of their visits and conversations. Yet they were only meeting so frequently to fulfil the terms of the debt of honour. At the end of the week the arrangement would cease and Amy would be free of his company. Feeling thoroughly grumpy now, Joss turned the phaeton in the direction of Covent Garden. Thinking about Amy was proving too problematical and he did not wish to question why. On the other hand, Harriet would be delighted to see him and that was not complicated at all. All the same, he knew that he was running away.

'Amy, I have been thinking.' Richard Bainbridge had caught his sister at the foot of the stairs as they waited for Lady Bainbridge to join them for the Carteret ball. Richard's fair, good-humoured face was creased with worry and this, together with the unusual information that he had been thinking, made his sister vaguely apprehensive.

'Yes, Richard? Whatever is the matter?'

'It's Joss Tallant.' Richard leaned a hand against the newel post and surveyed his sister with severity. 'Dash it, Amy, it just won't do, you know. Yesterday you were closeted with the fellow for nigh on two hours and today you vanish with him for a whole day! It makes me uncomfortable!'

Amy raised her brows. 'I thought that Lord Tallant was a friend of yours, Richard?'

Richard looked affronted. 'What has that to do with the price of fish? Joss is a friend of mine, but he ain't suitable as a friend of yours!'

Amy shrugged. She felt irritable. 'You know there is no harm in it! Besides, you did nothing to stop the wager at the time.'

Richard shifted uncomfortably. 'I thought that Joss would simply pay up. I never imagined him squiring you around Town in this devilishly attentive manner! People will talk, you know!'

'People always talk,' Amy said crossly. 'Dear Richard, I know that you have my best interests at heart, but you more than anyone must see how baseless your fears are! I know it is indelicate to mention it, but what would Lord Tallant be doing with me when he has Miss Templeton to…entertain him?'

Richard blushed. Amy found this rather endearing. 'Amy! You should not… I cannot…'

'Amanda and I saw you all together, remember?' Amy said with brutal candour. 'You, Parrish, Fleet and Joss Tallant in the Park with those ladies.'

Richard recoiled. The sound of Lady Bainbridge's tread could be heard on the landing above and he threw a hunted look over his shoulder.

Nicola Cornick

'For God's sake, do not mention this in front of Mama, Amy! She would have an apoplexy!'

'Why?' Amy raised her brows in mock ignorance. 'Surely she knows you have an actress in keeping—'

'Amy!' Richard backed away, rather as though she was an unpredictable dog that might bite at any moment. 'You know full well why you should not speak of it! Besides, Mama would be furious to discover that I had Kitty Maltravers in keeping! Papa was cheated at cards by Kitty's first protector and Mama never forgets something like that.'

Amy gave a snort of laughter. 'Oh, Richard, I am sure you are more worried about that than ever you are that I might be in danger from associating with the Earl of Tallant...'

'Now there you are wrong,' her brother said virtuously, straightening up as Lady Bainbridge, in emerald green and a startlingly large diamond necklace, started to descend the stair. 'I have your interests firmly at heart! By the by, if you think that Joss's amorous interests are focussed on Miss Templeton these days, you are far out! Why, he barely seems interested in the girl. I believe it will not be long before Miss Templeton is looking for another protector.'

'Truly?' Amy felt her heart lift in a most inappropriate and telling way. 'Not, of course, that it is any concern of mine... Mama!' She turned to Lady Bainbridge, grateful for the distraction. 'You look magnificent tonight! And those diamonds—I had no notion that you possessed anything so fine.'

'All paste, my dear,' Lady Bainbridge said, patting her chest fondly as she approved her reflection in the hall mirror. 'I tried to pawn them when we fell upon hard times, but I fear the pawnbroker was not interested! He said they were too gaudy!' She frowned and checked her reflection again. 'I cannot imagine what he meant!'

'I say, Amy,' Richard whispered, as they waited for the new carriage to be brought round, 'can you lend me a monkey, just for tonight? My pockets are to let.'

'How much is a monkey?' Amy asked innocently.

Joss arrived at Lady Carteret's ball very late in the evening and Amy, noticing him the moment that he walked through the door, thought that he looked slightly tousled, which in no way detracted from his startlingly attractive appearance. She watched as he greeted his hostess with a gallantry that had her ladyship blushing and smiling and made his way by very slow and slight degrees to Amy's side.

At first she had assumed that this casual approach was designed to quash any gossip. They had agreed earlier that Joss should not escort her to the ball, but Amy had thought that the arrangement had at least involved Joss arriving tolerably early and dancing with her a couple of times. He was the one who had added balls, parties and masquerades to her list, after all. They were not her preferred mode of entertainment. As the evening had wound on and he had failed to appear, Amy found that she had every dance spoken for. To start with she had thought to save one for him; now she was glad that she had not.

She was not sure how she knew, but when he finally bowed over her hand she immediately realised that he was out of temper and that the easy camaraderie that had been between them only that afternoon had vanished. A slight frown creased her brow as she studied him. Joss's dark auburn hair was casually dishevelled and he wore his clothes with a careless distinction. Some instinct suggested to her that he looked as though he had just got out of bed. And as she stared, her mind transfixed by the idea, she realised that it was true and, further, that he had not been alone. She blushed scarlet with mortification, snatched her hand away and muttered something incoherent.

'Would you care to dance, Miss Bainbridge?' Joss asked, sounding to Amy's ears as though the very thought bored him to death. She gave him a tight smile.

'Thank you, my lord, but I fear all my dances are taken,' she said. 'Here is Lord Holles come to claim me for the boulanger. Excuse me, if you please.'

Joss bowed. His face was studiously blank but there was an edge to his voice. 'Some other time then, Miss Bainbridge?'

'Perhaps,' Amy said, with an equal edge to hers.

She did not remember much about the boulanger other than that from her place on the floor she could see Joss and Richard making their way to the card room. That seemed to make everything worse, as though Joss was deliberately doing everything he could to anger her by arriving late, acting in an offhand manner and then heading straight for the gaming tables. When Amy told herself not to be foolish and that she had no right to censure his behaviour, it only served to make her feel worse. She could not understand why she felt so upset. She had known all along what manner of man he was, and, if he chose to go directly to visit his mistress after he had spent the afternoon with her, that was his concern. She was not interested in his sophisticated games. It was not as though she had any romantic claim to him.

Nevertheless, there was a hot pain in her chest and tears burned behind her eyes. She had known that the debt of honour was a foolish idea from the very start and she decided that it would be better to finish it now, before it was really started, and have done with the pretence.

The dance ended and Amy accepted Lord Holles's arm

back to her mother's side. The poor man had been doing his best to be agreeable and she realised that she had not taken in a word that he had said to her. All that she could think was that she would speak to Joss at the next opportunity and tell him that their plans for the rest of the week were cancelled. That way she need not see him again.

Joss was faring little better than Amy. He had not enjoyed his time with Harriet, despite the strenuous efforts to do so that had made him late for Lady Carteret's ball. Their physical encounters had always been satisfying before, even if he had never found Harriet a particularly stimulating companion in other ways, yet he had found the last few hours utterly unfulfilling. He was bored and irritable and had found it almost impossible to work up any enthusiasm for their lovemaking no matter how he tried, and Harriet's failure to notice this seemed only to serve to emphasise the gulf between them. Afterwards she had prattled on about trips on the river and the projected visit to Vauxhall, until Joss had been desperate to escape her company. When she had flung her arms about him as he left and pressed her scented body against him, he had felt physically repulsed.

All in all it was enough to put him into a very bad mood and for some obscure reason it had seemed to be the fault of Miss Amy Bainbridge. He had enjoyed his afternoon with her so much that it had made the following hours seem even more disappointing. Then, when he had finally caught up with Amy what seemed like hours later, she had greeted him very coolly indeed and promptly gone off to dance with some other gentleman. For his part, Joss had headed for the card room in habitual fashion, only to find that he could not concentrate on the game of hazard that was in progress. He emerged a short while later, prompted by the need to discover whom Amy was dancing with next.

He was not amused to see that it was Clive Massingham who was plying her with lemonade and attention in equal measure under the approving eye of Lady Bainbridge. There were a couple of other young ladies present and a gaggle of younger sons whom Joss cynically identified as hanging out for a fortune. Amy was looking rather pretty, he thought, in another of Madame Louise's confections, this time of pale pink gauze embroidered with tiny rosebuds. There were matching flowers on the bandeau that held back her ringlets and her hair gleamed golden brown in the light. She looked tiny and delicate and she also looked extremely cheerful and not at all reserved. Joss's hands clenched in an involuntary movement as he saw Amy laughing with unrestrained enjoyment at one of Massingham's anecdotes. He detested Massingham. The man was a fortune hunter and a libertine and Joss knew it was hypocritical, but he deplored Massingham's lack of morals. He could hardly bear to be near the man—the fact that Massingham had been lover to both the Marchioness of Tallant and now to her daughter Juliana made Joss feel sick.

He was also surprised to see Lady Bainbridge countenancing Massingham's attentions to Amy when it was well known that the man had an unsavoury reputation. As for Massingham himself—thirty thousand pounds would never be enough for him. Joss knew that he had refused to marry Juliana because she did not have enough money to tempt him.

'You're looking very grim, old fellow,' Sebastian Fleet commented as he passed Joss the glass of wine that he had thoughtfully procured for him. 'I would have thought that a few hours with the lovely Harriet would have put you in a better humour!'

Joss shrugged irritably. 'I was just reflecting that Clive Massingham was a rather inappropriate suitor for Miss Bainbridge. I wonder that her mother allows it.'

Fleet raised his brows. 'Surely Lady Bainbridge would be *aux anges* to see her nestling married off to anyone who offered. Miss Bainbridge may have a fortune now, Joss old boy, but it don't make her any less reserved—or less plain.'

Joss's jaw tightened. Somewhere, not far below the surface, he felt violence bubbling up inside him.

'It may be, Seb, that your taste only runs to the more obvious-looking female! Miss Bainbridge has a certain distinction.'

Fleet smothered a grin in his wineglass. 'I stand corrected. Clearly you have more discernment than I.'

Joss found he could not stop himself even though he knew Fleet was deliberately goading him. 'Miss Bainbridge is charming, Sebastian.'

'You must be grateful to Lady Juliana for the debt of honour,' Fleet said, a twinkle in his eye, 'if it has given you the opportunity to ascertain as much!'

Joss gave him a darkling stare. He put his empty wineglass down with controlled force.

'This ball is boring me. I believe I shall go.'

Fleet's smile grew. 'To White's, old fellow? Or to Covent Garden, perhaps?'

Joss paused. Neither of Fleet's suggestions held the slightest appeal and he realised with a strange pang that he was not at all sure where he would go or what he would do. A part of him wanted to stay at Lady Carteret's ball simply to be near Amy, but at the same time the thought of watching her dancing with other gentlemen irritated him almost beyond measure.

Even as he hesitated, Fleet touched his arm to draw his attention to the tableau across the room.

'I did not realise that Juliana was a particular friend of Miss Bainbridge?'

Joss turned. His sister had indeed come up to the group about Amy and was engaging in conversation that seemed most amicable, although her gaze was dwelling on Clive Massingham with a possessive intensity. Joss frowned. Surely Juliana did not imagine Amy a rival for Massingham's affections? It seemed absurd. Yet a vague sense of unease possessed him; he started across the room towards them and as he did so Juliana's drawling tones floated over to him.

'Lud, Miss Bainbridge, I had no idea that you were such a secret gambler—and such a successful one! First you lift over two hundred guineas from me at play, and then I hear that this mysterious fortune of yours is a lottery prize! We should be calling you the lottery heiress!'

There was a sudden lull in the conversation all around, as though all ears were out on stalks. Like everyone else, Joss had his gaze fixed on Amy's face and saw the colour fade from her cheeks before her chin came up sharply and an angry gleam came into her eyes. She spoke quietly but with emphasis.

'Thank you, Lady Juliana, but I should prefer no such soubriquet.'

Her eyes met Joss's and he saw the hurt and anger there before she turned away with contempt. Joss felt his own anger start to burn. He caught Juliana's arm in an iron grip and pulled her unceremoniously towards an alcove.

'That was not well done, Juliana.' He wanted to shake her

and only just managed to restrain himself. 'Sometimes your spite shocks even me, sister dear!'

Already word of Amy's lottery win was rippling away from the group, a frisson of excitement accompanying the whispered words as such a prime piece of gossip was passed on.

Juliana pulled a face. She shook his hand off her arm. 'Lud, what is it to you, Joss? I heard a piece of gossip and thought to tease a little, that is all—'

'You thought to damage Miss Bainbridge's reputation! You must know that Lady Bainbridge has put it about that the money was inherited.'

Juliana shrugged. 'I do so dislike dishonesty, don't you, Joss? If little Miss Bainbridge wishes to be courted for her money, all well and good, but at least let it be known where that money has come from!'

Her green gaze searched his face for a moment and then she smiled, her lazy smile. 'Lud, you do look angry, my dear. Can it be that you are developing a *tendre* for the innocent little Miss Bainbridge? How piquant! I declare that that would be a greater piece of gossip even than the lottery winnings!'

Joss's eyes narrowed. He was shocked at the anger he felt inside; anger with Juliana for her malice, mixed with the most astonishing desire to protect Amy from such spite.

'You will not spread such gossip, Juliana!'

'Shall I not?' Lady Juliana arched an elegant eyebrow. 'How so?'

'Because you are scarcely lily white yourself. I would not wish you to…damage…yourself in the process. A story about Miss Bainbridge could lead so very easily to a disclosure about you…'

For a moment they stared furiously at each other, then

Juliana lowered her gaze. A bright spot of colour burned in her cheeks. 'Bah, you are an odious wretch sometimes, Joss! You would do it, too!'

Joss bowed slightly. 'I would. You see, Juliana, little Miss Bainbridge, as you call her, is indeed a genuinely innocent girl, whereas you and I inhabit the sort of world that has nothing in common with hers, except superficially. I suggest that you leave her alone.'

Juliana smiled. 'Oh, I will, brother dear. Just as long as you do. You could damage her reputation far more than I ever could.'

Joss held her gaze. He knew she was right and he also knew he could not afford to give her any advantages.

'Which is why I shall be keeping well away from her myself,' he said coldly. 'There is no truth in your suspicions, Juliana. None whatsoever.'

Chapter Ten

Lady Bainbridge, close to indulging in a fit of the vapours, had wanted to retire from the ball immediately when the word of the lottery win was out, but Amy had refused to retreat in ignominy. It was not that she felt there was any further enjoyment to be obtained from the evening; on the contrary, it had been a disappointment from start to finish and the fact that everyone was talking scandal about her only served to confirm her poor opinion of society. However, she had a task to undertake and it was one that her anger would enable her accomplish. Tomorrow would be too late. She wanted to give the Earl of Tallant a piece of her mind.

It had to be Joss who had told Lady Juliana about the lottery win and she was furious with him for it. First they had hatched their stupid joke, calling it a debt of honour, and then they had humiliated her at the ball for good measure. If ever a brother and sister were kindred spirits, Amy thought angrily, it was those two. They deserved each other.

She could not see Joss anywhere in the ballroom and

thought that he might have left. There was no trace of him in the card room or the refreshment room, although there were plenty of prying eyes and sly smiles from those people who watched her. Her fury increasing by the minute, Amy was about to call her hunt off and retire, when she saw Joss just coming through the terrace doors. He appeared to be alone. She hurried across the ballroom and caught up with him before he had taken more than a few steps inside, planting herself directly in his path.

'Lord Tallant!'

'Miss Bainbridge?' Joss's tone was measured in comparison with her own and he sounded coolly bored. The thought made Amy's temper soar. Now she was well served for even thinking for a moment that they had established some kind of innocuous friendship. She had stumbled well out of her depth and should withdraw—but not until she had told him what she thought of him.

'I wish to speak with you, my lord.' Amy kept her tone steady although her pulse hammered hard. 'Immediately!'

Joss looked amused at her vehemence. He made a slight gesture. 'Please do so.'

'Not here!' Amy said, glancing around. The crowd in the ballroom was thinning a little because of the lateness of the hour but there were still plenty of people present and many of them were looking their way.

'We cannot step outside without causing further speculation,' Joss pointed out. 'If you wish to speak with me now, Miss Bainbridge, it will have to be in public.'

Amy glared at him. 'I am surprised that you scruple at causing further scandal, my lord! Perhaps you should have thought of that before you told your sister that I had won my fortune on the lottery. I asked you to keep that a secret and I trusted you to do so!'

Joss's eyes narrowed. 'Am I to understand that you believe that *I* told Juliana that you had won the thirty thousand pounds? Why should you think such a thing?'

Amy threw a quick glance over her shoulder. Now he sounded almost as angry as she.

'It must be you! Who else?'

Rather than answer, Joss took her arm and drew her out of the long terrace windows. He did not stop at the balustrade, but hurried her down the steps and on to the spruce-flanked lawn at the bottom. A full summer moon rode high in the sky so it was not entirely dark, but Amy shivered in the cool breeze. Already the ballroom seemed a long way away.

'Oh! Why did you do that? I thought you just expressed a wish to avoid scandal?'

'I judged that it would cause more scandal for us to quarrel in public than for us to take a small walk,' Joss said, through shut teeth. 'However, I am not detaining you, Miss Bainbridge. If you wish to return to the ballroom you may do so at once.'

Amy surveyed him in silence for a moment. Her anger had ebbed as soon as she had thrown the accusation at him and now, although he had not refuted it, she found that she no longer wished to argue with him.

'Were we quarrelling?' she asked in a small voice.

'Assuredly. And we shall continue to do so if you accuse me of breaking your trust.'

Amy frowned slightly. 'So you did not tell Lady Juliana?'

'I did not.' Joss's tone was uncompromising. 'As for who the culprit might be, there could be a number of possibilities.

Lady Bainbridge, perhaps, or your brother or even Amanda
Spry. I suppose you told her the truth of your situation?'

'Yes, but—' Amy had started to feel quite regretful. Perhaps she had jumped to conclusions. She probably owed him
an apology, except that now Joss had started to speak it was
difficult to offer one. She realised that he was very angry—
she had never seen him like this before.

'Then there were the gentlemen you were accosting at
Lady Moon's ball when you were trying to find the owner of
the lottery ticket,' Joss continued. 'Hallam and Dainty may
have been too slow to realise what you were about, but Sebastian Fleet is no fool!'

'No,' Amy said, 'but—'

'But what?' Joss's body was tight with tension. Amy could
feel it emanating from him in waves. 'None of the other suspects are as likely as I am? Is that what you wished to say,
Miss Bainbridge?'

Amy felt the need to justify herself. 'I am sorry. It is simply that Lady Juliana is your sister and as the two of you had
already colluded over Lady Juliana's debt to me, I thought...'
Her voice faded away then strengthened. 'I thought that it
was all part of some jest at my expense...'

'I see.' Joss's voice was very polite. 'You thought that I
had conspired with Juliana to make fun of you, despite the
fact that I had already assured you that was not true, and
you also believed that I had told Juliana about the money.'

Amy shivered again. 'You make it sound very foolish of
me.'

Joss shrugged. 'It merely proves that you do not trust me.'

Amy swallowed what felt like a huge lump in her throat.
She did not understand why the stark words should make
her feel miserable but they did. Nor could she deny them for

that was exactly what she had said to him only a few minutes previously. It was too dark to see his expression, but she was certain that she had hurt him in some way although the idea seemed manifestly absurd. She made a slight gesture.

'I am sorry if I made a mistake...'

'Under the circumstances, it is probably better that we cancel the rest of the arrangements for this week and that I pay the debt in full,' Joss said formally. 'You will have your two hundred guineas tomorrow morning, Miss Bainbridge.'

'Oh, no!' Amy said quickly, feeling that matters were going from bad to worse. 'That is, if you prefer it that way.'

'It is not what I prefer,' Joss said, still with immaculate courtesy, 'but rather what you favour, Miss Bainbridge.'

Amy made a slight, helpless gesture. 'I accept that I have misjudged you, my lord. I have no wish to make matters worse by insisting on receiving the money in lieu of your company! Besides, it is Wednesday tomorrow! We have already spent two days together—'

'Are you suggesting that I should be granted some kind of discount, Miss Bainbridge?' Now there was violence in Joss's tone. 'A concession for services already rendered?'

Amy put her hand on his arm. 'Please! I do not wish to quarrel with you! I should have thought what would happen...'

There was a silence, but for the breeze in the night-scented pines. Then Joss put his hand over hers where it rested on his sleeve. His touch was warm. His tone had softened.

'Do you trust me, Amy?'

Amy caught her breath. 'Yes.'

'And do you wish our...arrangement...to be at an end?'

'No.'

She did not. Ten minutes previously Amy had vowed to

tell him that she never wanted to see him again, but now she realised just how much she had hurt him with her accusations—and how much she would suffer if she were to deny herself his company. It was a matter that required some careful thought, for it was telling her something very significant about her feelings. Except that she could not think about it now. Now she was aware of nothing except Joss's hand on hers, the sound of his breathing, the expression in his eyes. All her senses were focussed on him. At the back of her mind was the faint belief that she was getting herself into the most dreadful danger, but it was a distant thought and it did not really trouble her. She made no move away from him.

Joss bent his head and kissed her. For a moment Amy was acutely aware of the touch of his lips on hers, their warmth, their gentleness. Then the effect of the kiss and the shock that it was Joss kissing her hit her simultaneously. Her knees weakened and his arms went about her, drawing her closer.

The feel of his mouth on hers was unfamiliar and a little frightening, for Amy had never been kissed before. Despite the strangeness she felt no urge to withdraw from the embrace and after a moment her fear receded, drowned by the delightful sensations that were flooding her body. A rush of warmth swept through her and she was shaken by the sweetest pleasure she had ever felt, and when his tongue touched hers with a featherlight caress she shivered all the way down to her toes.

Joss drew back, but he kept an arm about her.

'I am sorry.' His voice was a little husky. '*Now* do you wish our arrangement to be at an end, Amy?'

Amy blinked and moved away from him. She felt a little cold. The stars settled back into their courses and the outlines of the trees came back into focus, yet she had the strangest feeling that something had changed irrevocably.

'I...don't know.' She frowned a little. 'Why are you sorry? A rake does not apologise.'

She saw Joss smile and the sight of it gave her a strange, warm feeling. 'That's true when he plans a seduction. I did not plan this, Amy.'

'Oh!' Amy stole a look at him. 'Then what do we do now?'

She saw Joss's smile deepen and her heart lurched, but he did not take her back in his arms, which was the answer she really wanted.

'That depends on you,' he said. 'If I have offended you and you do not wish to see me again, we should settle the debt and have done with it. Otherwise I think we could continue as we were before—and forget that this evening ever happened.'

Decidedly this was not what Amy wanted. Her heart sank a little and with it went all the lovely warm feelings that the kiss had engendered. Joss's words seemed eminently sensible but it was not sense that she wanted now. Nevertheless, she knew that he was right. She had been missing from the ballroom for far too long, she was with the most notorious rake in London and common sense rather than starry-eyed romance was what was needed here. To Joss a kiss might be no great matter; to Amy, who had just received the first, heart-stirring embrace of her life, it was a different thing entirely, but she could still see the disparity in their positions.

'I think that your payment of the debt of honour should continue,' she said, as briskly as she could. 'We are engaged to see the exhibition at the Royal Academy tomorrow afternoon, remember, and on Thursday we are to visit the St Boniface almshouses.'

'I will see you tomorrow afternoon, then.' Joss took her

hand and pressed a kiss on it. Amy could detect nothing in his voice except good humour and it lit a spark of rebellion in her. It was not fair that he should be so calm when her senses were still humming with awareness. If he could be cool, so could she. She pulled her hand from his grasp.

'Good night, Lord Tallant.'

'Good night, Miss Bainbridge.'

Amy went slowly up the stone steps and slipped in at the ballroom door. The light seemed very bright. The ballroom was still full of chatter and over by the door Richard was supporting a tottering Lady Bainbridge out into the hall. It was time to go home. And nothing had changed.

Joss caught up with his sister Juliana as she was about to step into her carriage. She was not alone. She was leaning on the arm of Clive Massingham and it was obvious that they were leaving together. Equally obvious was the fact the Juliana did not care who knew, whereas Massingham looked slightly nervous to see Joss approaching them, though he soon covered it with his customary truculent expression.

Joss hesitated for the merest split second. 'Juliana, a word with you, please.'

Juliana yawned widely. 'Not now, Joss, not again! Can you not see that I am anxious to reach home—and my bed?'

Massingham laughed at the innuendo. Joss's expression tightened. 'Yes, now! It will take but a moment.'

Juliana turned a pettish shoulder. 'Lud, you become more like our father every day! I declare, Joss, you will be spoiling your bad-boy reputation if you turn into a moralist!'

Joss gave Massingham a look of calculated dismissal. 'What I have to say is private, Juliana. Perhaps you and Mr Massingham may meet up again later?'

Juliana laughed. 'Oh, very well. You had better come with me in the carriage, Joss. Clive, darling…' her voice sank to a throaty purr '…I shall be all of five minutes…'

'I will count on that.' Massingham took her hand and pressed a kiss ostentatiously on the palm.

Juliana gave a pleasurable shiver. 'Forgive me if I embarrass you, Joss,' she said with evident insincerity.

'Your behaviour does not offend me in the least, Ju,' Joss said coolly, 'but the company you keep is beneath you. What you see in Massingham—'

'Can you not imagine?' Juliana allowed him to help her up into the carriage. 'And I had heard that your imagination was so very…vivid…as well, Joss dearest, when it comes to matters of the heart! I hear that Harriet Templeton speaks so highly of you! But not recently. Recently I'm told she says your mind is distracted, darling…'

'We were speaking of you and Massingham, I believe.' Joss's voice was hard.

'Oh, yes.' The undertone of amusement had returned to Juliana's voice. 'Are you concerned about his past relationship with our mother, Joss? He says that I am better than she—'

Joss's fist hit the smooth leather of the seat with a smothered crash. 'That is enough, Juliana!'

'Oh, very well. I do but tease.' Juliana's eyes flashed. 'Which reminds me—when are you to marry little Miss Innocence? What a change that will be for you, Joss! So much purity—I declare, it quite goes to one's head!'

'I infer you are speaking of Miss Bainbridge?' Joss said coldly. 'I have warned you before, Juliana—'

'Oh, I will not speak of her to anyone else, of course, but you can confide in me, Joss.' Juliana gave her feline smile. 'Is she not the sweetest little thing? Too good for you, my dear!'

'Precisely,' Joss said, through shut teeth. 'I can never aspire to marry Miss Bainbridge, Juliana—'

'Stuff! Why ever not? When you are in love with her as well...'

'My feelings are beside the point here. Miss Bainbridge should marry someone who can make up for the sufferings she has already endured. A reputation besmirched by years of gambling and womanising is scarcely much to offer, is it? Why, it is asking almost as much as acceptance of years of financial ruin!'

'Lud, you are in love with her!' For a moment Juliana's voice had softened to something that Joss remembered. 'You are too honourable, my dear. Just because George Bainbridge made his womenfolk suffer, it does not mean that Miss Bainbridge would find you an unacceptable suitor—'

'Miss Bainbridge has exactly the right opinion of my gambling, Ju—she deplores it. Now—' Joss clamped down on his temper with an effort '—may we speak instead of the matter in hand? I wish to know who it was told you of Miss Bainbridge's lottery win.'

Juliana laughed. 'Then you will have to go hang, my dear, for I cannot tell you. I may need to use that source again sometime!'

'Was it Richard Bainbridge? I have yet to learn that he is in your thrall, but it may be so.'

'No,' Juliana said consideringly, 'it was not he. Though you do give me an idea, Joss. If Massingham fails—'

'Fails to do what?' Joss's voice had an edge to it. 'Offer you marriage? You'll be waiting a long time there, Ju!'

It was too dark to see his sister's face but, though she took every pain to erase the hurt from her voice, he knew her too well. He heard it and understood it.

'Lud, I am not hanging out to be Massingham's wife! No, a better title is all that could capture me—' Her voice broke and she hurried to cover it up. 'But I will never tell you my informant, Joss, so you need not press me.'

Joss knew she would not. But the field was narrowing. If not Richard, then possibly Lady Bainbridge herself, or the Duke of Fleet, or even Amanda Spry…

'I see you have taken up with Lady Spry again,' he said carelessly. 'Does it remind you of the old days?'

Juliana gave him a sharp look. 'You'll not catch me that way, Joss! No, Amanda Spry and I cannot be friends now. One grows apart from one's girlhood friends.'

'I see.' Joss said slowly. 'Perhaps seeing her reminds you too much of Myfleet? You were all friends once, were you not? He was a good man, Juliana—'

'The best.' Joss heard the edge of tears in his sister's voice. 'But now I have Massingham, remember? I fear I shall have to ask you to leave now, my dear. You are tedious dull tonight, and if there is one thing that I cannot bear, it is to be bored.'

'Amy dear, you seem most distracted this morning.' Lady Bainbridge's faintly querulous voice made Amy jump and she dropped her bread honey-side down on the carpet. There was just the two of them for breakfast and for most of the meal Lady Bainbridge had kept up a lament about the events of the previous night—how could the spiteful Lady Juliana ever have heard the truth, what sort of wicked rumours would be circulating that morning, what was to become of them all now…? Amy had barely noticed her diatribe, for she was struggling with difficulties of her own. Shortly she would have to face Joss in the daylight and pretend that the previous evening was forgotten, yet she did not feel the same about him and, more confusingly still, she was not even sure what she *did* feel.

'I beg your pardon, Mama,' she said. 'I was thinking about what to do—'

'Precisely!' Lady Bainbridge looked triumphant. 'We must come up with a plan. I knew I should not have worn the yellow slippers yesterday, for yellow is a most unlucky colour and I should have known something bad would happen. Oh, that wretched Juliana Myfleet! She always was a wicked girl and now she has ruined things for you, Amy. Ruined! You will not catch a respectable husband now, for *ton* society cannot look kindly on a fortune derived from gambling. Not in a woman!'

The blatant double standard in this jerked Amy out of her preoccupation.

'Well, that is the biggest hypocrisy I have ever heard!' she said indignantly. 'Fortunes are won and lost at the tables all the time, yet no one condemns the gamblers! Not that I wish to catch a husband, Mama, as I told you from the first!'

Lady Bainbridge chose to ignore this. 'It may be hypocrisy, but it is the way of the world. To win the lottery is *not* respectable. Oh, to think that I told all those people about Aunt Bessie's legacy and now they are all laughing at me. It is too much!'

Amy privately thought that her mother had already been halfway to believing in the late Aunt Bessie and her legacy, and would probably soon say that the rumours were not respectful to her memory. She knew that Lady Bainbridge must be suffering. Her mother had always been so concerned with society's opinion, a fact that had given her much mortification when George Bainbridge had embarrassed her with his financial disasters. This new gossip would be most hurtful to her, whereas Amy was tempted to tell all the scandalmongers to go hang.

'I think we shall just have to ignore the gossip, Mama,' she said. 'If we carry on as though nothing has happened—'

Lady Bainbridge looked horrified. 'Oh, that is not to be thought of! I could not possibly walk into another ballroom now. No, Amy, I have plans for us to retire from town at once. If we go to Nettlecombe for a space, matters may settle down and we may return next season. Of course you will be older by then, and there are those who already think you at your last prayers, but it cannot be helped. No, I am decided! We leave for the country at the end of this week.'

Amy made an exasperated gesture. 'Mama, I cannot bear for us to appear to be running away from this. It is not that important.'

Lady Bainbridge looked outraged. 'Of course it is important! We *are* running away.'

Amy sighed. It was the old pattern repeating itself, of course, for her mother had had only one way of dealing with the scandals that had surrounded her life. Whenever George Bainbridge had been financially embarrassed, his wife had suffered an equivalent social embarrassment. They had removed Amy from her schools and her friends, they had moved to different lodgings, they had retired to the country, all to save face as well as save money. Amy could not be surprised that her mother was reacting this way now. She made a last appeal.

'Mama, I have so many plans that I do not wish to put off. Why, Amanda and I were going to attend the victory celebrations in St James's Park.'

Lady Bainbridge shuddered. 'If you wish to be cut dead

by all of our acquaintance, Amy, then pray remain in town.
I shall be going to Nettlecombe as soon as I may arrange it!'

Amy could see the tears in her mother's eyes. She felt the
exasperation swell up and stifled it. To argue now would
only upset her mother further. She patted her hand instead.

'Very well, Mama. We shall go to the country if you wish
it.'

Lady Bainbridge's blue eyes swam with tears. 'Thank you,
my love. I confess that will set my mind at rest.' She frowned
a little. 'There is something else that concerns me, however—
that most unsuitable young man, brother to that hateful Juliana Myfleet. There has been talk, Amy—'

Amy stood up abruptly. She had been prepared to humour
her mother on other points, but she did not want to talk about
Joss. It felt like trying to walk on a twisted ankle.

'I collect that you mean the Earl of Tallant. He is suitable
enough to be a friend of Richard's—'

'Oh, yes, but that is quite different, for he is rich and if
Richard can win from him... But for you, my love it is quite
another matter. Though I suppose,' Lady Bainbridge said,
diverted momentarily, 'he is vastly handsome...'

'Well, you need not worry, Mama.' Amy moved towards
the door. 'Since we shall be leaving London soon I shall have
no more opportunity to see him.'

'No more you shall!' Lady Bainbridge said, brightening.
'That is all right then!'

'I am going to visit Mrs Wendover this morning,' Amy
said, pausing with her hand on the doorjamb. 'I thought to
take some food and some clothing for the children and books
for the school.'

'That is kind of you, my love,' Lady Bainbridge said. She
looked up sharply. 'You had better take Patience with you.

Oh, and you had better procure a hack! Do not take the carriage to Whitechapel, not when it is so new! I could not bear for it to be damaged!'

'I wondered whether you had seen this,' Amanda Spry said, reluctantly holding out a sheet of paper to her friend. It was the evening and Amy, out of deference to Lady Bainbridge's wishes, had cancelled her attendance at a musicale and chosen instead to spend a quiet evening at home with her friend. Yet even here, it seemed, gossip pursued her. She took the scandal sheet from Amanda's hand and perused the doggerel written there:

Little Miss B
Who lived retired
To gambling and marriage
Never aspired
Now tempted to sin
By a lottery win
She plays for high stakes
With the greatest of rakes.'

'Oh dear.' Amy put the sheet down gently. Her first impulse had been to thrust it into the fire before Lady Bainbridge saw it, but now she scanned the rhyme again. 'I am not entirely clear what they are lampooning me for? Is it for the lottery win or for the time I am spending with Lord Tallant?' she sighed. 'Both, I suppose.'

Amanda's blue eyes scanned her face thoughtfully. 'You do not seem much concerned, Amy! If it were me I should have left town already! I cannot bear people speaking scandal about me.'

Amy shrugged with an assumption of ease. 'It will die away when the next *on-dit* comes along! I know I am considered an original and society so dislikes someone who does not fit in! Give that person a fortune and...' She shrugged again. 'It is easy to see why I am unpopular.'

Amanda was still watching her with concern. 'And what of Lord Tallant's part in this? He does not seem concerned that he has made you an object of scandal.'

'That is putting it far too strongly.' Amy spoke firmly. 'Just because I have chosen to spend some time in Lord Tallant's company should not give rise to speculation!'

Amanda gave her a pitying glance. 'Perhaps it should not, but it has! A rake of Lord Tallant's reputation accompanying you to charity concerts and almshouses! Half the people are saying that he has been making a game of you and the other half that he must be hunting your fortune—'

She broke off at the angry flash in Amy's eyes. 'I beg your pardon, Amy. That was unpardonably rude of me.' She spread her hands in a gesture of appeal. 'It is simply that I am worried about you! Lord Tallant—'

'There is nothing scandalous between Lord Tallant and myself, Amanda,' Amy said, feeling herself blush. If only her friend realised how desperately Amy wished the reverse were true! Ever since the previous night, Amy had found her thoughts returning to Joss's kiss with tiresome repetition. She had been so tongue-tied in his company that afternoon that it had been fortunate they had been looking at an exhibition of art, for it gave her the excuse to keep quiet as she contemplated the pictures. Certainly Joss did not appear to have noticed anything different in her demeanour and he had seemed quite preoccupied himself.

'It will all blow over,' she said again, with more composure than she was feeling. 'It only requires a Countess to run off with her footman and I shall be quite forgotten!'

'I envy you your hardihood,' Amanda said. 'What if it *were* something truly scandalous, Amy, such as your sojourn in Whitechapel when you were a girl? How would you feel if that story got out?'

Amy raised her brows. 'Living in Whitechapel is hardly a scandal, Amanda, although it is not something that I would wish to be common knowledge. In the end I would have to say that if people wish to speak of it, let them do so!'

Amanda shook her head. 'I believe that you are deliberately misunderstanding me! There must be something that you have done in the past you would not wish people to know! Everyone has their secrets.'

Amy searched her mind for something so reprehensible that she would fear it coming out. Her memory remained obstinately blank. She shook her head.

'No. I fear that I have led a very dull life. No one could blackmail me for my fortune!'

A tinge of colour came into Amanda's cheeks. 'So you are to go to Nettlecombe. I think that I shall leave town when you do, Amy. It will not be so much fun without you.'

Amy stared. 'Why ever should you do that? You know that you adore the balls and parties and you have plenty of friends here.'

Amanda sighed. 'I do not have many real friends, Amy, only acquaintances.'

'But surely…there is Emma Wren and Lady Juliana—'

Amanda met Amy's eye. Her own were bright with some emotion that Amy could not identify. 'Oh, stuff! They are no friends of mine! Emma is too fast for me—her behaviour gives me quite a disgust! As for Juliana…' Amanda's voice slowed. 'Well, we were friends once, perhaps, but that was in the days when Lord Myfleet was alive. Juliana was different then. She was not so hard. Now...' Amanda sighed. 'I declare she is quite another person!'

'Perhaps she is unhappy,' Amy said. She did not wish to think kindly of Lady Juliana after the way that she had behaved towards her and yet something prompted her to be generous. Perhaps it was the echo of Joss's words: *My sister at one time seemed exceptionally happy with her husband.* If Edwin Myfleet had not died, matters might well have been very different.

'Perhaps so.' Now there was a hard edge to Amanda's voice. 'She is not the only one, however.'

Amy put her knotting to one side and took Amanda's hands in hers. 'Mandy, I had no idea...'

'It does not matter.' Amanda, whom Amy had always thought of as elegant to a fault, now gave a most inelegant sniff. She snatched her hands away and stood up hurriedly. 'It is nothing to the purpose. Excuse me, Amy, I must go home. I have the headache.'

'Oh, but—' Amy was at a loss, wanting to help her friend and yet realising that Amanda did not want to talk. 'I will see you before we leave town?'

'Of course.' Amanda gave her a watery smile. 'Excuse me,' she said again. 'I fear that the megrim always makes me tearful.' Upon which blatantly untrue note she went out, leaving Amy to wonder what on earth could be the matter.

Chapter Eleven

'You are fast ruining my bad reputation, Miss Bainbridge,' Joss said resignedly, as Amy leaned out of his phaeton to hand him a pile of blankets, a hamper of food and a bag of medicines. 'Yesterday I was delivering school books for the orphans of St Boniface and today I am visiting in Windsor! Whatever next?'

'It is most kind of you, my lord.' Amy passed him the remainder of the pile of provisions. 'I am persuaded that Nurse Benfleet will be very grateful. We must not stay long, however. I did not tell Mama what I was doing and I simply must be back before evening or she will be fretting herself to flinders.'

She felt Joss's gaze upon her and willed herself not to blush. There were several practical reasons why she had not told Lady Bainbridge of the trip to see Mrs Benfleet. Firstly was the undeniable impropriety of driving to Windsor with Joss, even with a groom in attendance. Amy had considered this, but had decided it could not be allowed to matter.

Mrs Benfleet had been ill and needed her help, and that was the most important thing. Then there was the fact that her mother had warned her not to see Joss any more. Amy knew that this would not be possible beyond the end of the week, for their move to Nettlecombe was now fixed for the following day. Selfishly, she wished to make the most of her time with Joss before then, storing up the pleasure of his company against the future.

As Joss helped her down from the curricle his touch was impersonal and he took his hand away at once. Amy deliberately avoided looking at him. The worst of her self-consciousness had faded now, for Joss was treating her in exactly the same way as he had done before that fatal night in Lady Carteret's garden. He was charming but somehow remote.

Amy had been first relieved at Joss's attitude and then, once she had overcome her shyness, she had been frustrated. Inside her something had changed, her feelings had shifted, and when she looked at Joss sometimes and caught him looking at her, she thought he must feel the same. Yet there was a reserve in his manner that told her more plainly than any words that he would not kiss her again, that he would not come any closer, and Amy, to her shock, found that she wanted to shatter his cool resolution.

She picked up the pile of blankets and made her way up the stone-flagged path to the door of the cottage. Joss had dismissed the groom to take the curricle to the nearby inn until it was needed, and he followed her with the hamper in one hand and the medicines in the other. Amy smothered a smile. She had to applaud the uncomplaining way in which Joss had accepted the terms of the debt. It was difficult to imagine such a man visiting orphans or attending charitable lectures under any other circumstances. Yet he had accepted it all with a good grace.

'Miss Amy! Whatever are you doing here! Bless my soul, what a surprise!'

Mrs Benfleet, a round, motherly body in a white apron and lace cap with lavender ribbons, looked understandably surprised but pleased to see them. She hugged Amy warmly, then ushered them hospitably inside. The cottage was spartan but clean as a new pin and its ceiling was so low Amy feared Joss would hit his head on a beam.

'I am much better, thank you,' Mrs Benfleet replied, in answer to Amy's anxious questions about her health. 'That last package of medicine you sent was just the trick. Pure poison to taste, so I could tell it was doing me good!'

'You always used to say such things to me when I was a child,' Amy said, smiling.

'Yes, well, look at you! It must have worked. You look as fresh as a flower, child!'

Amy saw Joss smiling and blushed. 'I am sorry, I forgot—this is a...a friend of mine, Bennie. Lord Tallant—Mrs Benfleet.'

Amy saw Nurse's eyes open very wide as Joss took her hand. 'My word, Miss Amy!'

'Yes, well, anyway...' Amy hurried on for sudden fear that Mrs Benfleet was about to comment on either Joss's title or his indisputable good looks or possibly, even more embarrassingly, ask his intentions.

'We cannot stay more than a few minutes, Bennie, nor do we want to tire you out, but we brought you a few more bits and pieces to help pick you up. Some honey and some tonic wine—'

'I should be mortally offended if you don't take a bite of

luncheon with me,' Mrs Benfleet said. 'There's a nice ham in the larder, and bread and apples and milk enough for three.'

Amy cast a quick glance at Joss under her lashes. It was impossible to imagine him sitting down to any kind of repast in this cottage.

'We really must not—' she began.

'A splendid idea, Mrs Benfleet,' Joss said, smiling. 'Thank you very much. May I help you with anything?'

'That's the spirit,' Mrs Benfleet said approvingly, leading the way into her tiny kitchen. 'You go out into the garden, Miss Amy,' she called over her shoulder. 'It's nice and warm over by the apple tree.'

Amy went. The pocket-handkerchief of a garden had a bench against the south-facing wall and it was hot with summer scents and the buzzing of bees. She sat down and closed her eyes. The sun beat against her closed lids. She could hear the murmur of voices from the kitchen. So Joss was actually speaking to Mrs Benfleet, not merely helping to carve the ham or to carry things for her. Amy frowned a little. Perhaps she had been unfair to Joss in imagining he would feel awkward or out of place in such a setting. Whatever his other faults, snobbery was not amongst them.

'Over there, if you please.' She opened her eyes to see Mrs Benfleet advancing with a loaded tray and Joss carrying a table, which he placed in front of them beneath the apple tree.

'I was just telling your young man that he ought to try my homemade cider.' Mrs Benfleet beamed, handing the tray over as Amy hastened to grab it from her. 'Oof, that's better!' She subsided on the bench. 'Sometimes I forget I've been poorly and try to do too much. Move up, Miss Amy! There's room for three!'

Amy shifted along the bench so that there was space for

Joss to sit down. It was a tight squeeze and she was acutely conscious of the press of his thigh against hers. Once or twice his hand brushed hers as they passed the food around. Mrs Benfleet was chattering now, regaling Joss with stories of Amy's childhood. The sunshine, Joss's proximity and, most of all, the cider were all starting to make her head swim. She yawned widely, and then jumped, opening her eyes wide. It would never do to fall asleep. 'Oh, pray excuse me!'

'You sleep if you want to, my lamb,' Mrs Benfleet said comfortably. 'I'm sure your young man will help me to tidy all away when we've finished.'

'He is not my young man,' Amy said sleepily. She turned her head and her hair brushed Joss's shoulder. Suddenly the urge to rest her head there seemed overwhelming. She straightened up quickly.

'Is there anything else that you need me to send you, Bennie?'

'No, my pet, you've been more than generous.' Mrs Benfleet smiled mistily. 'Though where you found the funds for it I just don't know!' She turned to Joss. 'A crying shame it's been, my lord, to see Miss Amy scrimp and scrape to make ends meet in that house—'

'Bennie,' Amy said pleadingly.

'I know I speak out of turn,' the nurse said defiantly, 'but it was a shocking thing, my lord, the way that Miss Amy was dragged from pillar to post by that papa of hers. How Lady Bainbridge tolerated it, I'll never know! But that's marriage, I suppose. For better, for worse. I'm fortunate that my Sam was nothing if not steady, God rest his soul! That was my idea of a marriage—good companionship! Ah, well.' She hauled herself to her feet and bent to kiss Amy. 'You doze out here for a while if you like, Miss Amy. I'll be going in for my rest now, but I do thank you for coming.'

Amy watched through closing eyes as Joss carried the lunch tray back inside. She felt a very strong resistance to going back to London. The warmth and the peace of Mrs Benfleet's garden were so soothing after the bustle of the city. Perhaps it would not be so bad to return to Nettlecombe after all. She had always loved the country...

'Amy?'

Amy opened her eyes. She thought that it was the breeze touching her skin, but now she realised that Joss was crouching down next to her and that he had brushed the hair away from her face with gentle fingers. For a moment she stared into his eyes. Such tenderness... And as she stared, she received a revelation as shocking as a dousing with cold water.

The afternoon sun struck across Joss's face, lightening the amber of his eyes. Amy seemed to see him in extraordinary detail. His hair, slightly windswept, was the deep, dark red of autumn leaves, thick and glossy. He narrowed his eyes against the sun and she could see the shadow of his eyelashes, spiky against his cheek. He smiled again and Amy's heart seemed to skip a beat then start to race, so that the blood tingled around her whole body and all her senses tightened with anticipation. In that second, Amy realised that not only did she desire him with a longing that was as shameless as it was strong but that, more importantly, she loved him, and that everything else seemed to dwindle into unimportance in comparison.

She looked at him for what seemed like hours whilst the exultation swept through her and left her shaking, then reality returned and she blinked and sat up hastily. Somehow, she had no recollection of quite how, she had slid down on the bench and had been dozing with her head against the armrest. Her bonnet was all squashed and her face felt hot.

'Oh, Mama will be beside herself! I have been out in the sun for hours without my parasol!'

Joss traced the line of her cheekbone with one finger. 'You certainly look a little pink. Perhaps you will get freckles—'

Amy gave a squeak. She was not vain, but better that he should suspect that than think that she was red in the face because of his touch.

'I suppose we must go back now.' She started to stand up and Joss put a hand under her elbow to help her rise.

'Yes, indeed. If you would care to wait here, I shall go to the Rising Sun to fetch the phaeton.'

'No,' Amy said, remembering that there was something she needed to tell him. 'I will walk with you. It will help me to wake up.'

They went back through the cottage. From upstairs came the rhythmic sounds of Mrs Benfleet snoring. They exchanged a look like conspirators and tiptoed out.

They walked a little of the way down the track to the village in silence. The sun was still high and Amy tried to keep into the dappled shadows. The birds were calling in the trees and the road was dry, baked hard in the sun. Joss strode easily along beside her. Amy smiled as she thought about the gentlemen of fashion who tottered about St James's, leaning on their sticks, complaining if they got a speck of dirt on their boots or if the breeze ruffled their neck cloth. Joss was not like that. Whatever his debauchery amounted to, it had hardly affected his physical or mental condition. There was a tiny frown between his brows and he seemed abstracted and Amy remembered that he had said he did not like the country. No doubt this bucolic sojourn was exactly the sort of thing he did not enjoy.

'Thank you for bringing me here today,' she said hesitantly. 'It was very good of you, for I recall that you do not enjoy the country.'

'It is simply that the country has held few attractions for me in the past,' Joss said. 'The hunting and shooting is all very well, I suppose, but I have always valued the entertainments of town above such things. Perhaps I was mistaken, however. It is very beautiful here.'

The warm breeze feathered across Amy's skin. 'I meant also to thank you for your kindness to Mrs Benfleet. I had no intention of staying for luncheon—indeed, when she invited us I thought that you would surely refuse—'

She broke off. Joss looked amused.

'My dear Miss Bainbridge, you have a very poor idea of my manners!'

Amy frowned. 'Yes, but there is a difference between accepting something because one's manners are good and accepting with a good grace, with genuine willingness, if you like...' She bit her lip. 'Oh dear, I have offended you—'

'Quite right. I like Mrs Benfleet enormously and it was no great effort of will on my part to stay and enjoy luncheon with her. Why should you think otherwise?'

Amy made a slight gesture. How to convey to him that the thought of a Corinthian like Joss sitting down to lunch in a cottage garden was quite absurd?

'I suppose...because it would not be your choice of entertainment... I thought—'

'You assumed that I was a snob.' Joss's tone was even. 'Admit it, Miss Bainbridge.' He smiled. 'I believe that, paragon of virtue that you are, you may actually be at fault here.'

There was a pause whilst Amy wrestled with herself. 'I suppose so. I beg your pardon.'

Joss's smile broadened. 'It does not matter. You will know me better in future.'

Amy's heart sank a little. That gave her a very neat opening to tell him of the plan to go to Nettlecombe and the fact that they would not be seeing each other at all in the future, but just for now she did not wish to spoil things. The day had been so enjoyable, warm and bright, with Joss's sole company to enjoy, and she was loath to spoil it.

'I suppose that it was rather improper of me to request that you escort me here today,' she said slowly, following this train of thought out loud, 'but Mrs Benfleet has been ill and I wanted to visit her...'

'And it was easier to ask me than to hire a carriage.' Joss was laughing. 'Besides, this whole week has been an education for me, Miss Bainbridge, as well as an opportunity for you to start using your lottery money to do good!'

Amy's eyes flew to his. She stopped walking. 'I do wish you would not say things like that! I told you before that I had no wish to improve you. It is not my place to do so. Anyway, I have the oddest feeling that I will find that you already give away half your income to charity, or that you fund schooling for rescued climbing-boys and have simply not told anyone.'

The smile vanished from Joss's face. 'You are quite mistaken. In fact, as usual, you give me too much credit. I have been a selfish creature all my life and have never done anything to oblige anyone else. I beg you not to think so.'

Amy frowned. 'You have been very obliging to me this week.'

Joss's expression softened. 'That is different. I have a duty to repay my sister's debt and...' his gaze lingered on her face

'…I find it very easy to be obliging to you, Miss Bainbridge. I think that I would probably do anything you asked of me.'

Amy caught her breath. The blood fizzed beneath her skin as though she had heatstroke. She dragged her gaze from his and started walking again, quite quickly.

'I must tell you, my lord, that the end of the debt tomorrow coincides with my departure from town,' she said. 'Mama intends for us to remove to Nettlecombe. She is most upset by the fuss that there has been about my lottery prize and would prefer to withdraw from town altogether.'

Joss caught her arm to slow her down. 'A moment, if you please, Miss Bainbridge. May we discuss this properly rather than on the run?'

Amy reluctantly slowed. There was a disused field gate to the left-hand side, beneath the shelter of a spreading horse chestnut tree. She drew into the shade and leant against wooden bars. They felt sun-warmed against her back.

'What do you wish to discuss, my lord? It is a foregone conclusion.'

'I see. Lady Bainbridge wishes to run from the speculation and you are humouring her?'

Amy blushed. 'For my part I would happily face it out, but Mama is not made of such stern stuff. She has been made very unhappy by all the gossip and she feels that if we were to go to Oxfordshire the scandal might fade away.' Amy shrugged. 'It seems a small price to pay to make her happy and I have always loved the country.'

'I see,' Joss said again, in an odd tone. 'So, we are not to meet again.'

'I suppose not.' Amy put out a hand. 'It is probably for the best. This debt has caused a great deal of talk—almost as much as the lottery win—and it will be good to let the gossip die down.'

Joss's gaze was intent on her face. 'Do you mind all the talk?'

'No, but then I am always being told that I have no society sensibility. Where there is no smoke I cannot see that there can be a fire.'

'Yet I suppose I must bear some responsibility.' Joss shifted slightly. 'I accepted the debt and caused a great deal of talk, all for the pleasure of your company, Miss Bainbridge.'

Once again Amy felt her heart leap. 'Indeed, you have been so very obliging, my lord.'

'So you said already. Well, as I have discovered the country anew today, perhaps I should come to visit you at Nettlecombe. Would you invite me, Miss Bainbridge?'

Amy gave him a small smile. 'Yes, of course.'

She could not believe that Joss would venture as far as Oxfordshire just to visit her. Why should he? With all the sophisticated delights of the town about him he would soon forget their rather strange association.

'So this is to be our final enterprise,' Joss said, with a slight smile. He leaned one hand against the top of the gate and smiled at her. 'As this is probably the only privacy we shall have before you leave, I want to tell you that I have enjoyed your company very much, Miss Bainbridge, and shall be sorry to see you go.'

'Thank you, my lord.' The sunlight falling between the shifting leaves was bright enough to make Amy blink. She swallowed hard, surprised by a sudden empty feeling inside. She felt small and lost. This was ridiculous. Here was Joss taking a light and charming farewell quite in keeping with their relationship, and here was she wanting…what? If only she had not tumbled so disastrously into love with him. In some ways it had been inevitable given the attention that he had paid her and yet in others she had thought herself quite safe. Intent on disapproving of him so heartily, she had barely noticed as her censure had slowly given way to enjoyment of his company. From there innocent delight had slid into something deeper and she was utterly lost.

'I hope that I have…ah…fulfilled all the duties required of me,' Joss continued. The sun was in Amy's eyes and she could not see his expression. 'If there is anything I have failed to do, then you have but a little time to rectify the omission.'

'Well, I…' A picture flashed through Amy's mind, a vision of the garden at Lady Carteret's ball. 'There is one thing.' Her voice sounded strange even to her own ears. She cleared her throat. 'You could…kiss me goodbye.'

As soon as the words were out she shrank back under the horse chestnut tree, seeking its cooling shade on her hot cheeks. She did not dare to look at Joss. She was seldom so forthright, but he had asked what else he could do for her and she had given an honest answer. As the silence stretched to several heartbeats, Amy wished fervently that she had lied.

'Once again you surprise me, Miss Bainbridge. Surely that is something we have already done—if you remember?' Joss's voice was light, unreadable, but there was something in his tone that made Amy start to burn, shade or not. She knew instinctively that he was not going to refuse her.

She raised her chin. 'Strictly speaking, my lord, that is incorrect. It was an action that you took of your own accord. It was not one of the stipulations of the debt. Besides, this is a kiss goodbye, which is different.'

Their eyes met. Joss's were very dark, but there was a smile lurking in the depths and it made Amy's toes curl.

'So, what would you like me to do?' His voice was smooth. 'As this is part of the debt and is therefore your call, Miss Bainbridge...'

'I would like you to come here.' Amy's voice was no more than a shaky whisper. Her legs felt weak and she was trembling. When Joss obligingly crossed the small space between them and came to stand directly before her, she thought she might give up breathing altogether.

'And now?' Joss's tone was very soft.

Amy cleared her throat. 'Must you make this so difficult for me?'

'I am sorry.' Joss smiled. 'Will this do?'

It was not a question that Amy could answer immediately. He kissed her with a thoroughness that left her breathless, his hands smoothing her body's curves against the hard length of his to a devastating effect. Amy felt the liquid heat race through her, kindled by his touch. She drew back with a gasp, leaning against the rough bark of the tree, relieved at the support its sturdy trunk provided.

Joss did not speak, only looked at her.

'Yes,' she gasped, 'that will do very well.'

Joss laughed. 'For you perhaps, Amy.' His tone was husky. 'Now I find that I need something on my own account.'

Amy's gaze was riveted to his and she jumped when his fingers touched the back of her neck, drawing her gently forward so that her lips met his again. A soft groan escaped her. The kiss was light and teasing at first, but still the heat returned to her body with an aching intensity that shocked her, yet somehow drew her on. She kept quite still allowing the sensuous excitement to course through her as his lips and tongue explored hers in ways she had never even imagined. Her hands came up to Joss's chest, to curl against his jacket, then slid of their own volition around his neck so that she could entangle her fingers in his hair and kiss him more deeply. It was only when Joss's hand slid from the nape of her neck to caress the hollow at the base of her throat then move lower still, that Amy recoiled, abruptly shaken back to reality.

She could not let this go any further, no matter how strongly she desired it. Already she could not bear the thought of leaving him. She did not want to set off for Nettlecombe with her heart broken and her future in tatters.

She stepped back, out of his embrace. 'Joss, please—'

Joss looked as though he was awakening from a dream. He removed himself abruptly from her proximity, putting at least three feet between them. 'Forgive me, Amy. I had no wish to frighten you.'

'I was not afraid,' Amy said tremulously, 'but it did not seem such a very good idea after all.'

She knew she was not expressing herself at all well and then she saw the expression on Joss's face, the lightning flash of pain in his eyes that was gone so swiftly it seemed almost as though she had imagined it. She put out a hand to him.

'Oh, Joss, I am sorry—I did not mean it to sound like that! Only you must see the folly of it! I am to leave London and you...' Her voice trailed away. She could not speak for him, she did not even know whether there was any equality in their situation. For her to be in Joss's arms was the sweetest thing, but for him? This was a man whose relationships with women were never sincere in the sense she wanted. She had to be a fool even to dream of it and in future her memories would be all she had.

She saw Joss's expression harden slightly, saw all emotion wiped from his face and he stood back to allow her to precede him back on to the track. It was only five minutes to the inn and from there it would be a swift journey back to London. And that would be that. She could go to Nettlecombe with a memory to warm her of the time that she invited the most notorious rakehell in London to kiss her. It had been an adventure. The whole week had been an adventure. And yet... Amy avoided looking at Joss as the outskirts of the village drew near. And yet it suddenly seemed too late to avoid a broken heart. If she was honest—and she always was—she knew that Joss Tallant had stolen her heart and soul.

'There you are, my love!' Lady Bainbridge was sitting by the fire in the parlour at Curzon Street and was feeding what looked like a large quantity of papers into the flames. Amy paused on the threshold. The room was like a furnace for the fire was roaring fit to set the chimney on fire and all the windows were closed. Amy's head, which had ached incessantly on the silent journey back to London, now felt as though it was about to explode. She had seldom felt so miserable in her life.

She had said a formal goodbye to Joss at the corner of the street. Under the interested eye of his groom he had thanked her for her company during the week and wished her well for the future. Amy had been equally cool and courteous. And, despite his previous assurance that he would visit her at Nettlecombe, Amy had thought it unlikely that she would see Joss again.

'Mama, what are you doing?' she asked mildly, striving not to take her pent-up misery out on her mother. 'Those look like letters—'

'They are, my dear! So useful.' Lady Bainbridge beamed. 'Now we do not need to use up any more coal!'

'It is quite warm enough to do without a fire,' Amy observed. 'Besides, Mama, we can afford the coal now. There is no need to scrimp and scrape any longer.'

Lady Bainbridge looked downcast. 'I fear I cannot stop, my love. I have got into such a habit now. Besides, who knows how long the money will last? Which is why you should not be giving it away to any of these people.'

Amy came up to the table and picked up the top letter from the pile that was being consigned to the flames.

'Dear ma'am,' she read, *'I here as you as won some money and was wondering if you could spare some for me. I am a widow woman and my little ones need food and medicine—'* She broke off abruptly. 'Mama, what is this?'

'Begging letters,' Lady Bainbridge said with a shudder. 'Now that the truth is out, people have been dropping letters in all day. This one here—' she thrust it under Amy's nose '—this is from Lady Belmarsh! She has signed it Mrs Otter and thinks I will not realise the real author, but I recognise the way she writes her letters! The "T" gives her away! To think that she has sunk to this!'

Amy frowned. 'I cannot believe… And you are burning them all! But there may be some genuine cases of hardship amongst them!'

'Undoubtedly, my dear.' Lady Bainbridge picked up another handful and stuffed them into the grate. The flames roared and the edges blackened. 'There are always genuine cases, but how to tell? Are you to spend all your days checking who is needy and who is not? Besides, there are those such as *this*—' Lady Bainbridge shuddered '—who do not deserve to be heard!'

Amy glanced down at the letter in her mother's shaking hand. *'You scheming bitch, that money should be mine—'* she read. She pushed it away, revolted. 'Oh, Mama!'

'I know!' Lady Bainbridge threw her a tearful look. 'Another good reason for us to leave London!'

Amy's shoulders slumped. 'I suppose so. I will go and start packing my bags.'

'Oh, I forgot!' Lady Bainbridge paused, her hands full of paper. 'Amanda Spry is waiting for you in the dining room. She says that it is urgent and she has been waiting a considerable time. I offered her tea in here with me, but she said she would wait in the cool. I suppose it is rather hot in here...'

Amy went back out into the hall, breathing the cooler air with gratitude. The door of the dining room was half open and she went in. Amanda was sitting on one of the hard chairs, her head down her, shoulders drooping. She looked as abject as Amy felt. Amy hurried forward.

'Amanda, I am so sorry to have kept you waiting so long! Would you—?'

She broke off as her friend raised her gaze to hers. Amanda's pretty face was swollen and tear-stained almost out of recognition. Amy went down on her knees on the carpet and clasped both of Amanda's hands.

'Amanda! Whatever has happened? What is the matter?'

Amanda burst into a fresh bout of sobs. She sounded as though she was almost exhausted with crying and she had already shredded her sodden cambric handkerchief between her fingers. Then she had started on her gloves. Amy could see that she had unpicked a whole seam.

'Oh, Amy, I am in such trouble and I need your help!'

Amy frowned. 'Well, of course, I will do whatever I can, but, Amanda, you must tell me—'

'Twenty thousand pounds!' Amanda said wildly. 'I need twenty thousand pounds at once, Amy! Please say you will help me! If you do not, I shall be ruined!'

* * *

Half an hour later, Amanda was tucked up in Amy's bedroom and Patience was fussing round with warm milk and a soothing draught of laudanum. Amanda was almost transparent with exhaustion and could barely keep her eyes open. Amy had already sent a reassuring message to Amanda's aunt explaining that Lady Spry would be staying with her that night and that there was no cause for alarm. Now, with the evening drawing on, she came to sit beside the bed and took Amanda's hand in hers.

'There now. Everything is organised and all will be well. You need do nothing except sleep and cease this worrying.'

Amanda's hand clung to hers. 'The money—'

'It will be yours. Do not worry about that now.'

Two small tears seeped from beneath Amanda's eyelids as though she were too weak to cry any more. The hair clung to her forehead with sweat. Amy thought it very likely that she was developing an ague.

'Oh, Amy, I have been such a bad friend to you,' Amanda wailed. 'You have been so kind and I have not even told you what the money is for!'

'You need not.' Amy pushed away the terrifying thought of parting with twenty thousand pounds and told herself stalwartly that she would still have ten thousand to stand between her and penury. Amanda was her dearest friend and she could not—would not—let her down, even if it meant that her own circumstances were reduced.

She patted her hand, anxious only that Amanda should not completely exhaust herself. 'Tomorrow will be soon enough to sort everything out. Now, take your draught.'

'No.' Amanda pushed her hand away. 'I must tell you everything first. I must!'

'Very well,' Amy could tell that her friend was so agitated that she would not rest until she had unburdened herself. 'Do not neglect your milk, though!'

'Very well.' Amanda took a sip. 'Where to start?'

'Where is the beginning?'

Amanda frowned. 'I am not sure.' She put the cup down with a rattle and knitted her hands together. 'I fear that I am being blackmailed.'

Amy stared. The idea seemed manifestly absurd. 'Amanda, who could want to blackmail you and more to the point, about what?'

Amanda looked away. 'I... I suppose that I must tell you everything.' She looked back at Amy. 'I have had an anonymous letter demanding twenty thousand pounds to prevent the release of certain...letters...to the *ton*. Love letters. Do you understand me, Amy? If I do not meet the blackmailer tonight and make arrangements for payment, he will publish my letters in all the scandal sheets. I shall be utterly ruined!'

Amy frowned. 'Amanda, if the letter is anonymous—'

'Oh, I know what you will say!' Amanda made a wild gesture that almost knocked her cup of milk over. 'If it is anonymous, how can I know the identity of the blackmailer? But you see, Amy, there is only one person who knows about the letters...and he has sent me one just to prove that he is in earnest.'

Amy tried to work this out. 'But who would do such a thing?'

Amanda sighed, closing her eyes. She was parchment pale. 'Let me tell you the whole story and then, perhaps, you will understand. I do not want you to think badly of me...'

'Of course.' Amy patted her hand.

'I never wrote to you much about my marriage, did I? That

was because I was so unhappy that I had no wish to talk about it. I allowed my mother to choose my husband for me, and Frank Spry was the man she chose. He...' Amy shuddered '...he was not kind to me.'

Amy sighed. 'I am sorry, Mandy. Did nobody know?'

'No, no one. I was so far away, you see. Frank was a gambler and when he was in his cups he would be free with his fists. He swiftly ran though my fortune and after that treated me with contempt. When I discovered that I was breeding he was furious—another mouth to feed, he said, when there was not enough for the two of us. We quarrelled and he...' Amanda shook her head. 'No matter. I lost the child and Frank was pleased, actually pleased!' Her defiant gaze met Amy's again. 'After that, well... I could never care for him again and I took a lover.' She gripped Amy's hand again. 'Please do not hate me!'

'Oh, Mandy!' Amy's throat closed. 'As if I could!'

'I know most people would be obliged to condemn me.' Amanda twisted uncomfortably in the bed. 'And it was not as though I truly loved him, which makes it so much worse! But I was unhappy and it was part misery and part revenge—' her voice rose '—and part just wanting to do *something*—' she screwed up her face '—anything to show my defiance! So I had an affair and I wrote the man some indiscreet letters, and Frank found out...'

'Oh, no...' Amy grimaced. 'What happened?'

'Frank was set to banish me when he fell into an argument over some card-sharping and died in a duel. So I was a widow and thought all safe. I had parted from my lover some time before and had thought...' Amanda plucked at the blankets '...that he had gone abroad. Alas for me that he has returned—and that he still has my letters! Even then I was slow to believe… I thought him a gentleman and not one to sink so low as blackmail!'

A cold breath touched Amy's heart. 'Who was he, Amanda?'

'It was Clive Massingham.' Amanda peered at her friend. 'Why, Amy, you look as white as a sheet! Whatever did you think?'

Amy took a huge, shaky breath. Not even to herself could she admit that she had thought—just for a split second—that it might be Joss Tallant. She had known that she distrusted Joss's reputation and deplored his relationships with women, but to have doubted him so far was a shocking betrayal.

'I thought it might have been Sebastian Fleet,' she said.

Amanda smiled tiredly. 'No. Oh, Fleet admires me and might wish to make me his mistress, but I have more sense than that now! No, I have learned my lesson the hard way, but it seems that, despite that, my sins will find me out!'

'If it were only your word against Massingham's—'

'But it is not. He has the letters.'

'Of course. He has proved it.'

Amanda nodded slowly. 'As I said, the blackmailer has sent me one of the letters. To help me make up my mind quickly, he said.'

Amy sighed. 'And you are to give him your reply tonight?'

'Yes. That was why it was so urgent that I see you. I am to go to an address in St James's later this evening.' Amanda struggled a little as she tried to get out of bed and sank back with a sigh. 'Oh, I feel so exhausted! I could think of nowhere to turn for the money except to you, Amy, although I knew you would despise me! But I have to pay or else Massingham will distribute my letters about the *ton* and I shall be ruined! Truly, I think I should kill myself!'

'Don't speak like that, Mandy,' Amy said quickly. 'I will

keep your assignation with the blackmailer and tell him that the money will be his as soon as I can arrange it. There is nothing for you to fear. You must stay here and rest.'

Amanda's gaze clung to hers. 'You are so good a friend, Amy, and I have been so poor a one to you!'

'Stuff!' Amy went over to her wardrobe and started to rummage through. She needed a dark cloak and a hat with a veil. 'Remember when we were at school and the others were always horrid to me because of my father being a gambler? I was lonely and miserable and you were always the one who defended me!'

Amanda looked as though she was about to cry again. 'I suppose that was so. Yet there is something else that I must tell you. It is nothing to do with this case—nothing at all— but you ought to know...'

Amy's hand stilled. She took the cloak from the wardrobe and came to sit down again. 'What is it?'

'It is Juliana Myfleet.' Amanda sniffed. 'You have remarked before that Juliana and I were friends in my first season. It was the year before you were out. Juliana was such fun but...' she smiled sadly '...she gambled even then, and even though she was unmarried. It was scandalous, of course, but there... Anyway, when I came back up to town this spring I was determined to avoid her, but she sought me out.' Amanda shrugged. 'Once again she tried to involve me in high play, but I have little money now and more sense. I accidentally let slip to her that you had come into a fortune and that was why she inveigled you to gamble with her that night. Not just that—I deliberately left you alone at the tables with her so that she could try to fleece you! I am so sorry, Amy.'

Amy's eyes narrowed. 'Amanda, were you the one who told Lady Juliana that I had won the money on the lottery?'

Amanda evaded her gaze. 'Oh, Amy!'

'Did you?'

'Yes!' Amanda burst out. 'I am sorry. I owed her money—a trifling sum—but she said that she was willing to trade it for information about your fortune! The only thing I could think to tell her was that you had won thirty thousand pounds! Oh, I cannot bear it!'

Amy sighed. 'It does not matter. I knew that it had to be one of you. I thought it might have been Richard, for Mama is indiscreet but fears society's disapproval too much to let such a matter slip. The only other person who knew was the Earl of Tallant and for a while I suspected him because I thought he might be in league with his sister over that foolish debt!'

Amanda gave a watery laugh. 'I doubt it, Amy! Joss Tallant keeps his distance from Juliana these days.'

Amy looked at her sharply. 'Why, what can you mean?'

Amanda hesitated. 'This is not really my secret to tell—you shall have to ask Lord Tallant about it, and...' she gave Amy a sweet smile '...perhaps you should, since I suspect you have feelings for him.'

'Amanda!' Amy said quickly. She was blushing. 'I am to ask him what?'

'Ask him why he took the blame for his sister's gambling debts all those years ago. Ask him why he allowed his father to believe it was *his* fault, not Juliana's, and why he has never told the truth about it.' Amanda yawned. 'Lord, I am so tired...'

'Yes, but—' Amy grabbed her arm and almost shook her. 'How do you know this? Everyone says that it was Joss who incurred those debts that almost brought the Tallants down. Why, it is common knowledge—'

Amanda shook her head, still yawning. 'As I said—I was

Juliana's best friend in her first season. She confided in me. She was different in those days, Amy.' Amanda sighed. 'There was something softer to her then, more gentle. She knew that she would be utterly disgraced if it all came out and she was desperate to marry Myfleet. 'Tis a pity he did not live—he was a good man and would have been a steadying influence. But Juliana was afraid that he would not have her if he knew... Ask Lord Tallant what happened next. I think he will tell you. All I can say is that no breath of scandal ever attached to Juliana's name and it was Joss who was banished in disgrace...' She slid down in the bed. 'Thank you so much, Amy. I am so sorry...'

It was only a few minutes before the laudanum took full effect and Amanda was asleep, but Amy sat beside the bed for much longer. Deliberating on Amanda's unhappiness and the ways to prevent blackmail, she also thought of Juliana Myfleet and her love for a good man, and of Joss Tallant, who might well prove to be a better man than ever he had been painted.

Chapter Twelve

Joss knew that he was in deep trouble. He had known it for a long time, but had refused to face up to it. He had known it when he had accepted Juliana's wager purely for the pleasure of spending time in Amy's company, he had known it when he had paid off Harriet Templeton and admitted to himself that he had no desire to set up another mistress, and he had known it when he had kissed Amy in Lady Carteret's garden. The only thing that he had not done was acknowledge the truth to himself, indulging instead in a whole range of activities designed to distract his thoughts from their one inevitable conclusion. Now, as he made his farewells to his gambling cronies at a scandalously early hour, Joss was conscious of nothing other than a relief that he had finally admitted the truth. He was in love with Miss Amy Bainbridge and he wanted to marry her.

The thought was shocking, exhilarating and nerve-racking all at the same time, and he had no very clear idea how it could possibly have happened. Since it had, however, he

realised that he had two distinct options: to ignore the mal-
aise and hope that it was of short duration or to act on his
impulses, ask for an interview and put his fate to the touch.
It was a terrifying thought because he did not flatter himself
that Amy would accept him.

Outside White's it was raining. The cold night air helped to
clear his head, although the thoughts that followed were not
encouraging ones. As he walked, Joss enumerated them in
his head. Amy thought him a gambler, a wastrel and a womaniser. She hated gambling because of her father's excesses.
She would never, never give herself to a man who had the
same weakness. Against his will, he remembered her words
when they had discussed marriage:

*'I am a lady of independent means and have achieved the
security I craved. To my mind that is much better...'*

He could hardly fool himself that his prospects were bright
and yet it only served to strengthen his resolve. He wanted
Amy Bainbridge with an ardour that made a mockery of all
his previous experience. He wanted to make love to her and
he wanted to protect her with the same passionate intensity,
and now that he had belatedly admitted to himself that he
loved her with all his heart, he had not a hope in hell of sup-
pressing his feelings.

Amy, with her quick wit, shy but astringent, sweet and
kind... Amy, small, soft and yielding in his arms... Joss
almost groaned aloud. If he had been able to go around to
Curzon Street and demand an answer at once, he would have
done so. As it was, he suspected he was in for a long, wakeful night.

It was raining. Somehow Amy had not been expecting that
and she stood in the darkness outside Number 12 St James's

with the raindrops dripping off the brim of her hat and pooling on her cloak. She felt damp and miserable and her wet veil kept sticking to her face. The blackmailer was not at home and now she was uncertain just what to do.

It had not occurred to her that he would not be there. Either Amanda had got the time or the place wrong, or this was a deliberate attempt to keep her waiting and make her more on edge. Amy suspected the latter. She had no desire to huddle on a street corner until Massingham deigned to return, but equally she did not want to leave Amanda to her fate. It was a dilemma.

She retreated on to the pavement and viewed the dark windows of Number 12 dubiously. Richard had not been at home when she left, or she would have asked him who lived there just so that she had some confirmation of Amanda's suspicions. She felt conspicuous and vulnerable, despite the thick darkness, and when someone touched her arm she almost screamed.

'Miss Bainbridge, it is you. I thought so, but I could scarce believe it! What the *devil* are you doing here at this time of night?'

There was an edge of furious exasperation in Joss's voice and he took her arm in a tight grip. Amy shook him off.

'Oh! It's you!' She looked at him doubtfully. 'Do you live here?'

'I live just across the road. What are you doing loitering in St James's, Miss Bainbridge?' Joss's gaze skimmed her in the gloom. 'And dressed like a shady widow as well? Good God, if I did not know better I should say you were visiting a gentleman—'

'I am.' Amy's teeth were beginning to chatter and a raindrop edged its cold path down her neck. She saw Joss's gaze whip round incredulously and she started to laugh. 'Oh, not in the way that you mean! May we discuss this inside? I am rather cold and wet.'

Joss took her arm again and turned her firmly in the direction of Curzon Street. 'No, we may not! That would be utterly improper. I am taking you home immediately.'

Once again, Amy freed herself. 'That would be quite pointless for I should only be obliged to turn round and come straight back. I cannot believe that the greatest rake in London is debating morality with me in the street at midnight! Please, my lord—'

A couple strolled past them and gave them a curious look. Joss gave an irritable sigh. 'Oh, very well! Come along!'

He hustled her across the road and in at the door. Amy looked about her with interest. Joss's chambers were a mirror of the man himself, stark and austerely decorated. Everything was in excellent taste, but it lacked a spark of warmth, as though Joss deliberately strove to eliminate emotion in his surroundings as much as in his life. Glancing at him, she saw that he was watching her and was immediately obliged to revise her opinion. There was enough heat in his gaze to scorch her. Amy turned hastily away, the danger of stepping into the rooms of a notorious rake hitting her just a little too late.

'Belton, a bottle of brandy, if you please, and some wine for Miss Bainbridge.' Joss was divesting himself of his cloak and hat and passing them to the valet, who had materialised silently in the corridor in front of them. Amy started to feel a little better. There was nothing more respectable than a servant.

'Once you have brought the drinks you may retire,' Joss continued.

'Certainly, my lord,' the valet said.

Amy bit her lip. 'Oh dear, how perfectly scandalous this is! Perhaps I should not have come in—'

'Of course you should not.' Joss ushered her into a drawing room where a cheerful fire burned and the candles were already lit. 'You are here now, however. Would you care to give me your cloak and that rather extraordinary hat?'

Amy started to struggle out of her disguise. Belton came into the room, set down a tray with the drinks and unobtrusively slipped out again.

'How well your valet copes with such disreputable goings-on, my lord!' Amy smothered a yawn. The warmth of the room made her feel sleepy. 'No doubt he has had much practice!'

Joss did not look amused. 'No, indeed. Belton and I live a very quiet life.' He scrutinised her. 'Amy, you look as though you should be on stage at Drury Lane rigged out in that garb! What *is* that ridiculous contraption on your head?'

Amy unpinned the black felt hat and looked at it sorrowfully. It had drooped in the rain and the veil was dripping water. 'It is dreadful, is it not? At least Mama was never fond of it!' She broke off as she realised that Joss's attention was focussed on her hair rather than the hat in her hand. The shining strands were tumbling straight about her shoulders but she could not see why that should be responsible for his slightly stunned expression. She flicked it back a little self-consciously.

'I suppose I look a fright! Would your valet be good enough to dry my cloak?'

'Of course.' Joss seemed to shake himself and took the soaking black cloak from her outstretched hands. He was careful not to touch her and Amy suddenly understood. A burning blush washed over her as she acknowledged that she was alone with Joss in his rooms at past midnight. It was, as he had said, utterly improper. Yet a small, traitorous tickle of excitement ran down her spine at the thought.

'I would not have expected you to be home at this hour, my lord,' she said, accepting the glass of wine that he passed to her. 'I thought that you would be gambling at White's, or—' She stopped, blushing harder. That was what one got for allowing unruly thoughts to get away.

There was a glimmer of a smile in Joss's eyes. 'I fear that you have improved me even if you did not desire to do so, Miss Bainbridge,' he said slowly. 'I am home so early because I find that you have ruined my concentration at cards. As for the rest...' his smile deepened '...I fear that holds little interest for me either!'

'Oh, well...' Amy attempted to achieve a coolness to match his own although she knew she was looking pink and flustered. 'Perhaps you will find some new pastimes in a little while.'

'Perhaps so.' Joss's gaze held hers intently for a loaded moment, and then he moved away, his manner becoming briskly businesslike. 'That is nothing to the purpose, however. Come and sit by the fire and tell me what is going on.'

Amy took a sip of her wine. It was warming and strong and she started almost imperceptibly to relax.

'It is a little difficult... I am here on behalf of another lady, you see. Oh!' She looked up as a thought struck her. 'Perhaps you could tell me who lives at Number 12, my lord? It is most important that I find out.'

'I could tell you,' Joss said, swirling the brandy in his glass, 'but not until you tell me the whole story.'

Amy frowned. 'That is not fair play! I am keeping a secret for another lady and am not at liberty to disclose the whole!'

Joss shrugged. 'You will not get something for nothing, Miss Bainbridge! Is the gentleman expecting you or will he be surprised to find the assignation kept by a different lady? I should warn you to be careful!'

Amy laughed. 'It is not that sort of assignation, my lord. I am here to assure the gentleman that…' she hesitated '…that he will receive his money in good time.'

'A blackmailer?' Joss's tone hardened. He sat forward in his chair, resting his elbows on his knees. 'Then I should also counsel you not to pay, Miss Bainbridge, for blackmailers are seldom satisfied with a single sum. He will return and bleed you dry.'

'I know.' Amy screwed up her face. She had already thought of this, but could see no immediate solution. If Amanda did not pay, she would be ruined; if she did pay, no doubt she would be called upon to do so again and again. 'I have told my friend this, but…'

Joss sighed. 'Your friend? Amy, are you sure that it is not you who are being blackmailed?'

Amy pulled a face. 'Of course not! What reason could anyone have to blackmail me? I have no secrets!'

Joss shrugged. 'If you say so, I believe you. It is just that when someone alludes to a mysterious friend, it is usually themselves they are referring to…'

'Oh, I know!' Amy took another draught of the wine. 'I realise it sounds most odd and unconvincing!' She hesitated. 'If I trust you with the whole—'

A light flickered in Joss's eyes. 'Would you do so?'

'Yes, I think I would,' Amy looked undecided. 'I feel a little disloyal all the same.'

Joss straightened up. 'Perhaps I can make matters easy for you. I would guess that your friend is Lady Spry and she is being blackmailed about some indiscretion, but because she has no money you have decided to help her pay—'

'Stop!' Amy held a hand up. 'You are correct in all particulars, my lord, and I can see that there is no point in withholding the truth from you! Amanda is in desperate straits and I have sworn to help her.'

Joss shook his head. 'You are not helping. The blackmailer will not accept a single payment, Amy. You know he will not! Whatever Lady Spry's secret, he will hold it over her head until she pays and pays again! It would be easier for her just to tell him to publish and be damned.'

Amy looked away. 'Like his Grace of Wellington? She cannot. She will be ruined.'

Joss made a slight gesture. 'What is it—a love affair? It might be uncomfortable for her, but she will live it down. She is a widow and cannot be ruined by so commonplace an indiscretion—'

'You do not understand. It was whilst she was married to Frank Spry and he threatened to banish her.'

'Even so—' Joss frowned '—Spry is dead and whilst such rumours would be unpleasant—'

'There are *letters*,' Amy said, with emphasis.

There was a silence.

'I see,' Joss said at length. 'That does make it considerably more difficult.'

Amy gave a slight laugh. She pushed the hair back from her face, where it was drying in silken strands. 'Difficult! If you could have seen her, Joss! She said that she would kill herself if the letters were ever to become public!'

'So you agreed to help her. Of course. How much money is he asking?'

Amy looked down. 'Twenty thousand pounds.'

'Two-thirds of your fortune. Amy, you said that now you had the money you felt secure at last—'

'It is nothing,' Amy said quickly. She swallowed hard. 'I have thought about this, Joss. Amanda has been a good friend to me. Besides, I shall still have ten thousand pounds—less the sum I have already spent...'

Joss said nothing. His face was shadowed and still. 'And the name of the blackmailer?'

Amy stared. 'It is Clive Massingham. Surely you knew? I thought... If he lives at Number 12...'

'No one lives there presently,' Joss said. 'It has been empty, which I suppose makes it a useful address for a blackmailer to take.' He stretched and stood up. 'I will go and see Massingham, Amy, and retrieve your friend's letters for her. In the meantime I suggest you return and reassure her that all is well. I will get in touch with you as soon as I have them.'

Amy got slowly to her feet. She felt relieved but puzzled by his offer of help. '*You* will go to see Massingham? But why?'

'To help you, of course.' Joss raised an eyebrow. 'He is not the sort of man with whom you should be arranging a midnight rendezvous. It will also save you wasting your winnings on him. He will never be a good cause.' He smiled. 'Now you should go home, Amy.'

Amy was watching his face. 'Yes, in a little... How will you make Massingham give up the letters if you do not pay him? He will not be persuaded easily!'

Joss's expression hardened. 'I think I can persuade him, though perhaps Lady Spry should be prepared to leave town for a little until the matter dies down.'

'I had thought of that,' Amy said. 'I plan to take Amanda to Nettlecombe with me for a space.'

Joss's face softened. 'I do not understand it, but it seems you must for ever be helping waifs and strays, Amy—'

Amy met his eyes very directly. 'It is not my sole prerogative, is it, Joss? What about yourself?'

Joss had been moving towards the door, but now he paused. 'What do you mean?'

Amy held his gaze. Now that the moment had come for her to ask for the truth she felt acutely nervous. 'Why, I mean that you are going to a deal of trouble to help me now, but that is nothing compared to what you did to help Lady Juliana.'

Joss's jaw tightened. She saw a muscle move in his cheek. He walked slowly over to the fireplace and laid his arm along the mantel, resting one booted foot on the fender. He looked relaxed, but Amy knew he was not. The tension in him was as taut as twisted steel.

'Who told you about that, Amy? I cannot believe that Juliana—' He broke off. 'It was a long time ago and no doubt you have heard a garbled tale.'

Amy moved across to him. She touched his arm very lightly. There was anger and gentleness in his eyes, warring for mastery, and it made her heart contract.

'I heard that you took the blame for all of Lady Juliana's gambling so that she should not be ruined and might marry Lord Myfleet. Is my informant wrong?'

For a long moment Joss stared down into her eyes, then he pulled away. His tone was clipped. 'No, she is in the right of it! Lady Spry, I presume? Juliana swore she had never told anyone, but I did not believe her!' He took an angry pace across the room. 'Damnation, of all the things that I did not wish you to know—'

'I do not understand,' Amy said tremulously. His anger shook her. 'I do not understand why you took the blame and allowed your father to banish you, and I do not understand why you did not wish me to know—'

Joss was looking furious. 'Oh, you understand well enough, Amy! I took the blame out of misplaced chivalry, in the same way in which you wanted to save Lady Spry from Massingham!' His tone was savage. 'Juliana is my little sister and she was a different girl then. Oh, she was wild, and she gambled too hard, but she was gentler—she could have been so different if our childhood had not been as it was!' Joss brought his fist crashing down on the mantelpiece. 'Juliana came to me in tears and told me that she had made huge losses at the gaming table. I confess that when she told me the sum I was shocked. She was in despair—Myfleet was on the point of proposing and I knew she was head over heels in love with him. I also knew that if the scandal of her losses came out our father would send her away and ruin it all for her. Myfleet would have forgiven her, but our father never would! He was always unbending and she...she had lost eighty thousand pounds! She almost brought the family down! To my father the dishonour was more important than anything else!'

Amy sank back down into her armchair. 'But how did you fool him?' she whispered.

'It was simple enough.' Joss shrugged indifferently. 'My father never comes up to town. Juliana had some hen-witted female as chaperon—the woman could not control her and knew nothing of her antics. And I was a young man about town who gambled sometimes... No one thought it strange that I should have incurred such losses.'

'But your father sent you away...'

'Yes—' Joss gave her a grim smile '—but Juliana married Myfleet and was happy and I thought...' His face twisted. 'I thought it might make up for all the callous indifference that our father had shown her over the years. I still believe that, if Myfleet had not died, Juliana would be quite different...'

Amy went across to him. 'But what about you, Joss?'

'What about me? I was luckier than Ju—he always suspected that she was not his daughter, you see. Whereas I had my father's attention, his good opinion—'

'Until you deliberately threw it away.'

Amy saw him flinch. 'It does not matter. It was all a long time ago.'

'It does matter!' Amy felt a surge of rage so powerful that she was shaking. 'Surely Juliana could tell your father the truth now? It could not hurt her after all these years! Whereas you have borne his disapproval and dislike unnecessarily for all this time—'

Joss moved away from her. His voice was cold, forbidding her to trespass further. 'It would make no difference now.'

Amy made an impotent little gesture. 'Do you not care?'

Joss gave her a sideways look. 'Not any more. Now...' his tone eased '...it is time that you were going.'

Amy stood her ground. 'You have not told me yet why you did not wish me to know.'

Joss stopped. 'I was afraid you would interpret it as a noble gesture, my dear, and I wished to avoid that above all things.'

Amy was stung by the contempt in his tone, though whether it was for her or for himself, she could not tell. She went up to him and put a hand on his arm. 'Well, and so it is a noble gesture—why deny it? What you did for your sister was truly generous and shows the essential goodness of your character.'

'It shows nothing! This is *exactly* what I knew you would say!'

'Then why make yourself out to be worse than you truly are—?' Amy stopped, at a loss.

'I shall tell you why!' Joss grabbed her arms. For a moment Amy thought he was about to shake her, but he just held her in an iron grip, his fingers biting into her flesh. 'One noble deed does not make a hero, Miss Bainbridge, and it is naïve and foolish to think otherwise.' His furious face was heart-stoppingly close to hers. 'Every other thing that you have heard of me, every stupid and dangerous and arrogant thing—the gambling, the women—everything is true. Probably it is worse than you have heard. *That* is why I cannot have you believing me to be good.'

He let her go as swiftly as he had grabbed hold of her. 'Now will you leave?'

'No,' Amy said. Her voice was shaking and distantly she realised it was because her throat was thick with tears. 'I will not go until I understand what you are trying to prove to me.'

With an infuriated groan, Joss wrenched her into his arms.

'Amy, you try me past endurance! Not two hours ago I was resolved to offer you marriage, but now I am indebted to you for showing me why it can never be! What can I do to make you see that we can never be together? Our worlds are so utterly different—'

'You do speak a deal of nonsense, Joss,' Amy said clearly. Her heart had leapt at his words, but now she schooled herself to calm. She raised her hand to his cheek and felt the stubble rough against her palm. Inside she was trembling but she knew she could not let it show. Any uncertainty on her part now would compound his own agonising doubts and then she could never break through them. The only way was to show absolute confidence, when inside she was terrified. This was the biggest gamble of her life.

'I am tired of being on a pedestal,' she said. 'I have made mistakes and misjudged people and thought that I knew best.

I do not want to be treated like a saint!' She pressed her fingertips against his lips. 'I want you, Joss.'

Amy felt Joss go very still. After such a declaration it would have been impossible to withdraw, even had she wanted to do so. Her hand fell to his chest, pressing against the smooth material of his jacket. Would he never move, never speak? She loved him so much that she could feel the desperation and longing rise within her in a devastating tide. She had gambled now—was she about to lose it all? She could not help the lone tear that slid down her cheek.

Joss bent his head and captured it, his lips following the salty trail to the corner of Amy's mouth. She was shaking like a leaf now. His lips brushed hers, the lightest of contacts, and she shivered and opened to him, the desire burning through her as the kiss deepened.

Joss swung her up in his arms and took two strides over to the sofa, where he sat down with her on his knee. Amy slid her arms about his neck and held tight. She found that she liked their new position; she turned her head and pressed her lips against his throat, inhaling the scent of his skin overlaid with the spice of sandalwood. Excitement flared inside her. She felt as though she was on the edge of some precipice, about to step into thin air, but in the knowledge that she could fly. Tentatively she parted her lips and touched her tongue to his skin, tasting, marvelling. She heard Joss groan, and then one of his hands came up to tangle in her hair and he turned her lips up to his again, plundering her mouth with his own. The world spun, ignited by their mutual passion.

When Joss finally broke the kiss and drew back, his breathing was ragged and his eyes dark with desire.

'Amy, believe me, I want nothing more than to keep you here with me and make love to you, but it must not be—'

Amy leaned forward and kissed him again, her teeth closing over his bottom lip, biting gently. Joss smothered another groan.

'Amy, damnation...'

Joss could feel his self-control slipping perilously. He had been fighting this ever since she had stepped into the room. When she had removed her ridiculous hat, the sight of her hair loose about her shoulders had transfixed him. When she had taken off the cloak he had wanted to ease her out of every other item of clothing that she was wearing. He had barely been able to concentrate on what she had been telling him about the blackmail attempt because all his senses were focussed on her and the devastating need that possessed him. He had thought that if he could only get rid of her, finish the discussion and send her home, he might at least have some chance of getting through the encounter with Amy unscathed. Then Amy herself had turned that upon its head and now...

His hands tightened about her waist, drawing her against him. He let her pursue the kiss, his senses tightening as she took the initiative and tentatively touched her tongue to his. Joss could feel her breasts crushed against his chest and his entire body clenched in anticipation. He eased her bodice down and her left breast, small and perfect, fell into his hand. He rubbed his fingers over the taut nipple and felt Amy tense in his arms.

'Oh, my goodness! *Joss*...'

She sounded dazzled and profoundly intrigued. Joss bent his head to take her nipple in his mouth. Amy stifled a small scream.

'Joss! Oh, please...'

In the firelight her skin was flushed warm and pink, too tempting to resist. He could see the dawning passion in her eyes, their topaz blue dazed and slumberous with desire. He kissed her again, his hand cupping her breast, and tumbled her beneath him on the sofa.

'Amy...' He brushed the shining hair back from her face. 'Sweetheart...you know what will happen if you stay...' In about ten seconds, he thought wryly, if I do not find my self-control. He drew away from her. 'You must go home.'

Amy reached up to slide her arms about his neck. 'I know.' Her words were a whisper. 'I love you, Joss.'

It was almost his undoing. He brought his lips back to hers, sliding his tongue into the intimate depths of her mouth, kissing her with all the pent-up desire that possessed him. Then, carefully, he drew away. His fingers were shaking as he helped her to rearrange her dress and to get to her feet.

'This is not how I want it to be between us, darling. Not some midnight tryst in my rooms with your reputation in ruins if it were to ever come out. No!' He warded her off when she would have come into his arms again. 'Grant me this, please. If I am to have you, then it must be done properly. I must ask your brother's permission and speak to you in form and...' he hesitated '...give you the opportunity to think about it in case you wish to refuse me...'

He saw the tender laughter in Amy's eyes and felt his heart leap.

'Very well, Lord Tallant,' she said demurely. 'In that case you had better escort me home.'

The streets were wet and dark, with a cool rain still falling. It felt like tears against Amy's cheek and she ducked under the shelter of Joss's umbrella to keep dry. She gripped his arm tightly and pressed close to his side, comforted by his proximity. Their earlier passion had melted into companionable warmth but under it a current of excitement still ran strongly. Every so often Amy would glance up at Joss's face and, even though it was dark and shadowed, she could see the faint smile that curved his lips. She felt so intensely happy that she could not stop herself smiling. She knew that she would not be able to sleep.

At the door of Number 3 Curzon Street, Joss turned to her very formally and kissed her gloved hand.

'I will go to see Massingham now and I will bring Lady Spry's letters for her in the morning. Then, perhaps, we may talk, Miss Bainbridge?'

'I should like that,' Amy said shyly.

Joss smiled and bowed, then turned and walked away. Amy watched him until the shadows swallowed him up and the echo of his footsteps died away.

A light still burned in the house and Marten came out into the hall when she opened the door. He showed not a flicker of surprise to see Amy returning alone at that hour of the night, informed her that Sir Richard had yet to return and wished her goodnight. Amy climbed the stairs slowly. The euphoria that had filled her in Joss's company had settled to a simmering of excitement now and the ache of unfulfilled passion had eased. She felt precious and, in a strange way, fiercely proud of Joss.

Patience had had the foresight to make up a bed for her in the small, spare room, and as Amy slid between the fresh, lavender-scented sheets, she thought of what Joss had said about Juliana, and about his relationship with his father. So much unhappiness and misunderstanding…

Amy was too tired to think properly but she knew there was one more thing that she had to do, one more wrong to be righted. Joss would deal with Massingham, but in the matter of Juliana's debts he would never tell his father the truth. Amy turned over on to her side, pressing her hot cheek against the cool pillow. She suspected that were Joss to discover what she intended, he would do everything in his power to prevent her. Which meant that she would have to leave London early and go to Ashby Tallant alone. On that thought, to her vague surprise, she fell asleep.

Chapter Thirteen

After Joss left Amy he did not, as she might have supposed, go back to Number 12, St James's but went instead to an elegant house in Cavendish Square, where a slightly flustered maid showed him into the drawing room and informed him that her mistress was from home but was expected back soon.

Sure enough, not five minutes had elapsed and Joss's glass of brandy was almost untouched when the front door banged and there was the sound of angry footsteps on the hall tiles, followed by the murmur of the maid's voice.

'Lord Tallant is here to see you, ma'am—'

'Joss is here? At this time of the night?'

The drawing-room door was thrust unceremoniously open and Juliana Myfleet swept in. Joss thought that she, too, looked flustered for one brief moment, then her expression changed to chagrin and finally amusement.

'Joss, dearest,' she said coolly, 'I scarce expected to see you tonight! Whatever can have brought you here?'

Joss smiled. 'May I pour you a glass of wine, Ju? You will

need it if you have been out in the rain. I always say it is so time-consuming owning two properties. One is called out at all times of the night!'

Since Lady Juliana was even now shaking the raindrops from her black cloak, she did not waste time on denials. She gave her brother a faint smile.

'A glass of port would be welcome, I thank you, Joss. But I repeat, what do you do here?'

'I came about a business matter,' Joss said. He poured for his sister and took the glass over to her by the fire before resuming his seat in the other armchair. 'Your business, to be precise. I fear that you have had a wasted journey, Juliana.' Then, when she made no move to reply: 'To Number 12 St James's.'

Juliana's gaze flickered slightly. 'I do not understand you, my dear—'

'I think that you do.' Joss's tone was very even. 'Lady Spry did not arrive for your assignation, did she?'

'I know nothing of a meeting with Amanda Spry.' Juliana gave a petulant little shrug. 'The apartment in St James's belongs to Massingham. He uses it for certain…business arrangements. It is so much more convenient. I was awaiting him there but he—' She broke off.

'He failed to arrive. I understand that Massingham is normally to be found in Covent Garden these days, enjoying the company of Miss Templeton. Why do you tolerate it, Ju?'

Juliana gave a slight shudder, so imperceptible that Joss almost missed it. 'Massingham's *amours* do not trouble me. A woman is a fool if she expects a man to be faithful and that little bitch was always for sale to the highest bidder! You know that, Joss! You were the one who left the vacancy!'

Joss put his brandy glass down gently. 'I am less concerned

with Massingham's *amours* than I am with your business affairs, Juliana. If you needed money, why did you not ask me, instead of trying to extort it from Lady Spry? That was needlessly cruel.'

They stared at each other for what seemed an hour. There was no sound but the crackle of the fire and the pale hiss of the candles burning down. Joss refused to break the silence and Juliana's composure smashed.

'I did not ask you because I detest being your pensioner, Joss, and I knew...' She swallowed a sob. 'I knew that you would not give me the money if you found out why I required it! Massingham and I are to go to Paris, but we cannot do so without the funds to support us and I knew you detest Massingham and would never pay! For once...' she gave him a self-deprecating smile that wobbled slightly '...I did not wish to lie to you and pretend that this was a gambling debt...'

'You mean that Massingham will not take you for love alone?' Joss's face twisted. 'Juliana, the man is worthless. Have done with this!'

'No!' Juliana's glass smashed on the marble fireplace. She jumped to her feet and swung round on him, the tears streaming down her face. 'I love him, Joss! Was that what you wanted to hear? You have driven me to say it. I love him without pretence or illusion and I still want him! If he will not take me without fortune, then fortune I must have!' She scrambled for a handkerchief. 'I do not expect you to understand.'

Joss handed her his handkerchief. His heart felt heavy. He knew that he had to let her go, had to help her, even against his better judgement. 'I do understand, Ju. I understand better than you might imagine.'

Juliana stared at him. 'Because of Miss Bainbridge? The cases are not the same.'

'No, they are not, but loving Amy has made me see that one cannot always control love as one might choose,' Joss sighed. 'If Massingham is what you want, Juliana, then I will give you the money to go with him. Now, come here.'

She came to him and he hugged her in much the same way as he had done when they were children. He rested his chin on the top of her head and spoke quietly.

'How did you come by Lady Spry's letters, Ju?'

He felt a shudder go through her. 'I found them. Clive had kept them all, bound in pink ribbon. Pink ribbon, for pity's sake! And I was so angry, Joss, so angry and jealous that I took them all. I was going to destroy them, to burn them all, but then Amanda Spry came up to town and I suddenly thought to have my revenge on her and gain something out of my loss...' She freed herself and scrubbed her cheeks viciously. 'I do not believe that Clive even knows that I have them.'

Joss shook his head. 'So much hatred, Juliana. And Lady Spry did not even have the money to give to you.'

'No, but I knew that she was thick with Amy Bainbridge and that Miss Bainbridge *did* have the money.' Juliana looked up and gave her brother a glimmer of a smile. 'I suppose I should have guessed that Miss Bainbridge would come to you, Joss, but I underestimated two things: the fact that she trusted you and the fact that you loved her. If anyone had asked me I would never have imagined it, not in a thousand years! I do not believe that I know my own brother well at all...'

Joss smiled and moved away. 'You know me well enough. I will give you your twenty thousand pounds in return for Lady Spry's letters—all of them, Ju.' There was a warning note in his voice. 'And I will wish you godspeed and say that no matter what happens I shall always want to see you again—'

'Enough!' Lady Juliana had regained some of her brittle composure and stepped away from him. The malicious gleam was back in her green eyes. 'You grow maudlin, Joss! If this is the effect that love has had on you I shudder to think what a doting husband you will make and I am glad I shall not be here to see it! Now, I will fetch the letters and I shall be obliged if I may draw on your bank…' She wafted towards the door. 'You are too good to me, my dear. It is a shame that you have been unfairly damned as the black sheep of the family, but I fear that when my latest exploits are known I shall inherit that role. I shall hope to bear it with fortitude.'

It was mid-morning of the following day when Joss reached Curzon Street and the rain of the previous night had gone, blown away by a fresh breeze. It felt like a day for new beginnings.

As Patience let him in to the house, he became aware of a certain tension in the atmosphere. The sound of Lady Bainbridge's voice came to him from behind the parlour door, rising and falling like a peal of bells.

'It is all very well for you to say that, Richard, but we were supposed to remove to Nettlecombe today and now that Amy is missing—'

Joss quickened his step. For a split second he had the most dreadful conviction that Amy had fled to the country because she regretted the events of the previous night. She did not want to marry him—she would never want to do so. She would never even want to see him again… He shook his head to dispel the images, remembering a little grimly that he had once told Amy that his family history was bound to make him wary of marriage. What he had failed to grasp, he thought now, was how inextricably his happiness had become bound up in Amy. She could break his heart so easily, but he had to have the faith that she would never do so. It seemed a monstrously difficult lesson to learn and he had only just started.

Lady Bainbridge, Richard and Amanda Spry were assembled in the parlour and the addition of another person made the room seem rather small. Richard was lounging by the window and looking irritated, Amanda was sitting with her hands clenched in her lap and looked very pale and Lady Bainbridge, her hair in drooping ringlets, her face creased with worry, was waving a piece of paper in her hand.

'She says in her note that she has had to travel to the country unexpectedly and will meet us at Nettlecombe this evening!'

'There you are then, Mama!' Richard said heartily. 'There is no mystery—' He broke off as he saw Joss and a look of relief crossed his face, though whether it was for the distraction or because he thought the newcomer might help Joss was not sure.

'Good morning, Joss! Perhaps you might be able to shed some light on this as you've been seeing a lot of Amy recently—' Richard broke off again, evidently aware of his infelicitous choice of words and his mother's frown. Joss came forward and bowed over Lady Bainbridge's hand, smoothing her ruffled temper with his most charming smile.

'Good morning, ma'am. Lady Spry...' He bowed to Amanda before straightening up and turning to his host. 'Do I understand that Miss Bainbridge is from home?'

'She has gone to Oxfordshire,' Lady Bainbridge wailed, brandishing the note, 'and she has travelled post! Post! It is so much more expensive!'

'Come now, Mama,' Richard said, with an apologetic look at Joss, 'you know you would prefer Amy not to travel alone on the common stage.'

'No,' Lady Bainbridge conceded, 'but I do not understand why she must go jauntering off in this manner at all!'

Joss caught Amanda's eye. It was clear that Lady Spry suspected that Amy had gone off on some errand connected with the blackmailer, but that she did not dare disclose her suspicions. If Amy had arrived back in Curzon Street too late to see her friend and had set off that morning whilst it was still early, Amanda might even now be labouring under the belief that the blackmailer was still at large. Joss gave her a reassuring smile.

'Before I forget, Lady Spry, I was commissioned to give this to you by Miss Bainbridge.' He passed her an anonymous brown parcel. 'Something that she has…procured for you, I believe. You will find that it is all there. I am to tell you that there was no charge.'

The colour flooded into Amanda's cheeks, changing her from tense and strained to pretty and animated once again. 'Oh! Thank you, sir!'

'A pleasure, Lady Spry.' Joss bowed and turned away. 'Lady Bainbridge, I beg you not to worry. I believe that Miss Bainbridge may have gone to Ashby Tallant to see my father. Would you like me to find her for you?'

Richard and Lady Bainbridge exchanged a look. 'To see your father?' Lady Bainbridge echoed faintly. 'But Amy does not even know the Marquis!'

'I feel sure it is an omission she is about to remedy,' Joss said, a little grimly. 'We had a conversation yesterday that leads me to suspect that Miss Bainbridge would wish to speak with him urgently. With your permission, I will ride to Ashby Tallant and find out for myself. Then I can escort Miss Bainbridge to Nettlecombe once the matter is settled.'

Lady Bainbridge looked understandably perplexed. 'Well, if you are certain, my lord...'

'Of course, ma'am.' Joss turned to Richard. 'You are in agreement?'

Richard was looking relieved. 'Of course, old fellow! Only surprised that you want to be bothered! Still, it saves me trouble. I'm already late for a game at the Cocoa Tree—' He caught his mother's admonishing look and broke off.

'If I might delay you a little longer,' Joss said smoothly, a twinkle in his eye, 'there is something rather particular I wished to ask you. It might also explain why I...er...would be bothering to follow Miss Bainbridge...'

He saw the light dawn in Richard's eye, heard Amanda catch her breath, and allowed himself a grin.

As Richard ushered him out of the room, Joss heard Amanda turn to Lady Bainbridge with the excitement vivid in her voice:

'Oh, Lady Bainbridge, is it not wonderful! Amy is to be a Countess!'

'Well, dear,' his future mother-in-law said, 'one should not refine too much upon these things, but it is more than I had ever expected for Amy! And it will be so much cheaper to have her off my hands at last!'

Richard closed the door very firmly and turned to Joss, offering his hand.

'Welcome to the family,' he said.

* * *

Amy had been impressed by her first view of Ashby Tallant. The lime avenue was very fine and the frontage of the house, red brick with a great hall and a tower at one end, was most imposing. Even in his most prosperous times, Sir George Bainbridge had never possessed a house like it and Nettlecombe, the only remaining Bainbridge property, was on a considerably smaller scale. Nevertheless, Ashby Tallant did not appear to Amy as a comfortable family home.

The liveried servant who answered the door informed her that the Marquis was out in the gardens but that if Miss Bainbridge would not mind waiting, someone would be sent to fetch him at once. She was escorted into a drawing room decorated in blue and faded gold. It was cold and dusty and Amy, perching on the edge of one of the hard chairs, felt a little over-awed as the chill seeped into her bones.

The house was quiet as the grave and the long wait gave her plenty of time to think. When Joss had confirmed the story that Amanda had told her, her first and overwhelming reaction had been fury—fury that Joss had taken all the blame for Lady Juliana's misdeeds and that the Marquis was so cold and censorious a character that he had never forgiven his son. The long journey from London had given her time to try to compose herself and she had admitted to herself that it was her love for Joss that had prompted such furious indignation. She could not bear to see him hurt any more and that alone obliged her to tell the Marquis the truth. She had no notion what her reception might be or whether it would make any difference at all, but she felt she had to try. At the back of her mind was also the thought that Joss would probably be quite angry with her for interfering, but she refused to think about that. Her stomach rumbled with hunger—it was past the hour for luncheon—and she could not repress a sneeze.

The door opened.

'His lordship will see you now, Miss Bainbridge,' the footman intoned.

The hall was a vast affair of white stone and dark wood, and on the other side of it the footman opened a door and stepped aside for her to enter.

'Miss Bainbridge, my lord.'

The Marquis of Tallant was standing before the huge fireplace, leaning heavily on a gold-topped cane. Amy had been uncertain what to expect but now the sight of the Marquis surprised her; he was stooped and his face was pulled with pain and his hair was white, but his eyes were the same amber as those of his son, and burned with the same fierce light.

'Miss Bainbridge,' he said, and his voice was beautiful, smooth as polished leather, 'this is a great honour.'

'I fear it is a great intrusion, my lord,' Amy said, suddenly feeling the whole weight of the Marquis's age and authority, and wondering how she would ever have the courage to blurt out her tale. 'I must thank you for seeing me.'

The Marquis gestured her to a chair. 'No imposition, Miss Bainbridge. We have never met, but I do believe that I knew your father once. Your family has property over Nettlecombe way, I believe? You have a great look of George Bainbridge about you.'

'Do I?' Amy was so startled that she was distracted from the purpose of the visit for a moment. No one had ever likened her to her father. Richard, with his glowing fair looks and blue eyes had always been the obvious comparison.

'You have his spirit,' the Marquis said, on a sigh. 'I see

it in your eyes. Would you care for some refreshment, Miss Bainbridge? I suspect that you have travelled a long way.'

Amy was tempted. 'Well, I confess I am a little sharp set, my lord. I left London very early and I was not sure how long the journey would take...'

'It must have been urgent, then,' the Marquis said. He gave the bell pull a sharp tug.

'Ah, Watson, a tray of food for Miss Bainbridge and... some wine?'

'Just a little, if you please,' Amy said, blushing. 'I am not accustomed to strong drink.'

'A small glass,' the Marquis instructed, 'and some canary for me.'

There was a short silence after the servant had left the room. Amy was aware that she should state her business and even more conscious that if she did so and the Marquis took exception to her words, she would be out of the house without any time for refreshment at all. She bit her lip as she tried to think of the best way to broach the subject. The Marquis, who had been watching her expressive little face, limped across to the other armchair and eased himself down.

'Take your time, my dear. I always say that there is no point in rushing an important matter.'

Amy gave him an agonised look. 'Oh, my lord, it is simply that I am fearful of what you will think.'

'Then do not be. I doubt that I could think badly of you and I shall certainly not turn you off before you have had your wine!'

Amy stifled a laugh. 'My lord, you say that now—'

'Allow me to help you to overcome your scruples,' the Marquis said. 'Does this matter concern my son, perhaps?'

Amy stared. 'Why, yes, but...how did you know?'

The question was not to be answered for a moment, for the footman reappeared with a tray laden with bread, cheeses, honey, ham and fruit for Amy and a glass and bottle of canary for the Marquis. By the time that everything was served and Amy had obeyed the Marquis's instruction to eat, the barriers had been broken down further.

'It is always a mistake to tackle high emotion on an empty stomach,' the Marquis said, watching with amusement as Amy attacked the food with enthusiasm. 'I always feel that food gives one an appropriate sense of proportion.' He took a sip of canary. 'As to how I knew—well, I cannot go to London much these days—confounded ill health, you know—but there are those who keep me informed and they told me that my son had recently abandoned his usual pursuits in favour of spending time with a certain young lady of... impeccable quality. You, my dear. I confess that I was delighted to hear it.'

Amy looked up and blushed. 'Oh, well, yes, but it was not as you might suppose.'

The Marquis raised an ironic eyebrow. 'Indeed? I had thought that perhaps Joss had taken to heart my strictures about taking a wife...'

Amy blushed harder. 'Yes...well, no! You see, Lord Tallant only spent time with me because his sister made a bet... Oh dear, this is difficult... I had not intended to tell you so much...'

The Marquis's sardonic smile melted into one of genuine charm. 'My dear Miss Bainbridge, why do you not simply tell me the whole? You will probably find it easier to come to the point if you tell the whole tale from beginning to end.'

'Yes, my lord.' Amy was also beginning to realise that it would not be possible to tell half a story. Nor did she wish to.

The Marquis was so very different from the image that she had in her mind that she was certain he would charm the truth from her by one means or another. He was just like his son.

'Before I begin, my lord,' she said impulsively, 'I wish you to know that I am aware of the...the lack of sympathy that there has been between you and your son.' She saw that he was looking at her inscrutably and hurried on. 'Oh, I know that this is none of my business and that in speaking thus I am guilty of the greatest impertinence, but I had to tell you! What I will relate must surely make you see that you are mistaken in Lord Tallant and that he is—essentially noble!'

The Marquis raised his eyebrows. 'Noble? I might say that you are coming it a bit strong, Miss Bainbridge, but I fear you would call me out! Your tale will speak for itself, I am sure. As for my opinion of you, nothing can alter the esteem in which I hold you.'

Amy smiled tremulously. She was not clear how the Marquis had come to have such a good opinion of her in such a short time, but she was fearful that she might lose it soon. Nevertheless, the story had to be told. She suspected that she might have given away something of her feelings for Joss in her last impassioned outburst, but that appeared to in no way have impaired his father's view of her. Maybe that was the key to his approval—he was so pleased that his son had apparently attached himself to a respectable female that he was willing to give her a certain latitude. On that thought she took her courage in both hands and plunged in.

She left nothing out. She told the Marquis how she had first met Joss at the house in Curzon Street, how she had won the lottery, how Joss had accepted Juliana's debt and spent the week doing good deeds. When she related that he had escorted her to the concert given by the children's charity choir and had gone to visit the St Boniface orphanage with her, the Marquis was overcome with a fit of coughing and Amy was afraid that he might choke.

'I can only assume that my son holds you in even higher esteem than I do, Miss Bainbridge!' the Marquis said, when he had regained his breath.

Amy saw the twinkle of humour in his eye and it disconcerted her. She hurried on to relate how Joss had given her his help in dealing with the blackmailer, omitting nothing but Amanda and the blackmailer's identity. Finally she reached the story of what had happened when Joss had saved Juliana seven years before, and at last she saw the Marquis become very tense and still, and he did not speak until she had finished.

When she had finally run out of words there was a long silence in the room. Amy felt exhausted and her heart was racing, but she also felt a tremendous relief that she had done what justice demanded. Her only remaining concern was the effect upon the Marquis. He seemed to have shrunk in his chair, turned in upon himself, shrivelled and aged. Impulsively she left her own seat and went across to kneel by his.

'I am sorry, my lord, so sorry to have had to shock you like this, but I thought that the truth must be told—'

'You did the right thing, Miss Bainbridge.' The Marquis's voice was no longer smooth but scarred and old. 'My only doubt is how I could have not realised this sooner. Oh, Joss was as wild as any other when he was young, but he had never given me serious cause for alarm. He gambled a little and I suppose there were women, but...' he sighed '...he was never excessive in his behaviour. Never before. But then this happened and his excesses bordered on madness and I felt him slipping away from me, and I could not get him back.' His voice faded, then strengthened. 'Truth to tell, I did not try. I was so angry and disgusted by his behaviour and every new outrage seemed to confirm my initial disappointment—that he had gambled away eighty thousand pounds, brought disgrace upon us and almost ruined the family in the process!'

Amy put her hand on his. 'My lord, do not distress yourself—'

'As for Juliana,' the Marquis said, 'there I failed even more badly.' His tone was bleak. 'I could never love the chit in the same way as I loved Joss, for I knew she was not mine. Yet that was not her fault—it should not have mattered. I should not have let it matter!'

Amy closed her eyes to stop the tears squeezing from beneath her lids. She had had no very high opinion of Juliana before and, even when Joss had spoken for her, Amy could find little sympathy in her heart. Nevertheless she could understand the bond between Joss and his sister—and understand the Marquis's agony.

'It is never too late,' she said quietly.

They sat for a little, very still, Amy's hand clasped in his, and then the Marquis stirred.

'So,' he said, and his tone had strengthened now, the authority showing through, 'it seems I have grossly misjudged my son, and the rest of the world has done so too. Yet...' he smiled down at Amy '...you have seen proof of his wildness, Miss Bainbridge. You must admit that Joss is not blameless—'

'No.' Amy got to her feet. 'Indeed, Lord Tallant said the very same thing himself. Yet when one can understand the reasons...'

'One can also forgive?' The Marquis's mouth twisted. 'If

you can do so, Miss Bainbridge, I shall find myself profoundly grateful to you—'

He broke off at the sound of a horse been ridden hard up
the drive, then lay back in his chair with a contented sigh.

'Ah, that will be my son, I think, come in good time. How
excellent to have my suspicions confirmed!' He saw Amy's
look of curiosity and gave her a smile. 'It is quite evident that
you love my son, Miss Bainbridge—so evident that I do not
scruple to speak of it. Logic suggested to me that if he had
one iota of the same feeling for you, he would follow you to
the ends of the earth, let alone to Ashby Tallant! It makes me
very happy to see that I am right. Oh, Miss Bainbridge—'
his voice halted Amy when she was already halfway to the
door, looking for somewhere to hide '—you shall oblige me
by staying here with me. I imagine that Joss will wish to
speak to you too!'

Chapter Fourteen

A couple of hours later, Amy walked with Joss along the top terrace and down the steps to the Ashby Tallant gardens. There were four terraces in all, flanked by huge cedar trees, each with their own name and character. The top garden, nearest the house was the most formal; the bottom one, the wilderness garden, was an overgrown Eden with medieval fishponds and tumbling walls.

'I played here as a boy,' Joss said, tracing the lines on a stone-carved sundial as they stood in the central grassy court and looked at the tangled profusion all around. 'It was an exciting place for a child.' He gestured to a stone bench under the shade of a weeping willow. 'Shall we sit?'

Amy sat down. She was feeling strangely shy and it did not help that the only conversation between them since they had left the house had been of the most formal kind. She had wondered if Joss had just been waiting for a little privacy, waiting for the opportunity to rebuke her for coming to Ashby Tallant and having the audacity to set his circumstances before the Marquis. She wondered if he was angry and could not tell. The amber gaze, the living replica of the portraits on the wall, was as inscrutable as he had always been. She wished it was not so. She could not stand the uncertainly.

'Are you angry with me?' she burst out, when she could stand it no longer. Her fingers plucked nervously at the cambric of her dress. 'I am sorry, Joss, but I felt I had to come.'

Joss took her hand in his and her words dried on her lips. The look in his eyes was tender and rueful.

'Amy, I might wish that you did not rush so precipitately towards doing what you think is right, but I cannot be angry with you.' He smiled a little. 'Indeed, now that I am in a fair way to establishing a better understanding with my father, I suppose I should be grateful to you! It will take a little time for us to be on better terms, but we have made a beginning.'

Amy felt a rush of relief. 'I am glad that you were able to speak with him,' she said shyly. She moved a little closer to him. 'He was very kind to me, Joss. I like him very much.'

'He likes you,' Joss said drily. 'He told me that he would disown me for good this time if I let you slip through my fingers. But we will talk of that presently. I wanted to tell you first that Lady Spry's letters are safe and that I have returned them to her. I believe she has nothing further to fear in that quarter.'

Amy let go of his hand, but only so that she could throw her arms about him. 'Oh, how did you manage that?'

Joss released himself, laughing. 'It was not difficult.' The light went out of his face. 'It was Juliana who had the letters, not Massingham.'

'Juliana!' Amy frowned. She sat back. 'But Amanda was sure that Massingham had them.'

Joss shifted uncomfortably. 'You may have guessed that

Juliana is Massingham's mistress. She had found the letters and used them for her own ends. As soon as you told me the tale, I suspected her. She has tried to pull such a trick before, you see.' He looked Amy in the eye. 'Juliana loves Massingham and she has been very unhappy. Do not judge her too harshly, Amy. For my sake, I beg you do not.' He took a deep breath. 'We could all have made things so very different for her.'

'Your father said as much to me,' Amy said softly. 'I cannot judge her, Joss. If all is well and Amanda is safe, those are the only things that truly matter to me.'

Joss's expression lightened. 'Lady Spry is very well. I left her discussing the remove to Nettlecombe with your mama. And Juliana is leaving for the continent for a space. I will tell you the whole in a little while, Amy, but I would rather speak of happier things.'

'There is one thing I have to ask first,' Amy said softly. 'Did you tell your father that the blackmailer was Juliana?'

Joss nodded. 'It is only fair that he knows the whole. Then, when the time comes for him to be reconciled with Juliana, there will be no secrets.'

'I hope that will be soon,' Amy said. There was a lump in her throat and she bit her lip to prevent the tears. 'Oh, I do hope so...'

'I hope so too.' Joss pulled her to her feet. 'Enough of this doom and gloom! May we speak on something I hope will be a happier subject?'

Amy nodded wordlessly. He was looking very serious. Her heart started to race.

'I have your brother's permission to pay my addresses to you, Amy,' Joss said formally. 'However, it is your good opinion that I value the most. If you consent to accept my proposal I shall be the happiest man alive, but I think that you should be very certain you are doing the right thing—'

Amy pressed her fingers against his lips, effectively silencing him. She tugged on his hand and he came to sit down beside her on the bench again.

'Joss, I must know why you are so persistent in trying to make me refuse you.'

She saw the laughter creep into his eyes, warm as sunshine, banishing the cold doubt there.

'Amy, you once told me that you detested gamblers and that your greatest happiness was when you won your money and achieved the security you craved.' Joss's fingers, long and strong, interlocked tightly with hers. 'You would be a fool to throw all that away to bind yourself to a man who embodies all that you despised—'

This time Amy silenced him with a kiss. 'Joss, it is not folly, it is love.' She freed herself and sat back a little so that she could see his face. 'I confess that at first I disliked you for your reputation—'

'No, you held me in contempt. That is far, far worse.'

'If you prefer.' Amy smiled slightly. 'Alas for me, my dislike was soon undermined by the pleasure that I took in your company. I was slow to realise it and when I tried to pull back it was too late.' Her voice sank to a whisper. 'I did not wish to avoid you. When I thought that I should not see you again it was the most dreadful torment.'

Joss pulled her close. He pressed his lips to her hair. 'Amy, you know I am a wastrel—'

'Stuff and nonsense! You do not gamble to excess and anyway, you always win! You told me so yourself!'

Joss gave a muffled groan. 'You know that makes no difference. Besides, I have been a rake.'

'Yes—' Amy raised her face to his '—but I shall be happy if you confine your attentions to me in future. Indeed, I have been hoping to see evidence of your rakish tendencies for I fear they have been overrated.'

Joss bent his head until his lips touched hers. 'I will let you be the judge of that. I do believe that you have disposed of all my objections, Amy.'

He made to kiss her properly, but Amy drew away from him. 'I have some concerns of my own, Joss. I mean that there are matters about which I feel *you* should be concerned...'

'Oh?' There was a light in his eyes now that made her heart skip a beat. 'What are they, my love? Can it be that your gambling is a far greater obsession than I had previously thought?'

'No...' Amy smiled despite herself, and then hesitated. 'It is simply that... I feel that I should be counselling you to think very carefully. You always said that you were wary of marriage, Joss, and I could not bear it if you were to find that it did not suit you after we were wed...'

Her hand was against his chest and she could feel the steady beat of his heart against her palm. It felt strong and reassuring.

'Amy!' Joss drew her to him again and this time she allowed herself to go. 'It is true that until recently I had absolutely no wish to marry. I could not imagine a time when I should ever feel differently. Worse, I dreaded sitting at one end of this cold mausoleum of a house whilst my wife inhabited a set of rooms as far away from me as possible. It seemed so bleak.' He smiled at her. 'Then I met you. At first I had no notion that I was falling in love with you. I knew that I enjoyed talking to you and found your company stimulating. I thought that there was no more to it than that, but...'

he shook his head '…fool that I was, I did not realise that I was already in love.'

Amy made an inarticulate noise and pressed closer to him. She slid her arms about his waist and pressed her cheek against his jacket.

'Oh, Joss, that is by far the nicest thing that anyone has ever said to me! I have always been so plain and shy, and had no admirers—'

'That,' Joss said, tilting her chin up so that he could kiss her gently, 'is the most blatant fishing for a compliment that I have heard in a very long time! Let me oblige. For almost the whole time I knew you, I found myself looking at you and thinking how beautiful you were, Amy. You did not need the lottery money to buy pretty clothes.'

This time they kissed with rather more fervour and less gentleness.

'Besides,' Joss finished, 'if I discover that any other man has been professing himself in love with you, I fear I should have to call him out!'

'There is always poor Bertie Hallam,' Amy said thoughtfully. 'Proposing to me has become such a habit of his that I hope he may soon find another object for his gallantry!'

'He should confine his attentions to his cards,' Joss said callously, 'and then perhaps he might start winning!'

He drew Amy's arm through his and turned towards the steps. 'Come, let us go and tell my father the good news. I am happy that at last I have fulfilled one of his expectations!'

They were married two months later in the chapel at Ashby Tallant. Sir Richard Bainbridge gave the bride away and Amanda, Lady Spry, was matron-of-honour. The Duke of Fleet acted as groomsman and Lady Bainbridge graciously accepted the escort of the Marquis of Tallant to the wedding feast, where she was seen slipping several large slices of ham into her reticule to consume later. Mrs Benfleet travelled from Windsor in the Bainbridge carriage and Mrs Wendover and her children came from Whitechapel, travelling in the Tallant carriage, which miraculously kept all its wheels even whilst waiting in the street in Whitechapel.

Later, when the guests had departed, the bridal suite had been prepared for the happy couple and Lady Bainbridge had imparted some words of maternal wisdom to her daughter, Amy was finally left in peace to contemplate her wedding night.

Although she had spent a large part of the previous three months in Joss's company, she felt apprehensive and suddenly a little shy. As the wedding day had approached and the bustle of preparation had taken over it had been so difficult to hold on to the things that were really important. Even her charitable ventures had been curtailed through the necessary evils of dress fitting and consultations with Lady Bainbridge about the menu for the wedding breakfast. It felt to Amy as though there had been a buzz of activity about her for as long as she could remember and now all was suddenly silence.

Not quite silence. She could hear the sound of Joss's voice in the next room as he spoke quietly to his valet. Soon he would be joining her. Her head ached with the tension. The huge, opulent bedroom seemed unbearably stuffy.

She scrambled from the bed and flung up the window, leaning out and inhaling the fresh, summer air. It was not quite dark and a tiny crescent moon was rising above the lime avenue. The breeze caressed her face. Amy closed her eyes and felt a little of her tension evaporate.

'Amy?'

Amy jumped and almost hit her head on the window. She had not heard the connecting door open but now Joss was standing just behind her, the light burnishing his hair to dark bronze and shadowing his eyes. Amy felt her throat go dry. She swallowed hard.

'Oh. Joss. I… I did not hear you. I needed some fresh air. I have the headache.'

As soon as she said it she realised how lame it sounded, as though she were having second thoughts about her wedding night. Panic and shyness gripped her but, before she could blurt out that she did not mean to send him away, Joss had taken her hand, drawing her gently towards him.

'There is a balcony in the other bedroom. Let us go outside for a little. It has been an unconscionably long and tiring day.'

Grateful for his understanding, Amy went with him through the dressing room and into another, much smaller bedroom where one candle still burned. Joss drew back the heavy curtains and opened the long windows. A breath of wind stirred the wall hangings and set the candle flame dancing. They went out on to the balcony. Immediately the cool twilight wrapped about them.

The moon was riding high above the trees and the first of the stars were coming out now. The cupola on the top of the great hall was outlined in black against a midnight blue sky. Amy stared entranced at the parkland, spread out before them in the fading light.

'Oh! It is so beautiful! It makes me feel quite wild! I want to run downstairs and out of the doors and across the grass in the moonlight—'

'Perhaps we may do that tomorrow night,' Joss said, a smile in his voice, 'and scandalise the servants.'

Amy sighed. 'Yes, I suppose... For tonight it would not be at all the thing. But I do thank you, Joss, for not going all stuffy and saying that that would be most unseemly and that I must always act with a decorum that becomes a Countess.'

Joss pulled her into his arms with a swiftness that took her breath away. 'Amy, if you wish to run barefoot through the gardens clad only in your shift you shall not find me far behind!'

Amy turned her blushing face against his chest. 'Thank you. So...' she felt brave enough to address the subject on her mind '...how is this difficult matter of our wedding night to be managed? I feel a little self-conscious—'

'How is it to be *managed*?' Joss loosened his grip a little, holding her at arm's length so that his gaze could sweep over her comprehensively from her bare feet to her tumbling hair. 'Like this, I imagine...'

Before Amy was aware of what he was about, he had swept her up into his arms and carried her through the open windows, laying her on the tester bed. With one swift move he had drawn her silky dressing robe away from her. 'I suspect that you will soon forget your difficulties...'

'Yes, but—' Amy struggled to sit up. 'The bridal bed is all prepared in the other room—'

'We shall go back in there presently. This will do perfectly well in the meantime.'

'Oh, but—' Amy lost the thread of her thoughts as Joss stripped off his own robe. In the candlelight his body was hard and lean and it was plain to see that he was aroused. Amy, whose experience of such matters was nil, felt her self-consciousness return even as something inside her responded to him.

'Joss, I am feeling even more apprehensive now,' she said in a tiny voice.

Joss smiled. He joined her on the bed, stretching out beside her and resting one hand gently on her stomach. Amy could feel the warmth of it through her gauzy nightdress and felt a delicious squirmy sensation inside.

'There is no need to be afraid, Amy,' Joss said softly. 'I swear I shall do nothing that you do not want.'

'It is not so much that I do not want it,' Amy said, eyes wide, 'simply that I am not sure how it will work.'

'Then it is best not to worry and just see what happens.' Joss's voice was as soothing as honey wine. Amy could feel herself letting go—at the same time as part of her was feeling very tense and excited indeed.

'Very well, I shall try...'

Joss bent and kissed her throat and she could not help the tremor that went through her. His hand slid to her hip, and she shivered again, eyes closing. When he started to unlace her nightdress she opened her eyes, but before she could speak he had silenced her with his lips on hers. The kiss was gentle but there was something hot beneath its sweetness. Amy wriggled, running her fingers into Joss's hair, holding him closer. She heard him groan against her mouth, then the kiss deepened and became hard and hungry, and she was swept with the most intoxicating sensual excitement she had ever felt.

'Oh, that is so very agreeable...'

Amy had not noticed when her nightdress had fallen open, freeing her breasts to Joss's touch. Now she arched against him as she felt his fingers brush one rosy nipple, circling, caressing. Then the nightdress came away altogether and she felt the warmth and hardness of Joss's naked body against her own, his hands pulling her closer still, and thought she might faint from sheer pleasure.

'Joss!'

Joss's eyes had darkened with desire and now he kissed her again with a concentrated passion. Amy knew instinctively that he was very close to losing control and the knowledge made her feel wicked and excited and powerful. Eagerly she returned kiss for searing kiss, sliding her hands over the strong muscles of his back, digging her fingers into his shoulders.

His hands and lips moved over her, provoking a blazing sensual awareness in her as they lingered on her breasts. Amy had long ago ceased to be afraid, ceased to think, wanting only the necessary consummation of all her desires. She shivered as she felt Joss's hand on her thigh, his fingers stroking the soft skin before he moved to touch her with an intimacy that was shocking but exquisitely exciting. Her mouth formed a silent 'oh' of pleasure and longing and he repeated the caress, moving on top of her, sliding one leg between hers. Amy squirmed, desperate to appease the delicious ache inside.

Joss took her face between both his hands. 'Sweetheart, I love you. I will try not to hurt you—'

As soon as the words were out his hands moved to her hips and he captured her mouth with his in an urgent kiss. He slid into her and smothered her instinctive gasp with his lips on hers.

The shock was enough to shake Amy out of the sensual trance that possessed her, but then Joss was kissing her again lingeringly, bending his head to her breasts with exquisite patience and skill, moving in long slow strokes that quickly built up the excitement to fever pitch again. Amy gasped and clung to him and felt his body go taut within her and watched his face as he took her, and the sheer excitement and the knowing pushed her over the edge, to shatter into a hundred shimmering pieces before she floated slowly down to earth. She lay entangled in Joss's arms, feeling his heart rate slow down and the sweat cool on their skin and she thought, *He is mine, now and for always.* Her heart swelled with love and she burrowed closer to his warmth and fell asleep.

'Amy, sweetheart, there is something that I must tell you.'

It was the following afternoon and Amy had taken Joss's arm for a stroll on the terrace after luncheon, for all the world, she had said laughingly, like an old married couple. Joss had stayed with her all night and most of the morning, first in the tester bed in the smaller room and then in the bridal bed, whose pristine perfection had been most satisfactorily disordered. He had finally dragged himself away only to dress and they had somehow managed to get themselves downstairs to eat.

The sun was warm and Amy felt drowsy. She leant against the terrace balustrade and smiled at him sleepily. 'You had better be quick then, for I fear I shall fall asleep soon! I think I need to take a nap this afternoon.'

'That will be delightful,' Joss said promptly. 'I will join you.'

Amy blinked at him. 'In the afternoon? But surely that would be most scandalous—'

Joss shrugged. 'I said that we should shake this old house up, did I not? I intend to start as I mean to go on. And tonight we may run barefoot through the gardens and—'

'Enough!' Amy held up a hand. 'I thought that you had something to tell me?'

'I did. You distracted me.' Joss came across and kissed

her very gently, taking both her hands in his. 'Amy, when I tell you this I beg you not to be angry with me.'

Amy was starting to feel concerned. 'Joss, what is this?'

For once Joss seemed at a loss. 'I did think about never telling you—'

'Joss!' Amy broke in sharply. 'You are making me so nervous that I beg you will tell me at once!'

'Very well.' Joss gave her a lopsided smile. 'It is the lottery money, Amy. I have to tell you that it was my ticket that you found. It was my thirty thousand pounds.'

Amy stepped back, eyes narrowing. 'Yours? But you said that it was not! Are you making this up to tease me? What was the number?'

'Two thousand five hundred and eighty-eight,' Joss said obligingly. A smile was twitching the corner of his mouth. 'Oh dear, you look very angry.'

'I am not angry, precisely...' Amy was struggling with a variety of emotions. Indignation won. 'Well, upon my word! I have heard of people claiming prizes that do not belong to them, but why refuse a prize that does? It makes no sense! Why did you not tell me?'

Joss drove his hands into his pockets. 'I am not sure.'

Amy frowned. 'But I asked you! I asked you directly if it was your ticket and you said that it was not!'

Joss shook his head, turning slightly away. 'I would only have gambled the money away and I thought that you were more deserving...'

'You let me keep it out of pity?' There was a note of hurt in Amy's voice. 'Perhaps you thought that I might buy myself some pretty dresses and look halfway presentable—'

Joss caught her in his arms. 'To my mind you look most presentable without your clothes—'

'Joss!' Amy beat her fist against his chest in mock anger. She could feel her indignation melting like ice in the sun. 'Oh, this is too bad! To trick me like this! To marry me under false pretences! I suppose you thought that I needed the funds to pay for my charitable ventures?'

'The thought did cross my mind. I was so enjoying sharing them with you, sweetheart!'

Amy struggled. Joss held her fast and after a moment she relaxed against him.

'I suppose,' she said in a mollified tone, 'that the fact that you let me keep the money is really evidence of your noble nature, Joss. I have always said that you are an honourable man—'

'Minx!' Joss said. 'If you mention my noble nature one more time I shall kiss you until you reconsider your words.'

Amy smiled and tilted her face up to his. 'Is that a promise?'

She saw his eyes darken as they took in the captivating line of her lips. He lowered his head until his mouth was an inch from hers. 'It could be...'

They kissed again, breathless, happy.

'But, of course...' Amy pulled away and put her hand against his lips '...you have possession of my fortune now, Joss, so that you have regained your lottery win!'

'There is always the interest to pay on the sum,' Joss murmured. He moved her hand aside and bent closer, his lips an inch away from hers. 'You also owe me for the money you have already spent...'

Amy smiled as his mouth touched hers in a butterfly kiss. 'I fear you will never regain it. You will be forever out of pocket. You have gambled and lost, Joss Tallant.'

'No.' Joss was smiling at her with so much love it made

her quite dizzy. 'I gambled and won, Amy Tallant, for I gained far more than the lottery prize.' He swung her up in his arms. 'That you cannot dispute. Winner takes all.'

* * * * *

The
Chaperone Bride

Chapter One

June 1816

The coach from Leeds drew into the yard of the Hope Inn at Harrogate in the late afternoon and disgorged a number of passengers. Although it was still quite early in the season, the spa villages of High and Low Harrogate were starting to fill up with visitors coming to take the health-giving waters and on this occasion there were seven new arrivals. First to descend was a family of four: mother, father, a boy of about sixteen and a girl a year or so older, both with smiling faces and a lively interest in what was going on around them. Next descended an elderly lady wrapped up in a vast shawl and attended by a solicitous young man who might or might not have been her nephew. The other arrival was Annis, Lady Wycherley, carrying a small leather case and dressed in practical black bombazine and an unbecoming bonnet.

Annis Wycherley was not a newcomer to Harrogate, for she had been born near the town and had spent many happy holidays there with her cousins during the times that her papa had been on leave from the navy. The late Captain Lafoy had even bought a small estate out towards Skipton, which Annis had inherited almost a decade before and visited whenever she had the opportunity. She was not in Harrogate as often as she would like, however. Her employment, as a chaperon to spoilt society misses, took her to London or Brighton or Bath, although this latter was considered rather *déclassé* these days, a shabby genteel place that was not popular with the fashionable crowd. Harrogate, with its romantic setting in the wilds of nowhere, its unpleasantly smelling but healthful spa waters and its rustic northern charm, was fast becoming the new Bath in the eyes of the *ton*.

Annis, espying her cousin Charles in the crowd thronging the inn yard, hurried across and gave him an affectionate hug. He hugged her back, then held her at arm's length, looking her over dubiously but with a twinkle in his very blue eyes.

'Annis, whatever have you done to yourself?'

Annis gave a little giggle. 'Dear Charles, it is lovely to see you too! I collect that your horror stems from seeing me in my chaperon's attire? I always dress the part, you know.'

'It puts years on you.' Charles gave the black bombazine a bemused look and frowned at the bonnet. 'Lord, Annis, it's wonderful to see you again, but I barely recognised you!'

'You know that it is always a mistake to travel in your best clothes. You end up either mud spattered or dusty. Besides, as a professional chaperon I cannot look too elegant.'

'No danger of that.' Charles tried to hide his grin. 'Was the journey good?'

'A little precipitate,' Annis said. 'I suppose that is why the coach is called the Tally Ho? The driver certainly seemed to take that to heart!'

'I would have sent the carriage to Leeds for you, you know,' Charles said, gesturing to a smart black chaise that stood in the corner of the yard. 'It would have been no trouble.'

'There was no need,' Annis said cheerfully. 'I am accustomed to travelling on the stage.' She waved at the family of four as the landlord escorted them inside the inn. 'Dear Mr and Mrs Fairlie... Amelia... James... I shall hope to see you all at the Promenade Rooms before long.'

'You make friends easily,' Charles observed as the couple bowed and smiled in return.

'One must beguile the long journey somehow, you know, and they were a very pleasant family. Not like that young man over there...' Annis nodded across at the young gentleman who was helping the elderly lady up into a barouche. 'I am sure he is after her money, Charles. If I hear that she has passed away, I shall be most suspicious!'

'Annis!'

'Oh, I am only joking,' Annis said hastily, remembering belatedly that her cousin could be a bit of a high stickler. 'Pay no attention! Now you...are you well? And Sibella?'

'I am very well indeed.' Charles grinned. 'Sib is flourishing. She and David are expecting their fourth, you know.'

'I had heard.' Annis smiled, tucking her arm through his. 'She has been very busy whilst you and I, Charles, have let the family down sadly! You are not even married and I only look after other peoples' children!'

Charles laughed and patted her hand where it rested on his sleeve. 'Plenty of time for the rest of us. But it is fortunate

Sibella did not come to meet you, Annis. She would have disowned you as soon as look at you!'

'Sibella is lucky in that she can indulge herself as a lady of fashion.' Annis looked around for her trunks. 'I am obliged to work for my living. Nevertheless I am grateful to you for swallowing the family pride and coming to meet me, Charles. I know I do you no credit!'

Charles laughed again. 'It was shock, that is all. I barely recognised you in all that frumpish black. You used to be such a good-looking girl...'

Annis gave him a sharp nudge. 'You used to be quite handsome yourself! Where did it all go wrong, Charles?'

Charles Lafoy was in fact a very good-looking man, as most of the female population of Harrogate would testify. Like his sister Sibella, he had the fair, open features of the Lafoys, the honest blue eyes and engaging smile. As lawyer to Harrogate's most prosperous merchant, Samuel Ingram, he had a prestigious position in village society. There was no shortage of inn servants queuing up to help his groom put Annis's luggage in the carriage. Everyone knew that Mr Lafoy always tipped most generously.

Annis Wycherley was almost as tall as her cousin, having a height unfashionable in a woman but useful in a chaperon, since it helped to assert her authority. Her eyes were hazel rather than the Lafoy blue, but she had the same rich, golden blonde hair. In Annis's case this rarely saw the light of day, being hidden under a succession of lace caps, ugly bonnets and ragingly unfashionable turbans. She had learned early on that no one took a blonde chaperon at all seriously; it could, in fact, be positively dangerous to display her hair, for it made gentlemen behave in a most inappropriately amorous manner.

The shapeless gowns in dowager black, purple and turkey red were all designed and worn with one intention in mind—to make her look older and unattractive. This was a necessity of her profession. Just as no one would take a blonde chaperon seriously, so would nobody entrust their daughter, niece or ward to a girl who looked as though she had only just left the schoolroom herself. Annis was in fact seven and twenty and had been widowed for eight years, but she had a fair, youthful complexion, wide-spaced eyes, a snub nose and a generous mouth that all conspired to undermine the sense of gravity required by a professional chaperon. Prettiness combined with poverty had always struck her as a recipe for disaster, so she did her best to disguise those natural assets she possessed.

'I thought that we would go straight to the house in Church Row,' Charles said, as they made their way across to his carriage. 'You will have the chance to settle in comfortably before Sibella calls on you this evening. When do your charges arrive?'

'Not until Friday,' Annis said. 'Sir Robert Crossley is escorting the girls up from London himself and Mrs Hardcastle accompanies them as duenna in my absence. I am persuaded that she will have licked them into shape before ever they darken my door!' She shivered a little in the breeze. 'Gracious, Charles, I can scarce believe that it is June. The wind off the hills is as cold as ever.'

'You have gone soft from living too long in the south,' Charles said affectionately. 'These charges of yours, the Misses Crossley—do they have a large fortune?'

'Big enough to buy half of Harrogate!' Annis said. She grimaced, remembering the interview that she had had in London with the Crossley girls before she had agreed to take them on. 'I fear that even that will not be sufficient to sweeten the pill of Miss Fanny Crossley's bad manners, however. The girl is as sharp as a thorn and only passably good-looking. She may well be my first failure!'

'I doubt it.' Charles grinned at her. 'Even here in Harrogate we have heard of the striking success of that matchmaker *par excellence*, Lady Wycherley! They say that you could catch a husband for any girl, be she ugly as sin and poor as a church mouse.'

'One or other, perhaps, but not both together!' Annis laughed. 'You are not hanging out for a wealthy bride, are you, Charles?'

'Not I!' Her cousin watched as the last bags were strapped onto the platform of the chaise. 'I do have a client who is looking, however. Sir Everard Doble, a very worthy but rather dull man with an estate mortgaged to the hilt. We shall arrange a meeting for him with your charges.'

'Dear Charles,' Annis said gratefully. 'I feel my task is already half done. And Miss Lucy Crossley, unlike her elder sister, is a sweet girl who should make a match easily enough amongst all the half-pay officers who seem to crowd the place. I do not imagine that either sister will make a dazzling match, but it should be possible to settle them creditably. So...' Annis sighed '...I may get them off my hands and then spend some time at Starbeck. It was the real reason that I accepted Sir Robert's commission to chaperon his nieces, you know. I wanted to spend some time at home.'

Charles frowned slightly. 'Ah, Starbeck. You know that

I have not been able to keep a tenant there for the last few months and that the house is in a poor state? I need to talk to you about it at some point, coz.'

Annis looked at him sharply. There was something odd in his tone, a reluctance that made her heart miss a beat, for it boded ill. The small estate of Starbeck was a drain on her limited income and she knew that Charles thought she was a sentimental fool to hold on to it. He had administered the estate for her since her father died and he had been urging her to sell for several years. The house was tumbledown and swallowed money in constant repairs, Charles had been unable to find a tenant who would stay there for any length of time, and the home farm was so poor its owners could barely scratch a living. Since Annis had no money other than what she earned plus a small annuity, it was financial nonsense to continue to support Starbeck, and yet she did not want to let it go. She had had a peripatetic childhood following her father about the country from posting to posting and travelling abroad with her parents on several occasions. Starbeck was home, the only certainty she knew, and for that reason she did not want to lose it.

'Of course we may talk—' she began, but broke off as a green and gold high-perch phaeton swept into the inn yard, scattering the ostlers like nervous chickens.

'For pity's sake!' Charles flushed red in annoyance and skipped out of the way as the offside wheel almost ran over his foot. Annis tried not to laugh. Her cousin had always been slightly stuffy, the responsible one amongst the three of them. Perhaps it stemmed from the fact that Charles was the eldest, or more likely it was because he was the only boy and as such was now head of the Lafoy family. Whatever the case, he deplored frivolity.

The phaeton was gleaming and new and contained two occupants, a lady and a gentleman. The lady, a buxom brunette, was swathed in furs. She was laughing and clutching a saucy hat on her dark curls. Her vivacious brown eyes scanned the assembled company, rested thoughtfully on Charles's red face and dismissed Annis's plain one, before she took her companion's hand and jumped lightly down to join him on the cobbles of the inn yard. The landlord had emerged and was bowing enthusiastically, waving them towards the inn door.

'Ashwick!' Annis heard Charles say, under his breath.

She cast him a quick glance. Once again there was an odd note in Charles's voice, one that she could not place. It was neither envy nor even disapproval, both of which might have been understandable from the country lawyer to the dashing peer of the realm. Annis knew of Lord Ashwick, of course; no one who had sponsored girls in *ton* society for the last three years as she had could fail to be aware of a man whose recent career consisted mainly of playing high and keeping low company. Adam Ashwick was a friend of such luminaries as the Duke of Fleet and the Earl of Tallant, who had scandalised the town with their exploits for years. Tallant was married now and had become disappointingly uxorious, but the gossips were still entertained by the activities of Sebastian Fleet and Adam Ashwick. It seemed extraordinary to find him in so out of the way a place as Harrogate.

The couple had to pass them to reach the inn door. Annis drew back against the side of the coach, having no wish to push herself forward for notice. To her surprise, however,

Adam Ashwick paused in front of them and gave Charles the briefest of bows.

'Lafoy.' His tone was cold.

Charles's own bow was correspondingly slight. 'Ashwick.'

There was a silence that prickled with tension. Annis, looking from one to the other, sensed all kinds of undercurrents that she was at a loss to explain. Ashwick was watching Charles, an unpleasant smile on his lips, and Annis took the opportunity to study him whilst his attention was diverted.

At first glance, she did not consider him to be a good-looking man in the conventional sense, for his face was too swarthy, and its hard angles were too stern and uncompromising to be considered handsome. His eyes were wide set and a cool grey beneath straight black brows. Although he could only be in his early thirties, his thick, dark hair was turning silver, which added a certain distinction to his looks. He was above average height and had a sportsman's physique, but he was dressed with what appeared to be deliberate understatement, in tight dove-grey riding breeches and a pristine black coat that made his linen seem a very pure white indeed. Instead of Hessians he was wearing a fine pair of leather riding boots with turned-down cuffs. He had the appearance of a man of action rather than the dissipated aristocrat Annis had been imagining, and he exuded latent power. Annis could feel the effect. It was different from the confidence that Charles possessed as a successful professional man; Ashwick's authority was instinctive, unquestioned.

His cool grey gaze switched to her and Annis hastily lowered her eyes. She did not wish him to think that she had been staring. Adam Ashwick bowed again, with scrupulous courtesy this time.

'Madam.'

'My cousin, Annis, Lady Wycherley,' Charles said, with such obvious unwillingness that Annis felt her lips twitch. She was not sure if Charles's reluctance to introduce her sprang from disapproval of Ashwick's reputation or a more personal dislike. A split second later, she realised that Adam Ashwick was also considering the reasons for Charles's protective concern. As their eyes met he raised a quizzical brow and they were drawn into a moment of shared amusement. Annis broke the contact hastily, feeling a little disloyal.

She held out her hand politely. 'How do you do, my lord.'

'Your servant, Lady Wycherley.' Adam took her hand. She felt compelled to look at him again, then wished she had not. He was studying her thoughtfully, his gaze moving over her features with deliberation. There was a definite masculine interest in that appraisal and Annis recognised it with a shock. She felt a little shiver go through her and withdrew her hand from his.

Ashwick's beautiful companion was getting restive at the lack of attention. She pulled on his arm.

'Are you not to introduce me, Ashy, darling?' Her French accent was slight and very pretty. She peeked up at him under the brim of the dashing hat with the charm of a wilful child.

Ashy! Annis thought, trying not to laugh at the diminutive. She caught Ashwick's eye again and looked quickly away, for fear that he might read her mind again. She did not seek such affinity with him.

'Margot, may I present Annis, Lady Wycherley, and her cousin Mr Charles Lafoy?' Ashwick sounded pleasantly indifferent now as though the moment of enmity with Charles had never occurred. The lady nodded to Annis and batted her eyelashes at Charles in exaggerated fashion. Annis felt slightly amused and rather more irritated. The whole inn yard seemed to have stopped in order to stare at the Beauty and Annis wondered, as she had on many previous occasions, just why people were always drawn to the obvious. She had lost count of the times that débutantes with charm and fine looks were overlooked when something flashier came along. It was the same here. The ostlers were gaping, the other travellers were staring in admiration and some of the guests were even peering from the inn window to admire Ashwick's fair companion.

'I am Margot Mardyn,' the lady said, with the air of one making an important announcement. 'You have heard of me, *non*?'

'Of course,' Annis said hastily, as Charles looked blank. 'I hear that we are will be privileged to have you perform at the Theatre Royal this summer season, Miss Mardyn. My cousin and I shall be sure to attend.'

Margot Mardyn nodded, whilst smiling bewitchingly at Charles. 'I shall hope to see you after the show,' she said graciously to him.

She squeezed Ashwick's arm. '*Viens*, Ashy, I am cold. This "north" of yours is a shockingly barbaric place. Why, do you know...' she turned back to Charles confidingly '...at some of the inns along the way we were obliged to drink in the common tap? *Alors*! Along with all the hoi polloi! Come along, Ashy!'

Annis looked at Lord Ashwick and was taken aback to see that he was still watching her. He inclined his head and gave her a faint smile, which Annis found even more disturbing. She fidgeted with the seam of her gloves and hoped that her colour had not risen. Famously impervious to the good looks of eligible young gentlemen, she found it very odd that she should be drawn in this curious manner to a man whose style of life was so far removed from her own. Yet she could not deny it; the air between them was sharp with awareness. It was extremely disconcerting.

'I shall look forward to meeting you again, Lady Wycherley,' Ashwick said politely. 'I hope that you enjoy your stay in Harrogate.'

'Who was that?' Charles asked in a bemused tone as Ashwick steered his fair companion through the inn door and the excitement in the yard subsided. Annis, observing the rapt expression on his face as he watched Miss Mardyn's departure, sighed to herself.

'That was Lord Ashwick,' she said drily. 'I collect that you are acquainted with him?'

'Of course I know Ashwick.' Charles turned to her impatiently. 'His family have owned property around here for hundreds of years.'

'Of course.' Annis remembered this herself now. The Ashwicks had been part of the long and turbulent history of the Yorkshire moors for centuries, from the time that the first baron had served at the court of Charles II and had been given an estate in the back of beyond for his pains. Presumably Lord Ashwick was in Yorkshire to visit that very estate. Annis found herself wondering if she would see him again.

Charles was still looking over his shoulder in the direction that the couple had gone.

'Annis? Are your wits wandering? I meant the lady—'

'Ah, the lovely Miss Mardyn. She is a dancer and singer who has recently graced the stage at Drury Lane.' Annis looked at him sardonically. 'Charles, I should be obliged if you would help me up into the carriage. We have been standing here these ten minutes past and, as Miss Mardyn so succinctly observed, it is rather chilly.'

She waited until they were settled back on the fat red squabs of the Lafoy carriage, then added, 'I heard on the journey up that Miss Mardyn is to entertain us with *Harlequin's Metamorphoses, Escapes and Leaps.* Mr Fairlie was telling me about it and he was most excited. I believe the show will sell out, so you had better hurry to get your ticket.'

'That...child, a dancer?' Charles's mouth seemed permanently propped open. 'She cannot be above seventeen, surely?'

'Thirty-five if she's a day,' Annis said cheerfully, reflecting ruefully that men were always distracted by a pretty face and could never see what was under their nose, 'and hailing from the Portsmouth Docks rather than Paris, I hear.'

Charles looked appalled and fascinated all at the same time. 'Good God! And her connection with Ashwick?'

Annis gave him a speaking look.

'Oh!' Charles said.

'Well, it is entirely possible that Lord Ashwick was escorting Miss Mardyn as a favour for a friend,' Annis said fairly. 'When I left London the *on dit* was that she was the Duke of Fleet's inamorata. Who would have thought that such a bird of paradise would alight in Harrogate, of all places?'

'You are very free in your conversation, Annis,' Charles said, his mouth turning down at the corners. 'It must be the effect of London living. I hope you do not encourage your charges to listen to gossip.'

Annis laughed aloud. 'I am sorry if I offend your sensibilities, Charles. I had no idea you had turned into such a puritan!'

The coach trundled out of the inn yard and turned on to Silver Street. It was only a step to the house that Charles had hired for Annis in Church Row, but with her trunks it had clearly been impractical to walk. Annis leaned forward to look out of the window at the open ground of The Stray, bathed in the late afternoon sunlight.

'Oh it is quite delightful to be back! I do believe the last time was two years ago, and a flying visit at that. Tell me, Charles—' she turned back to look at him thoughtfully '—what is the nature of your quarrel with Lord Ashwick? I was not aware that the two of you knew each other.'

Charles shifted uncomfortably. 'I met him last year when his brother-in-law died. It is a little difficult, Annis.' Charles sighed. 'The late Lord Tilney, Ashwick's brother-in-law, was involved in a business scheme with Mr Ingram, but it failed and Ingram bought all his debts. When he died, Humphrey Tilney owed Ingram a deal of money. Ashwick agreed to pay the debt to save his sister from penury. The situation caused some difficulties.'

Annis raised her brows. Samuel Ingram, Charles's most powerful client, was a man who rode roughshod over all those who opposed his business dealings. She could imagine a nobleman of Lord Ashwick's calibre deeply resenting being in debt to such a man.

'What was this business venture?'

Charles looked gloomy. 'You probably remember it. It was in all the newspapers. Ingram and Humphrey Tilney were joint owners of the *Northern Prince*, the ship that went down carrying goods and money to the colonies eighteen months ago. There was the devil of a fuss.'

'I imagine there would be.' Annis frowned. 'Was there not a fortune in gold on the ship?'

'That is correct, and banknotes and silver and God alone knows what other valuables in addition.'

'Surely it was insured?'

Charles shifted uncomfortably. 'Yes, but Humphrey Tilney had overreached himself financially to fund his part in the enterprise in the first place. Under normal circumstances he might have recouped his losses within a couple of years but, as it was, he ended thirty thousand in debt. Ingram bought his debts up to help him rather than let him fall ever deeper into the hands of the moneylenders.'

'How charitable of him,' Annis said drily, thinking that a man such as Samuel Ingram seldom did anything out of the goodness of his heart.

Charles frowned to hear the note in her voice. 'See here, Annis, Ingram charged a very reasonable rate of interest—'

'And you wonder at Lord Ashwick resenting the fact!' Annis said, even more drily.

Charles subsided like a pricked balloon. 'That is the way that business works...'

'I dare say. I suppose there was no doubt that the ship actually went down? Ingram has not compounded his sins by defrauding the insurers?'

Charles looked horrified. 'Devil take it, Annis, of course not! Of course the ship went down! For pity's sake, do not go around saying such things in public!'

Annis was startled at his vehemence. 'Very well, Charles, there is no need to roast me for it! I only asked the question.

Speaking of Ingram, I read in the *Leeds Mercury* that there had been a fire at his farm at Shawes. Is foul play suspected?'

Charles gave her a very sharp look. 'Not at all. Why do you ask?'

Annis gave him an old-fashioned look. 'No need to pretend to me, Charles! I know that Mr Ingram is not popular hereabouts. I have read all about the arson and the threats to his property.'

Charles looked shifty. 'Yes, well, I will concede there has been a little local difficulty over the enclosure of the Shawes common, and there has been some discussion about rents this year—'

'You sound like a lawyer!' Annis said with a sigh.

'Well, so I am. And Mr Ingram's lawyer at that. It is my place to be dispassionate.'

'I would have thought that Mr Ingram would see it as your place to support him,' Annis said drily. 'That is what he pays you for.'

Charles blushed an angry red. 'See here, Annis, must you be so blunt? I'm astounded you ever find a match for those girls of yours if you are as outspoken with their suitors as you are with me!'

'Fortunately the gentlemen are marrying the girls and not me,' Annis said cheerfully. 'I do not seek to marry again, as you know, Charles.'

'Can't think why not. At least you would not need to work then.'

'Thank you, but I prefer to be independent. You know I dislike to be idle. Besides, I found that the married state did not suit me.'

'Not surprised if you spoke to John as plainly as you do to me!'

Annis locked her gloved hands together and looked pointedly out of the window. It was no secret that she and her elderly husband had been unhappy together, but even after eight years of widowhood the memory caused an ache.

'Sorry, Annis.' Charles sounded remorseful. 'I did not mean to offend you.'

'It is no matter, Charles.' Annis spoke briskly. 'You know that John had decided opinions about women and their place. Now that I am no longer required to respect those views, I fear I have become quite outspoken.'

'I suppose there are some men who like their wives to read the newspaper and have decided opinions,' Charles said dubiously.

'Are there? I have never met any of them.' Annis smiled. 'So perhaps it is fortunate that I do not look to marry.'

The carriage slowed before a grey stone house with neat sash windows, then turned through a small archway into a cobbled yard with stables along one side.

'There is a walled garden at the back,' Charles said eagerly, 'and I have engaged a couple of servants for you. You indicated that Mrs Hardcastle was to be housekeeper, so I imagine that she will wish to have the ordering of the household affairs once she arrives.'

'Of course. Hardy will soon have everything organised.' Annis looked about her with approval. 'You seem to have done us proud, Charles.'

'There is a drawing-room and walk-in cupboards in the bedrooms,' Charles offered, still trying to make amends for his earlier insensitivity. 'It is all very modern. I am sure that it is just what you require, Annis.'

'Thank you.' Annis took his hand as she descended from the coach. 'There is a most pleasant aspect to the front.'

'And the shops are not far away.'

'I assume that it is a quiet neighbourhood and one suitable for the Misses Crossley? No undesirable alehouses or rowdy neighbours? I would not wish my charges to be subject to unsuitable influences.'

Charles had opened his mouth to reply when there was a loud tally-ho from the road and a green and gold phaeton shot past, its occupants shrieking with laughter. It turned neatly through the archway of the house behind. Annis raised her eyebrows.

'My new neighbours, I presume?'

'Oh, dear,' Charles said unhappily.

'Ashy dearest,' Margot Mardyn said sweetly, draping herself over the arm of Adam Ashwick's chair, 'whatever would your mama say if she knew that you had brought me here?'

Adam glanced up briefly from the *York Herald*. The diva's cleavage was inclining tantalisingly close to his nose. It was plush and pink, and smelled cloyingly of roses. Adam looked thoughtfully at it, then returned to his paper.

'Margot, my sweet, do go and sit down. You are blocking my light. I am sure that Tranter will be in with the tea in a moment.'

Miss Mardyn flounced away to lay herself seductively along the sofa. 'Ashy…' her voice fell several octaves '…you have not answered my question.'

Adam sighed and laid his newspaper aside. He knew there

was not the least chance of him finishing the item until Miss Mardyn had partaken of tea and been delivered to her palatial suite of rooms at the Granby Hotel. His original intention to deliver her directly there had been thwarted when one of his horses had thrown a shoe, necessitating the stop at the Hope Inn. After that, Margot had insisted that nothing but tea in Church Row would soothe her ruffled sensibilities.

'I am persuaded that Mama would be delighted to find you here, Margot,' he said. 'She will be quite cast down to have been out of town.'

'But now that we are here,' Miss Mardyn purred, with a soft fluttering of her lashes, 'we might find a pleasant way to pass the time, Ashy...'

Adam raised his brows. 'Indeed we might, sweet. We could talk, and take tea and even...' he smiled at her '...plan a trip to Knaresborough!'

Miss Mardyn scowled unbecomingly. She did not take kindly to teasing.

'I had something so much more exciting in mind, Ashy!'

'Did you?' Adam murmured. 'I doubt that Seb would appreciate it, my love, if I took you up on that offer!'

'Sebastian will never know,' the diva replied. She sparkled at him. 'Please, Ashy. I am most curious. I beg you to indulge me. Lydia Trent says that you were *magnifique*—a stallion, *en effet*!'

'I am indebted to Miss Trent for her enthusiastic description,' Adam drawled. 'Alas, the answer is still no, my sweet. Sebastian Fleet might not know, but I would know that I had betrayed his friendship!'

'You men and your honour!' scoffed Miss Mardyn. 'Am I not worth it, Ashy?'

The answer, Adam reflected, was a decided 'no' but even he, renowned as he was for plain speaking, could hardly be so unchivalrous as to say so. He had been widowed for nine years and during those years he had sampled the favours of quite a few opera singers, actresses and dancers like Miss Trent, with the addition of several bored society ladies as well. Even so, he felt he could scarcely lay claim to the title of rake, for all that others awarded it to him. Despite Miss Trent's extravagant praise, sexual conquest was not even an activity that particularly interested him. There was something deplorably mechanical about the amorous liaisons of many of the *ton*, whereas he, having once experienced true love, was at heart a real romantic.

Six months before, the past had finally and unexpectedly caught up with him and put paid to any rakish tendencies for good. They had taken dinner at Joss Tallant's house that night, he, Seb Fleet and a number of other friends. Gradually the others had drifted away to the clubs and balls, leaving Joss and he partaking of a malt whisky and talking over times past and the time to come. At some point, late in the evening, Amy Tallant had come in, kissed her husband goodnight and warned him not to be too late to bed. From the look in Joss's eye, Adam had guessed that it would not be long at all until he was politely ejected from the house and Joss went hot foot to join his wife. And that was when it had happened. Adam had felt the most sudden and shocking jolt of jealousy and misery go through him like a sword thrust. It was not that he envied Joss his wife, serene and charming though Amy was. It was that for the first time in years he remembered the warmth and intimacy and pure pleasure of marriage, and he felt sick to think that he had had it and lost it all.

Joss had seen the stunned look in his eyes and, old friend that he was, had challenged him on it. They had ended up talking until the morning and finishing the bottle of whisky between them. Adam had sent Amy a huge bunch of flowers the following day with his apologies for keeping her husband from her side. But the ache of loss had not been alleviated and Adam knew he would never find what he was looking for in the scented bordellos of Covent Garden. He would not even try. The favours of Margot Mardyn, so eagerly sought by so many men, were not for him.

Miss Mardyn was aware that his attention had slipped from her. She wafted over to the window and stood twitching the drapes and peering out inquisitively.

'*Alors*, Ashy, it is that so-proper Englishman we met at the inn! I do so adore men like that—so prim, so correct. It makes me want to tear off all their clothes and shock them to the core!'

'I am sure that Lafoy would be delighted were you to do that to him,' Adam rejoined drily. 'Do leave that curtain twitching alone, my love. It is so bourgeois!'

But Miss Mardyn was enjoying herself too much to obey him. 'I do believe they must be your neighbours, Ashy. Oh, do come and look! The freakish cousin is with him. Have you ever seen anything so ugly as that bonnet?'

Adam felt a rush of irritation that had nothing to do with Miss Mardyn's constant chatter. Why he should feel so protective of Charles Lafoy's cousin he had no notion, but protective he was. When he had first seen Annis Wycherley at the inn he had thought her a drab creature of that class that were instantly recognisable as governesses and schoolmistresses, frumpish, proper, and dull. Then, when their eyes had met and he had seen the decided twinkle in hers, he had realised his mistake. He had watched her during the conversation and seen her covert amusement at both Margot's affectations and Lafoy's discomfort. It argued a certain sophistication of mind that intrigued him, hidden as it was behind the chaperon's dull exterior. Yet she had also seemed an innocent, so much so that she was not quite able to hide the fact that she was not indifferent to him. It had charmed him—and he had wanted to see her again.

He could see her now, walking under the fruit trees at the bottom of the garden. The garden of his own house sloped down from the terrace to a narrow lane and the wall of the neighbouring garden backed on to it. Under normal circumstance it was not an arrangement that would have met with his approval. He was a man who guarded his privacy jealously, and the Harrogate town houses were too close together to suit him. He preferred his estate at Eynhallow—remote, unspoilt and not overlooked.

Adam watched as Charles Lafoy gave his cousin his hand to help her back on to the path. He disliked Lafoy intensely for his part in helping Samuel Ingram fleece his brother-in-law. Whilst he was able to accept that the sinking of the *Northern Prince* was nothing more than devilish bad luck, Adam still bitterly resented that Ingram had persuaded Humphrey into a partnership in the first place. Humphrey Tilney had been a weak man, easily led by the thought of making a fortune. Instead he had ended up losing one and bequeathing to his wife the uncomfortable role of Ingram's debtor.

When Humphrey had died the previous year and Adam had discovered the extent of his debts, he had felt honour-bound to pay them off and rescue his sister from ignominy.

It had been a humiliating and infuriating episode. Ingram made no secret of his amusement at the deal and Adam hated him for it.

He could hardly blame Lady Wycherley for her cousin's sins, however. Finding out that she was a neighbour leant a curious attraction to what would otherwise have been a dull stay in Harrogate. Adam had originally intended only a short visit to his nearby estate at Eynhallow, but now he thought he might stay a little longer and find out about Annis Wycherley as well. It might prove interesting.

'Look!' La Mardyn was pointing at Annis now. 'What a shocking frump! I shudder, darling, positively shudder, to think that there are women like that in the world!'

'You are such a cat, Margot,' Adam said lazily. He smiled to himself as he saw that his fair companion was not sure whether to laugh or pout at his unflattering assessment of her character. Eventually she pouted.

'And you are so cruel, Ashy. I do believe that you are the rudest man in London.'

'Nonsense! There are plenty with manners far worse than mine. I merely speak as I find.'

'Then pray do not speak at all.' Miss Mardyn turned her shoulder. 'Or, if you must, tell me what you truly think of Lady Wycherley and her ugly bonnet.'

Adam sighed. He could see Annis walking slowly up the path and chatting to her cousin as she went. Certainly the black bombazine dress was unflattering, one might almost say disfiguring. It seemed to weigh her down and take the colour from her, leaving her drab and pale. On the other hand, he noticed that she had a slender figure that swayed

with unconscious elegance as she walked. As for the offend-
ing bonnet, it was fit only for destruction.

As he watched, Lady Wycherley loosened the ribbons of
the bonnet and, with one impatient gesture, flung it away
from her. It bowled across the grass and came to rest under
one of the trees, and Annis Wycherley laughed. Adam heard
her. The late afternoon sunlight fell on her face, upturned
to that of her cousin. She looked young and free and happy.

'Well, bless me,' Miss Mardyn said, forgetting her accent
for once and sounding both older and irredeemably English,
'look at her hair!'

Adam looked again. Then he stopped. And stared. Loose
from the bonnet, Annis Wycherley's long, blonde hair had
come cascading down around her shoulders in a tumble of
gold. It shone in the sun like a newly minted coin and framed
a heart-shaped face that suddenly looked piquant and pretty.

'I'll be damned!' Adam found that he was smiling. 'What
do you say now, Margot?'

'Why, I think that she must be an even greater fool to
hide such beauty,' Miss Mardyn said acerbically. She had
recovered her poise and now flounced away from the window. 'Such a thing is *incroyable*! She would make a pass-
able courtesan with hair like that and a good figure. Not as
attractive as me, perhaps, but all the same...'

'I rather think she disguises herself because she is a chaperon,' Adam said. He had never met Annis Wycherley in
London, but he remembered quite well that she had a reputation for being able to settle even the most unpromising of
girls. Now he could see that she had quite a lot of promise
herself. 'No one is going to employ her as a companion if
she outshines her charges!'

Miss Mardyn looked uncomprehending. '*Eh bien*, why be a chaperon if one can be a cyprian? I do not understand that, me!'

'No,' Adam murmured. 'I do not suppose that you do.'

He watched Annis Wycherley for a moment, then strolled back to his chair and picked up the paper again as Tranter, the butler, came into the room, accompanied by a footman with the tea tray. There was an item about Samuel Ingram buying the lease to the local turnpike and building new tollhouses on the Skipton road. One of them would be near Eynhallow...

'What do you think of the current state of the turnpike trusts, my dear?' he asked Miss Mardyn, as the teacups were handed around.

Miss Mardyn bent a charming smile on the dazzled butler, then turned back to her host. 'I have no opinion on it, Ashy darling. You should know better than to ask me. Politics, economics...pah! The whole business bores me. I never read the papers.' She looked at him thoughtfully. 'If I had realised that you were turning into such a dead bore yourself, I should have agreed to play Cheltenham rather than Harrogate this summer. I hear the shops are better!'

Adam smiled. 'I do apologise for being such poor company, my dear. Perhaps you will find other gentlemen who please you more. Mr Lafoy, for example.'

La Mardyn dismissed Charles Lafoy with a wave of one white hand. 'Oh, the conquest would be fun, but after that is over...*pouf*... I expect he is as dull as ditchwater. Are there no other eligible gentlemen in Harrogate, Ashy? I must amuse myself.'

'I see that the Earl and Countess of Glasgow are here to take the waters this season,' Adam said, consulting the paper, 'though I fear the Earl may be a little infirm for you, Margot, and not very plump in the pocket to compensate. There is Lord Boyles—Boyles by name and by nature, I believe, so again, a gloomy prospect. Ah! Sir Everard Doble. He is a young man, and not ill favoured, if memory serves me. He might be a possibility.'

'Sir Everard Doble...' Miss Mardyn repeated. 'Well, we shall see, Ashy. And how will you amuse yourself?'

Adam's gaze fell on the paper again. 'Oh, I have plenty to occupy me, Margot. Estate business will keep me quite busy, I fear...'

From the garden came the sound of feminine laughter, spontaneous and infectious. Adam's gaze narrowed. He resolved that he would definitely find out more about Annis Wycherley. She seemed a most uncommon chaperon.

'That sounds lamentably boring, darling,' Margot Mardyn said, yawning widely.

'On the contrary,' Adam said, with a smile. 'I have the feeling that my stay could be very interesting indeed.'

Chapter Two

Tickets for Miss Mardyn's performance proved to be the most sought-after items in Harrogate, and it was a whole fortnight before Charles Lafoy could book a box at the Theatre Royal. Thus it was that, on a Thursday evening two weeks later, Annis sat in the theatre and reflected that acting as chaperon to two high-spirited girls at the same time was utterly exhausting. The Misses Crossley had taken to Harrogate society like ducks to water, and every day had been packed with outings and every evening with parties and entertainments. Indeed, a trip to the theatre was a rare luxury, for it allowed Annis to keep an eye on both girls at once and sit down at the same time. On this particular evening she was further blessed, for she had the pleasure of her family's company as well. Charles, Sibella and Sibella's husband David had all accompanied them to the theatre that night.

'That was very...entertaining, was it not?' she said, joining in the applause as Margot Mardyn executed her final spin and ran gracefully from the stage. 'Miss Mardyn is really quite talented.'

Annis caught her cousin Sibella's gaze. Sibella was an indolent blonde who had been an accredited beauty in her youth and still had the fair Lafoy looks, blurring a little into comfortable plumpness now. Sibella glanced towards the men and rolled her eyes expressively.

'I hear that dancing is the least of Miss Mardyn's talents!' she said.

Annis laughed. The sight of the shapely Miss Mardyn in her gauzy finery had transfixed the male members of the audience. Miss Mardyn might not be a particularly skilful dancer or indeed an above average singer, but no one in the audience cared a whit for that, Annis thought. Harrogate had never seen anything quite like her and the whole auditorium was buzzing with excitement. Annis could not help wondering whether it had been a suitable entertainment for the Misses Crossley. Perhaps the more provocative of Miss Mardyn's dance movements had passed them by. She hoped so.

She consulted her theatre programme. 'I see that there is an interval now. Would you care to stretch your legs, girls?'

'No, thank you, Lady Wycherley,' Fanny Crossley said pertly. 'Lucy and I shall do very well where we are. We are... admiring these country fashions...'

The two girls dissolved into giggles and Annis sighed inwardly. She knew perfectly well that the Crossley girls were hanging over the edge of the box so that they could assess all the young gentlemen in the audience and be admired in return. Miss Fanny, attired in a fussy dress of yellow silk that Annis privately thought much too old for her, was making waspish observations. Miss Lucy was agreeing eagerly.

Miss Crossley and her echo, Annis thought. There was no malice in Lucy Crossley, for her elder sister had enough for two, but Lucy did so like to agree with everyone.

'Look at that strange gentleman there, Luce—' Miss Crossley was pointing with her fan into the pit. 'Why, he is as scruffy as a scarecrow and I do believe the candle wax has dripped on his bald head! How absurd he looks!' She stifled a giggle.

'Quite absurd,' Lucy echoed dutifully.

'That is the Marquis of Midlothian,' Annis said. 'He is a most highly respected gentleman.'

During the first two weeks of the Miss Crossleys' visit, when Annis had been getting their measure, she had corrected Fanny's bad manners and barbed remarks. Now, in the third week, she had realised that there was little point in trying to improve the elder Miss Crossley. Fanny was vulgar through and through, and, unlike her sister, was disinclined to accept guidance. Indeed, any attempt to improve Fanny's behaviour often had the reverse effect, for she was like a wilful small child. As a result, Annis often held her tongue and concentrated instead on the large sum of money that Sir Robert Crossley was paying her to chaperon his tiresome niece. She simply hoped that she would not be tempted to strangle the goose that laid the golden eggs before the egg actually materialised.

'A marquis!' Fanny looked put out, then brightened. 'Oh, but as it is an Irish title one cannot be surprised that he looks all to pieces. I hear the Irish aristocracy are a ramshackle bunch.'

'They may well be,' Annis said, 'but Midlothian is a Scottish title.'

Fanny turned her shoulder to Annis and leaned towards Lucy again. 'Look at the shocking quiz in that purple feathered turban,' she said, in a stage whisper. 'I do declare she is the greatest frump in creation!'

Since Annis herself was wearing dowager purple and a turban that night, it was easy to see at whom Fanny's shaft was aimed. Lucy flushed an embarrassed pink, cast Annis an agonised look and muttered something unintelligible. Annis smiled at her reassuringly. It took more than a few malicious words from a slip of a girl to discompose her. Lucy was more upset than she was.

Annis turned her attention to the crowds milling in the pit and aisles. Everybody who was anybody took a box, of course, but during the intervals they all went for a stroll and greeted their acquaintances. Some even went out onto the green in front of the theatre to get a breath of fresh air, for on a hot summer night the temperature inside could become stifling. The general scene in the auditorium was one of immense, cheerful disarray now. Gentlemen were leaning over the green rails of the gallery and accosting their friends below. Ladies preened and fluttered their fans. Annis, watching, felt a warm pleasure to be back home.

'I see that the Ashwicks have taken a box tonight,' Sibella said, leaning forward to speak in Annis's ear. 'It has been so awkward this year past, Annis, for although Lord Ashwick had mostly been in London, the rest of the family have stayed at Eynhallow and frequently come to Harrogate. I have scarcely known what to say to them, for it is such a small town one cannot avoid one's acquaintance. Yet everyone knows of the difficulties between the Ashwicks and Mr Ingram, and I have felt so uncomfortable because of Charles's involvement...' Her voice trailed away and she looked unhappily at Charles, who was chatting in an undertone to David at the back of the box.

Annis patted her hand comfortingly. Sibella, like Lucy Crossley, wished everyone to be happy, but sometimes it was simply not possible.

'Charles has a job to do—'

'I know.' Sibella gripped her hand. 'I know he does not have the funds to do anything but work for a living. Neither of us inherited anything from our father. Yet I do not like Charles's job, Annis. Particularly when it obliges me to be polite to Samuel Ingram and his wife! Speaking of which, I do believe that they are coming this way...'

Annis followed her gaze. It was many years since she had met Samuel Ingram, but he looked very much the same. He was a tall man, stout and with the prosperous air of consequence of the self-made merchant. His waistcoat was just a little too ornate with its gold embroidery and a large signet ring shone on his right hand. Beside him, Venetia Ingram glowed like a rare jewel. Annis watched as Ingram solicitously escorted his wife through the crowd, a hand in the small of her back. He shone with pride, like a preening turkey cock. There were those who said that Ingram's only weakness was his young wife. When it came to the fair sex, Annis knew that there was no fool like an old fool, for she had taken advantage of that fact herself, when finding suitors for some of her charges.

'Who is that lady over there, with the old man?' Fanny Crossley said, and in her voice Annis heard all the cruelty and envy of youth. 'She is so very beautiful...'

'That is Mrs Ingram,' Sibella said. She caught Annis's eye and grimaced. 'Mr Ingram is not so very old, Miss Crossley—'

'I expect that he must be rich, to be married to such an incomparable,' Lucy Crossley said wisely, and Annis sighed. She could not rebuke Lucy for so accurate an observation. Money marrying beauty was, after all, the way of the world in much the same way as money married a title.

'Come along now, girls,' Sibella said, with surprising firmness. 'It will do you good to have a little exercise. Did you not know that if you sit still all the time you will become fat and then what will the gentlemen think of you? We shall go down into the foyer for a few minutes. David, if you would be so good as to give me your arm, you may take Miss Lucy on your other side. Charles, I know you would be delighted to escort Miss Crossley.'

Annis threw her a grateful look. Sibella was indolent to a fault, but she was kind-hearted and she was also sensitive. Sibella knew that Annis found the Crossley girls very tiresome at times, but she had put herself out to take the girls out shopping and introduce them to other young ladies and chaperons who might share the burden a little. Annis had been extremely touched by her cousin's kindness for she knew that given a choice, neither Charles nor Sibella would have come near the Crossleys girls with a barge pole. Unfortunately, she herself could not be so choosy. Her livelihood depended on chaperoning the nieces, wards and daughters of cits and minor gentry and she counted herself fortunate that most of them, unlike Fanny Crossley, were pleasant company.

'Luce, it is Lieutenant Greaves and Lieutenant Norwood!' Fanny, having espied some red-coated gentlemen in the gallery, turned to grab her sister's hand. 'You remember—we met them yesterday at the Promenade Rooms!' She frowned slightly. 'I do hope they have not taken seats in the upper gallery. They only cost a shilling each!'

'Lieutenant Norwood!' Lucy's face was suddenly poppy red. 'Oh, let us go down. Quickly! We shall miss them else!'

The two girls scampered out of the box like a couple of puppies and Sibella subsided into her seat again. 'You shall never teach those girls how to go on, Annis,' she said, watching as the Crossley sisters rushed out into the pit and waved energetically at the gentlemen in the gallery. 'Miss Lucy has possibilities, but is led astray by that hoyden of a sister, and as for Miss Fanny, the best thing you can do is to promote the Doble match as quickly as possible and get rid of her. How does it progress?'

'Quite well, I think,' Annis said. She had been disappointed that Sir Everard Doble had not been able to join them at the theatre that night, for his courtship of Fanny was advancing, based on the need for a fortune on his part and the desire for a title on Fanny's.

'The problem with Fanny is that I fear she may go off at a tangent at any moment and ruin the whole plan. If she sees someone she likes better...' Annis looked over at the officers, who were strolling down from the gallery to greet the girls. 'Lieutenant Greaves looks very dashing in his regimentals, I know, but he has not two pennies to rub together and is a sadly unsteady character into the bargain. It is a shame that he is such a great friend to Barnaby Norwood, for I wish to encourage the one and discourage the other! Lieutenant Norwood has taken quite a fancy to Lucy, I think.' She started to her feet. 'You know, Sib, I had better go down and keep an eye on things. I do not trust Fanny at all.'

'I will go,' Sibella said resignedly, struggling up again. 'Come, David, you may escort me down and content yourself with the thought that you are doing Annis a splendid favour. You might as well come too, Charles, in case we need the extra authority!'

Once left on her own, Annis sat back and closed her eyes. She let the hum of the crowd wash over her. Normally she enjoyed the theatre, but tonight there were too many other things going on. She had the feeling that if she gave Fanny an inch, the little hoyden would take a mile.

She opened her eyes abruptly, feeling a prickle of awareness, a sudden conviction that someone was watching her. The crowd in the theatre was dissipating a little now and Annis caught a glimpse of Charles, talking to someone behind one of the tall ornamental pilasters. His companion moved slightly, and Annis saw that it was Della Tilney, Adam Ashwick's sister, a vivacious, dark-haired beauty who always looked supremely elegant. Annis frowned slightly. It seemed curious that Charles and Lady Tilney should be on such good terms when he worked for Ingram and she was the widow of the man Ingram had ruined...

A second later she forgot all about Della Tilney when she realised that Adam Ashwick was looking directly at her. He was leaning against a nearby pillar and he did not look away as she caught his gaze. Annis saw him incline his head slightly to acknowledge her then start moving towards her, cutting a path through the crowd with an easy authority. He did not take his eyes off her the whole time.

Annis felt a little flustered. She did not understand why Adam Ashwick should have this effect on her and it only made her more disturbed that he should do so. She fidgeted with her fan, smoothed her skirt and looked away in an attempt to calm herself, hoping that Lord Ashwick might in fact have some other destination in mind. Sibella and David had joined Fanny and Lieutenant Greaves now, breaking up their cosy tête-à-tête whilst leaving Lucy and Barnaby Norwood together. Annis smiled her appreciation at Sibella's tactics.

'And serve you right, you little minx!' she said aloud.

'Good evening, Lady Wycherley.' Adam Ashwick's voice came from behind her, smooth and betraying a hint of amusement. Annis jumped and spun around in her chair. So he *had* been intending to seek her out. The thought made her go quite hot all over.

'Lord Ashwick. How do you do?' She forced a polite smile. 'I do apologise. I was not... I did not... I was not addressing you.'

'I guessed as much.' There was a glimmer of a smile in Adam Ashwick's eyes. He gestured to the chair beside her. 'May I?'

'Oh, of course!'

Annis had assumed that he would not be staying and now felt surprise and another emotion she could not quite place. She did not look to be distinguished by Adam Ashwick's attention and to be so set her a little on edge. It was something to do with the speculative interest she saw in his eyes, an interest he made no effort to hide. When they had met at the inn she had felt a curious tug of affinity with him and it was the last thing that she had expected or wanted. She was accustomed to living without male companionship and after an unhappy early marriage had no intention of changing that state. Yet it was disconcerting that, for all her seven-and-twenty years and her relative experience, there was a man who could disturb her equilibrium.

'I hope that you are enjoying your return to Harrogate, Lady Wycherley,' Adam said lazily. 'I understand that it is several years since you were here?'

'Indeed it is, my lord.' Annis smiled. 'I shall always think of this as my home even though I have spent so much time away. It is pleasant to be back here. Do you find it so?'

Adam smiled back. 'I find Harrogate enjoyable enough for a short space of time.'

Although they were talking quite conventionally, Annis was acutely aware that Adam was watching her intently. It was as though he was making the first moves in a game—a game he showed all the signs of pursuing. Annis caught her breath at the thought.

She raised her brows coolly, determined that his appraisal should not discomfort her. 'You do not appreciate the Yorkshire countryside, my lord?'

'Oh, the countryside is extremely beautiful. It is the society of a small town that I find somewhat restrictive. The same company, the same balls and parties night after night...'

'Rather like London during the Season, in fact,' Annis said, with just a hint of asperity in her tone.

Adam laughed aloud. 'You put me neatly in my place, ma'am! Yes, I suppose the Season in London does bear a striking resemblance to the Season anywhere else, be it Brighton or Harrogate. It is simply on a grander scale—and I have my own friends and entertainments.'

'So I hear!' Annis said sweetly. She saw that he was not offended by her directness; on the contrary, the laughter lines deepened about his eyes and there was amusement in their grey depths. She imagined that it would be very difficult to discommode Adam Ashwick. He had far too much experience.

Annis shifted slightly in her seat, wishing that she did not feel quite so hot. It was a humid night and, with the candles, the heat was almost overpowering. Then there was her purple turban, which was making her head itch and ache. First the black bombazine and now the dowager purple, Annis thought ruefully. It was a very long time since she had wanted a man to see her in anything other than her drab chaperon's clothes. Now though, Adam Ashwick's cool grey gaze was fixed appraisingly on her face and Annis was vain enough to wish that she were appearing to slightly better advantage. It was a novel experience for her to want a man to admire her and it was contrary to every sensible precept that governed her actions.

'You are often in London, are you not, ma'am?' he asked. 'How comes it that we have never met there before?'

Annis gave him a very straight look. 'It is hardly surprising that we have not met, my lord. I believe that you do not attend débutante balls and I never attend events of any other sort.'

'Then that is one advantage that a small town confers,' Adam observed. 'Here we may all meet and mingle together. A decided benefit, Lady Wycherley, for otherwise I might never have met you.'

Annis laughed, refusing to be flattered. 'You are very apt with your compliments, my lord.'

The smile deepened in Adam's eyes. 'Do you imply that I am not sincere? I assure you that you are quite mistaken.'

Annis flicked him a look. His whole attention was focussed on her in a manner that was decidedly disconcerting. She looked away.

'Oh, men offer compliments when it suits their purpose! I could not have worked as a chaperon for so many years without realising that fact, my lord.'

Adam grimaced. 'You are a cynic, ma'am, as no doubt a chaperon should be. I expect it helps you sort the genuine suitors from the rakes when you are trying to make a match for your charges.' He leaned back in his chair and fixed her with a challenging look. 'Let us test your assertion. What is my purpose tonight?'

Annis frowned a little. 'I beg your pardon?'

'You said that men offer compliments when it suits their purpose. So what was my purpose in complimenting you?'

Annis looked away, vexed to realise that she was blushing. She had the feeling that she was straying towards dangerous ground here and was not going to be lured into offering a view. She gave Adam a reluctant smile.

'As to that, I have no notion.'

Adam shifted slightly. 'I think that you do. You suspect that I want something and am therefore making myself agreeable.'

Annis laughed. 'I apologise. I was judging on past experience, my lord. Most gentlemen try to charm the chaperon if they are interested in her charges. Perhaps you are looking to marry and are wanting an introduction to the Misses Crossley, Lord Ashwick?'

Adam kept his face straight. 'I thank you, but no. *They* do not interest me. You, on the other hand, Lady Wycherley, are a different matter.'

Annis kept her lips tightly closed and vowed to make no

more unwary comments that evening. Adam Ashwick was altogether too quick to take her up on them. And Adam, who evidently knew to a nicety when to leave matters in his dealings with the fair sex, smiled slightly and turned the subject.

'Did you enjoy Miss Mardyn's dancing tonight, ma'am? I am not entirely sure that Harrogate was quite ready for the experience.'

Annis smothered an unexpected smile. 'I found it very imaginative, my lord. I can see why Miss Mardyn is so popular.'

There was an answering smile lurking in Adam Ashwick's eyes as he took in all the things that Annis had carefully omitted to say.

'I believe that we have *The Death of Captain Cook* after the interval,' he said. 'That should be something of a contrast. Will it be melancholy, do you think?'

'Almost certainly,' Annis said cheerfully. 'If your taste runs to something more classical, my lord, you might wish to return next week, for I believe Mr Jefferson will be appearing in *Hamlet, Prince of Denmark*. Or is Shakespeare too sober for you?'

'On the contrary, I like a good tragedy,' Adam said easily. 'However, I am not entirely certain that I shall be here next week. I have business at Eynhallow, my estate towards Skipton, and shall be back and forth to Harrogate during the next month.'

'Of course,' Annis murmured. She had forgotten that the Ashwick estate bordered her own land at Starbeck. Starbeck could scarcely aspire to be called an estate, for it was too small, and almost entirely surrounded by its more powerful neighbours. There were the Ashwicks and then, of course, there was Samuel Ingram's property at Linforth.

'I understand that your cousin has property in the same direction,' Adam continued. 'That charming little house at Starbeck is his, is it not?'

Annis smiled slightly. 'Starbeck is mine, my lord,' she said, aware of the hint of pride that crept into her voice. 'Charles administers the property for me, but it belongs to my branch of the Lafoy family.'

For a second Adam looked surprised. 'Does it, indeed? But I thought—' He broke off, a hint of speculation in his eyes.

Annis raised her brows. 'What did you think, my lord?'

'Why, merely that Starbeck belonged to Mr Lafoy rather than yourself.' His voice dropped. 'It is pleasant to think that I am not entirely surrounded by hostile forces.'

Annis laughed, despite herself. 'I am sure that it cannot be as bad as that, my lord.'

'I assure you that it is.' Adam's gaze was resting thoughtfully on Samuel Ingram as he chatted to an acquaintance in the theatre pit. He turned back to Annis. 'You cannot have failed to hear of my…dispute with Mr Ingram, Lady Wycherley, so I do not scruple to mention it. May I hope that you are more sympathetically inclined than your cousin?'

Their eyes met and held. 'You will find that I am most independently inclined, my lord,' Annis said coolly. She had no time for Samuel Ingram, but she did not want Adam Ashwick casting her as an ally against Charles.

Adam nodded. 'I imagine that is the best I can hope for?'

'I believe so.'

'Then we understand one another.' Adam smiled at her.

'You seem a most unusual chaperon, if I may say so, Lady Wycherley.'

Annis gave him a cool look. 'From what perspective, my lord?'

'Well, most chaperons do not own their own estates. One has the impression that they have to work for a living, whereas you, Lady Wycherley...' Adam gave her a thoughtful look '...you give the impression of choosing your profession. As I said, it is unusual.'

Annis laughed. 'Oh, I have to earn my living, my lord! It is true that I enjoy my work most of the time, and that I prefer to be busy rather than to wither away as some kind of genteel poor relation, but—' she shrugged '—it is not truly a matter of choice.'

'I see.' Adam did not seem put out to discover her lack of funds but then, Annis thought, if he had ever seen Starbeck he would know that she was scarcely flush with money. 'One gets the strong impression that you value your independence, ma'am.'

Annis was a little startled. She had not been aware that she had given away so much about herself. Normally she was remarkably guarded in speaking of herself, particularly to strangers. Particularly to gentlemen of Adam Ashwick's reputation and experience, who saw far more than they were told.

'I value my independence almost above all things, my lord,' she said slowly. 'And being a chaperon is vastly superior to being a governess or schoolteacher, you know. I may choose when I work and whom I chaperon. I travel and meet people—' Annis broke off, thinking again that she was offering far too much personal information and wondering why she was telling him such a great deal. It did not help that

Adam was giving her his undivided attention, watching her animated face with a faint smile on his lips. She fell silent in something of a confusion.

'As I said, you are a most unusual chaperon,' he murmured.

Annis rallied. 'Do you know many chaperons in order to make such a comparison, my lord?'

'No, I concede that I do not know many at all.' Adam was watching her with a lazy amusement that made Annis's skin prickle. 'As you correctly surmised, ma'am, I move in vastly different circles.'

'I imagine that most chaperons can only be grateful for that, my lord,' Annis said tartly. 'One must be constantly vigilant for the safety of one's charges and a gentleman who is not interested in matrimony might be pursuing them for a wholly different purpose!'

Adam laughed. 'My dear Lady Wycherley, I am not interested in marrying your charges, but I equally uninterested in endangering the virtue of innocents! Only the most hardened of rakes would be so inclined!'

Annis nodded. 'I see. You make a distinction between yourself and such gentlemen, Lord Ashwick?'

Adam raised his brows. 'Certainly I do. I am no rake, although I see by your expression that you remain unconvinced, ma'am!'

Annis's lips twitched. 'I imagine that it matters little to you what I think, my lord. We shall not be having much conversation in the future.'

'How so?'

Annis gave him an old-fashioned look. 'Must I spell matters out, my lord? I am a very *proper* chaperon with two young ladies to look after. You are...' She paused.

'Yes? I am…what?'

'A gentleman that I would warn my charges to avoid. I am therefore unlikely to set the bad example of courting your company myself.'

Adam burst out laughing. 'My dear Lady Wycherley! You are harsh towards me. And most direct.'

'I beg your pardon.' Annis steadfastly held his gaze. 'I always feel that honesty helps one to avoid misunderstandings later.'

'I will grant you that, although I deplore your poor opinion of me, ma'am.' Adam was still smiling. 'Perhaps if we had met when we were younger you would not be so wary of me. Indeed, I am surprised that we did not meet, given that we shared a childhood in this very place. I remember your cousins well from my youth.'

Annis smiled. 'Everyone remembers Sibella, my lord.'

'Of course! The incomparable Sibella Lafoy! My brother Ned was heartbroken that she preferred David Granger to him. But where were you, Lady Wycherley?'

Annis looked away. 'I was not brought up near here, my lord. My father was in the Navy and my family travelled a great deal. I visited Starbeck but rarely.'

'I see. And when you were married? Did you live in London then, ma'am?'

'No.' For the life of her, Annis could not prevent a slight shiver. 'We resided in Lyme Regis.'

She turned away and made a business of looking for Lucy and Fanny in the crowds milling below. Both of them were firmly under Sibella's supervision, though Fanny was still casting enticing glances over her shoulder at Lieutenant

Greaves. Despite the fact that her attention was diverted, Annis could tell that Adam Ashwick was still watching her.

His gaze was steady and perceptive. After a moment he said gently, 'I am sorry. Have I said something wrong?'

Annis looked back at him, then quickly away. There was no coolness in those grey eyes now, only a searching look that was as disturbing as it was observant. She fidgeted with her fan.

'No, not at all. Of course not! It is just... I am sorry...' She floundered, hearing the arch brightness in her own tone. That would convince him of nothing other than the fact that she was disturbed by something. She sounded as socially inept as a schoolgirl. Taking a deep breath she looked him in the eye. 'I beg your pardon. It is simply that I do not talk about my marriage.'

'Why not? Were you very unhappy?' Adam's tone was soft.

Annis blinked. She was not accustomed to such plain speaking, especially with a man who was virtually a stranger. Yet something in his own directness called an answering candour from her.

'Yes, I was. Which is why I do not like to speak about it, sir.'

She thought that he would let the matter drop, but Adam touched the back of her hand lightly. 'I am sorry to hear it, ma'am. Forgive my impertinent questions. When I want to know something I tend to be blunt.'

Annis forced a smile. 'Please do not apologise, my lord.' She frowned a little. 'I am simply uncertain of how we come to be speaking on matters of such intimacy when we are barely acquainted.'

Adam smiled at her. Annis watched the lines deepen about his eyes again and felt a strange pang deep inside her.

'Natural affinity, I suppose,' he said softly. He touched her hand again, the lightest of touches. "I shall always be happy to speak with you on any matter you choose, Lady Wycherley.'

'Annis!'

Annis tore her gaze away from Adam and swung round abruptly. Charles Lafoy had returned to the box and he looked to be in a very bad temper. Annis suspected that this was due in part to the Misses Crossley, who were chattering like a pair of magpies as Sibella ushered them back to their seats, but it was also indubitably the result of finding her deep in conversation with Adam Ashwick. To her own annoyance, she felt herself blush.

Adam got to his feet in unhurried fashion. There was a mocking glint in his eye. 'Evening, Lafoy. Granger, Mrs Granger, it is a pleasure to see you again...' He bowed to Sibella before turning back to Annis. There was a decided twinkle in that cool grey gaze now. 'I have enjoyed consorting with the enemy, ma'am. We must do it again some time...'

'Good night, my lord,' Annis said repressively.

Adam smiled at her and withdrew.

Sibella sighed, a little wistfully. 'Oh, he is as charming as they said he was...'

Charles slid into Adam's vacated seat. 'Annis, what the devil were you about, flirting with Ashwick of all people?'

Annis kept her own voice low. 'I am sure that one may greet an acquaintance without fear of censure, Charles. As you know, I never flirt.'

'Yes, but Ashwick!' Charles ran a hand through his fair hair. 'He is a loose fish. Gambling, drinking, women...'

'Show me a man who isn't,' Annis murmured. 'Or one who has not indulged at some point in his life.'

Charles looked disapproving. 'You might at least have some regard for my own situation, if nothing else! Ingram cannot approve—'

'Fortunately I do not have to be governed by Mr Ingram's approval.' Annis smoothed her skirts and threw her cousin a warning glance. 'You refine too much upon this, Charles. Lord Ashwick is a neighbour and was only doing the pretty. Now, the second act is about to start. May we call a truce?'

The rest of the show was quite spoilt for Annis, who hated to quarrel with either of her cousins. *The Death of Captain Cook* proved to be a melodramatic tale of tragedy that was ruined anyway by Fanny and Lucy Crossley chattering incessantly. Charles stared ahead with a frown on his handsome brow, completely ignoring the play. When Annis followed his gaze she saw that he was looking across at the Ashwick box, but he was looking not at Adam but rather at the serene countenance of Della Tilney, illuminated by the pale candlelight. When he noticed Annis's regard, Charles immediately looked away.

It was a subdued group that assembled in the foyer to take their coaches home. Fanny and Lucy Crossley were quite worn out with flirtation and gossip, Sibella, who was increasing, looked fatigued and leaned heavily on David's arm, and Charles was still preserving an abstracted silence. As Annis shepherded the girls up into the coach, she spotted a closed carriage pulling away from the side entrance to the theatre. The light from the coach lamps fell briefly on

Margot Mardyn's pretty little face before she twitched the curtain back into place. Annis felt flat and cross at the same time. No doubt Miss Mardyn was being spirited away to join Adam Ashwick somewhere. It was just like a man, Annis thought irritably, to be escorting his mother and sister out of the front door of the theatre whilst whisking his *chère amie* discreetly out of the back. It should not have mattered to her, but unfortunately she found that it did.

Chapter Three

The morrow brought an invitation for Fanny and Lucy to spend a couple of days with their friend, Clara Anstey, under the auspices of her mother, Sibella's bosom-bow Lady Anstey. Given this unexpected break from her chaperonage duties, Annis decided to borrow Charles's carriage and make the journey out into the Dales to visit Starbeck. She had every intention of spending a few weeks there once Fanny and Lucy were off her hands, for she had no engagements until she returned to London for the Little Season. However, an advance visit to Starbeck would prove doubly useful; Annis wanted to assess the state of the house before she discussed its future with Charles, and she also wished to see what would be needed to make the house habitable for her stay.

It promised to be a hot day. The wind had dropped and the sun was already high above the Washburn valley. The grey stone villages dozed in the sunshine and higher up, the heather clad moors shimmered in a heat haze.

They stopped at one of Samuel Ingram's new tollgates

on the Skipton road. At present it was simply a wooden hut and a chain across the road, but a group of men were working conspicuously hard on the construction of a neat stone house beside the road. Their factor, a bare-headed young man whose chestnut hair gleamed bright in the sunlight, was standing close by and keeping a wary eye on them. Annis recognised him as Samuel Ingram's agent at Linforth, Ellis Benson. Ingram tended to surround himself with the impecunious sons of the gentry, Annis thought wryly. Perhaps it was some manifestation of snobbery that he, a self-made man and son of a lighthouse-keeper, should employ those whose birth was so much better than his own.

Ellis saw her and his grim expression lightened in a smile as he lifted a hand in greeting. The tollkeeper came shuffling out of the hut to take their money and Annis leaned out of the window, recognising him as the former schoolmaster of Starbeck village.

'Mr Castle! How are you, sir?'

The tollkeeper raised one hand to shade his eyes from the sun. His parchment-grey face crinkled into genuine pleasure.

'Miss Annis! Well, I'll be... I am very well, ma'am. And you?'

Annis opened the carriage door and let the steps down. The sun felt hot on her face and she could feel the warmth of the road beneath her feet. She tilted the brim of her bonnet to shield her face, feeling grateful that today she had abandoned her chaperon's turbans for a straw hat and a light blue muslin gown.

'I am well, thank you, Mr Castle.' Annis shook hands with tollkeeper. 'I am back in Harrogate for the summer, you know, and shall be staying at Starbeck next month. But you...' Annis gestured to the tollhouse. 'What happened to the school, Mr Castle?'

A strange expression crossed the tollkeeper's face and for a moment Annis could have sworn it was guilt.

'I can't do both, Miss Annis. Besides, Mr Ingram pays me well to take the tolls for him. Nine shillings a week I'm making here.' He shuffled, turning back to the coachman. 'That's ninepence for a carriage and pair, if you please.'

There was a clatter of wheels on the track behind them and then a horse and cart drew up on the road beside the carriage. The carter and his mate jumped down and started to unhitch the horse from between the shaft. A richly pungent smell of dung filled the air. Mr Castle, who had been about to move the chain from across the road so that Annis' carriage could pass, gave an exclamation and hurried across to the cart.

'Now see here, Jem Marchant, you can't do that!'

The carter pushed his hat back from his brow and scratched his head. 'Do what, Mr Castle?'

'You can't unhitch the horse. Horse and cart is fivepence together.' Castle looked at the cart. 'Sixpence, as you've got narrow wheels.'

'Horse and cart are only thruppence apart!' the carter returned triumphantly. 'None of us can afford to pay Mr Ingram's prices. Daylight robbery, so it is.'

The aroma of manure was almost enough to make Annis scramble back into the carriage and put the window up, but she suddenly caught sight of what looked like a pile of bricks hidden beneath the manure and leaned over for a closer look. The carter's accomplice gave her a wink and shovelled some more dung over to hide it. Castle walked around the back of the cart and looked suspiciously at the load.

'What've you got here?'

'What does it look like?' The carter started to lead the horse towards the tollgate, tipping his hat to Annis as he went. 'Mornin', ma'am.'

'Good morning,' Annis returned. A small crowd of villagers was gathering now to see what was going on, appearing from the fields and lanes as though drawn by some mysterious silent message. A few came running up the path from Eynhallow village to see what was happening, whilst the farm workers abandoned their tools and hastened over to the tollbooth. It seemed to Annis as though they were scenting trouble and had come to watch.

The workmen, meanwhile, were leaning on their spades, the carter's mate was grinning, hands on hips, and Ellis Benson looked as though he thought he should intervene to support the tollkeeper, but really did not want to get involved. The carter unhooked the chain from across the road and urged the horse through.

'Tell you what, Harry Castle, you've made yourselves no friends taking coin from that Ingram. Bloody thief, that man is.'

Castle was sweating, the beads of perspiration running down his face.

'I'm only trying to make an honest shilling from an honest day's work, unlike you, Jem Marchant! What you got under that manure, then? Something you should be paying for, I'll warrant!'

'Why don't you look then, nosy?' The carter's mate stuck his chest out aggressively. 'Don't like to get your hands dirty, do you?' He spat out the straw he was chewing with deliberate insult in the direction of the builders. 'Incomers!' he said with disgust. 'Ingram 'as to bring men in and pay them over the odds to do his dirty work for 'im.'

A growl went through the ranks of the assembled workmen. Despite the hot sunlight the atmosphere seemed suddenly chill. The workmen were shuffling and looking as though they would like to use their spades on the carter and his mate, and only a sharp word from Benson held them back. The villagers were also angry, swaying like corn with the wind coming up. Annis realised that at any moment the whole situation could go up like a tinderbox.

She backed towards the carriage, wishing now that she had not got down in the first place. The movement drew the attention of the carter's burly mate.

'Ain't that Mr Lafoy's carriage?' He looked at Annis with sudden suspicion. 'They're all 'ere today, ain't they? All Ingram's vultures.' He took a menacing step towards Annis.

'Now just a minute,' Castle said, the sweat dripping off his chin as he looked anxiously from Annis to the crowd, 'this is Lady Wycherley from Starbeck, and no enemy of yourn. She may be a Lafoy, but she's got nothing to do with Ingram.'

It was enough to give the carter's mate pause. He tugged his forelock a little bashfully. 'Beg pardon, ma'am. Dare say you cannot help being Mr Lafoy's cousin.'

'Not really,' Annis said. 'It was something I was born with.'

The carter tied his horse to a fence post and came bustling up. He thrust his face close to Annis's own. 'All the same, ma'am, you tell that Mr Lafoy that we don't like turncoats up here in the valley. If he shows his face around here, he'll be sorry—'

Ellis Benson started forward, obliged to intervene at last. 'How dare you threaten Lady Wycherley, man—'

It was the spark that set light to the tinder. Within a second it seemed to Annis that the fists were flying as the villagers pelted Ingram's workmen with stones and the carter and his mate set about Benson and Castle with gusto. Annis sidestepped the carter's wildly swinging right fist and tried to gain the shelter of the carriage, but just as she reached it a stone hit the Lafoy crest on the bodywork beside her head and splintered into pieces. Annis felt a sharp sting along her cheekbone and put up a hand in astonishment. Her fingers came away with blood on them.

There was a drumming of hooves on the road and the dust swirled up. Annis spun around. An arm went about her waist, scooping her off her feet, and the next moment she was on the saddlebow of a huge bay stallion, whose rider brought the dancing creature sharply under control with a single flick of the reins. The whole experience, so quick and so sudden, literally took her breath away; looking down from what seemed a great height, she realised that it had had a similar effect on the carter and his mate. Both had dropped their fists and were gaping up at her rescuer as though the hand of God had intervened.

'What the *devil* is going on here?' Adam Ashwick's incisive tones cut across the fight and brought all the men there to their senses. They fell apart from each other, panting heavily, hanging their heads, dropping the stones and shovels that had served them as weapons. Castle put up his sleeve to staunch the blood running from a cut on his forehead. Benson, who seemed to have had the best of the fight owing to a promising amateur career in pugilism, straightened up and pushed the hair back from his forehead.

'Lord Ashwick!'

'Benson.' Adam's tone was menacing. 'I do not believe that your employer pays you to come to fisticuffs on the king's highway?'

Benson's glance turned to Annis. 'I beg your pardon, Lord Ashwick. I was attempting to defend Lady Wycherley.'

'Very commendable of you, Benson.' There was amusement now in Adam Ashwick's tone. 'You may safely leave Lady Wycherley's defence to me now.'

Annis felt his breath stir her hair. She tried to turn to look at him, but he was holding her too tight and too close, with one arm still about her waist and the other holding the reins, and effectively trapping her in front of him. His chest was hard against her back and Annis could feel the beat of his heart. She kept very still.

'Yes, my lord.' Benson sketched a bow to Annis and turned away to marshal his workmen, and Adam reined in the chestnut stallion, which was tossing its head skittishly at the crowd. He raised his voice again.

'Get back to work, all of you! Don't you have better things to do than stand around here causing trouble?'

'No, my lord!' someone shouted. 'This is as good as a play, and cheaper!'

There was a rumble of laughter. The tension was dissipating now and the crowd started to chatter and melt away. Annis felt Adam's arms relax a little about her, but he showed no signs of letting her go. He looked down at the hapless carter and his mate.

'As for you, Marchant, and you, Pierce, I should haul you before the magistrates for breach of the peace!'

The carter looked sheepish. 'No harm done, m'lord. Apologies, my lady. We never meant to hurt you.'

'Pay your toll and get going,' Adam said abruptly. He turned his head and spoke in Annis's ear.

'And now, Lady Wycherley, what the deuce are you doing here?'

Annis turned in his arms and found that his face was very close to hers. There was a frown between his brows and his gaze was very stern. At such close quarters Annis could see his features in perfect detail. His eyes, so cool and grey, were fringed by thick black lashes. There was a crease down one cheek that deepened when he smiled. His skin had a golden sheen and there was a trace of stubble darkening his jaw and chin. It felt odd to be so close to him. Odd in an entirely pleasurable way. Annis felt warm and a little light-headed. Her body softened almost imperceptibly against Adam's and, as his arms tightened about her again, she saw a flash of desire mirrored in his eyes, hot, sudden, shocking.

'What are you doing here?' Adam repeated, very softly.

Annis straightened up hastily.

'I was paying my toll, my lord,' she said acerbically. 'As one does.'

Adam's gaze went from her flushed face to the carriage, and back again. 'You are here alone?'

Annis was starting to feel guilty as well as flustered. It made her more annoyed. 'No. I am not alone. I have my coachman and groom.'

'Lafoy's coachman—and Lafoy's coach.'

Annis sighed sharply. 'As you see, my lord. Would you let me down, if you please? Whilst I appreciate your intervention, I should like to continue to Starbeck now.'

Adam shook his head. 'Presently. I would like to speak with you first, if you please.'

Annis opened her eyes wide. 'Here?'

'Why not?' Adam gave her a crooked smile. 'I find I rather like…our current situation.'

Annis was not in a position to argue. Adam drew rein alongside the coach and leaned across to address the shaken coachman.

'Drive up to the first crossroads. It leads to Eynhallow and you should have no trouble there. I shall bring Lady Wycherley along in a moment.' He pulled the horse back and raised his whip in salutation as the coach lurched ahead of them, following the cart up the track. Then he tossed a coin to the tollkeeper and swung down from the saddle, holding his arms out to help Annis dismount.

Annis was both disconcerted and annoyed that she had no other choice but to accept his aid. It was a long way down to the ground and she had no desire to turn her ankle by trying to jump. She placed her hands lightly on Adam's shoulders and slid down, feeling his arms close about her again to steady her. For a second his cheek brushed hers, his dark hair soft against her skin, then he stepped back and released her gently.

'You are importunate, my lord,' Annis snapped, thoroughly ruffled now, 'both in the way you…you picked me up and the way you set me down!'

Adam raised a quizzical brow. He looped the horse's reins over his arm. 'I beg your pardon if I disturbed you, Lady Wycherley.'

Annis turned slightly away and smoothed her skirts down in self-conscious fashion. Adam had disturbed her—very much—but she did not want to admit it. After a moment she was able to regain her composure and fall into step with him on the sun-baked road. The echo of the carriage wheels was dying away up the track and the builders had returned to their work on the tollhouse, and there was no sound but for the birds in the trees and the faint bleating of the sheep in the fields.

'You are not too shaken, I hope, Lady Wycherley,' Adam asked, casting her a look of concern. 'I doubt that they would have hurt you—you simply became caught in the crossfire.'

'I know.' Annis put her fingers to her cheek again. The bleeding had stopped, but it felt a little sore. 'I suppose I was ungracious just now, my lord, and I should thank you for your prompt action. It was kind of you to come to my rescue.'

Adam smiled. Annis's errant heart did a little flip at the sight of it. 'It was the first time that I have swept a lady off her feet,' he said slowly.

The air between them seemed to sizzle with the heat of the day—and something else.

'I doubt that,' Annis said, trying to remain practical, 'and, as a chaperon, I must object to being swept.'

Adam raised one dark brow. 'Why is that? Do chaperons never experience any adventure, my lady?'

'Certainly not. It goes against the grain.'

Adam stepped closer. 'I should imagine that the most useful experience for a chaperon would be to undergo all the things that might happen to one of your charges, in order to be able to advise them what to do in each circumstance.'

Annis choked on a laugh. 'An outrageous suggestion, my lord!'

Adam shrugged. 'Tell me if you change your mind, Lady Wycherley.'

Annis started to walk again, her fingers straying to her cheek where the cut was feeling hot and itchy in the sunshine. She saw Adam glance at her and then he took her arm.

'Come into the shade,' he said abruptly. 'I want to have a look at that scratch on your cheek.'

Annis tried to pull away, feeling panic stir in her again. 'It is nothing—'

'Nevertheless, I would like to make sure.'

Adam drew her into the shade of a spreading oak tree, dropped the horse's reins and left the stallion grazing docilely on the bank. He turned to Annis, taking her chin in one hand and tilting her face up to the light. His gaze was intent, his touch was gentle and impersonal, but Annis nevertheless felt as though it was branding her. She tried not to jump away. No one had touched her for a very long time. No one had *ever* touched her with such tenderness.

'Hold still…' Adam's voice was barely above a murmur, his fingers as light as the stroke of a feather. 'There is a graze on your cheek, but I do not think it will leave a scar.'

'It is nothing.' Annis said again. Her voice was shaky. 'Please, my lord—'

Adam dropped his hand. His gaze fell to her lips. Suddenly the air between them, hot and heavy already, seemed even more heated.

Annis found that she was shaking. 'I must rejoin my carriage, my lord,' she whispered. 'I am expected at Starbeck—'

There was a pause, then Adam stepped back. 'Of course. It is only a little further up the road.'

There was a stiff silence between them as they scrambled back down on to the track. When Adam offered her his hand to help her down, Annis hesitated before taking it. Finally, when they were once more walking up towards the cross-roads, Annis spoke slowly.

'How is it, my lord, that it has become dangerous for me to travel alone in the countryside I have known all my life?'

Adam shrugged. 'These are unhappy times, my lady. Mr Ingram is tightening his grip on a populace already worn down by hunger and poverty. You saw the hostility to the imposition of the tolls just now. It is an even choice as to who is hated more here—Ingram for his greed and meanness or your cousin Charles Lafoy, who was one of them and has now become Ingram's creature.'

Annis's lips tightened. She felt indignation on Charles's behalf but she was afraid for him as well. She had had intimations of this in her letters from the Shepherd family at Starbeck, but this made it all much more real. And more serious.

'Is it truly so bad? I had not realised. I have read in the papers about the riot over the enclosure of Shawes Common and the arson attacks on Mr Ingram's property, but—' she frowned '—I had not imagined the hostility to be so strong.'

Adam cast her a look. 'Even in Harrogate it is sometimes easy to forget the feelings that run high out in the country-side. Perhaps your cousin does not yet realise how much he is disliked, or perhaps he feels that it is worth it for what Ingram must pay him.'

Annis flashed him a look of dislike. 'I do not believe you should make such an assumption, my lord! You can have no idea why Charles chooses to work for Mr Ingram.'

Adam gave her a cynical look. 'Do *you* know why he does? You are very loyal, Lady Wycherley, but perhaps that loyalty is misplaced. Unless I miss my guess, it will be put to the test all too soon.'

Annis stopped abruptly in the middle of the dusty road. 'Pray explain exactly what you mean by that, my lord!'

'With pleasure. I am speaking of Starbeck. It is common knowledge that Mr Ingram wants that property. Perhaps he has already made you an offer for it.' His searching gaze studied her indignant face. 'No? He will. He is waiting for Lafoy to do his dirty work for him.'

Annis raised her brows haughtily. 'And?'

'And Lafoy has already been preparing the ground. The reason that you have not had a permanent tenant at Starbeck for the past two years, Lady Wycherley, is that your cousin has deliberately avoided finding one. He wishes the house to fall down and for you to be unable to afford the repairs. That way Mr Ingram can step in—and make a lower offer.' Adam laughed. 'Did you not suspect any of this?'

'No!' Annis said hotly. She recovered herself. 'Nor do I believe you, sir. You are stirring up trouble because of your dislike for Mr Ingram.'

Adam shrugged easily. 'I cannot deny that I detest Ingram. That is beside the point, however. You will soon see that I am right.'

Annis glared at him from under the brim of her straw hat. 'You are an odious man, Lord Ashwick.'

'Why? Because I tell the truth?' Adam quirked a brow.

'No. You know what I mean. To set me against my cousin…'

Adam's expression became grimmer. 'I am sorry that you see it like that, Lady Wycherley.' He gestured to the carriage, drawn up ahead of them at the crossroads. 'Go to Starbeck! See for yourself.'

'I will!' Annis said. She was afraid that she sounded sulky, but could not quite help herself. She was very afraid that all the things Adam was saying might be true. He put his hand on her arm.

'But before you go, Lady Wycherley, just how odious do you think me?'

'I...oh...' Annis's gaze fell before his searching look. 'I beg your pardon, Lord Ashwick. I meant that what you said was odious, and not that you yourself...' She faltered. 'That is, I thought it unkind in you to speak as you did.'

'I see,' Adam said. He gave her a crooked smile. 'I suppose I should be grateful that you make a distinction.' He took her hand and pressed a kiss to the palm. 'Good day, Lady Wycherley.'

Aware that her face was now as red as a setting sun, Annis scrambled up into her carriage with absolutely no decorum. She tried to ignore Adam's hand outstretched to help her, but he outmanoeuvred her by the simple expedient of taking her elbow to help her up. He stood back and raised his hand in mocking farewell.

'Drive on!' Annis said crossly to the coachman, well aware that even as the coach turned the corner and Adam Ashwick was left behind, her palm still tingled with the imprint of his kiss.

Annis's journey home that evening was uneventful, which was fortunate as she had plenty to think about. Whenever she tried to concentrate on the shocking dilapidation of Starbeck, she found herself thinking instead of Adam Ashwick, and not of the Adam from whom she had parted in a temper, but the one who had held her with such heart-shaking tenderness. She was out of all patience with herself by the time she reached Church Row and was glad to partake of a solitary supper. She had just finished the meal when there was a knock at the door.

'Your cousin is here,' Mrs Hardcastle announced, coming into the dining room and wiping her hands on her apron. The housekeeper had been with the Lafoy family for years and, when Annis had returned to England, had gladly accepted a post in her household. Her husband, who had died some ten years previously, had been the family's coachman. These days Annis made do with a very small staff, of which Mrs Hardcastle was the undisputed matriarch. She was a tiny woman with bright dark eyes and a bosom encased in black that jutted like a shelf. It was unfortunate, Annis thought, that the bosom was what always drew the eye first. Plenty of gentlemen had been accused of 'sauce' for staring incredulously at Mrs Hardcastle's figure, when in fact it was difficult to look elsewhere.

'Powerful big bunch of flowers Mr Lafoy's got with 'im,' Mrs Hardcastle continued. She fixed Annis with a disapproving eye. 'He ain't come courting 'as he, Miss Annis?'

Annis put her book aside a little regretfully. She had been enjoying the peace. 'I doubt it, Hardy. Charles does not appear interested in the Misses Crossley and he has never shown any urge to marry me!'

Mrs Hardcastle sniffed. 'Well, I haven't seen a bouquet so large since Mrs Arbuthnot's funeral, Miss Annis. You bin reading books at the table again? T'ain't good for you, you know. You need a bit of company.'

'I like my own company,' Annis said, getting to her feet. 'Still, as Charles is here I suppose I had better see him. Please show him into the drawing-room, Hardy.'

When she went into the room, Charles was standing before the fireplace, a bunch of pink roses in one hand. He was fidgeting a little nervously with his neckcloth. When he saw Annis he looked simultaneously anxious and relieved, and came over to kiss her.

'Annis? You are well? Benson rode over this afternoon and told me what had happened at the tollhouse.'

'That was nice of him,' Annis said composedly. 'Are those flowers for me, Charles? How kind of you.'

'They are from Mr Ingram,' Charles said, holding the bouquet out to her a little awkwardly. 'He was most distressed to hear what had happened.'

'Please thank him from me.' Annis laid the flowers on the sideboard. 'It was an unpleasant experience, but I assure you I came to no harm.'

She sat down and, after a moment, Charles did the same, taking the chair opposite. He adopted such a concerned look that Annis was hard put to it not to laugh.

'Truly, Charles, I am very well. Lord Ashwick arrived before too much harm was done. I fear your carriage has suffered a few dents, however.'

'Never mind the carriage.' Charles sat forward. 'Ellis said that Ashwick had turned up. I suppose I should be grateful to him for rescuing you.' He sounded both dubious and unwilling. 'The trouble is that every time I hear of Ashwick's involvement in one of these situations I am convinced he has stirred up the trouble in the first place!'

Annis raised her brows. 'I think you may acquit him of

that, Charles. He was nowhere near the tollhouse when the altercation broke out. It was a carter called Marchant and his companion who started to goad the workmen.'

'Ellis told me,' Charles said glumly. 'Trouble is, Annis, there is more than one way of stirring rebellion. Ashwick's brother is the rector of Eynhallow, you know, and preaches fierily against exploitation.'

Annis sighed. 'If he is anything like Lord Ashwick, I imagine he is not subtle about it!'

Charles looked rather amused. 'I say, Annis, what has Ashwick done to upset you?'

'Oh, nothing,' Annis said quickly. She did not want to let her cousin know that it was Adam who had told her about Starbeck, for that did smack of making trouble. 'I find him somewhat brusque, that is all.'

Charles looked amused. 'I thought that you liked him.'

Annis gave him a straight stare. She was not about to admit to a partiality for Lord Ashwick, no matter that there was a grain of truth in Charles' words. 'Did you, Charles?'

Charles crossed his legs. 'Do not seek to gammon me, Annis! At the theatre the two of you looked more than cosy together.'

'As far as I am aware, Lord Ashwick is cosy with Miss Mardyn rather than anyone else.' Annis shifted a little. She knew that she was turning a little pink. 'Now, Charles, do not seek to distract me. I must speak with you about Starbeck.'

There was a knock and Mrs Hardcastle came in with a tray and two glasses of wine. She slapped it down on the sideboard.

'There you are, Mr Lafoy. Get that inside you. My nephew's best elderflower cordial, that is. Got yourself a wife yet, have you?'

She thrust a glass at Charles, who looked revolted for a second but manfully covered his lapse. 'Thank you, Hardy. No, I fear I have not yet found a lady willing to take me on.'

'You should ask your cousin to find you an heiress,' Mrs Hardcastle said, with a grim nod at Annis. 'Powerful good at settling these girls, Miss Annis is. Why, you should see her with these two little minxes we have now! As good as betrothed already, they are! Though why anyone would want to marry the elder girl—'

'Thank you, Hardy,' Annis said, a little desperately.

'Vulgar, vulgar, vulgar!' Mrs Hardcastle finished triumphantly. 'Excuse me, miss. I have to finish up in the scullery this evening. There's a mouse's nest in there. Quite a plague there was this last winter.'

'How on earth you cope with her I'll never know,' Charles said, as the door closed behind the housekeeper. 'I know she has been worked for the family for years, but surely it is time to pension her off?'

'Hardy would go into a decline if she were not busy all the time,' Annis said. 'She is like me in that respect, Charles. She would never forgive me if I told her we wanted to lose her services.'

'Have you asked her?' Charles enquired. 'She might be grateful to hang up her apron.' He took a sip of the wine and grimaced. 'Ugh! This is too sweet for me.'

'Pour it on the trailing ivy,' Annis instructed, waving towards the impressive collection of greenery that decorated a corner of the room. 'It thrives on the cordial! I have watered it often enough with mine.'

'So you wished to speak of Starbeck,' Charles said, when he had regained his seat. 'How did you find it, Annis?'

Annis looked him in the eye. 'It was shockingly bad, Charles. The roof leaks so much that one of the bedrooms has an impromptu indoor waterfall and the wood of the front door has swollen in the damp of the winter, then dried out in the summer and cracked across the frame. Several of the windows are broken and the place is infested with mice.' Annis made a hopeless gesture. 'And about it all is an air so tumbledown and neglected that I think it would take a fortune to put to rights. You know as well as I that I do not possess such a fortune.'

Charles was looking tired. He ran a hand through his fair hair. 'I have tried, Annis. The money you have sent me has all been passed to Tom Shepard to spend on the upkeep of the home farm. There is simply not enough to go round.'

'He told me.' Annis passed her cousin a glass of brandy from the decanter. 'He said that there were insufficient funds and that you had too little time to spend there.'

Charles flushed guiltily. 'It is true that I have been very busy of late. My work for Ingram...' He shrugged expressively.

'Tom was telling me that there has been a poor harvest these two years past and a bad winter this year. People are barely surviving, Charles.'

Charles shifted, leaning forward. 'Annis, I know you are opposed to selling, but for the sake of the estate you must consider it.'

Annis jumped to her feet. Her instinctive reaction was to refuse. 'No!' She swung around. 'Charles, one of the reasons that Starbeck is in such a parlous state is that there has been no permanent tenant for over two years.' She hesitated. 'Have you tried—truly tried—to find one for me?'

There was a moment when her cousin looked her in the eye and she was convinced he was going to tell her the truth. Adam's words rang in her ears: *The reason that you have not had a permanent tenant at Starbeck for the past two years, Lady Wycherley, is that your cousin has deliberately avoided finding one. He wishes the house to fall down and for you to be unable to afford the repairs. That way Mr Ingram can step in...*

Then Charles looked away and fidgeted with his empty brandy glass.

'Annis...' His tone was reasonable. 'Of course I tried...'

'I see.' Annis felt a chill. 'Yet you found no one.'

'It is not all bad news,' Charles said encouragingly. 'Mr Ingram would be interested in buying Starbeck from you, Annis.'

Annis glared at him. 'I am sure that he would, Charles.'

Charles got to his feet. 'I must go. Please think about Ingram's offer, Annis. It would solve your difficulties.' He came across to kiss her cheek and it was only by an effort of will that Annis did not pull away.

'Goodnight, Charles,' she said tightly.

After her cousin had gone, Annis sat by the window and looked out over the twilit garden. She could not bear to sell Starbeck. It would be like selling a part of her independence. As for Charles, for all his denials, she did not trust him. It had all happened just as Adam Ashwick had predicted.

Annis found that she was looking across to the houses opposite, where the lights burned in the house Adam had taken. She wondered if he had returned to Harrogate that afternoon or whether he had stayed at Eynhallow. Then she wondered when she would see him again, and then wondered *why* she was wondering! Finally, in a burst of irritation, she twitched the curtains closed and went up to bed, to dream, blissfully, about being swept off her feet.

Chapter Four

Fanny and Lucy Crossley returned the following day, full of chatter and excitement about their stay with the Anstey family. There was a ball that night at the Granby, and on the following morning, Lucy vouchsafed that Lieutenant Norwood had suggested a carriage outing to the River Nidd at Howden.

'It is not very far and should prove a pleasant trip for a summer day,' she begged, when Annis expressed reservations about the plan. 'Oh, *please*, Lady Wycherley, do let us go!'

Annis was torn. On the one hand she had seen the growing regard between Lucy and Barnaby Norwood and wished to encourage it, Mr Norwood being a most eligible young man. On the other hand, Lieutenant Norwood's best friend was the dashing Lieutenant Greaves, and the last thing that Annis wanted was to throw Fanny and Greaves together. In the end, unable to resist the mixture of hope and pleading in Lucy's eyes, Annis agreed, consoling herself with the thought that she would be able to keep a close eye on Fanny and that Sir Everard Doble was also to be one of their party.

The young baronet arrived for the outing with a volume of poetry clasped under one arm and a boater with coloured ribbons adorning his head, and Lucy and Fanny were hard put to it to conceal their mirth.

Mindful of the heat of the day, Annis had discarded her evening blacks for a muslin gown in pale pink, with a straw hat with matching ribbons and a pale pink parasol. When she first appeared, Lucy's eyes lit up like stars.

'Why, Lady Wycherley, you look famously pretty!'

Fanny screwed up her hard little face. 'You look too young to be our chaperon,' she said disagreeably, and Annis, smiling widely, reflected that that was as close to a compliment as she was ever likely to get from Fanny.

It was a glorious day and the party was in high spirits as they set off. Lieutenants Norwood and Greaves kept up a flow of easy conversation with the girls, whilst Sir Everard sat reading his poetry and Annis looked out of the carriage window at the view. Howden was an attractive little village and there was a charming riverside path that ran along the bank under the dappled shadow of the willow trees. Fanny and Lucy chattered constantly, seemingly unimpressed by the natural beauty around them. Annis, having ensured that Fanny took Sir Everard's arm rather than that of Lieutenant Greaves, was content to stroll along behind, enjoying the cool shade.

They reached a place where the bank opened out into a wide meadow. Lieutenant Greaves started to recite some poetry, in evident mockery of Sir Everard, who frowned at such levity and walked off on his own. The girls giggled. Annis turned away, irritated, and caught sight of a man standing beneath the weeping willows, gazing out across the water meadows to where the spire of a church cut the heat haze. At the sound of voices he turned impatiently and looked as though he was about to stride away. Then he checked. Annis, with a mixture of surprise and hastily repressed anticipation, recognised Adam Ashwick.

She hesitated. His stance was very much that of a person who wished to be left alone, but it seemed churlish to ignore him when it was obvious that they had recognised one another. After a moment she walked across to join him in the lee of the willows, and Adam sketched a slight bow.

'How do you do, Lady Wycherley?'

Annis could not tell from his tone whether he was pleased to see her but she thought that probably he was not. She suspected that he was annoyed that she had brought a group of chattering youngsters to spoil the peace.

She tilted her parasol to shadow her eyes. The reflection off the water was blinding.

'Good afternoon, Lord Ashwick. This is a beautiful spot.'

Adam Ashwick's lips twisted into a smile. 'It is indeed, Lady Wycherley. I often come her when I am looking for a little solitude.'

There was only one way to take that. Annis blushed and felt vexed, with him for his frankness and with herself for originally being pleased to see him when he so clearly wished to avoid company.

'Then I beg your pardon for spoiling your retreat, sir.'

She made to walk away, but Adam put a hand on her arm. 'Lady Wycherley. Forgive me, that was unconscionably clumsy of me. Will you not stay for a little?'

Annis hesitated. She had enough of an excuse to walk away if she wished, for Fanny and Lucy were now shrieking and running around in a most unladylike fashion. Lieutenant Greaves and Lieutenant Norwood were making impromptu boats from twigs and arranging a race down the river. Sir Everard stood a little apart, arms folded, looking disapproving. He had an unfortunate habit of looking down his nose, Annis thought. Even if he did not mean to appear superior, that was the effect it had. Within the light-hearted group he stood out like a sore thumb.

'Please,' Adam Ashwick said, persuasively, recalling her attention to him. 'If there is anyone I would care to share the view with, it is you, ma'am.'

The blood fizzed beneath Annis's skin as she blushed again under Adam's appreciative scrutiny. 'I am happy to rest a moment in the shade if I am not disturbing you, my lord,' she temporised. 'I may only be a moment, though.'

Adam gestured to a wooden seat set back a little from the water's edge. They sat down.

'I hope that you have recovered from your experience at the tollbooth the day before yesterday,' Adam said. 'I trust you took no lasting hurt?'

Annis laughed. 'I am in no danger of being overset by the experience, I thank you, my lord.'

A smile crept into Adam's eyes like sunlight on the water. 'I had not imagined that you would be, but it is conventional to ask. You do not strike me as a frail flower, Lady Wycherley.'

'Well, I should rather hope not. I could not make my own way in the world if I was forever wilting!'

Adam sat back a little and laid one arm along the back of the seat. Annis found she was strangely aware of his hand resting close to her shoulder. 'And you have made your own way for…how long, ma'am?'

'Since my husband died, my lord. Eight years, in fact.'

'You had no relatives to whom you might apply for help when you were widowed?'

'Oh, of course.' Annis made a slight gesture. 'Sibella and David offered me a home, as did Charles, but I did not wish to be a burden.' She smiled. 'Besides, I am a managing female, my lord. I could not bear to spend my time arranging flowers and taking tea when there are so many other things to do.'

'And you have Starbeck to support.'

'Indeed. I could not let Starbeck go.' Annis hesitated. 'It is my safe haven. Except—' she frowned '—it is not as sound as I would like it to be. It was quite a shock to see it two days ago.'

Adam nodded. 'I was afraid that you would find it so.' He looked at her very directly. 'I apologise if I offended you with my remarks about your cousin and Starbeck.'

Annis looked away. She felt hot and bothered, torn by several conflicting loyalties. 'Please do not apologise, my lord. I have already spoken to Charles.'

'And sorted matters out, I hope. It is a melancholy thing to be at odds with one's relatives when you are otherwise alone in the world.'

Annis felt a little pang inside her; for herself, for Charles, for the fact that Adam Ashwick understood how she felt even though she had never told him. 'It is indeed, sir. Sibella and Charles are all I have and I value them exceedingly.'

Adam nodded. For a moment they looked out across the river in silence.

'My late wife used to love this view,' Adam said abruptly.

'We would often walk along the river bank and stop here to rest. I had commissioned a painting of it for her, but she died before it was finished.'

A ripple of breeze ruffled the surface of the river and carried the shouts of the men and the excited calling of the girls to them. Annis could see Fanny hanging over the packhorse bridge to watch the progress of the race. Lieutenant Greaves was leaning over her shoulder, pointing and laughing. There was no sign of Sir Everard.

'I am sorry,' Annis said softly. 'I heard that you married young and were most attached to your wife.'

Adam gave her a lopsided smile. 'She was the light of my life for five years, Lady Wycherley,' he said softly.

There was a fierce ache in Annis's throat. 'I envy you, my lord.' She stood up abruptly. 'Please excuse me. I do not like to leave the young ladies for too long.'

Adam stood up too. He did not speak again, but Annis was very conscious of his gaze following her as she walked back across the meadow. There was a pain in her chest and she miserably acknowledged its cause. She was jealous; jealous that her own marriage had in no way lit up the world for anyone and, ignominiously, hotly envious of Adam's happy relationship with his wife. When she reached the bridge she looked back to where they had been sitting. She could not help herself. But Adam had gone.

Fanny and Lucy Crossley retired early that night, but Annis sat up with her book for a while, enjoying the solitude that only came to her after her charges had gone to bed. Finally, when she heard the clock strike a quarter past midnight, she put her book aside with a little sigh. She felt restless and knew that she was unlikely to sleep. Nevertheless her eyes were tired from peering at the print in the candle-light and the heat of the day was at last fading, and she knew she should go up to bed.

Annis blew out the candles, taking one with her into the hall, and went slowly up the stairs.

Fanny Crossley's bedroom door was ajar and a slight draught skittered along the landing, raising the corner of the rugs. Annis frowned. Fanny hated the cold and was always complaining that Harrogate was a miserable, chilly place, so it seemed odd that she should have her window open. Annis pushed the bedroom door a little wider and held the candle a little higher. The breeze from the window caught the flame and set it spluttering, sending dancing shadows across the bed. The empty bed.

During the previous month, Fanny had done plenty of things to try Annis's patience, but this was something else entirely. This was the worst thing that could happen to a chaperon. An empty bed, turned down for the night but pristine and unruffled. Open window, empty bed, missing débutante... The conclusion was inevitable. Fanny had either eloped or she had slipped out for some lovers' tryst.

Annis revised her first opinion. It was not as bad as it might be. After all, Lieutenant Greaves might have been *in* the room with Fanny, or even in the bed for that matter. Not that Annis had ever made such a shocking discovery, but she knew other chaperons that had. She checked the room again. The little minx had been so sure of herself that she had not even stuffed the bolster down the bed to make it look as though she was asleep. That was Fanny all over. Thought-less, arrogant, risking all for a light flirtation...

Annis berated herself for allowing the Misses Crossley two days under Lady Anstey's lenient guardianship—two days which Fanny had no doubt turned to her advantage. She walked across to the open window, setting the candle down on the nightstand. There was no note, which rather suggested that Fanny had not eloped. Annis crossed to the closet and quickly checked through the dresses hanging there. All appeared to be present and there was no suggestion that Fanny had packed a travelling bag. Annis gave a little sigh of relief. There were girls who would run away taking almost nothing with them, believing that love would conquer all, but Fanny Crossley was not such a débutante—at least, not unless her importunate lover had a title.

Annis sighed and leaned out of the window to see how Fanny might have escaped. There was no convenient ladder leaning against the wall and no drainpipe or clinging ivy to provide a foothold. Annis frowned in puzzlement. She had been in the drawing room all evening, but she had not heard Fanny slip downstairs. Yet it was evident that she had gone somewhere and Annis was convinced that Lieutenant Greaves was the key. Fanny wanted to make an advantageous marriage to a titled man, which was why she had fastened upon Everard Doble. But Sir Everard was dull and Fanny also wanted a little illicit excitement and a few stolen kisses. Hence the Lieutenant. Annis had always known that he would be trouble.

She latched the window. Fanny would probably be in the garden at the back of the house, clasped firmly in Lieutenant Greaves's strong arms beneath the summer moon. Annis closed the bedroom door behind her and slipped along the corridor to her own room to collect a cloak, hat and shoes.

On the way she paused to peep around Lucy Crossley's bedroom door. Lucy's outline was a solid lump in the bed, her breathing deep and even. Annis pulled the door closed with a soft click and tiptoed to the top of the stairs, down into the hall and out through the garden door into the night.

In the house that backed on to Annis Wycherley's own, a light still burned in Adam Ashwick's study. Adam and his younger brother Edward were sharing a bottle of brandy and a game of cards. The brothers looked very alike, with dark, watchful faces and thick dark hair, though there was no grey in Edward's. He was stockier than Adam, with less of the sportsman's muscular physique, but he had a readier smile.

'So many invitations, Ash,' Edward said with a grin, nodding towards the mantelpiece, which was groaning beneath a pile of embossed cards. 'Mama, Della and I are never so popular when you are out of town!'

Adam grunted, unimpressed. 'Am I supposed to feel flattered?'

'Well, I would,' Edward said frankly. 'People throwing their wine cellars and their daughters open to you.'

'An unpleasant thought. I fear I shall not be accepting either offer, for I have too much business to attend to.' Adam tossed his cards down on the table. 'You win, little brother!'

'That makes a change.' Edward gathered the cards up and shuffled them. 'I was surprised that you came back from Eynhallow so soon, Ash. Can Miss Mardyn be the draw?'

'Hardly.' Adam flashed him the ghost of a grin. Edward was one of the few who knew that Margot Mardyn was not and never had been his mistress. The rest of Harrogate speculated at will. 'I am sure there are many other gentlemen only too happy to dance attendance on the diva.'

'It is usually the one who gets away that the lady wants,' Edward said sagely.

Adam laughed aloud at that. 'Wise words from a vicar, Ned!'

'I am sure that I see more of life here in Harrogate than you do in London,' Edward returned.

'Very probably. But I still maintain that Miss Mardyn will not miss my attentions. Why, when we last spoke she had been driving with a certain Lieutenant Greaves who is, I understand, a cousin to Lord Farmoor and in line for a pretty title of his own. She had also taken the spa waters with Sir Everard Doble and had her eye on Charles Lafoy. Quite enough for one woman to be going on with, even one so famously energetic as Miss Mardyn.'

Edward spluttered into his brandy. 'I say, Ash!'

'Did you not see one of her admirers spiriting Miss Mardyn away from the theatre the other night?' Adam asked. 'I'll say this for Margot—she works fast!'

'I believe the whole town thought that that was your carriage,' Edward said.

'They may think what they will.' Adam shrugged. He was notoriously impervious to public opinion. 'It was an interesting evening,' he added drily. 'I thought it civil of Della to speak to Charles Lafoy when he is Ingram's man of business.'

'I thought so too.' Edward hesitated. 'I sometimes wondered—' He stopped.

'What?'

'Oh...' Edward's ruddy face flushed redder. 'Nothing. I

just wondered sometimes why Della has stayed in Harrogate after Humphrey died.'

Adam raised his brows. 'Surely because Eynhallow is her family home?'

'I suppose so.' Edward looked as though he was about to say something else, then thought better of it. 'She always enjoyed the bright lights of London when she was younger, but perhaps she don't care so much for that any more.'

'She has only been widowed twelve months,' Adam pointed out. 'Maybe when she is out of mourning she will choose to go back.'

Edward nodded. 'Poor Della. She was very young to be tied to a sickly wastrel.' He cast Adam a sideways glance. 'Much the same age as your Lady Wycherley, I suppose.'

'She is not *my* Lady Wycherley,' Adam said coolly, picking up his next hand of cards and studying them for a second. He found he was not concentrating. The idea of *his* Lady Wycherley seemed to have lodged in his brain with the tenacity of a burr. He looked up to find his brother's speculative grey gaze resting on him. 'Devil take it, Ned, what is it?'

'Nothing,' Edward said again. 'I thought that you seemed very cosy with Lady Wycherley at the theatre, that is all, and then you did mention that you rescued her from that mob at the tollhouse.'

Adam smiled. 'And I met her again today!'

'So?'

Adam sighed. 'So…what?'

'So, do you have an interest there, Ash? And must you be so deliberately obtuse?'

Adam grinned. 'I beg your pardon. I enjoy talking to Lady Wycherley and I do believe that it makes Lafoy nervous for his cousin to be speaking with the enemy. It is an excellent way to annoy him!'

Edward frowned. 'Are you using Lady Wycherley, Ash?'

Adam sobered. 'Certainly not. I like her.' He hesitated. 'In fact, I like her a great deal.'

Edward gave a low, soundless whistle. 'I see.'

'Hold fire, Ned! I am not suggesting that the banns should be read.' Adam sighed. 'Annis Wycherley has an aversion to marriage, so I understand. I formed the distinct impression that she holds her independence in high esteem. She is a most unusual female, to protect her liberty so zealously.'

'As she was married to Sir John Wycherley, I can understand her reluctance to remarry,' Edward said.

Adam raised a brow. 'Oh?'

'Wycherley was a dreadful old sea dog.' Edward shook his head. 'I don't believe he distinguished himself in any way in the navy, but he treated his wife like he treated his men, so I hear. With a rule of iron! I'm surprised the poor girl didn't mutiny!'

Adam pulled a face. If that was the case, it explained a great deal of Annis's aversion to the married state. He wondered why she had chosen to marry Sir John Wycherley in the first place. She had said that she had been widowed a long time, which meant that she must have married at a young age. Perhaps she had been seeking security. It was common enough...

'I thought that you said you went to Howden today,' Edward remarked. 'Was that where you met Lady Wycherley?'

'It was. I was walking down by the river where I used to go with Mary. Annis Wycherley arrived with those dreadful girls of hers, plus a couple of likely-looking young officers and that stick-in-the-mud Everard Doble.'

'I had heard that Doble was looking for a rich bride.' Edward looked cynical. 'Can he believe that Miss Crossley will grace Hansard Court?'

Adam laughed. 'Her fortune will certainly grace the place.' He took a swallow of his brandy, thinking back to the encounter with Annis Wycherley. There was something about her that drew him strongly and he had been thinking about her on and off for the rest of the day. Her candour and her innocence were both exceptionally attractive. They called forth an equal openness from him. He had been astounded to find himself speaking to her of his love for Mary, for he had seldom shared his feelings with anyone, least of all a mere acquaintance. Yet he had felt quite comfortable speaking to Annis.

Adam frowned. Innocence was not the first quality that one expected to find in a widowed chaperon, particularly a lady who had travelled as widely as Annis Wycherley and had also been her own mistress from a young age. If it came to that, innocence was not an attribute one came across very often at all, particularly not in the circles in which he moved. It was not that Annis Wycherley was naïve—far from it. There was simply some bright, open quality about her that attracted him. When he had seen her by the river in her pale pink muslin dress with the wind ruffling the ribbons of her straw hat…

'Ash? Ash, your concentration is wandering,' Edward chided. 'You have just discarded the Queen of diamonds, which I'll wager you need, and you have ignored my repeated question into the bargain!'

Adam grinned. 'I am sorry, Ned. What was it you were asking me?'

'Nothing of importance. I was merely enquiring whether you would be returning to Eynhallow within the next few days.' Edward picked up the brandy bottle and refilled their glasses.

'I imagine so.' Adam sighed, his mind turning from Annis to less pleasant thoughts. 'I need hardly tell you, Ned, that there is much work to be done there and, since paying off Humphrey's debt to Ingram, I have had precious little spare money to spend. Still, that does not excuse the greater neglect. I am sorry I have been such an absentee landlord these nine years past.'

Edward gave him a straight look. 'I understand your reasons, Ash. Do you feel you have put enough distance between yourself and the past now?'

Adam shifted uncomfortably. His life with Mary had been bound up in the hills and the moors of Yorkshire, and after she had died it had seemed that every view held a painful memory. London, with its impersonal bustle, had been a far easier place for him to live. He had neglected Eynhallow for nine long years because he had not wanted to be reminded of his wife. Yet today, when he had walked beside the river, though he had still felt an ache of memory, the pain was gone.

'I believe I have,' he said slowly.

Edward smiled in wordless satisfaction and raised his glass in a toast. 'Here is to Eynhallow, then!'

They drank the toast.

'And to the future,' Edward added.

Adam smiled. He thought again of Annis Wycherley. When he had first met her he had thought casually that it would be interesting to know her better. Since then he had seen her a handful of times, yet already his feelings were stronger. Already he wanted more. That required some serious thought.

He got to his feet and drew back the curtain, unlatching the long doors that led on to the terrace. They swung open with a gust of summer breeze. 'I need some fresh air before I go to bed. I will see you in the morning.'

'Good night, Ash,' Edward said, draining his brandy glass.

Adam stepped over the threshold and went out into the dark.

It was a clear July night. The wind was blowing down from the moors again, chasing rags of cloud across the full moon. The trees that lined the gardens of the town houses tossed their branches and cast long shadows in the moonlight.

Annis had searched the whole garden by the light of the moon and had found no sign of the amorous couple. She was a little surprised, for the walled gardens of the town houses provided excellent cover for a pair of lovers. She could scarcely imagine Fanny being so lost to propriety that she would hold an assignation in the street. The thought troubled her, for it pointed to the likelihood of the girl having eloped after all. She was about to go back inside the house and raise the alarm, when a scrap of white on the grass caught her attention.

It was a handkerchief and it lay by the back gate. Annis picked it up. It was crisp white cambric and it held a faint trace of the lavender water that Fanny habitually wore. Annis sighed and unfastened the gate. It unlatched with a soft click that was lost in the soughing of the wind. Outside, in the lane that ran between the gardens, the shadows were deeper and the light of the moon barely penetrated between the high walls. Annis hesitated, not because she was nervous, but because, in spite of the evidence of the handkerchief, it seemed so unlikely that Fanny would be out here. She was a girl who liked all the comfort that money could buy, and a fumbled tryst in a dark alleyway seemed quite out of character in Annis's opinion. She took a few steps down the lane, peering into the darkness, then decided to go back. Fanny was not here, and Annis was becoming quite out of patience with the whole business. When she finally caught up with the girl she would give her a piece of her mind. She turned abruptly, took a step forward into the dark, and quite unexpectedly collided with someone who had been standing almost directly behind her.

'Ooof!' The air was knocked out of Annis's body. This was definitely not Fanny's diminutive figure, nor indeed did it appear to be Lieutenant Greaves, who was a willowy gentleman who looked as though a puff of wind might blow him over and disarrange his dandyish finery. This man—and Annis was quite aware that it was a man—was large and decidedly more unyielding. She tried to take a step back to free herself, but he had both arms about her and she could not put any space between their bodies. She could see nothing of him in the darkness, but she could hear his breathing above the thud of her own heart and feel the warmth of his hands through the thickness of her cloak. Despite the darkness and the suddenness of her ambush, his touch conveyed reassurance and she felt herself start to relax. The smell of him, the mingled scent of brandy and sandalwood and masculinity, wrapped up in the cold fresh night air, was insidiously attractive. He felt familiar, which gave her a wholly inappropriate sense of intimacy.

This was dangerous. Annis knew that she had to act, before her traitorous body failed her completely. Sharply, and completely against her instincts, she raised her knee and felt it make a satisfyingly accurate contact with his groin.

Adam felt sick and cold and breathless. The whole encounter, so unexpected and so startling, had lasted only a few seconds. One minute he had been holding a woman in his arms—a woman he had already mysteriously managed to identify as Annis Wycherley—and the next moment she had released herself in the most efficient way imaginable. He wondered vaguely who on earth had taught her that trick.

'Lord Ashwick? Lord Ashwick! Are you injured at all?' Her urgent tones cut through his pain. Adam leaned one hand against the garden wall and tried to regain his breath. The wave of nausea was receding a little now but he still felt damnably uncomfortable. He raised his head.

'Of course I'm damn well injured, Lady Wycherley! I thought that was your intention?'

There was a silence.

'I am most dreadfully sorry,' Annis said. Adam grudgingly allowed that she did sound genuinely remorseful. 'I did not realise that it was you, Lord Ashwick. Had I done so, I would not have hurt you.'

There was a pause whilst Adam's better nature slowly asserted itself. 'You did the right thing,' he said, still grudging. He straightened up slowly. 'Why wait to be sure? By then it might be too late.'

'That is exactly what my papa used to say.' Annis sounded relieved. 'He told me not to hesitate.'

'You evidently took his advice to heart.' Adam still felt bruised and bad-tempered. 'You were precisely on target.'

'I am grateful that you have taken the matter so well, my lord.' Annis was briskly practical now. 'Of course you really should not have grabbed me so roughly in the first place, and then it would never have happened. It was entirely your own fault.'

Adam gritted his teeth. He knew that there was an element of truth in what she said, but he had been taken by surprise as much as she. 'Thank you. I shall remember not to grab you should the occasion arise again.' He took a deep breath. 'I apologise, Lady Wycherley. I believe I swore at you.'

'Your apology is accepted.' Now she sounded almost prim. 'After all, I suppose I dealt you quite an injury.'

'You did.'

There was silence but for the wind in the trees. A night coach rattled past on the cobbles of the street, then there was a deep quiet.

'How did you know that it was me? It is too dark here to see clearly.' There was an odd tone in Annis's voice, as though she was asking against her will. She sounded intrigued but also wary, as though she did not really want to know the answer. Adam thought that he knew why. Whatever she had claimed, she *had* recognised him in the dark, just as he had known her. She did not understand why and it troubled her, but even so she could not resist asking…

Adam hesitated. The truth was that it had been one part deduction and nine parts intuition. When he had first caught hold of her his senses had been swamped with information, despite the darkness. A strand of her hair had brushed his face and it was soft and smelled faintly of honey. Her breathing had been light and quick, feathering his cheek. Her body had felt soft and yielding beneath the velvet slipperiness of the cloak. All these thoughts had gone through his head in a split second and his senses had stirred in response to her nearness. Then her knee had made contact with his groin and any stirrings had died a swift death.

Until now. Now he felt stirred all over again, disturbed by her proximity, thrown off balance by her presence there in the dark with him. It was unexpected. And exciting.

'I recognised you as soon as I touched you, Lady Wycherley.' Adam smiled a little as he heard the quick, indrawn breath Annis could not hide. 'Having once held you in my arms, I was bound to recognise you again. You have a most deliciously curved shape—'

'Lord Ashwick!'

Adam laughed. 'Surely all chaperons are aware that men are all the same, Lady Wycherley?'

He heard Annis smother a laugh. 'Oh! I should be angry with you, but... Anyhow, I *have* warned my charges many a time about men like you!'

'Well, then...' Adam's voice dropped '...no doubt you know exactly how to deal with me, ma'am.'

'I doubt it.' Annis sounded a little breathless and Adam smiled to himself. 'I have no personal experience of fending off rakes, my lord.'

'No? Well, I am not a rake.'

'Indeed?' She sounded doubtful. Adam was charmed. The Annis Wycherley he had met before had been in control. Now she sounded younger and less sure of herself. It intrigued him that the proper chaperon should have a softer edge.

'I confess I had seen no evidence of your rakishness in the daylight, sir, but—'

'But?'

'One cannot be too careful. I do not know you well.'

'I assure you that I am utterly harmless.' Adam took her hand in his. His fingers, long and strong, interlocked with hers. 'You may remember that when we met at Eynhallow I suggested that all chaperons should have the relevant experience to advise their charges. Tell me, Lady Wycherley...' he spoke very softly '...if you were advising one of your young ladies on how to deal with this situation, what would you suggest?'

He heard Annis take a deep breath. 'Firstly I would tell her that she should step into the light, sir. The darkness is altogether too intimate.'

'Ah. It is indeed.'

'Then...' her voice faltered a little '...I would tell her to bid you a brisk goodnight.'

'That is eminently sensible advice.' Adam smiled. The longer they talked, the more acutely conscious he became of her physical proximity and he was certain that she felt the same way, in spite of her wariness. Something was holding her there in the darkness, talking to him. He was determined to prolong the encounter.

'Perhaps you might also have taught her the elements of self-defence? Nothing is so ruinous to the intentions of a potential rake than the blow you dealt me just now.'

'Oh...' He heard a breath of a laugh as Annis answered him. 'It is a useful if extreme strategy, my lord. It was all I could think of at the time. If I had had my pistol I might have shot you, of course.'

'That might also be a useful deterrent, I suppose. Except that you do not have it with you now.'

'Fortunately for you.'

Adam sighed. 'I am only sorry that you felt you needed to defend yourself against me in the first place. If you had already recognised me, you must have known that I would not have harmed you.'

There was an odd pause. The darkness was indeed creating an atmosphere of intimacy between them and Adam felt instinctively that Annis would be honest with him.

'I did not know it was you, Lord Ashwick. I thought perhaps it might be, although how I knew...' She sounded confused. 'I did not feel that I was in danger, but one cannot always trust to intuition.'

Adam took her hand and drew out of the shadows and into the moonlight by the garden gate. The pale silver light fell on her face. She looked absurdly young to him, despite her composure. All her features were as neat and precise as she was herself, except for her mouth, which was the most unconsciously sensual thing that he had ever seen. He found it was all he could do to stop himself kissing her. His pulse quickened. He brought his hand up to touch her hair, a fleeting touch, there one moment, gone the next. It felt soft and silky beneath his fingers. He wanted to tangle his hands in it and tilt her face up to his. Her eyes were dark and wide in the moonlight.

From their first meeting at the inn there had been something between them, some affinity. He remembered that encounter now—that moment when their eyes had met and she had looked hastily away. And whenever he met her there was the same pull of awareness, though he knew she had tried very hard to repress it. This sensation, though…this was something else entirely. Now he felt an attraction stronger than anything he had ever experienced. Perhaps it was the fact that they had bumped into each other in the dark and he had therefore had no preconceptions about chaperons, or frumpish dresses or her being Charles Lafoy's cousin. Perhaps it was her perfume, honey and cinnamon, teasing his senses. It brought to mind soft skin and tumbled sheets. He thought of the matchmaking matrons in *ton* society. Never in his life had he responded to a chaperon in the way he was reacting to Annis Wycherley now. He wanted to catch hold of her and crush her to him.

'You did not tell me why you were out here in the first place.' Adam spoke a little abruptly. He knew that he was going to have to let her go soon, but he did not want to do so. He saw something in her face change, as though she had suddenly remembered something very important. She pressed a hand to her mouth.

'Oh! I had forgot! I am out here because I am looking for someone.'

Adam raised his brows. 'One of your charges?'

'Yes…' Annis whisked through the garden gate, clearly recalled to a sense of duty. 'Please excuse me, my lord. I must go.'

Still she hesitated, standing under the spreading branches of the apple trees whilst the moonlight, filtering through the dancing leaves, patterned her in black and white. It was as though she could not quite tear herself away.

Adam put out a hand.

'Wait!'

She paused. 'My lord?'

'May I call upon you tomorrow?'

He saw her frown. 'I think not.' She hesitated, on the edge of flight. 'You are aware that I am a chaperon.'

'Yes. So?' It seemed irrelevant to him.

'So it would cause conjecture if you were to visit. People would judge me to be flighty, entertaining gentlemen callers. It is simply not appropriate.'

Adam was not inclined to give up so easily. 'I cannot see why it should be unsuitable for me to call,' he said. 'Surely you must have some time to yourself?'

Annis gave him a faint smile. 'Unfortunately not. A chaperon always needs to be vigilant. Which is why I am out here in the first place. Now, please excuse me. I really must go.'

'Wait.' This time Adam spoke in a murmur. One of her hands was resting on the top of the gate and now he put his hand over hers. Before she could divine his intention he leaned forward, drew her closer and kissed her very lightly on the mouth.

She felt sweet and soft, and, as soon as his lips touched hers, Adam wanted to pull her into his arms and kiss her until she was breathless. She seemed frozen with surprise, as though she had never been kissed before. Without pausing to think or, more importantly, to allow her to do so, he slid an arm about her waist, drawing her hard against the wooden panels of the gate, and kissed her again.

This kiss was deliberate and skilful. His lips teased hers, coaxing them apart, moving with persuasive insistence. He felt her yield and drew her closer still, cursing the cold solidity of the gate between them. This was far, far more intoxicating than he had ever imagined. As he felt her tentative response to him, desire exploded within him. He ran one hand into her hair and held her head still, plundering her mouth with his. Then he felt a shudder go through her and she stepped back from him, her hands against his chest, warding him off.

'No, please…' Her face was bemused in the moonlight, her breathing ragged. 'I cannot do this.'

He sought to recapture her hands. 'Why not?'

'Because…' her expression showed her uncertainty '…I do not do things like that.'

'You just did. And I dare swear that you enjoyed it.'

'I… Yes… No. That is nothing to the purpose.' She was regaining control. He wanted to kiss her until she lost it again.

'Why did you kiss me?' She sounded genuinely puzzled.

'Because I wanted to.' Adam shifted a little, releasing her. He felt bereft without the touch of her hand. 'And also because I was afraid that if I asked you first, you would say that it was inappropriate for a chaperon to be kissed.'

She laughed a little disbelievingly. 'Why, so it is, sir. I cannot quite believe that you did it.'

'Believe it. And that I would like to do it again.'

'Oh, no.' Now she took several decided steps back. 'I am no easy entertainment for a rake.'

'I hardly thought you so and I have told you I am no rake. I do not make a habit of kissing chaperons. In the main they are too old and unattractive.'

She laughed again. 'You are absurd, my lord. And unpardonably rude as well.'

'I know. Open the gate.'

'Certainly not.'

'Open the gate. Please, Annis.'

She hesitated visibly. A flash of sheer masculine triumph went through him as he saw the struggle she had with her own feelings and desires. He waited.

'No, I shall not.' Determination gave strength to her tone. 'I have a position to maintain, my lord, and I shall not compromise it further.'

It would be easy enough for him to open the gate himself—or to vault over it. She could not prevent him. They both knew it. The breeze whispered in the branches above them whilst they waited, her gaze holding his. His desire for her was simmering now, but Adam knew it could be rekindled at a second's notice. Yet something held him back. Passion, he was accustomed to, although perhaps not as intense a desire as this. Respect was something else. He admired Annis's strength of will and her determination to do the right thing, even as he thought of overriding her and taking what he wanted. Her resolve was part of her attraction. Passion…and respect. It was a powerful combination. He found he had to honour it.

'Goodnight then, my lady,' he said reluctantly. 'I shall look forward to seeing you again.'

'Goodnight, my lord.' Her tone had eased. Relief? Reluctance? Both, perhaps. 'I see you spoke the truth. You are not such a rake after all.' There was no challenge in her voice, only amusement.

He laughed ruefully. 'I told you I was no such thing. But… I would still like to see you again.'

He saw the shadow of her smile. 'I am persuaded that you will change your mind, my lord. Everything always looks different in the daylight. Goodnight.'

She disappeared up the path to the house and her footsteps died away. Adam was left to make his way back up his own garden and on to the terrace in thoughtful silence.

His wife, Mary, had died when he was only twenty-three and for a while, after the initial grief had dulled a little, he had briefly indulged in all the superficial hellraising of a rake on the town. His efforts to forget Mary had been hopeless. His liaisons had seemed tawdry and supremely unfulfilling, and every time, the cool, sweet memory of her had reasserted itself easily, reminding him that he had not buried his grief at all. Eventually he had joined the army, gone abroad, and fought his battles against the French rather than struggling against his demons at home.

He had been so young when he had fallen in love with Mary that he had never cultivated the hard, dismissive attitude to women that he saw reflected in so many of his contemporaries. To him it had been impossible to see his wife merely as an ornament to grace his home, the mother of his heirs. He had wanted her to be both of those things but they had also been intimately attuned, madly in love. Adam recognised now that it had been a first and very special love that he had had for Mary, but there was no reason to suppose that, had she lived, it would not have matured into something deeper and wiser.

Alas that it had not been meant to be. After he had returned from the Peninsula, he had hardly eschewed all women, but he had never met anyone that he wanted to marry. He had never even considered it. But in the nine years of his widowerhood he had never been moved to passion the way that Annis Wycherley had moved him tonight. He thought ruefully that he must have been without a woman for too long, to want someone so irrationally and so immediately. The only other person that he had ever been drawn to so quickly was Mary.

Annis Wycherley. Fair and sweet, not an innocent young girl and yet strangely untouched. He remembered once again her hesitancy, the way her lips had softened beneath his, warming in response. Such unpractised sweetness could not be feigned and just the memory of it made his body tighten in response.

She had taken a step back from him in more ways than one that night, distancing herself from the disconcerting affinity that had bound them together in the darkness. As a chaperon, he could understand her reserve, but it did not discourage him. He wanted Annis Wycherley and he knew that she was also attracted to him. He was determined to know her better.

Annis closed the garden door and locked it behind her. Just for a moment, out in the darkness, she had forgotten all about Fanny and the urgent need to find her, and that was unforgivable. Just for a moment, when Adam Ashwick had kissed her, she had forgotten that she was a chaperon.

She shivered slightly. She met plenty of eligible men in her work, but almost all of them were looking through her to see her charges and the fortunes that they brought with them. Annis could not blame them. In public she dressed with deliberate, self-effacing dullness and behaved with stultifying propriety. It would have been impossible for her to do anything else, for surely no one would employ a flighty duenna. Yet Adam Ashwick had not looked through her. He had seen her, even in the dark. Seen her, pursued her, almost caught

her. She could barely believe that she had let him kiss her.
Or that she had kissed him back.

'*I do not do things like that.*'

'*You just did. And I dare swear that you enjoyed it.*'

She had, too. No one had ever kissed her like that. In fact,
no one had really kissed her at all. Not with passion and intensity and a sweetness that had melted all her resistance. It
had taken her completely by surprise.

'*I cannot quite believe that you did it.*'

'*Believe it. And that I would like to do it again.*'

She did not doubt him. No false modesty, nor convention,
nor reserve could deny the fact. He had wanted to kiss her
and she had wanted him to do so, wanted it with an ache that
she could still feel deep within her.

Annis drew a deep breath. Such a situation was not part of
her plans at all. She had married young, for security. There
had been nothing of love about it. She certainly did not wish
to be ambushed by romance now, at the advanced age of
seven and twenty, when she had a living to make and an
estate to support and no intention of falling for a man who
could turn her untried emotions inside out.

She frowned a little. She had known that she was drawn
to Adam Ashwick, but she had severely underestimated the
extent of that attraction. The direct, complex and perplexing man that she had met in the daylight had given no hint
of this other deep and passionate side to his nature. Annis
shivered convulsively. These were dark and uncharted waters and she would do better to avoid them.

Except that she had already encouraged him. She knew
she had, seduced a little by the moonlight and the romance
and more than a little by Adam himself. He had surprised

in her a depth of passion she had not known existed. Now that she was alone again it felt like folly, but at the time it had been very sweet.

She hurried along the garden corridor. She had told Adam not to call and no doubt he would not put himself to the trouble of contradicting her. Which was just as well, for she was not at all sure what she could say to him if she were to see him again. It would be awkward. It might be embarrassing. Matters always looked different in the cold light of day, and this was one incident that was best left to moonlight and memory.

And now, she had to find Fanny.

A sliver of light from beneath the door of the servants' quarters caught Annis's eye as she went down the corridor to the hall. In these small town houses the servants' quarters were small, consisting only of a tiny office for the butler, the kitchen and a small dining room. Annis did not employ a butler, and had only four indoor servants—five if one included the maid who waited on Fanny and Lucy. All of them should have been abed by now.

Annis opened the door and went down the stairs. There was a furtive rustling sound, as though a large mouse was running wild in the kitchen. Flickering candlelight betrayed the litter of a large feast: breadcrumbs, chunks of cheese, slivers of ham. At the end of the table sat Fanny, her cheeks bulging, crumbs scattered down her nightdress. For the first time in the acquaintance, Annis thought that Fanny looked discommoded.

'Oh! Lady Wycherley! I was a little hungry...'

'So I see,' Annis said. She felt simultaneously vastly relieved and slightly irritated. 'Tidy up after yourself, Fanny, and go up to bed. You are like to have nightmares with all that cheese.'

'Yes, ma'am,' Fanny murmured submissively. Her sharp eyes took in Annis's outdoor clothes. 'Have you been out, ma'am?' she asked innocently.

'Only into the garden,' Annis said. 'I thought that I heard an intruder and went out to check that everything was secure.'

'How brave of you, ma'am!' Fanny said, eyes huge. 'That is just what I would expect of you. I would never venture out in the dark alone, of course, for my aunt, Lady Mary Crewe, says that it is not at all the done thing.' She stuffed the remaining piece of cheese into her mouth, adding as an afterthought, 'Was anyone out there?'

'No,' Annis said, turning away. 'There was no one at all.'

Chapter Five

Annis was accustomed to keeping her own counsel, but she was surprised to find how strong was the urge to confide when she had luncheon with Sibella the following day. Her cousin had a nose for gossip and an insatiable interest in all things romantic or matrimonial; indeed, Annis often thought that when Sibella was on a scent she was more tenacious than a terrier. It was with this in mind that she told her only the bare outline of her encounter with Adam Ashwick, leaving out all the bits that Sibella would be interested in. What would Sibella say if her notoriously down to earth cousin confessed to kissing a man who was almost a stranger and further, admitted that she had found him shockingly attractive? She would scent a romance and would be forever trying to throw Annis in Adam Ashwick's path, which would be both embarrassing and unhelpful. Annis loved Sibella, for she was warm and comfortable company, but she was not subtle.

'So,' Sibella said, when Annis had finished the tale, 'did you ask Lord Ashwick what he was doing lurking in the lane in the middle of the night?' She stirred another spoonful of sugar into her cup of chocolate. 'It seems a strange time to be taking the air. Do you think that he was waiting for Fanny or Lucy Crossley? Perhaps whilst Fanny was attending to her midnight feast, Lucy was intending to creep out?'

'I think it most unlikely, Sib.' Annis helped herself the last half scone. 'Lucy Crossley has a *tendre* for Barnaby Norwood, as you know, and unlike her sister she is unlikely to do anything foolish to put a potential match at risk. Barney is young and handsome, as well as being the younger son of Lord Norwood, and Lucy is head over ears in love with him.'

'Well, Lord Ashwick is young and handsome, if it comes to that.'

'I do not consider a man of two and thirty to be young,' Annis said. 'Nor is Lord Ashwick precisely handsome.'

Her cousin arched her perfectly plucked brows. 'Lord, you are very exacting! Where does youth end for you, Annis, and middle age begin?'

Annis laughed. She had had this discussion many times before with her cousin, who stubbornly refused to acknowledge that they were growing older. 'Oh, at six and twenty, I think. And you and I, my dear, are both on the shady side of that!'

Sibella looked down at her comfortably spreading figure, clothed today in a gown of blue-and-white striped sarcenet. 'Then I *like* being middle-aged!' She asserted. 'I have three delightful children, a doting husband and a comfortable home.'

'And all before you reach the age of thirty.'

'Hush!' Sibella shuddered. 'I will not have that word spoken in this house.'

'Why not?' Annis smiled maliciously. 'David is already thirty and looks very well upon it and Charles will be thirty in December and I myself will be thirty—'

'Stop!' Sibella held up her hand. 'You will not be thirty for at least two and a half years.'

'You look very well preserved for your age,' Annis said commiseratingly, a twinkle in her eye. 'No one would believe you a day over five and twenty, Sib!'

'Thank you.' Her cousin patted her blonde curls. 'Unlike you, Annis. Where did you get that atrocious dress? It puts years on you! I fear I shall not be going out in public with you if you affect such frightful fashions!'

'Fortunate that no one saw me arriving at your door, then,' Annis said, 'or you would lose your position as Harrogate's most fashionable hostess once and for all. You know that I almost always wear bombazine and a turban, Sib! What self-respecting chaperon would not?'

'Well, you look like a ape-leader! Surely you did not purchase that at Mr Frankland's shop?'

'I did.' Annis stroked the grey bombazine dress lovingly. 'He bought it in especially for me, you know. Apparently everyone else is wearing silk and muslin this summer.'

'Of course they are. It is cooler, for one thing.' Sibella put her head on one side and viewed her cousin with a jaundiced air. 'You know, Annis, you could be quite good looking if only you tried harder. You are lovely and slender—'

'I am considered too tall for a woman.'

'But you have a most elegant figure. If only you did not disguise your curves under those drab clothes—' Sibella broke off as Annis blushed bright red. 'Oh! Whatever have I said?'

'Nothing,' Annis said hastily, putting her plate down with a clatter. She remembered Adam's words: *'You have a most deliciously curved shape'* and she almost ended up spilling her tea as well, her hand shook so much.

Sibella was looking at her strangely. 'What is the matter, Annis? You look very red.'

'The heat!' Annis said hastily, fanning herself vigorously. 'I feel a little warm.'

'Well, I did warn you about the bombazine.' Sibella frowned. 'Where was I? Oh, yes, I was suggesting improvements to your appearance.'

'May we please change the subject, Sib?' Annis asked desperately.

'In a minute. Do you not wish for the benefit of my advice? Your hair is a very pretty blonde colour if only you would let it show—'

'It is unfashionably without curl,' Annis snapped. She pushed away the memory of Adam touching her hair in the moonlight, running his hands through it as he tilted her head up to kiss her. The whole encounter seemed extraordinary. She still could not quite believe it. Adam Ashwick had kissed her. She, Annis Wycherley, a widowed chaperon of seven and twenty, who did not have a romantic bone in her body. She drained her teacup and reached for the pot again. Tea was always efficacious in soothing ruffled sensibilities, so Mrs Hardcastle said.

'You have a beautiful complexion,' Sibella was saying, determined to continue with her appraisal.

Annis sighed. 'And freckles! That, as you know, is death to any pretensions to beauty. Now, may we end this litany?'

Sibella, an accredited beauty since her girlhood, sighed as

well. 'All I am saying is that if you did not dress as a dowd it would be a start.'

Annis had herself back in hand by now. 'If I did not dress as a dowd, as you put it, no one would send their wards and daughters to me to chaperon. Remember the fuss that time I went as a governess and did not have the sense to cover up my hair! One would have thought that a glimpse of blonde hair was enough to send a man into a love-struck daze!'

'Oh, it is,' Sibella said, smiling a little self-satisfied smile. 'I have always found it so.'

'Well, I have not—' Annis broke off, realising that this was not entirely true. Adam certainly seemed to have liked her hair. She wriggled a little uncomfortably on the sofa, wishing that she had never raised the subject of Fanny's jaunt the previous evening. It had also raised some other memories that had kept her awake long into the night.

Sibella was still looking at her oddly. 'Are you sure you are quite well, Annis? You seem strangely distracted today and not at all like your usual self. Perhaps your meeting with Lord Ashwick has disturbed you more than you make out.'

'It has nothing to do with Lord Ashwick,' Annis said quickly.

'I see. All the same, it must have been splendidly romantic to meet him out in the garden—in the dark.'

Annis swallowed hard. She had a strong urge to change the subject, but she knew that Sibella would view that as deeply suspicious. Her best option was to affect a cool and casual air, but she was not sure she could carry that off. Whatever else she felt, cool and casual was not it.

'Umm. I would not say that it was romantic. I was looking for Fanny, of course, and Lord Ashwick... Well...' Annis fidgeted slightly as she tried to think of something to say without giving herself away '...he was very pleasant...'

'Pleasant! Annis!' Sibella rolled her eyes. 'Half the ladies in Harrogate would have given their diamonds to be in your shoes last night and the only word you can come up with is pleasant!'

Annis looked defensive. 'What would you have me say? I suppose there are those who would reckon Lord Ashwick charming.'

'How half-hearted you sound!' Sibella's big blue eyes opened wide. 'The *York Herald* was far more fulsome in its comments.'

'Of course. Its publisher wishes to sell many papers and to have all the ladies swooning over Lord Ashwick must surely increase its circulation.'

'Lud, what a cynic you are, Annis!'

'I fear so.' Annis smiled. 'Experience breeds cynicism.'

Sibella tutted. 'What nonsense. I am sure Lord Ashwick is well worth swooning over.'

'If one is the swooning kind one could do worse, I suppose.'

'He has quite a reputation.'

Annis smiled. 'These London gentlemen always do. Some women find those sort of dark good looks unbearably attractive.'

'But not you?' Sibella gave Annis an arch look. 'At least you could have some sympathy with his situation. He has a tragic past.'

'Yes...' Annis thought of the time by the river when Adam had told her of his love for his wife. She felt a little low. The encounter in the garden had been romantic and passionate, but it seemed trivial in comparison to the devotion Adam had felt for Mary.

'I imagine Lord Ashwick's past will encourage many a young lady to think that she will be the one to help him love again!' she said, with deliberate flippancy. 'And how odiously mawkish would that be?'

'You do not have any finer feelings, do you, Annis?' Sibella was looking very irritated now. 'You are handed an opportunity that most right-thinking women would clamour for and what do you do—precisely nothing! I despair of you.'

'Next time that I meet Lord Ashwick in the dark I shall be sure to take your advice,' Annis said, getting to her feet. 'You are a blessing to any indigent chaperon in search of a lord!'

She tried to duck the cushion that her cousin threw with surprising energy and accuracy. 'Ouch! Sib, I did not deserve that.'

'You did,' her cousin asserted. She put out a hand and rang the bell for the maid. 'When do the Misses Crossley return? I could scarce believe my luck when you arrived unaccompanied today!'

'They are back tonight, after a visit to the theatre with the Ansteys. Miss Mardyn is not dancing tonight, I am glad to say. It is *The Forest of Hermanstadt*, which I understand to be a melodrama, so it should suit Fanny very well. Poor Clara Anstey, I doubt she will enjoy the company for all her mother pretends she does. Fanny makes her cry.'

'I am not surprised.' Sibella yawned. 'That child will be one of society's most spiteful, cattish creatures in a few years, Annis. Do you know, she told me that she thought I had quite good taste for a cit's wife! The little madam.'

Annis smothered a smile. 'Oh, dear, she is a dreadful girl.

Although I do think that comment merely lacked polish, Sib. Fanny needs more practice before she is truly malicious!'

Sibella sniffed. 'She is quite impertinent enough for me. Besides, David is not a cit! He is a gentleman.'

'How lucky you are. Many of us have to earn money to survive.'

Sibella shuddered. 'Oh, do not be so blunt about it, Annis!'

'Oh, Sib, do not be such a snob!' Annis laughed. 'Money makes the world go round, they say.'

'No, I am sure that that is love!' Sibella frowned.

Annis, quick to avoid a return to Sibella's favourite subject, made for the door. 'If you will excuse me, I shall have to run. Days without Fanny and Lucy are so precious and I am trying to squeeze so much into today.'

Sibella brightened. 'Do you go to the shops?'

'I do. To Gilbertson and Holmes for some new fabric to make an evening gown, and to Wilson's Library, of course.'

Sibella struggled to her feet. 'If you will but allow me fifteen minutes, I shall join you.' She saw the look on her cousin's face and said pleadingly, 'No, Annis, it will not take me an hour to get ready, I swear! Besides, we may take the carriage, which will be quicker. You will not be wasting any of your precious time.'

Annis sighed and gave in. 'Oh, very well. But I know you. You will be wanting to go to Robey's to buy that china ornament of the girl with the apple basket that we saw last week, and once you are in there you will spy something else to your taste...'

Sibella smiled happily. 'Oh, I do hope so. After all, Annis, I need to purchase some trifle to compensate me for being seen with you in that hideous bombazine!'

'You are such a good influence on me, Sib, that I feel I may end up buying poplin instead,' Annis said, as her cousin hurried out of the drawing room, calling for her maid as she went.

'Poplin?' Sibella said over her shoulder. 'For an evening gown? Dearest Annis, I shall not rest until you are arrayed in silk!'

'Did anyone call whilst I was out, Hardy?'

Annis, laden with a roll of muslin, three books from the circulating library and two week-old copies of the Leeds Mercury, which Hargrave's bookshop always let her have for free, entered the hall of her town house in Church Row and put her parcels down with a sigh of relief. Mrs Hardcastle promptly picked them up again, putting the books on a side table, the material at the bottom of the stairs and the papers under her arm to be taken into the drawing room.

'Mind what you do with those parcels. You know I cannot abide mess, Miss Annis.'

'I am sorry,' Annis said. She tried to sound casual. 'So, did anybody call, Hardy?'

'"Appen they might've done.' Mrs Hardcastle put her hands on her hips and watched as Annis drew off her spencer, gloves and bonnet. She took the spencer and laid it gently over the back of the hall chair. 'Were you expecting someone, Miss Annis?'

'No, not really,' Annis said. It would have been both troubling and pleasing of Adam Ashwick to pay his compliments in the daylight, but perhaps on balance she should prefer to forget the whole incident. 'I thought that Mrs Bartle might call,' she said hastily, seeing that Mrs Hardcastle's suspicious gaze was still upon her. 'She said something about a trip to the theatre next week.'

'Aye, well, she didn't pay a visit.'

'Oh. Well, never mind—'

'Lady Copthorne called,' Mrs Hardcastle said. 'She said that you had done a right good job on Miss Fanny and she wondered whether you would consider taking her Eustacia to London for the Little Season.' Mrs Hardcastle sniffed. 'I said as I'd ask you. Between you and me, Miss Annis, you'd do better to refuse.'

'Would I?' Annis looked intrigued. 'I would have expected you to encourage me to accept gainful employment for the autumn, Hardy.'

'Aye, well, if you thought Miss Fanny was bad, Miss Copthorne is worse,' Mrs Hardcastle said darkly. 'Don't say as I didn't warn you, Miss Annis!'

'I shall remember that,' Annis said meekly, thinking that it was a shame she could not always be choosy in her employment. Much of the money she had earned from chaperoning the Crossley girls was already earmarked, intended for improvements to Starbeck.

'A gentleman called,' Mrs Hardcastle added, as Annis started up the stairs. Annis paused, feeling a tickle of anticipation.

'Indeed? Which gentleman was that?'

'Mr Flitwick,' the housekeeper said. There was a twinkle in her berry black eyes. 'Said he needed to measure your foot again for those new winter boots you ordered.' She made it sound as though the cordwainer had suggested some unspeakable perversion. 'To my mind, Mr Flitwick is a bit too anxious to take your measurements, Miss Annis. 'Tis my belief he sees you as a most suitable wife for a prosperous merchant.'

Annis grimaced. 'Oh, dear. Hardy, surely you are teasing me? Mr Flitwick cannot wish to marry me!'

Mrs Hardcastle looked triumphant. 'He doesn't wish to now. I told 'im as you were too good for the likes of him!'

'Oh, Hardy, you didn't!' Annis looked horrified. 'The poor man! He was probably not interested in the first place and now he will be hopelessly embarrassed.' Another thought struck her. 'And I will never get my boots, for he will not speak to me again!'

'Gimson's make boots as well,' the housekeeper pointed out, 'and what's more, Mr Gimson is very happily married already.'

Annis sighed. Mrs Hardcastle had always protected her with the enthusiasm of a mother bear looking after a single cub, but sometimes that enthusiasm went a bit far.

'Thank you, Hardy,' she said. 'I shall bear that in mind when I choose my purchases in future.'

Mrs Hardcastle beamed. Annis ascended another three steps.

'A *second* gentleman called,' Mrs Hardcastle said. This time her tone suggested that Annis was a hussy to have so many gentlemen on a string.

Annis raised her brows. 'And was he good enough for me, Hardy?'

'Don't know about that.' Mrs Hardcastle frowned. 'Mebbe. Francis Ashwick's boy—mind those books, Miss Annis!'

The library books tumbled from Annis's hand and bounced down the stairs to land at Mrs Hardcastle's feet.

'Mess!' that lady mourned, bending creakily to pick them

up. Then, 'Thank you, Miss Annis,' as Annis ran back down the steps and put a hand under her elbow to help the housekeeper straighten up.

'This gentleman,' Annis persisted. 'Lord Ashwick, you said—'

'Aye?'

'What did he say when he heard that I was out?'

'Said that you'd told him not to call.'

Annis felt a little deflated. 'Yes, I did.'

'So I asked him,' Mrs Hardcastle said triumphantly, 'why he had bothered to call if you'd told him not.'

'And he said?'

'That it had been a pleasure to meet you in the moonlight and he wanted to pay his respects in the daylight.'

'Very pretty of him.' Annis smiled a little. 'One cannot fault his turn of phrase.'

'Handsome is as handsome does in my book,' Mrs Hardcastle sniffed. 'T'would be a very unusual gentleman who would be good enough for you, Miss Annis.'

Annis's shoulders slumped a little. 'I do not look to marry again, Hardy, truly I do not.'

Mrs Hardcastle patted her hand and passed the books over again. 'Don't blame you after that Sir John, love. Shockin' martinet, that man was. But not all men are like that.'

'I know.' Annis hesitated, a hand on the banister. 'It is just that I could not bear it again, Hardy—accounting for my every move, being allowed no liberty to read, or walk out on my own, or do any of the simple things that give me such pleasure—' She broke off. 'Excuse me. I think I shall go up and rest for a little.'

'What you need is a nice glass of elderflower cordial to

refresh you,' Mrs Hardcastle said comfortingly. 'I'll bring it up for you. And don't worry about that Lord Ashwick, love. He'll be back. I'd stake my life on it.'

Annis looked at her and Mrs Hardcastle thought that she looked very young. Young and bewildered.

'Will he?' Annis said. 'But the trouble is, Hardy, I do not know if I want him to. I do not know what I want at all.'

The following day was hot and cloudless. Annis and her charges spent the morning shopping in High Harrogate, where Fanny purchased a bonnet and Lucy, rather sweetly, bought a gift of Whitehead's Essence of Mustard Pills for their uncle. Annis then suggested a walk on The Stray, which was not popular. Fanny hated to exert herself and was inclined to sulk.

'Must we do so, Lady Wycherley? The poor people graze their sheep there and it is uncommonly dirty!'

At that moment, Lucy espied a group of gentlemen riding towards them. 'Oh, look, Fanny! It is Captain Hammond, Lieutenant Greaves and...' she blushed '...Lieutenant Norwood. Lady Wycherley—' she turned a flushed, eager face towards Annis '—may we walk a little way with them? Just across to the livery stables at the Granby?'

'Of course, Lucy,' Annis said gravely, amused at how attractive a walk had suddenly become. She was certain that Lieutenant Norwood was going to declare himself soon and so was making sure that he and Lucy had every opportunity to be together.

The gentlemen dismounted and there was a flurry of greeting. Lucy took Barnaby Norwood's arm and Annis watched in secret entertainment as Fanny tried to decide whether to walk with Captain Hammond or Lieutenant Greaves. Captain Hammond had the rank, of course, but the Lieutenant was decidedly more dashing. *And whichever one she rejects,* Annis thought, *will end up having to escort me!* Her lips curved into a little smile at the thought of the young man having to hide his disappointment.

'Good morning, Lady Wycherley.'

Annis jumped and spun round. She recognised Adam Ashwick's voice, although his tall figure was little more that a silhouette against the sun. Annis suddenly wished that she were carrying a parasol like the girls. Not only did she feel decidedly too hot in her grey bombazine, she also felt strangely vulnerable. She raised a gloved hand to shade her eyes.

'Good morning, Lord Ashwick.'

Adam smiled at her. 'May I offer you my arm across The Stray, ma'am? It looks as though your party is headed that way.'

At the same moment, Fanny made her choice in Lieutenant Greaves's favour and turned back to Annis.

'You may have Captain Hammond, ma'am, which is only appropriate as he is senior and so are you—oh!'

Her gaze fell on Ashwick and narrowed slightly. 'Lord... Ashwick, is it not? I believe we saw you at the theatre, sir.'

Adam bowed very slightly. 'Miss Crossley.'

Fanny fluttered, transparently intent on monopolising him. She dropped Lieutenant Greaves's arm and bustled forward, placing herself between Annis and Adam. 'Well, this is famous, sir! We met in London earlier in the Season.'

'I recollect.' There was something in Adam's tone that suggested his memory of her was not a particularly outstanding one. 'I hope that you are well, Miss Crossley. Miss Lucy...'

He bowed and Lucy Crossley blushed, as well she might.

'Are you settled in Harrogate for a space, my lord?' Fanny was gushing now and Annis watched, torn between amusement and embarrassment on the girl's behalf. She had a dreadful feeling that Adam was about to deliver a crushing set-down.

'For a while,' Adam said, a slight hardness entering his voice. 'At the moment, however, I am here to escort Lady Wycherley wherever she wishes to go.'

Fanny turned to Annis and her gaze sharpened. 'Lady Wycherley? But…did you know that she is our chaperon, my lord? I was not aware that you even knew her.'

Adam looked at Annis. There was a smile lurking deep in his eyes.

'Well,' he said, 'I do.' He held out his arm to her. 'Shall we proceed, ma'am?'

There was an edge of authority to his voice that no one cared to gainsay. Fanny turned back to the spurned Lieutenant and in short order she had taken his arm, Lucy had fallen in with Lieutenant Norwood again and the luckless Captain Hammond had taken charge of the three horses and was leading them back to the livery stable.

'Oh, dear,' Annis said ruefully, as she and Adam fell into step behind the other four, ' I was so afraid that you were about to give Miss Crossley a most tremendous set-down, my lord. I must thank you for your forbearance.'

'It is more than the silly little chit deserves,' Adam said. There was a flash of anger in his eyes. 'Did I know that you were their chaperon, indeed! She should be grateful for that privilege instead of being intolerably snobbish about it! You have all the qualities she needs to learn and yet she has the impertinence—' He broke off, scowling blackly.

Annis glanced at him, a little shaken by the vehemence of his tone. His grim gaze was fixed on the back of Fanny Crossley's head and there was a frown between his brows. When he saw Annis looking at him, however, his expression lightened and he smiled.

'I beg your pardon, ma'am. I should not have said that.'

Annis smiled back. 'Do not apologise, my lord. I know that some of my charges think themselves better bred than I—'

'And some, knowing they are not, are even more ill behaved, I'll warrant!' Adam laughed grimly.

Annis made a slight gesture. 'Whatever the case, it does not upset me. I take their money and I do my work.'

There was a small silence between them.

'I am glad that I have caught up with you at last, ma'am,' Adam said in an undertone, as they fell back a little from the main group. 'I called to see you yesterday, but found only your housekeeper at home.'

Annis nodded. 'Mrs Hardcastle. Yes, I understand that she quizzed you shamelessly about your visit.'

'I remember that her mother was much the same,' Adam said, ruefully. 'Did you know that her family worked for my father at Eynhallow? They are true Yorkshire stock, calling a spade a spade.'

'At least one knows where one stands with such blunt honesty,' Annis said.

'Indeed. I believe that you are also Yorkshire born and bred, Lady Wycherley? There is about you the same sort of frankness. It is refreshing and unusual to find in *ton* society.'

Annis smiled slightly. 'I hope that I am not so forthright

as Hardy! But I am certainly Yorkshire born, my lord, if not bred. My father being in the navy, we travelled about a great deal.'

'Of course. I had not forgot.' Adam's gaze was warm as it rested on her and Annis felt herself blush a little. She had been fearful that when they met again Adam might approach her with some familiarity, which would be embarrassing, particularly in public. Now she realised that she need not have feared this. Though there was a shadow of a smile about his mouth as he watched her, she could not fault him for his manner to her. He was as respectful as ever she could have demanded. She felt herself relax a little.

'What of your own antecedents, my lord?' she queried lightly. 'Can you claim a true Yorkshire pedigree?'

'Certainly, for both my parents are from the county. Further back the bloodline is more mixed.' Adam squared his shoulders. 'I do believe there have even been some instances of Ashwick and Lafoy alliances, Lady Wycherley. Our two families go back a long way.'

'I cannot believe that, for we have always been of yeoman stock,' Annis said, laughing, 'and far too far beneath the notice of the Ashwick lords! Mrs Hardcastle says that your family has grown mighty high in the instep, my lord!'

Adam looked amused. 'I see that people have been talking.'

Annis looked at him from under her lashes. 'People do talk about you. It is only natural when you are one of the most...' she hesitated '...one of the most prominent landowners in the locality.'

Adam sighed. 'I accept that but I think it unfair that you

should set me so high when you are the granddaughter of a Marquis and connected to half the noble families in England!'

Annis laughed. 'If you have heard that, you must also have heard that my mother's family do not acknowledge me. When one's mother runs away with a sea captain I fear it is inevitable.' She made a slight gesture. 'It is perfectly understandable that people should discuss *you*, my lord, but I cannot believe that anyone has been talking about *me!*'

Adam stopped and took her gloved hand in his. 'I have been asking about you,' he said softly.

There was something in his tone that brought the blood up into Annis's cheeks. She knew that this was the moment she had to make certain things clear between them.

'Then pray do not ask about me in future, sir.' There was a note of entreaty in her voice. She freed herself and walked on. 'I have a job of work to do, and it does not allow for an idle flirtation with the local lord of the manor.'

It was Adam's turn to laugh. 'How charmingly medieval you make that sound, as though I go around taking my pleasure with the local populace! I do assure you, ma'am, that is hardly my intention.'

'No...' Annis looked troubled '...but when we met two nights ago...'

'Yes?'

'I feel that I must tell you... Oh, how difficult this is!' Annis raised her eyes to his face. 'I fear that you must have received a certain impression of me which is quite false, my lord. I do not generally go around embracing strange gentlemen in the garden—' She broke off in acute embarrassment.

Adam gave her a brief smile. 'You need not tell me that, Lady Wycherley. I never imagined that you did.'

Annis gave him a glance that was half-ashamed, half-grateful. 'Thank you, my lord. So we are agreed that it should never have happened.'

Adam straightened slightly. 'I certainly did not say that. That is a different matter entirely.'

Annis shot him a pleading look. 'But surely—'

'I am not going to pretend that I did not enjoy it.' Adam met her gaze very directly. 'You would want the truth from me, I know, and the truth is that, given the opportunity, I would do exactly the same thing again.'

Annis's face flamed. He was not making this easy for her. In a town the size of Harrogate it would be well nigh impossible to avoid him and her chaperon's duties meant that she was obliged to enter into society. She could not escape Adam, but she had already resolved that the two of them should behave as though the moonlight encounter had never occurred. Now Adam was telling her he did not want to forget it.

'Please understand that I have a living to earn, sir,' she said urgently. 'Whatever it is that you want, whatever game you are playing at my expense—'

Adam stopped abruptly and turned to her. His face was stern. 'I play no games, Lady Wycherley. What I want is to know you better. There, it is said and now you cannot misunderstand me. Yet if you do not desire the same thing, tell me now and I shall not trouble you again.'

There was a silence whilst Annis struggled with her feelings. She could not deny that she found his company enjoyable, but the demands of her profession were strong and stronger still was her fear of losing her independence for a second time.

'You left it too long,' Adam said quietly.

Annis looked at him. There was a spark in his gaze that lit something within her, something that made her shiver.

She frowned. 'You are very direct, my lord. You compel me to answer.'

'I am renowned for my frankness,' Adam said. He smiled. 'What is your answer?'

Annis gave him a very straight look. 'My circumstances do not allow for me to pursue your acquaintance, my lord. Regardless of my feelings, as a chaperon I cannot afford to give rise to gossip and conjecture through my behaviour. That is all there is to it. Please say that you understand.'

Adam sighed. 'I understand your reasoning. I even admire your resolve. I simply do not agree with you.'

'It does not need for you to agree, my lord,' Annis said, a shade acerbically, 'only accept.'

Adam shrugged. 'Then I respect your position, ma'am.' His expression eased a little. 'However, I hope you will at least accept my escort across The Stray?'

'Of course. Thank you.' Annis tried to smile, but her heart felt leaden. This had been her choice and yet now she felt quite miserable to have given him his *congé*. She had seldom felt such a conflict between her feelings and her inclination and she did not care for it.

She became aware of Fanny's inquisitive face peering at her. The girl was almost tripping over as she tried to see what Annis and Adam could be talking about together. Annis gave herself a little shake and rearranged her face into the blandest of expressions. She raised her voice slightly.

'Do you find it strange to be no longer in the military, Lord Ashwick? I understand that you sold out a few years ago?'

Adam saw the direction of her gaze and took his cue from

her. 'In some ways I find it odd, Lady Wycherley. It gives a structure to life that can be lacking otherwise. But I have Eynhallow, and an unconscionable amount of work to do to get the estate back into shape.'

He smiled at her. 'And what do you do with your time, ma'am? I find myself intrigued to know of the entertainments available to young ladies—and their chaperon!'

Annis smiled self-deprecatingly. 'I am sure that you do not, my lord. I can think of little that would interest you less.'

Adam quirked a brow. 'I assure you that I am very interested to know how you spend the day, ma'am. You are always so busy.'

'Well...' Annis made a slight gesture '...there are plenty of activities for the young ladies to indulge in. We might visit Wilson's Circulating Library, or the shops, or go for a small walk, as you see.'

'And in the evenings I suppose there are always the dances at the Granby or the Crown or the Dragon.'

'Every evening is accounted for by some social outing,' Annis agreed. 'The Theatre Royal has a show on alternate nights to the balls, and then there are the private parties, of course. Sometimes we even venture out of Harrogate to visit the surrounding countryside.' She laughed. 'Fountains Abbey was a great hit with the Misses Crossley, you know, and Knaresborough even more so. The castle ruins could have been taken straight from one of Mrs Radcliffe's books, complete with clanking chains and resident ghost!'

Adam smiled at her. 'Did they like the Dropping Well?'

'Miss Lucy did. Miss Crossley found it a little slow and said she was afraid she would be turned to stone herself with the boredom of it all!'

They laughed together. And stopped together. And looked at each other in a silence fraught with possibilities. Then Adam sighed.

'You are not making this easy, Lady Wycherley. You are delightful company, you know, and I would not deliberately deny myself that pleasure.'

Annis looked away. 'Thank you for the compliment, my lord.'

'I find it astonishing that you have not married again, particularly as you must meet plenty of gentlemen in your line of work. Can there be a rational explanation?'

Annis laughed unwillingly. 'There is a simple one. I always try to divert the attention of the gentlemen towards my charges. *They* are the ones requiring to make an advantageous match, not myself.'

'My dear Lady Wycherley...' Adam drew her slightly closer '...you could not divert my attention to them if you tried!'

Annis bit back an answering smile. It was the devil's own job to resist that charm. The warmth, the dangerous intimacy, was still there between them despite her refusal to acknowledge it and her determination to avoid him.

'I am happy to say that the Misses Crossley are both already spoken for, my lord, so you would be too late, anyway,' she said primly.

'And yourself?'

Annis allowed a tinge of coldness to creep into her tone. 'As you are aware, sir, I have already been married and have no inclination to repeat the exercise.' She tilted the brim of her bonnet slightly to block his view of her face.

'You must have married very young.' Adam's tone had softened.

'I did. I was seventeen.' There was a lump in Annis's throat and she had no notion where it had come from. She turned to look at him and the sun dazzled her momentarily. With relief she realised that they had reached the far side of The Stray and were almost at the Granby.

'Thank you for your company, my lord,' she said formally. 'I believe our ways part here.'

'And you are certain that I am not to see you again? I cannot convince you to change your mind?' He was dangerously persuasive. Annis steeled herself against that charm.

'In a town the size of Harrogate I imagine it will be inevitable.'

'That was not precisely what I meant.'

'I did not think that it was.' Their gazes locked. Annis took a deep breath. 'The answer to your question, my lord, is no. I explained why earlier.'

Adam gave a sharp sigh. Annis could see the annoyance in his eyes. 'I cannot agree—' He broke off, running a hand through his hair. 'Confound it! This is not what I had wanted. I cannot believe that I have agreed to your strictures.'

Annis gave him an appealing look. 'Please, my lord! We did agree...'

Adam sighed again. 'I know. I am regretting my promise deeply.'

Fanny and Lucy were busy disentangling themselves from their escorts with much chatter and giggling. Annis gave Adam her hand.

'Thank you, Lord Ashwick.' She was not speaking of his escort and they both knew it. 'I am indebted to you.'

Adam gave her a faint, rueful smile and bowed. 'Good day, Lady Wycherley.'

He walked away. Fanny and Lucy stared after him, mouths inelegantly agape.

'He is very handsome,' Lucy ventured.

'No, he is not!' Fanny snapped. 'He is too plainly dressed. And his manners lack polish.'

Annis's lips twitched. Fanny had evidently taken offence that Adam Ashwick had not shown more of an interest in her.

'Come along, girls! Let us take a little luncheon here and rest in the shade before we take a carriage back home. We need to have plenty of time to prepare for the ball tonight.'

Lucy brightened but Fanny was still staring after Adam's departing figure, her lower lip stuck out.

'Did you know that Lord Ashwick ran off with the vicar's daughter, Lady Wycherley? How frightfully vulgar is that?'

'I should have thought it was of all things romantic,' Lucy said bravely.

Fanny gave her sister a scornful glance. 'He has a shocking reputation,' she said. 'Why, they say that after his wife died, he became the greatest libertine in London! He is not at all suitable company for a chaperon and I am surprised that you allowed him to approach us at all!'

'Thank you, Fanny,' Annis said tranquilly, mentally counting the number of days until Sir Robert Crossley came to take his nieces away. 'It is thoughtful of you to warn me. I do not believe that any of us were in imminent danger and, anyway, I never listen to spiteful gossip.'

She turned and shepherded her charges into the inn, and the door swung closed behind them, hiding Adam Ashwick's tall figure and taking away the temptation for her to watch him into the distance. She had sent him away, and stopped something before it had really started. It had been the only thing to do, yet she could not help wondering what would have happened if she had given in to her instincts and agreed to meet him again. Now she would never know.

Chapter Six

'Had you thought about dosing yourself up with the spa waters, Ash?' Edward Ashwick enquired over dinner one evening a week later. 'They say that it is sovereign for ill humours and you have been like a bear with a sore head this week past.' He shot his brother a grin. 'I do not scruple to mention it because the whole family is aware of your bad temper.'

'The whole house is aware...' Adam's sister Della murmured.

'Probably the whole town,' the Dowager Lady Ashwick finished.

Adam allowed his gaze to move around the table from one to the next. Both his siblings and his mother were watching him with identical expressions of sympathy in their grey eyes. The Dowager Lady Ashwick, a diminutive brunette who had been married from the schoolroom and was still extremely well preserved, even though she was on the very shady side of forty, gave him a fond maternal smile.

'We thought that it might be difficult for you returning to Harrogate after so long, darling,' she murmured. 'We *do* so sympathise...'

'Of course,' Della echoed compassionately. 'Pray be as unpleasant to us as you wish, Adam. We shall not take offence.'

A reluctant smile pierced Adam's gloom. 'I beg your pardon. I had no idea that I was being so ill humoured.'

'Surly,' Edward confirmed.

'Testy,' Della agreed.

'Grumpy,' the Dowager said sadly. 'I suppose it is all to do with Lady Wycherley.'

Adam put down his knife and fork and gave his brother a hard stare. 'What have you been saying, Ned?'

'I? Nothing, I swear.' Edward looked the epitome of virtue. 'Della happened to comment to me that she had seen you walking on The Stray with Lady Wycherley last week—'

'The devil she did!'

'And I observed that you had spent some time in that lady's company and that you seemed to admire her.'

'Which we already knew, Adam,' The Dowager said. 'Ned was breaking no confidences, I assure you. We all saw you at the theatre that night. You looked positively *épris*! We were so happy for you, darling.' A tiny frown marred her brow. 'Except that you do not seem so cheerful now. Whatever can have gone wrong?'

Adam frowned ferociously. He could scarcely be indelicate enough to tell his mother that he ached for a woman he could not have, but that was the nature of the problem. He had not seen Annis Wycherley for seven days now and she haunted his thoughts and his dreams. He had even found himself walking past the house in Church Row hoping to catch sight of her. It was juvenile and sentimental, but he did not seem able to help himself. He had fallen hard and no one was more surprised than he.

'Lady Wycherley and I are mere acquaintances,' he said shortly. 'She has indicated that she does not wish to take our association any further.'

'Ah,' Edward said significantly. 'That explains everything, of course.'

'Has she misunderstood about Miss Mardyn's position?' Della enquired innocently. 'That might account for a reluctance to pursue the acquaintance. If so, perhaps I could explain to her—'

Adam scowled. 'Pray do not even think of doing so, Della.'

The Dowager was looking puzzled. 'I do not entirely understand, Adam. Lady Wycherley indicated that she did not wish to see you and you…agreed?'

Adam's scowl deepened. 'I did, Mama. One cannot force one's attentions on an unwilling lady.'

Della smiled. 'Very noble of you, Adam. Yet Lady Wycherley seemed to be enjoying your company when I saw the two of you together. Whatever can you have done to give her a dislike of you?'

Adam threw down his napkin and got up from the table. He was sorely tempted to tell his interfering family to mind their own business, but he knew that they had his best interests at heart. Besides, he owed them an apology for his bad moods. He found himself providing a reluctant explanation.

'It cannot have escaped your notice that Lady Wycherley is a chaperon.'

'A very proper one.' The Dowager nodded.

'Indeed. Thank you, Mama. That is exactly it.' Adam swallowed his glass of wine and walked over to the window with an impatient step. 'A proper chaperon cannot entertain gentleman callers without losing her reputation. Lady Wycherley drew this fact to my attention and I was forced to agree with her. It is as simple as that.'

'I can understand her point of view,' Della agreed. 'People can be so gossipy and cattish. Yet if your intentions are honourable, Adam… At least, I take it that you *do* have honourable intentions?'

Catching Edward's amused eye, Adam reflected on the difficulties of even attempting to engage in a courtship under his family's eye.

'I would have if I was given the chance!'

'Then we may help you,' Della said.

'Yes, indeed,' Lady Ashwick said. 'If you have honourable intentions, Adam, I pledge my support as well. I should like it above all things to see you wed again.'

Adam felt slightly bemused. His family seemed to be working even faster than he was. 'Thank you. Would you vouchsafe to me exactly what you intend to do?'

The Dowager waved an airy hand. 'There is no great difficulty. Della and I shall contrive for Lady Wycherley to speak with you again.' She gave her firstborn a fond smile. 'After that, it is entirely up to you, Adam, and if you do not take your opportunity you will not deserve her anyway!'

'And if you would take the spa water in the meantime, Ash, it will be the better for all of us,' Edward added.

The sound of the bell broke into their laughter. The butler's footsteps approached.

'Mr Ingram has called, my lord,' Tranter said expressionlessly. 'I have put him in the study. He asks for a moment of your time.'

Some of the warmth and laughter seemed to drain from the room. Della had turned pale and now she rose to her feet, steadying herself against the edge of the table.

'Mama, I believe that I shall retire. No, pray do not concern yourself. I am quite well. I simply do not wish to meet Mr Ingram.'

The Dowager nodded. She took her daughter's arm. 'Neither do I. Come, let us go upstairs and decide on our gowns for the next ball. Adam, Edward…you will excuse us? I trust that that man will not take up too much of your time.'

'Do you wish me to leave you to see Ingram alone, Ash?' Edward asked, as he and Adam went out into the hall. 'Whatever your preference.'

Adam shook his head. 'I would rather that you were with me, Ned. The man is a slippery customer and I would rather have a witness—and some moral support.'

Edward nodded and they went into the study together. Ingram was standing before the fireplace, examining the invitations that adorned the mantel. He turned to look at them. Neither Adam nor Edward spoke.

'Good evening to you, gentlemen both. Ashwick… Reverend… I apologise for calling in the evening but when a man is busy at work during the day…' Ingram's greeting was breezy but his eyes were shrewd as they moved from one brother to the other.

Edward inclined his head slightly. A faint, cold smile touched his lips for a fleeting moment before he moved away and took up his station by the fire, one booted foot resting casually on the marble step, his arm along the mantel. As a means of making Ingram move away, it was admirable. Adam remained just inside the door, his stance wary, his expression closed.

'Good evening, Ingram.' Adam's voice was smooth but not at all welcoming. He did not offer Ingram his hand. 'What can I do for you?'

'I'm come to ask a favour of you, my lord,' Ingram said. He had a cultured voice, but where Adam's tones held a careless patrician drawl Ingram's were a little too carefully cultivated. Very occasionally, when under stress, he would waver back to the flatter vowels of his childhood.

'How intriguing,' Adam said politely. He could feel Edward's gaze on them, full of suspicion—and warning. Ned knew that he had a hot temper buried deep under the easy exterior and if anyone could provoke it, this man would. 'I was under the impression that our business was concluded, sir. The debt is paid.'

Ingram nodded. He removed his gloves and came forward to the fire, dry-rubbing his hands before the blaze. 'I know I'm not welcome in this house. The matter of your brother-in-law's debts was unfortunate, but business is business, my lord.'

'It is certainly unfortunate that the one business that you and Lord Tilney ventured into together did not prosper,' Adam agreed, with an edge to his voice. He hated this fencing, this polite fiction, when they both knew that this man had brought the Ashwick family close to ruin. The debt, thirty thousand pounds, had been huge and the Ashwicks had never been rich.

'Aye, the debt is settled, right enough,' Ingram said now, his tone friendly but his gaze piercing. 'There was another matter, however, which I believe that both you gentlemen may help me with.'

'And that is?' Edward spoke for the first time. He took a draught of brandy, but his gaze never left Ingram's face.

'Property, influence…' Ingram thrust his hands into his jacket pocket and rocked back on his heels, turning towards Adam again. 'You have a very pretty parcel of land that abuts my estate at Linforth, my lord. I hear that the farm there is not so profitable for you, but I could make it turn in a tidy income. With some of my improvements it would soon be on its feet again.'

'I hear that people do not like your improvements, Ingram,' Edward said coolly. 'There is discontent in the villages—'

Ingram barely flicked him a glance. 'They'll learn to live with it.' He looked at Adam. 'If you could see your way clear to selling the farm to me, my lord—at a reduced rate, of course, seeing as how it's in poor shape…'

'I cannot do that.' Adam felt the anger rising in him and forced himself to crush it down. He kept his tone even. 'I have a tenant in that farm, Ingram, and even if I did not I have no wish to sell.'

There was a taut silence in the room.

'Ah, well,' Ingram said, after a moment, 'you might wish to reconsider in a moment, my lord. But first I had a favour to ask, like. On behalf of my wife.'

Adam raised his eyebrows. Ingram shifted a little.

'Venetia—my wife—has taken it into her head to enter society. And as you are so influential in those circles, my lord, we thought you might smooth our way, sithee. You and your brother…' he gave Edward a mocking bow '…have the entrée to so many events that we, alas, do not.'

Adam turned away. He knew it was Ingram, not his wife, who had overweening social ambitions and he was damned if he was going to assist him. 'You are already prominent in local society, Ingram. I do not see how I may help you.'

'There's society and society, is there not, my lord?' Ingram said. His tone matched Adam's for blankness. 'Now I may be welcome to attend the town assemblies on account of my money, but there are some drawing rooms where I cannot enter—' He broke off as he caught the ghost of a smile that passed between Adam and Edward. 'I see you understand me, my lord. Society is a mighty tricky thing for a self-made man. So much snobbery...'

'Disgraceful as it is,' Adam said coolly, 'I do not believe that I can change that for you, Ingram.'

A faint flush came to Ingram's cheek. 'Like I said, my lord, you may wish to reconsider. It would be embarrassing if I were to make public the details of your brother-in-law's debt...'

Adam's head came up sharply. 'I understood that we had a gentleman's agreement that the details would never be published, Ingram.'

Ingram spread his hands in a helpless gesture. 'Not being a gentleman, my lord, I would not understand the principle of such a thing. However, I could learn very quickly if you were prepared to host a dinner for Venetia and myself, just as a start, like...'

Adam took a deep breath. This was blackmail, no more, no less. He had agreed to settle the debt and had thought that he had got off fairly lightly with the settlement that Lafoy had negotiated. Now he saw that that had just been the beginning. First there was the property. Ingram had chosen to strike when he knew that the Ashwicks were weak through payment of Tilney's debt. He would whittle away at the Eynhallow lands to expand his own estate, making life a misery for the tenants and villagers should Adam choose to cut his losses and sell. Then there was the more intangible issue of influence. There was no doubt that Adam could, if he chose, bring Samuel Ingram and his wife into fashion. He had the social power to do so for, in a small society like Harrogate, plenty would follow his lead. He felt revolted at the thought. To have to compromise his own principles and toady to Ingram simply because his brother-in-law had made a bad business decision... It was intolerable. It was not just pride or snobbery talking, Adam thought furiously. He hated to be coerced by any man.

'I am sorry but I cannot help you, Ingram,' he said, very firmly. 'I do not choose to enter Harrogate society myself and therefore cannot undertake to sponsor anyone else.'

Ingram shrugged. 'No hasty decisions, lad. I am sure that you would not wish Lord Tilney's poor judgement to become a matter for common tittle-tattle.'

Adam felt his temper slipping. 'If you understood more about being a gentleman, Ingram, you would know why I say tell everyone and be damned!' he said, through his teeth. 'Although I would deplore your behaviour, I would not lower myself to comment upon it in public!'

Ingram's mouth thinned to a tight line. 'Well, well, my lord, there's plain speaking! You might be so hardy, but what would your dear sister say? Such a charming lady, but not strong since her husband's death...not strong at all.'

Once again there was a tense silence. Adam caught Edward's look of mingled warning and disquiet. He knew his brother well and he knew that look. Ned was telling him to play for time, to give them a little breathing space. Adam made a final attempt to clamp down on his anger. An expression that was colder still hardened his lean, masculine features.

'Very well, then, Ingram. I will give consideration to your proposals, but you must give me a little time.'

Ingram relaxed. 'That is very sensible of you, lad. I'll call again in a day or two. My Venetia is not a patient woman, you see, and would like an answer soon as maybe.' His eyes narrowed to slits. 'See to it, laddie.'

Adam gave him a stony look. 'I hear you, Ingram.'

Edward moved across to the door and held it open. Ingram, showing the first signs of hesitation he had displayed all evening, paused for a moment before he marched through.

'Good night, my lord. Good night, Reverend.'

He appeared to expect some response, but when none was forthcoming his expression hardened and he stomped out, his footsteps echoing across the stone flags of the floor.

There was an ominous calm in the study until the sound of Ingram's footsteps had faded away and then the front door closed. Edward was the first to break the silence.

'As well that Della had already retired for the night,' he observed. 'She can scarcely bring herself to be civil to Ingram if she has the misfortune of bumping into him. She ain't *weak*, though! Ingram is barking up the wrong tree there!'

Adam's face was a mask that splintered suddenly into vivid anger. 'God *damn* the man! I feel like a fish wriggling on the end of his line!'

Edward took his brandy glass from his hand, moved

over to the oak sideboard and poured more brandy for both
of them.

'Your metaphor is not apt,' he said slowly. 'I was watching
you and a wolf at bay springs more easily to mind. Ingram
should have a care not to push you too far.'

Adam took the proffered glass and stalked across to the
fire, kicking a log deeper into the glowing embers. There
was a hiss of flame.

'Steady,' Edward observed. 'Hoby will never forgive you
if you set fire to those boots, Ash. Besides, imagine the figure you would cut, hopping around on one leg as you try to
remove them without the help of your valet! Not worth it,
old fellow.'

Adam's dark expression lightened with a glimmer of a
smile, but he did not pause in his restless pacing. 'If only
there had been one iota of evidence to suggest that the business with the *Northern Prince* was not above board.'

'Wishful thinking, old chap.' Edward swallowed his
brandy in one gulp. 'The ship went down right enough. It
was just our bad luck.'

'Then if not that, how did Ingram persuade Humphrey to
invest in the first place? Perhaps he was blackmailing him.'

Edward shook his head. 'Ash, Humphrey may have shown
bad judgement in borrowing heavily at a time of economic
uncertainty, but sadly that was in character.'

Adam was silent. He knew that this was true.

He threw himself down in his armchair. 'If I could find
any suggestion that Ingram's business dealings are illegal—'

'Others have tried that. The man is too clever to be caught.
Besides, just because Ingram is ruthless in business does not
make his dealings illegal.'

Adam brought his fist down hard on the arm of his chair in impotent anger.

'Damn it, Ned, the man is provably a blackmailer! What was he trying to do this evening?'

Edward shrugged. 'I concede that, but his methods are cunning. He would say that all he has asked of you is a favour...'

'And if I do not comply, he will drag Humphrey's name through the mud.' Adam swallowed a mouthful of brandy, frowning hard at the flames in the grate. 'Well, devil take it, he will have to make good his threats. I will not become Ingram's pet poodle and entertain him and his wife, and I am sure that Della will understand my reasons!'

'You may find that Ingram has greater matters on his mind soon,' Edward observed. 'I hear he has offered the tenant farm at Shawes for an exorbitant rent. The villagers already hate him for enclosing Shawes Common, and if we have a poor summer and wages are low, that hatred will erupt.'

There was a silence, but for the sigh of the wind in the trees outside.

'There was already trouble at one of the new tollhouses this week and it is only half-built.' Adam frowned. 'Do you think that matters will get worse, Ned?' He knew that Edward, as Rector of Eynhallow, had far closer an understanding of what went on in Harrogate's surrounding villages than any of the landowners could hope for.

'We have all the ingredients.' Edward looked grim. 'If there is a food shortage and a poor harvest, there will be crime and unrest. We've seen it happen before, Ash. And Ingram is turning the screw on a populace already sunk in poverty. I have a bad feeling...'

'It's an interesting prospect, albeit it a damned unpleasant one.' Adam shifted a little in his chair. 'There's already been the fire at Shawes.'

'Arson,' Edward said, nodding. 'It was meant as a warning, but Ingram is so thick-skinned it would take more than that.'

'What can we do?'

'Keep an ear to the ground. If there is trouble in the villages, there may be a way to take advantage…'

Adam raised his brows. 'Devil take it, little brother! Is that really a man of the cloth speaking?'

'God helps those who help themselves,' Edward said righteously.

'Does he? I don't believe I've ever read that bit of the Bible! Would it be next to the passage about men of God stirring up trouble from the pulpit?'

Edward looked positively angelic. 'I am sure you overestimate my influence, Ash.'

'I am sure that I do not.' Adam gave him a straight look, which Edward met with one of his own.

'Of course,' he said reflectively, 'we should dwell on the one matter that requires our gratitude…'

Adam raised his brows enquiringly.

'That Ingram at least has no daughters of marriageable age!' Edward said, with a grin. 'Or we should both be leg-shackled before you could say thirty thousand pounds in debt!'

'It gives a whole new meaning to the phrase parson's mousetrap,' Adam agreed gravely.

The weather broke the following night and it rained for the whole of the next day, putting Fanny and Lucy in a fretful mood and echoing Annis's own feelings of gloom. She sat on the window seat in the drawing room, watching the rain streak the glass and the passers-by hurry along the pavements, head into the wind, umbrellas held before them like bayonets. Fanny and Lucy picked at their needlework and chattered. Annis sat quietly, wishing that Adam would call and reminding herself that he would not since she had specifically asked him not to. Nevertheless, she missed him.

In the evening they were invited to dinner at Hansard Court, Sir Everard Doble's home just outside Harrogate. It was both an opportunity for Fanny to inspect the house and for the widowed Lady Doble to inspect her prospective daughter-in-law, and everyone was on tenterhooks. The dinner was poor and the house dark and dismal, but Fanny's desire for a title outweighed all else and she sparkled, making Annis wince with only a few ill-mannered remarks. After dinner, whilst Fanny entertained them on the pianoforte, Lady Doble plumped herself down next to Annis on the sofa.

'The chit will do well enough, I suppose.' Lady Doble did not trouble to lower her voice, and Annis reflected that her future mother-in-law might almost outdo Fanny in vulgarity. 'How much money will she be bringing?'

'Forty thousand pounds,' Annis said, lowering her voice.

'Forty thousand, eh?' Lady Doble bellowed. 'Perfect!'

After that it was only a matter of form for Sir Everard to whisk Fanny off to the conservatory to propose and to be accepted. Annis left Hansard Court feeling deeply relieved for a great many reasons, and wrote to Sir Robert Crossley that very night.

* * *

It was Miss Lucy Crossley's turn to receive a declaration the following week, when Barnaby Norwood came up to scratch and delivered himself of a romantic proposal in the drawing room. Annis congratulated Lucy wholeheartedly, wrote a second letter to Sir Robert, and felt almost euphoric with relief. Even Fanny, whose pride was satisfied to be marrying a baronet rather than a mere Honourable, was gracious to her little sister.

The Monday night ball the following week took place at the Dragon and both Crossley sisters were boasting about their engagements. It was another humid night. Annis sat amongst the chaperons, fanning herself ineffectually and wishing that she had not chosen turkey red for her gown that evening. With the current heat it was likely to be a close match for her face. The combination of a crowded ballroom, a hundred candles and a hot summer night was not a happy one. Even the feather in her turban was wilting.

She turned her head slowly to scan the dance floor. Lucy was dancing the quadrille with a half-pay officer, but was behaving with the perfect decorum of a girl whose future was already assured. Barnaby Norwood was watching indulgently and chatting to a group of fellow officers. Annis smiled to herself. Lucy was a sweet girl and deserved her happiness. Fanny was dancing with Sir Everard and looking very pleased with herself. Annis's smile became a little cynical. Fanny knew that all eyes were upon her, envying her the good luck and forty thousand pounds that had secured Sir Everard's title.

The door to the ballroom opened and a number of latecomers pressed their way into the throng. The Master of Ceremonies was bowing and scraping, and Annis's smile turned wry as she recognised the new arrivals. Samuel Ingram and his youthful wife Venetia were always warmly welcomed to the town's social events. It mattered little that Ingram was the son of a lighthouse keeper and the beautiful Venetia was a first-rate shrew. Their money, like Sir Robert Crossley's, cast a golden glow.

There were those who disapproved, of course. Annis's position amongst the chaperons gave her the perfect opportunity to witness the tight-lipped displeasure of some of the town's high sticklers. Old Lady Cardew and Lady Emily Trumpton were whispering malignantly like a pair of witches. Annis caught the phrases 'appalling drop in standards' and 'any old riff-raff at these events'. There were some circles in which the Ingrams would never be welcome. The Cardews and Trumptons would never invite them to grace their drawing rooms.

Following Mr and Mrs Ingram through the door were Charles, Sibella and David. Annis felt a mixture of strong affection and annoyance. She could not bear the way in which Charles in particular was in Ingram's pocket, and at times like this it stuck in her throat to see her family in Ingram's retinue. She was guiltily aware that she had been avoiding Charles since the issue of the sale of Starbeck had arisen. She had pleaded her work as an excuse and had been glad to put him off. Now she rather suspected Charles would press his case. What was worse was that she would be obliged to do the pretty to the Ingrams tonight for Charles's sake. Samuel Ingram always treated her with courtesy and Annis had a suspicion that he did so because of her title and because he was not sure of her exact social position. She had to work for a living, but the fact that she was a Marquis's granddaughter and the widow of a knight certainly confused the issue in his eyes.

The country dance ended and Annis watched as Sir Everard offered Fanny his arm and guided her over to an alcove where they could converse together. Fanny was behaving very pleasantly that evening, but Annis knew better than to take her gaze off her. Out of the corner of her eye, she saw that Lucy was now dancing with Lieutenant Norwood, and a very pretty pair they made. Annis relaxed slightly. From that point of view the evening was going well.

She stifled a yawn. Nothing particularly exciting ever happened at the Harrogate assemblies. In the summer the residents of the town were joined by the fashionable throngs who came north to take the spa waters, but the place still had a genteel quality, which she was sure the raffish London crowd found rather quaint.

Sibella waved at her across the ballroom and gestured that she would be coming over in a moment. Annis waved back and smiled. Some very late arrivals were just entering the ballroom. The Master of Ceremonies was bowing so low he had almost doubled himself up. Someone of more consequence than Mr and Mrs Ingram, then. Annis raised her brows.

Adam Ashwick walked in, accompanied by his brother and the Dowager Lady Ashwick. Annis's heart jumped once in recognition, then settled to a steady beat. She deliberately looked away, hoping that her colour had not betrayed her brief moment of confusion. She doubted they had noticed. Generally speaking, no one ever looked at chaperons very closely. Annis fidgeted on her rout chair. She felt confused and strangely out of countenance to see Adam again, regardless of the fact that he would probably not approach her. She had missed him and something had felt out of kilter ever since she had dismissed him. Nevertheless, she knew that she could not weaken now.

There was no doubt that the Ashwick party was working its way towards her quarter of the room. The Dowager Lady Ashwick and her younger son were both well known in Harrogate society and were stopping to speak to their many acquaintances. Since the new Lord Ashwick had spent much of the previous nine years either abroad or in London, he was being introduced to new arrivals and reacquainting himself with old friends. Annis took a deep breath to steady her nerves.

She allowed her gaze to rest on Adam's face for a moment, making sure that he did not catch her watching him. He looked very elegant in pale fawn inexpressibles and a black swallowtail coat and his neck cloth was tied in intricate folds that only a London valet could achieve. He was smiling as he answered some question from Lady Cardew and he looked charming, distinguished, everything that Annis might ever have wanted. She felt a pang of mingled regret and longing.

Annis forced her gaze away and looked at Della Tilney, elegant in the lavender of half-mourning, and from there to the Dowager and to Edward Ashwick. Unlike his elder brother, Edward did not have the figure to carry off evening dress well. His was a more rotund and rather comfortable figure and though his features were very similar to Adam's, his face was much more open, with a pleasing warmth of expression. Annis found herself warming to his easiness of manners as she watched him greet Lady Cardew and Lady Emily Trump-ton. He soon had the old tabbies eating out of his hand.

Adam Ashwick looked across at her and caught her gaze, and Annis felt a wave of heat wash over her from the top of her head to the tips of her toes. She stood up and started to edge away from the crowd milling about the Ashwicks. She had reckoned without Della Tilney and the Dowager, how-ever, who now excused themselves from Lady Cardew and cut off her retreat without appearing to do so. It was neatly and seamlessly done.

'Lady Wycherley, how charming to see you again. How do you do?' The Dowager was only a small woman, but some-how she appeared to be blocking Annis's path and Annis knew that she could scarcely dodge around her. Della Tilney was approaching on the left now in a clever flanking ma-noeuvre that Annis could have sworn was deliberate. She drew to a reluctant halt.

'Good evening, Lady Ashwick, Lady Tilney...'

'I believe that you are already acquainted with my elder son, Lord Ashwick,' the Dowager said. For a second Annis was certain that she saw a spark of mischief in her eyes.

She cast Adam a brief glance. 'Good evening, my lord.'

'It is a pleasure to meet you again, Lady Wycherley.'

Adam Ashwick's voice was smooth and amused. He took her hand in his. Annis risked another look at his face. His cool grey eyes were smiling into hers and in that moment she read all his suppressed amusement at the sight of her in her matronly red dress and matching turban. A vision came into her mind of herself as she had been the night they had met in the garden: the black cloak, her hair free about her shoulders, abandoned and wild. She felt herself blush like a débutante at her first ball and looked away hastily.

The Dowager had excused herself, taken her daughter's arm and moved on, leaving Annis and Adam together. It had been very neatly done.

'I wondered if you would care to dance, Lady Wycherley,' Adam continued. The pressure of his fingers on hers increased slightly until Annis was obliged to look up again. She met his gaze with a straight look of her own.

'I thank you, my lord, but chaperons do not dance.'

Adam raised his dark brows arrogantly. 'Why not? Is there some law against it?'

Annis frowned faintly. 'Not exactly—'

'Then you need to consult nothing but your inclination, Lady Wycherley. Besides, I did not ask whether chaperons danced. I asked if you would care to dance with me, which is a vastly different question.'

Their gazes locked. Annis bit back a smile.

'I see that you are as forthright as ever, my lord. You put me in an impossible position! How am I to refuse without giving offence?'

Adam grinned. 'You cannot. Give in to your fate.'

'Then I suppose that it would be quite pleasant to dance with you.'

His hand was warm on her arm as he steered her on to the floor.

'Only quite pleasant? You are severe, ma'am.'

It was a quadrille. They drew together, clasped hands and drew apart again.

'It is delightful to see you again,' Adam said, in an undertone. 'You observe how good I have been in obeying your strictures and staying away from you.'

Annis gave him a cool look. 'I imagined that you had been busy at Eynhallow, my lord.'

'Did you? I assure you that I would have abandoned all my plans to spend some time with you. Still, it is pleasant to know that you have been giving my circumstances some thought. I have missed seeing you, Lady Wycherley. Did you miss me too?'

Annis gave him a speaking look and he laughed. 'So you did. How encouraging.'

'I have been far too busy,' Annis said primly.

'To good effect, I understand. I hear that you are to be rid of your charges in a few weeks, and that they are likely to depart in a blaze of glory. An engagement to Sir Everard Doble for one, I understand, and the younger Norwood son for the other. I congratulate you.'

Annis smiled. 'Thank you. I hope that congratulations will be in order, my lord, but I am making no assumptions.'

'Once the Misses Crossley have left you will no longer be a chaperon, will you?' Adam continued, with limpid innocence. 'How do you plan to pass your time then, ma'am?'

Annis gave him a sharp look. 'I shall then be a chaperon on holiday, my lord,' she said sweetly. 'I intend to spend some time at Starbeck before going to London for the Little Season.'

'Do you accompany another young lady to London?'

'Of course. It is my job. I shall be chaperoning Miss Eustacia Copthorne.'

Adam gave a soundless whistle. 'You must enjoy a difficult challenge, ma'am. I declare your choices become more testing each time! You would do better to give it all up and spend some time with me.'

'Would that be less challenging, Lord Ashwick?'

Adam smiled. 'Maybe not, but it would be more enjoyable. For both of us.'

They parted, turned, crossed hands and drew together again. Annis took the opportunity to check that Fanny and Lucy were both well in view. They were—and they were gawping at her, along with half the population of the ballroom. As Annis had said, chaperons simply did not dance. It was as though most people assumed they were either incapable of dancing or somehow exempt from the normal entertainments of society.

The dance was ending and Adam offered her his arm for the customary circuit of the floor.

'That was not so bad, was it?' he enquired lightly. 'Perhaps you might give me permission to call on you at Starbeck, ma'am—before you become a chaperon again?'

Before Annis could reply, Charles was at her elbow, pointedly proprietorial.

'Good evening, coz. Your servant, Ashwick…'

The men exchanged polite bows. Once again there was an air of constraint between them, then Charles said, a little awkwardly, 'Mr Ingram asks if you would care to escort my cousin over to join his party, my lord.'

Annis hesitated and felt Adam stiffen as well. It felt suspiciously like some sort of trap. Charles had delivered the invitation with the unmistakable ring of a royal command and Annis could see that Ingram was watching them across the room with something approaching a gloating pleasure. Evidently he did not expect a refusal.

She saw the angry colour come into Adam's face, saw him hesitate as though he was searching for the appropriate words, and with a flash of insight wondered what hold Ingram had over him. Whatever it was, it seemed dangerous. Adam looked as though he would happily throttle the man.

After what seemed an age, Adam turned to her and bowed with scrupulous courtesy. 'You must excuse me, Lady Wycherley. I have no wish to offend you, but I fear I cannot accept Mr Ingram's invitation.'

He kissed her hand, turned sharply on his heel and strode away.

'Well!' Charles said, as he and Annis turned as one to watch Adam go. 'Of all the dashed poor manners—'

'Can you truly blame Lord Ashwick for declining Mr Ingram's invitation?' Annis demanded. 'It seems to me quite natural that he should want nothing to do with him, and rather insensitive of Mr Ingram to push himself on Lord Ashwick's acquaintance!'

Charles looked defensive. 'Yes, but the old man asked me specially to make sure of Ashwick—'

'Oh, I see! You are worried for yourself and fear that you will be in bad odour with your employer because you failed to bring in the prize catch!' Annis looked at him in exasperation. 'Really, Charles, are you a man or a mouse? There must be plenty of other business in Harrogate and around even were you to forfeit Ingram's favour—'

She knew that she was beating her head against a wall even as she spoke. There was a stubborn, closed expression on her cousin's face and after a second Annis sighed and took his arm. 'Both you and Mr Ingram will just have to make do with me, Charles, and I only do it as a favour to you because you are my cousin. I don't like the man either!'

Chapter Seven

Fifteen minutes later, Annis had said all that was polite to Samuel Ingram, exchanged a few words with Sibella and David, and was looking round a little anxiously to try to locate Lucy and Fanny. She was conscious that she had allowed them rather too much latitude that evening. What with the unexpected invitation to dance with Adam Ashwick and the unwelcome summons to join the Ingrams' party, her chaperon's duties had come a poor third. Naturally there was a price to pay, and that price was that Fanny had disappeared.

As Annis reached the edge of the dance floor, Lucy Crossley, pretty in a pale blue dress that matched her eyes, came up and caught her arm.

'Lady Wycherley, I am a little worried about Fanny...'

'Yes?' Annis kept her voice discreetly low, looking round covertly to make sure that their conversation was not attracting any attention.

'She said that she was going to the ladies' withdrawing room, but I am afraid...' Lucy hesitated and Annis saw concern warring with a surreptitious glee in her face '…that is, I know she has a *tendre* for Lieutenant Greaves and I wondered if they had gone out into the gardens.'

'I see,' Annis said.

'I am not trying to get Fanny into trouble…' Lucy had a look of limpid innocence that contradicted her words.

'Well,' Annis said, clamping down on her irritation, which was only made worse by the gleam of hopeful spite in Lucy's eye, 'I hope that Fanny may remember that she is affianced to Sir Everard Doble, and the Lieutenant may remember that he is a gentleman.'

Lucy giggled. 'Lord, I don't think so, Lady Wycherley! Barnaby says that Lieutenant Greaves is the worst flirt in Harrogate!'

'Yes, very well, Lucy!' Annis frowned. 'I will go to find Fanny, though I am sure this is all a hum. Now, please stay with Lieutenant Norwood until I come back with Fanny, and if Sir Everard Doble comes over, pray tell him that we shall come out to the carriage in a moment.' She fixed Lucy with a severe look. 'I trust that you, at least, will behave with discretion!'

'Oh, yes, Lady Wycherley.' Lucy assumed her most angelic look.

'Good. I am sure that there is no call for concern. I shall see you directly.'

Annis sighed. She liked Lucy a great deal more than Fanny, but she supposed it was no surprise that the girl was relishing her elder sister's apparent fall from grace. Fanny had seldom treated Lucy with kindness and now Lucy was having a small revenge. Annis had absolutely no faith that Lucy would hold her tongue. She was a sad rattle and Annis knew she would tell Barnaby Norwood what was going on and then the story would be round Harrogate in no time. Fanny would be branded a flirt, Sir Everard might cut up rough, and all before Sir Robert Crossley had come up with Annis's payment.

A search of the ladies' withdrawing room confirmed what Annis had already suspected; Fanny was nowhere to be found and the attendant had not seen her. Annis retraced her steps to the passage and paused for thought. There were no gardens at the Dragon and the possibilities for private conversation were therefore very limited. Could Fanny and Lieutenant Greaves have gone into one of the public rooms, hoping to grasp a few moments on their own? If so, Annis thought they were taking an enormous risk of discovery, but perhaps that might add to the excitement.

First though, before she panicked, Annis thought that she should try the supper room. Given Fanny's penchant for food, it was entirely possible that she might be found tidying up the crumbs left over from supper. Annis had noticed that Fanny had been particularly partial to the pigeon pie that evening...

Fanny was not in the supper room and the servants who were clearing the food away had not seen her. Annis went out into the Dragon's impressive entrance hall and opened a door at random. It was the library and it was quite deserted at this time of night. The fire was lit and one candle burned, but the room was empty. Next door was the writing room, and as Annis opened the door she heard voices.

'I 'eard as you were looking for information about Mr Ingram, my lord. I've got something that might interest you, but it'll cost you...'

'How much, Woodhouse?'

Annis recognised Adam Ashwick's incisive tones and paused, her hand still on the doorknob. Neither man appeared to have heard the door open for they were standing at the far end of the room in the window embrasure. The long windows were, in fact, slightly ajar. Woodhouse had his back to the door and Adam was half-turned away from it. Annis heard the clink of guineas. She could also smell the strong scent of ale. Every time Woodhouse moved another wave of it filled the room.

'For two hundred I could guarantee to point you in the right direction, m'lord.'

'I will pay you three hundred, you old scoundrel.' Distaste and amusement warred in Adam's voice, 'Here is half that on account and the rest will be on delivery, but for that I expect the best quality information. And proof, Woodhouse. Otherwise Ingram will tell me to go hang!'

Annis drew a sharp breath. She knew that she should withdraw, for Fanny Crossley was certainly not here and whatever Adam was discussing with Woodhouse was none of her business. She had known that he was no friend to Ingram and if he sought information to bring the man down, then that was his affair. She was about to tiptoe back the way she had come, when she heard Woodhouse mention Charles's name. She paused.

'A little tip, my lord...' Woodhouse gave a cackle of laughter. 'You should look into Mr Lafoy's activities. There's a gentleman that could do with watching. Ingram's right-hand man, so he is.' He hiccupped loudly. 'What you're after is treasure, my lord. Buried treasure. Or sunken treasure perhaps. Look to the skies and into the depths. That's my advice!'

Adam sounded impatient. 'What the devil are you talking about, man? You're so drunk you're not making sense—'

A draught from the open window tugged the knob out of Annis's hand and the door swung to behind her, closing with a soft, stealthy click. Both men spun around. Woodhouse swore and dived for the open terrace door and Adam came quickly across the room towards her.

Annis experienced a moment of pure panic when she wanted to run away. This would be ridiculous, however, and within a second she realised that she would have to brazen it out. She put her hands behind her back, resting her palms against the door panels, and waited for Adam to join her. His greeting was typically blunt.

'What the devil are you doing there, Lady Wycherley? Eavesdropping?'

Annis blushed a furious red. 'No, of course not, Lord Ashwick! I have lost Miss Fanny Crossley and thought that she might be in here. I can see that she is not, however, so I shall leave you.'

She turned towards the door. Adam was quicker than she. He leaned one hand against it and held it closed.

'Just a moment, Lady Wycherley. Do not be so hasty.'

Annis gave him a haughty look 'My lord?'

Adam grinned. 'Pray do not turn starchy with me, ma'am.'

Annis glared. 'Then do not prevent my egress from the room, sir.'

Adam stood back with exaggerated courtesy. 'You are, of course, free to go. I should be grateful if you would grant me a moment, however.'

Annis sighed sharply. 'Very well, my lord. You have a minute only. I must find Miss Crossley.'

'Of course. There was something I wished to ask you. Did you hear my conversation with Woodhouse?'

Annis met his gaze. 'I heard some of it.'

'I see. Were you deliberately listening?'

'No, indeed! Why should I? I have not been *spying* on you, Lord Ashwick!'

Adam's lips twitched. 'I beg your pardon. I was not suggesting that you were dogging my footsteps! I merely thought that if you had heard something of interest, you might have stopped to listen.'

Since this was precisely what Annis had done she felt a little awkward. 'I…heard a little. Not all.'

'So you know that Woodhouse has offered to furnish me some information about Mr Ingram's business dealings?'

'I know that you are paying him to do so,' Annis said coldly. 'I fear that you are wasting your money, my lord. Woodhouse is three parts disguised for most of the time. I doubt that he has any useful information to sell you at all.'

'We shall see,' Adam said imperturbably. 'What concerns me more now is what you intend to do about my activities, Lady Wycherley. Will you tell Lafoy?'

There was a silence. Annis had not thought that far but now that she did, she realised she had no idea what she would do. She said, with no hint of challenge, more out of simple curiosity, 'How would you stop me?'

To her surprise, Adam laughed. 'My dear Lady Wycherley, I could not begin to try! I can only tell you that whilst it is true I might be interested in information to discredit Ingram, I have no direct quarrel with your cousin, and I beg you to keep quiet.'

Annis hesitated. 'If you bring down Ingram, you will inevitably hurt Charles in the process.'

Adam's gaze was very direct. 'That might be true.'

'I cannot agree to that.'

Adam sighed. He drove his hands into his pockets. 'I suppose I would not expect anything else of you, ma'am. May I suggest a compromise? I will tell you what I discover—if you will keep my secret.'

Annis sought his gaze. 'You will tell me before you take any action?'

'I shall. I give you my word.'

'Then I agree to your terms, my lord. I will keep the secret.'

There was a pause. 'As easy as that?' Adam said, in an odd tone.

'Of course. What did you expect—that I would extract some kind of payment?' Annis put her head on one side. 'Now I come to think of it, that would be useful. I am always so lamentably hard up—'

Adam laughed again. 'What I meant, as you well know, is that you are a woman of principle. As such I could not imagine you condoning my behaviour. I should be interested to hear your reasoning, ma'am.'

Annis shrugged. 'It is simple. I do not approve of Mr Ingram's methods. As long as you do not hurt Charles—'

'I shall not, I promise you.' He took her hand and kissed it. 'Thank you, ma'am. Against all the odds I think you must trust me.'

His voice was a little husky. Looking up, Annis saw the flash of expression in his eyes, the desire, sensual and disturbing. She tried to pull her hand away. He held her fast. For a second they stood quite still, whilst Annis' heart started to hammer.

'My lord—' she began, but he covered her mouth with his before she could say another word. The room shifted and spun and Annis brought her hands up to clutch at Adam's jacket to steady herself. He kissed her with languorous slowness, teasing a response from her, repressing his own urgency beneath a gentleness that seduced her. Annis slid her hands over his shoulders and tangled them in his hair, pulling him closer.

Adam needed no urging. His kiss claimed her lips again and this time it was insistent, hot and wild with need. Annis made a little sound of surrender deep in her throat. She was conscious of nothing except the sensation of pleasure he aroused in her, and a deep longing to be closer still.

A door closed quietly down the corridor and Annis jumped, pulling away as though she had been stung. Adam caught her elbow to steady her. She felt shocked and light-headed. Her hands were shaking and her voice was shaking too.

'This is scandalous behaviour for a chaperon! I am supposed to be preventing Miss Crossley from behaving in just such a fashion rather than indulging in a flirtation of my own in the library! I cannot think what I was doing... I cannot believe...'

'Is that what you think this is, Lady Wycherley? A light flirtation?' Adam sounded almost as breathless as she. He also sounded angry. 'Devil take it—'

Annis looked at him. Adrift with a mixture of disbelief and condemnation for herself, she had not thought how Adam might feel. She took a steadying breath. 'I beg your pardon. I did not intend to make it sound—'

'Demeaning?'

Now she was sure that he was angry. She stopped and looked at him, her hazel eyes wide.

'Of course I did not intend to make it sound demeaning! Nor light and frivolous, for that matter. I only meant that I should not be indulging in such behaviour—'

'Should you not?' Before Annis could guess his intention, Adam moved so that he had his back against the door. He put out a hand and pulled her negligently back into his arms. 'I am not sure what I should do with you, Lady Wycherley. Kiss you until you admit this is not merely a meaningless flirtation?'

His lips were an inch from hers. Annis could feel his anger and his desire, latent in the lines of his body. She met the blazing grey eyes.

'Very well, I confess it is no mere flirtation,' she whispered.

Adam kissed her hard, then let her go. 'I feel sure we shall talk of this again, but for now we had better find your charge. But first...' He scrutinised her and shook his head, the smile back in his eyes. 'Oh, dear, Lady Wycherley. For once it *does* look as though it is the chaperon who has been kissed in the conservatory.' He held the door of the writing room open for her. 'That is exactly where I should look for Miss Crossley, if I was you.'

Annis was trying desperately to gather her shattered composure. *Later,* she told herself fiercely. *Later you may think about this and decide what you are going to do. For now you must find Fanny and fulfil your chaperon's duties.* She stole a look at Adam's face. Being a chaperon had never been quite so difficult as it appeared to be at the moment.

'The conservatory…' Annis tried to concentrate. 'I had not remembered that there was one.' She looked at Adam suspiciously. 'Did you see Miss Crossley go in there, my lord? You should have told me earlier.'

'No, I did not. It is merely a guess.' Adam hesitated. 'I am a little acquainted with Miss Fanny Crossley—or at least with her behaviour.'

Annis narrowed her eyes. 'You have said nothing before.'

'Certainly not. I was aware that I could ruin her prospects if I chose and then you, Lady Wycherley—' Adam sketched her a mocking bow '—would not receive your fee!'

'Oh!' Annis felt cross and curious in equal measure, but curiosity won. 'Well, I do think it most underhand of you not to tell me, my lord, but you may make up for it now.'

Adam smiled. 'Very well. You are aware that Miss Crossley was in London for the Season?'

'Of course.'

'She managed to attract the notice of the younger brother of a friend of mine.' Adam sighed. 'We all thought that John was making a frightful ass of himself over her, but he is young and Miss Crossley can be quite charming when she tries. Alas, when she discovered that he was not the heir to the Canvey title as she had supposed, she threw him over and tried to seduce Lord Burley instead. In the conservatory!'

Annis shot him an appalled look. 'Good God!' She quickened her pace. 'Does Miss Crossley know that you are aware of her history?'

'I doubt it. I said nothing, but you know how people talk, Lady Wycherley.' Adam shot her a look. 'I believe that was the reason why Miss Crossley failed to catch a husband in London. There were plenty interested in her fortune but her reputation was not so sweet.'

'I *knew* there must be a reason—' Annis broke off. 'Sir Robert insisted that there was nothing wrong, but I suspected there was a reason why his nieces had not taken.'

They reached the door of the conservatory and Annis pushed it open. She heard Fanny's voice at once, impassioned, and very much in the style of Mrs Siddons.

'Ever since we met in London I have been hopelessly in love with you.'

'Oh, lord,' Annis said, under her breath. 'If only I had been quicker I could have averted this! I fear Miss Crossley is quite carried away with her own eloquence!'

Lieutenant Greaves's fluting tones interrupted Fanny, sounding amused. 'Lud, Miss Crossley, it was only a bit of fun! If I'd thought you were after anything other than a flirtation—'

'Oh, but you did! You knew I cared for you!'

The two protagonists were standing behind a rank of huge potted palms and were therefore most taken aback when Annis and Adam Ashwick materialised suddenly beside them. Lieutenant Greaves paled and dropped his weary man-of-the-world stance at once, looking suddenly far more like the young and painfully inadequate youth that he was. Fanny burst into tears.

'Conduct both ungallant and unbecoming to a gentleman in the Light Dragoons,' Adam said pleasantly, as the luckless Lieutenant Greaves tried to flatten himself against the glass window. 'I should think twice before toying with a lady's affections again, lad.'

'Sir, yes, sir!' The Lieutenant shot Fanny an agonised glance. 'All a misunderstanding, sir...'

'I am glad to hear it,' Adam said, turning to Annis. 'Lady Wycherley, are you agreed that this is all an unfortunate mix-up?'

'Yes,' Annis said.

'No!' Fanny said. Her face was as red as Lieutenant Greaves's was pale. It was clear she did not wish him to get away with it—or away from her.

'I think,' Annis said, iron in her tone, 'that you will agree it is all a misunderstanding, Fanny, when you have had time to think about it.'

Adam gave the Lieutenant an ironic bow. 'Run along, Greaves!'

'Sir!' The Lieutenant drew himself up ramrod straight, almost saluted, and practically ran out of the conservatory.

'Silly young fool,' Adam said. 'I hope that will teach him to be more circumspect in future.' He turned to Annis. 'I will leave you to deal with this, Lady Wycherley.' His gaze softened. 'I have not forgotten that I am in your debt. At your service, Miss Crossley...'

He strode out of the room. Fanny started to sob.

'Now, come along, Fanny,' Annis said briskly, 'I am sure that you do not wish Lucy and the others to think that you have been crying. Nor Sir Everard, for that matter.'

Fanny muttered something unintelligible.

'After all,' Annis continued, shepherding her charge out into the corridor, 'it would not do for people to think that there was anything wrong. Sir Everard might think that you did not wish to marry him.'

'I do not!'

'Nor wish for a title or the pleasure of dancing at your sister's wedding as the new Lady Doble!' Annis finished, playing several of her trump cards in one hand.

There was a small silence. Annis could tell that Fanny, a practical girl at heart, still found it difficult to abandon her dream, no matter how foolish.

'I want to marry James Greaves,' the girl said mutinously. 'You could have made him marry me, Lady Wycherley, if you had kicked up a fuss!'

'I do not think so, Fanny,' Annis said coolly. 'Men like Lieutenant Greaves are not interested in settling down. Besides, it was very bad of you to try and entrap him, you know. It grieves me to say so, but you could have ended up as a laughing-stock and with a ruined reputation into the bargain!'

There was another silence whilst Fanny digested this. Annis took the opportunity to collect their cloaks and to send a maid into the ballroom to fetch Lucy. Eventually, when she thought that Fanny had reached the self-pitying stage, she added mendaciously, 'Of course, Fanny, you do realise that Lieutenant Greaves is not good enough for you, don't you?'

Fanny sniffed, wiping her nose on the edge of her cloak. 'He is heir to Lord Farmoor. I have only just discovered it.'

Which explained a good deal, Annis thought. Fanny's discovery about the handsome Lieutenant had turned him from a flirtation into a marriage prospect, and knowing that she had not very long, Fanny had acted quickly.

'I fear your intelligence is only partially correct, Fanny dear,' she said. 'As I understand it, Lieutenant Greaves is Lord Farmoor's heir at the moment, but his lordship has just married a young bride. It would be a tremendous risk, and just when you have secured a baronet as well.'

'Oh!' Fanny looked thoughtful.

Annis sighed. 'I know it must be very painful for you now, but you will soon see that I am in the right of it to discourage the match. Look at the Lieutenant's behaviour tonight! It was scarcely that of a gentleman. Oh, no, Fanny dear, it is better this way. Now look—Lucy is coming and Sir Everard. We shall just behave as though none of this has happened, and the day after tomorrow your uncle will be sending the news of your betrothal to the *Gazette.*'

Fanny gulped and nodded, rubbing away the evidence of tears. 'Very well, Lady Wycherley. I can see that your advice is sound. After all...' she brightened '...I may marry a lord next time, may I not?'

'Indeed you may, Fanny,' Annis said, realising that Fanny already had her widowhood planned before the knot was tied. *That is if you can find one to take you!* she added silently.

Later, in the privacy of her bedchamber, Annis removed her turban, unpinned her hair, took off the turkey-red dress and poured herself a generous glass of madeira.

She felt that she deserved a strong drink for saving both Fanny and herself from disaster. The foolish chit had come within an ace of ruining her own betrothal and Annis's future into the bargain, but all could now run smoothly. Sir Robert Crossley would be making the journey to Yorkshire the following week to take his nieces back to London for the purchase of their trousseaux. Then Annis would be free to go to Starbeck for a space and take a well-deserved rest.

She brushed her hair slowly. The long, lustrous strands fell about her face and down to her waist. She knew that the sensible course of action would be to have it all cut off since she spent so much time hiding it, but some spark of vanity prompted her to keep it long.

Annis paused, hairbrush in hand. Not even the business with Fanny could make her forget what else had happened that evening. She started to think about Adam kissing her, then deliberately forced her mind away and made herself concentrate on the curious scene Adam had had with Woodhouse in the hotel writing-room. Could the man really know something to the discredit of Samuel Ingram—and of Charles? Would Adam keep his word and tell her if he discovered any evidence? Annis shook her head thoughtfully. She was not entirely sure what impulse had prompted her to promise to keep Adam's dealings a secret. Certainly she deplored Ingram's behaviour, but anything he did touched Charles too, and she would do nothing to harm her cousin. Annis wriggled uncomfortably. It was odd, but she did trust Adam Ashwick and she did not know why. The same impulse that had prompted her to trust him the night they met in the dark was at work now. And impulses could be so very dangerous...

Annis finished undressing, climbed into bed and reached for her novel, but she did not read it and soon set it aside, staring instead at the candle flame. It had been blissful to be held in Adam's arms. His kisses had set her senses ablaze. She could not deny it. And it was not just a light flirtation. She knew it had angered him to have their actions cheapened thus. So now she was being honest. She had never wanted a man as she wanted Adam Ashwick. Truth to tell, she had never really wanted—needed—a man at all. She had thought that she never would. She had been naïve.

Annis sighed. As far as she could see, there were three courses of action for a woman in a position like hers. She could continue to work for a living, she could become a shady widow living off the generosity of men in return for her favours, or she could marry respectably again. A small smile curved Annis's lips. She had never previously considered becoming a courtesan, but now the idea held distinct possibilities. If she were to be the mistress of such a man as Adam Ashwick... Her smile vanished. She knew enough of the world to know that such arrangements seldom lasted. Was she to become like a parcel, passed from hand to hand, slightly tatty about the edges? That was not so appealing an idea. Besides, she had the strong belief that Adam would not countenance such an arrangement. He wanted her—she knew that he did. Yet she was also certain that he was a man of honour and would propose marriage. She might seduce him, but he would still insist on marrying her. And his will was as strong as hers.

Marriage. Annis's gaze narrowed. Most women would not think twice. Most women would be delighted. She was not most women. She shuddered to remember the horror of her marriage to John Wycherley and the way he had tried to control even the smallest aspect of her life. Preserving her independence was the only answer and she would do well to remember that.

She picked up her book again. Before long, her eyelids were drooping and the book fell from her hand to rest on the coverlet. It was left to Mrs Hardcastle, tapping at the door because she could see that there was still a light burning, to blow out the candle on the nightstand and leave Annis to sleep.

'There's a letter for you this morning, Miss Annis.' Mrs Hardcastle, pin neat in black bombazine, held the missive out to Annis as though it was in somewhat questionable taste.

'Tom Shepard brought it. Tom the younger, that is. Apparently his father is laid up with the lumbago.'

'Dear me.' Annis unfolded the letter. As though there were not enough difficulties to deal with at Starbeck, without Tom Shepard falling ill. 'Did Tom the younger not wish to come in?'

Mrs Hardcastle looked shocked. 'He came into the kitchen, ma'am! He certainly would not come in *here*.' Mrs Hardcastle gave the drawing-room a disapproving look. 'Why, he might have met one of your young ladies!'

'I am sure that they would have been delighted to meet him,' Annis said drily. Tom Shepard the younger was exceptionally good looking and as a farmer's son would have a certain rustic appeal to the Misses Crossley.

'Him's too bashful,' Mrs Hardcastle said, shaking her head. 'I was hoping he'd make a match with my youngest niece, Cicely, but he was too shy and now she's been snapped up by Jim Durkin, over Saltaire way.'

'It would have been quite safe for Tom to come in,' Annis said. 'Fanny and Lucy are gone to visit the Promenade Rooms with Sibella this morning, for I have an appointment in town and Sib promised to escort them on my behalf.'

Mrs Hardcastle wiped an invisible speck of dust from the table with the corner of her apron.

'It's you that young Tom is sweet on, Miss Annis, not the girls! I heard him tell that you rode like an angel and were the most gracious lady he'd ever met. Then there's Ellis Benson, over at Linforth. They say he was a holding a torch for you for ever so many years.' Mrs Hardcastle looked disapproving. 'You never see what's under your nose, Miss Annis.'

Annis looked up in the liveliest astonishment. 'Ellis Ben-

son? Tom Shepard? Really, Hardy, you make me sound like…
like a female Casanova!'

Mrs Hardcastle pursed her lips. 'Well, there's talk, Miss
Annis. Mostly about you and that fancy Lord—'

'Lord Ashwick?' Annis started to open the letter. 'I do not
want to hear any gossip, Hardy.'

'No? All right, then.'

Annis unfolded the paper. 'What are they saying?'

'Knew you wanted to know,' Mrs Hardcastle said with
satisfaction. 'Only that he means to marry you—'

'What?' It was such a sudden and unexpected confirmation of her thoughts the previous night that Annis dropped
the letter on the floor.

'Everyone has noticed 'im courting you.'

'There is nothing to notice!' Annis stood up in agitation
and walked over to the window. 'Lord Ashwick is not courting me, Hardy. I am a chaperon. I make matches for other
people.'

Mrs Hardcastle sniffed. 'Can't see what's in front of your
face if you ask me, Miss Annis. Too busy arranging mar-
riages to see when someone wants you instead of your girls!'

'I assure you that you are completely mistaken!'

'Well, we'll see,' Mrs Hardcastle said, massively unconvinced. 'Another pot of tea, ma'am?'

'Thank you. That would be nice.' Annis raised her brows.
'What will you be doing today, Hardy? Waging war on the
mice again?'

'No time for that when I have the young ladies' rooms to
clean out,' Mrs Hardcastle said. 'Tomorrow, mebbe. There
is another mouse nest up in the attic.'

'I am aware of it,' Annis said. 'Last night the little creatures were scampering across the ceiling at all hours. It sounded like an army marching through!'

After Mrs Hardcastle had gone, Annis poured herself a second cup, lay back in her chair in a most hoydenish fashion, and gave a huge sigh. Mrs Hardcastle's representation of her as Harrogate's *femme fatale* seemed quite unreasonable, particularly as Miss Mardyn was visiting the town and was surely more worthy of gossip. With another sigh she turned her attention to the letter.

'Dear Lady Wycherley,' it read, in careful print, 'Mr Ingram's agent has called again, telling us that you intend to sell the farm and that the rents will go up. You know that we could not abide to be Ingram's tenants, nor could we afford it. We cannot believe that you would sell to him, madam. Please tell us what is happening as we do not know what to believe. Some of the sheep have been taken again and we are in dire straits. Respectfully yrs, Tom Shepard.'

Annis crumpled the letter up in her hand. A huge, hot fury took her as she thought of Tom and Eliza Shepard out at Starbeck, trying to scrape a living from a farm that barely brought in enough income to support one person, never mind a family, and being bullied by Ingram's agent into the bargain. Their elder son, John, had left to find work in the nearby town of Leeds in the last year, defeated in his attempts to wrest a living from the poor soil and the few sheep that grazed the upper pastures. Annis had promised to look after Tom, Eliza and their remaining family, just as her father had always done, but now that Ingram was sniffing around the farm and the estate, she felt frighteningly vulnerable. This was the second time that Tom had written asking for advice, and in a way it was timely, for she had an appointment to see Samuel Ingram that very morning. She had decided to tell him once and for all that she was not interested in his offer for Starbeck.

Annis stood up, tension making her fidgety, and walked across to the window. She would have liked to ask Charles for advice, but as Ingram's lawyer it was hopeless to expect him to be impartial. Annis knew that he would tell her that the Shepards should sell—and so should she. In some ways to sell Starbeck would be a huge relief, but in others it was quite out of the question. She had inherited the welfare of the villagers along with the house and she was not prepared to shirk that responsibility. Besides, she hated Ingram's bullying tactics and was determined not to give in. He would be the worst landlord she could ever wish upon her tenants.

She thrust the letter into her reticule and went to don her pelisse, bonnet and half-boots. There had been a thunderstorm the previous night and it had left the air fresh and pleasantly crisp, making it a nice morning for a walk. Ingram's chambers were only just around the corner. As she turned into Park Row she saw a smartly dressed couple just disappearing around the corner in front of her. The lady was Miss Mardyn, resplendent in a chic gown of striped brown satin and nodding ostrich plumes. Annis could only see the back of the gentleman's head, but he was tall and dark. Adam Ashwick, perhaps. The thought made her feel even more bad-tempered.

In her anxiety, she was early and found herself obliged to wait in a small antechamber, where a supercilious clerk shuffled paper and watched her out of the corner of his eye. Annis tried not to fidget. After fifteen minutes she was certain that Ingram was deliberately keeping her waiting and as time ticked by she became more and more angry. Eventually the door of Ingram's inner sanctum opened and Annis's heart sank as her cousin Charles came to escort her in. Behind him she could see Ingram himself—and Woodhouse, whom she had last seen only the previous night, talking to Adam Ashwick. The clerk gave her a look like a startled rabbit and ducked his head, as though trying to melt into the furniture. Annis had no intention of breaking her word to Adam, but the sight of the clerk made her feel even more uncomfortable to be there.

Ingram came forward to bow over Annis's hand, his manner odiously smooth and yet somehow managing to convey that his time was precious and he could only spare her three minutes of it.

'Lady Wycherley. What may I do for you, ma'am?'

'Thank you for seeing me, Mr Ingram,' Annis said coldly. She took the chair that he indicated, and then wished that she had not when he remained standing. 'I am sure this will not take long. It concerns the proposed sale of Starbeck, the estate and the farm.'

'Ah!' Ingram gazed vaguely out of the window and across the street, as though the view was far more interesting than Annis. 'Yes. I hope that you have seen the sense in selling, Lady Wycherley.' He laughed mirthlessly. 'Although I fear that Mr and Mrs Shepard seem disinclined to become my tenants!'

'Mr and Mrs Shepard are tired of being harried by your agent!' Annis said. 'They have empowered me to tell you so, Mr Ingram. They would appreciate it if you called your man off and did not press the matter any further. And whilst we are on the subject, so should I. I do not wish to sell the Starbeck estate—'

'Estate!' Ingram gave a short laugh. 'You set yourself high, ma'am, to call it thus! A ruined house and few acres of land!'

Annis kept a grip on her temper. 'A few acres that you evidently value highly, Mr Ingram! Your agent has been most pressing!'

Ingram shrugged. 'Benson will continue to press until you all see sense, Lady Wycherley.'

'By taking our sheep and making matters even more difficult?' Annis was incensed. She cast a glance at Charles, but he did not meet her eye. He was looking flushed and unhappy.

'Surely you do not think that there was any connection between the sheep disappearing and Benson's visit?' Ingram seemed amused. He hooked his thumbs into the pockets of his shiny black waistcoat. 'Tut, tut, what an imagination you do have, ma'am!'

'Annis,' Charles said suddenly, 'please try to see reason—'

Annis swung round on him. 'All I can see, Charles, is that you appear to have misplaced your family loyalty!'

'Your cousin is in a difficult position, Lady Wycherley,' Ingram said. 'He can appreciate the value of my plans. Now, he is the head of the family, so do you not think you should be guided by him? He has your best interests at heart, you know. And those of your tenants.'

Annis, who had been waving the Shepards' letter about in the air, stuffed it in her bag and stalked towards the door.

'Our ideas of what is in the best interests of Starbeck are clearly divergent,' she said coldly. 'I will bid you good day.

Both of you,' she added sharply, as Charles moved to escort her out.

'A moment, Lady Wycherley—' Ingram said quickly. Annis turned.

'I am persuaded that you may come around to my point of view, ma'am,' Ingram said. 'There are usually ways to help people see that it is in their own interests...'

Annis knew that the colour had left her face. She felt a little sick and the bright room suddenly seemed darker. She felt frighteningly vulnerable.

'Are you threatening me, Mr Ingram?'

'Good gracious me, no, ma'am!' Ingram gave a puffy laugh. 'But you know how difficult it is to eke a living from Starbeck and its surrounding farms. You have mentioned yourself that the sheep go missing. If there were to be a fire, for instance, and the livestock killed or the buildings damaged, that would make life even more difficult for you and your tenants. Or there is your own line of work...' His voice changed subtly, became even more silky. 'A word dropped here or there about your suitability as a chaperon... One has to be so very careful of a reputation, and there are those who say that you have been consorting with Lord Ashwick...'

Annis's eyes flashed. 'There are those who say that you consort with the devil, Mr Ingram! One must not believe every foolish rumour that one hears. Good day to you. Pray do not trouble to show me out, Charles.'

When she reached the bottom, white-painted step outside, Annis hesitated for a moment, a hand on the railings, drawing a lungful of fresh air to try and calm herself. There was a step behind her and Charles's voice:

'Annis—'

'Charles,' Annis said with dangerous calm, 'do not speak to me, I beg.'

'Annis...' Charles ran a hand through his fair hair '...in a little while I may be able to help you.'

Annis waved his excuses away. 'All you have to do,' she said dully, 'is to show a little family feeling, Charles. I used to rely upon you.' The sunlight was making her eyes sting. She hoped that she was not going to cry. 'I do not want to talk about it. I do not even want to think about it! Go away!'

She left him standing on the steps and set off down the street. She was not certain whether it was busy or not. The figures of the passers-by blurred before her eyes and she scrubbed her face sharply. If Ingram should start to drop hints that she was unreliable or that there was something scandalous in her behaviour... Her financial survival was tenuous enough as it was, and no one would employ her if they suspected that her reputation was damaged. She was to all intents and purposes alone in the world and gossip was so harmful, even when it was untrue.

Then there was Starbeck. Her father had bought the estate as a place to retire; although he had died before he had returned to England, Annis had been happy to take on the house and its obligations. That had been before the sheep stealing had become rife and the villages began to seethe with hatred towards Ingram, a hatred which she felt so strongly herself now. She detested bullies.

Annis tried to think about her options, but her mind was a scramble of images. Sibella's household could not afford to support her as a pensioner and the last person she would accept help from was Charles. He had paid for her little town house in Church Row, so if they became estranged she would have to leave… Perhaps she would have to leave Harrogate altogether and go and live at Starbeck herself and become a farmer…except that she knew nothing about farming and she had little money and Starbeck was barely inhabitable…

She swiped at some nearby railings in helpless and hopeless anger. 'Hell and damnation!'

'Lady Wycherley?'

Annis swung round. Adam Ashwick was standing a bare few yards away, having evidently witnessed her unladylike attack on the railings. He was looking at her with amusement and speculation in his grey eyes. Annis inclined her head with haughty composure, trying to hide that fact that her thoughts were all mixed up. Along with images of herself locked in Adam's arms the previous night were thoughts that at least she was not wearing her turban this morning, followed by the unwelcome idea that Adam had probably come straight from his mistress. She blushed.

'Good morning, Lord Ashwick.'

'It is a very pleasant morning in fact, Lady Wycherley,' Adam said politely. 'However, you do not appear to be finding it so. I trust that you have not damaged your umbrella?'

Annis looked down at the umbrella a little self-consciously. 'I do not believe so. I am afraid that I was venting my dissatisfaction.'

Adam raised his brows. 'I see.' He smiled at her. 'I hope that the problem is not insurmountable. May I be of service to you in any way?'

Annis hesitated. It was tempting to pour out her difficulties about Starbeck as she needed an ally and she already knew that Adam was in dispute with Ingram. Yet there was still

Charles to consider, for even if he had apparently forgotten family loyalty, she had not…

'I thank you, but no, my lord. And I must apologise for my ill manners. A trifling business transaction is going a little awry. I am persuaded that all will be well soon.'

'I see,' Adam said again, slowly. His thoughtful gaze moved from her to the door of Ingram's offices and back again.

'May I escort you back to Church Row, ma'am?'

'Thank you, but I have some shopping to do first.'

'Then perhaps I might walk with you to Park Street? I too have a few errands to run.'

It was difficult to refuse. Annis rested her hand lightly on Adam's proffered arm as they strolled along the pavement.

'I hope that your difficulty with Miss Crossley last night was successfully resolved,' Adam said. 'Is the betrothal to Sir Everard still current?'

Annis smiled a little. 'It is, I thank you.'

'Then that cannot be the source of your displeasure.' Adam frowned. 'Let me guess. That means it must be Starbeck, I suppose.'

'You are partially correct, my lord.' Annis laughed. 'There are two causes for vexation and one of those is indeed Starbeck. My cousin—' She stopped, feeling guilty. 'It seems that everyone feels I should sell, but I do not wish to do so.'

She felt Adam stiffen. 'Am I to understand that Mr Ingram has made you an offer for the estate?'

Annis cast him a swift sideways look. He was frowning abstractedly. 'Yes, he has,' she said. 'You may be easy however, my lord. I have refused it.'

Adam shot her a look from under lowered brows. 'That

cannot have made you popular. I infer that you are under a deal of pressure from Lafoy as well as Ingram?'

Annis nodded unhappily.

'And can you afford to run the estate yourself?'

Annis shook her head. 'No. I can stave off ruin for a little, but I have only a small annuity. That and what I earn—' She stopped, aware that she was vouchsafing a great deal of personal information to him. He seemed all too easy to confide in.

It appeared, however, that Adam was prepared to be equally frank in return.

'I cannot abide the thought of Ingram owning the land, but you know my parlous financial state. I cannot afford to buy Starbeck from you myself or I would surely do it.'

Annis gave a little, dispirited shrug. 'I am sure that I shall think of a solution, sir.'

'You mentioned two problems,' Adam said. 'If Starbeck is the first, what is the second?'

Annis glanced at him under her lashes. 'The second is more personal, my lord. I do not think… That is, it would not be right for me to tell you.'

Adam looked amused. 'Good God, why not? Is Ingram blackmailing you, Lady Wycherley?'

Annis looked at him. 'No. At least, not exactly. He exerts pressure where he knows it will have the greatest effect.' She remembered the scene in the ballroom and Adam's hesitation to do Ingram's bidding. 'Is he blackmailing *you*, my lord?'

Adam looked startled. He stopped walking and spun round towards her. 'Why would you think that?'

Annis smiled. 'I believe that is the first time you have not given me a straight answer to a straight question, my lord. It leads me to suspect that I am correct.'

Adam sighed. 'Like you, ma'am, I am under pressure. You are aware that my brother-in-law was in debt to Ingram. He is using the threat of releasing the detail of that debt as a lever.'

'To gain what? Surely not Eynhallow?'

Adam looked grim. 'No, he has yet to go that far. Influence is what he wants from me, Lady Wycherley. Social recognition...acceptance... He may whistle for it!'

'Oh!' Light dawned on Annis. 'Last night at the ball, when Charles invited you to join Ingram's party, was that a part of his plan to gain acceptance?'

'I imagine so. I think he believed that I would give him countenance, but I was not prepared to accede to his wishes. The man is nothing but a contemptible bully.'

Annis stifled an unexpected giggle. 'Oh, dear, he must have been so vexed with you! I know that I should not laugh, but it is pleasant sometimes to see Mr Ingram gainsaid. And Lady Emily Trumpton and Lady Cardew were muttering last night about what a jumped-up nobody he was and how they would never accept him. It is fortunate that you did not agree to sponsor him, my lord, or they would have thought you had taken leave of your senses!'

Adam laughed. 'I would rather not offend Lady Cardew if I can help it for she is a fearsome old battleaxe. But you have not told me what Mr Ingram's hold is over you, Lady Wycherley. What could you possibly have done to give him the means to blackmail you?'

Annis's laughter faded. 'It is nothing as desperate as that, I assure you, my lord, just some nasty threats—'

'About what?'

Annis sighed. 'I have explained to you before that a chaperon's reputation is a vulnerable thing, my lord. Mr Ingram has also noticed that fact.'

'He seeks to threaten you with gossip?' Adam said slowly. 'About what?'

'About you, my lord,' Annis said candidly. She saw him frown and added hastily, 'Oh, have no fear—if it were not that I am sure that he would find something else. You said yourself that the man is adept at finding a lever.'

'The man crawls in the gutter,' Adam said, and there was such anger in his tone that Annis was taken aback.

'Please... I am sorry that I mentioned it to you.'

'I am not.' Adam gave her a very straight look. 'I was not aware, however, that there had been any conjecture about us.'

Annis remembered what Mrs Hardcastle had said and hastily disregarded it. 'I am persuaded that there has not. It is all manufactured.'

Adam was frowning. 'What if that was not the case, Lady Wycherley?'

'I beg your pardon?'

'What if the gossip was true and I was paying court to you? You know that from the first my sole interest has been in you. We could make the gossip true and then there would be no scandal.'

Annis stared at him. She had been grappling with the difficulties of Ingram's blackmail and this latest idea took her quite by surprise.

'I...but...' Annis pulled herself together. 'We have spoken of this, my lord. You know that I would have to discourage your attentions. It is clearly impossible.'

'How so?' Adam closed the gap between them.

Annis's gaze fell. 'Because... Because I... I have already

explained to you that my situation as a chaperon does not allow it.'

'That situation will end when the Misses Crossley leave, will it not?'

'For the time being. But it is my profession. I am to go to London for the Little Season. It is all arranged.' Annis gestured distractedly with her hands. Adam caught them both in his.

'So that is your first objection. What else?'

Annis had the desperate feeling that she was fighting a losing battle. 'There are many. I prefer to be independent.'

'I could change your mind.'

Annis frowned. For the first time, a tiny corner of her mind whispered that he might be right. 'That is very arrogant, my lord.'

'Very well. We shall see. What else?'

'There is your mistress. I saw you with her earlier.'

Adam laughed. 'I collect that you mean Miss Mardyn?'

'Who else?' Annis looked at him severely. 'Unless you have more than one mistress in keeping?'

'I have none, I assure you. I have no interest in Miss Mardyn. Whoever you saw with her, it was not I.'

'Well, never mind.' Annis had belatedly realised that she might sound jealous. It was true, of course, but she did not wish Adam to know that. Nor did she wish to give credence to the idea that she was actually considering his suggestion seriously. She freed her hands.

'This is ridiculous. You cannot wish to pay court to me. Such things simply do not happen to me.'

Adam smiled. 'I hesitate to contradict a lady, but it just has done. Do you truly find it so surprising that I might wish to pay my addresses to you?'

Annis frowned. 'I suppose I must believe you, but...' Her troubled gaze searched his face and she burst out, 'This is foolish, my lord. We have only recently met—'

'That is true. It does not mean that we need to remain strangers, however.' Adam smiled. 'I thought that you liked me a little.'

Annis sighed. 'You know that I am attracted to you, my lord.'

She saw the flash of all-male satisfaction in his eyes. 'Then give me a chance.'

Annis hesitated. The pull was very strong. But so was the pull of memory and she knew that marriage was not for her. She would never forget that stifling feeling of being trapped. She shook her head. 'I am sorry, my lord. I cannot do that. I must bid you good day.'

As she walked off she knew that he was still watching her and as she turned the corner she could not resist a look over her shoulder. Sure enough, he was standing where she had left him and there was a rueful smile still on his lips. When he saw her turn to look at him he inclined his head, very deliberately, as though reminding her that she might have held her resolve this time, but that he was determined too, and he knew she was weakening.

Chapter Eight

Sir Robert Crossley came to collect his nieces the following afternoon. There were many false professions of affection from Fanny, some genuine ones from Lucy and sincere gratitude and a fat purse of money from Sir Robert himself. After the carriage had drawn away, Annis went back into the drawing room, kicked off her satin pumps, plumped herself down on the sofa, and tossed her turban in the air.

Sibella called at three o'clock and she had a treat for Annis up her sleeve.

'I have had such a good idea,' she began, as they descended from her carriage outside the Crown Hotel. 'I thought that you deserved a reward, Annis, for refraining from strangling that odious Miss Crossley, so I have arranged for us to bathe. Far better to take a hot spa bath than to drink the waters! Mr Thackwray is very busy this afternoon, but he has squeezed us in.'

'Oh good,' Annis said glumly. It was kind of Sibella to

have thought to offer her a treat, but it was many years since Annis had taken the bath cure and she knew there must be a reason for that. Probably it was because the water was disgustingly malodorous. She could smell it already as they followed Mr Thackwray up the Crown's imposing mahogany staircase. The place was thronging with guests.

'I forget how popular Harrogate has become in the high summer,' Sibella commented. 'Why, it seems more crowded every year!'

Mr Thackwray beamed. 'The sulphur cure is remarkably efficacious, ladies, and, if I may say so, Harrogate has a certain quality that is lacking in other spa towns. Some of the southern spas have become decidedly *déclassé*, I fear...'

'At least the Bath Spa has a Pump Room,' Sibella whispered to Annis when their host's broad back was turned. 'Here we have to make do with a well with a canopy over! I heard one London lady say that she expected no better from the North, although she supposed that the lack of refinement added to Harrogate's rustic charm!'

Annis laughed. 'Surely the town is rich enough these days to build a Pump Room? Although it would not surprise me if Mr Thackwray opposed any such development. Why, he must make a fortune by offering medicinal baths here in his hotel!'

Sibella, who swore by the sulphur cure, frowned. 'You must own that rheumaticky patients are far more comfortable here than having to dip themselves in the sulphur well, Annis! I think Mr Thackwray offers a fine service.'

Mr Thackwray's suite of rooms was indeed comprehensive. Stretching along the whole of the first floor of the hotel were a series of small bedchambers with bathrooms in between, all interconnected to offer the opportunity for guests and visitors alike to sample the pleasures of the spa bath. The hotelier now stood aside to usher them into a small room in which two wooden baths stood side by side. The air was thick with steam and the smell of rotten eggs. An aproned attendant was emptying a copper pan into one of the baths and smilingly offered to help them off with their outdoor clothes. Mr Thackwray, bowing, beat a discreet retreat.

'Ugh!' Annis said, hanging back as her cousin went behind a screen and divested herself of her clothing, 'why, it smells to high heaven in here and looks hot enough to broil a lobster! Why do you do this to yourself, Sib?'

Sibella discarded her dressing robe and slipped into the water. She lay back, closed her eyes and smiled beatifically at her cousin.

'It is splendidly enjoyable, Annis, once you get used to it. I can only have the waters warm at the moment because of my condition, but I find it very soothing. What is more, it is a sovereign cure for all sorts of maladies from the rheumaticks to the smallpox. It helps to cure the lesions, you know.'

Annis stared hard into the water. The thought of what might be lurking in there was deeply unappealing. 'You do not have the lesions, Sib. They do change the water for each customer, do they not?'

'Of course!' Sibella turned her head and opened her eyes. Her short blonde hair was already sticking up in damp spikes. 'Now be a good girl and get in. You will soon see how thoroughly pleasant the experience can be!'

The attendant helped Annis to unbutton her dress, then left the two ladies to bathe, informing them that she would be back in an hour's time to help them dress. Annis dipped one toe in the water and grimaced.

'Ouch! That is very hot!'

'That,' Sibella said patiently, 'is the point, Annis.'

'It is all very well for you, sitting there is a warm tub! I am broiling here!'

Annis lowered herself gingerly into the bath. The sides were steep and the tub bore an unfortunate resemblance to a coffin. The water came up to her chin and it was extremely hot. The smell of sulphur rose from it like a cloud. Annis wrinkled up her nose and tried not to sneeze. The idea of a coffin seemed most apt—if the scalding water did not cause a heart attack and carry you off, the smell surely would. That was if the rheumaticks had not got you first, of course.

'Ugh!' Annis tried not to inhale. 'I have seldom felt the need to take the waters before. Now I know why!'

'You must breathe, Annis,' Sibella said, turning her head in her cousin's direction. 'Otherwise you will not have the benefit of the efficacious vapours. They are renowned for clearing the head.'

'That I can well believe.' Annis found the smell of sulphur was so intense that it felt as though it was splitting her skull in two. Not for nothing was Harrogate's spa also known as the 'Stinking Spaw'. Visitors might travel from miles around to take the waters and townsfolk like Sibella might claim it to be healthful, but Annis suspected that it was all some huge jest at their expense. No doubt Mr Thackwray was even now rubbing his hands at the thought of the gullible parting with their money for the fashionable cure.

'It is very good of you to introduce me to the pleasures of the spa,' she said, 'but a little shopping would have sufficed!'

'We can do that as well,' Sibella said sleepily. 'Oh, Annis, it is good to have some time with you. You seldom have the chance to chat when you are chaperoning those wretched girls and I know you are off to Starbeck in a few days. For all that it is only four-and-twenty miles away, it sometimes feels like hundreds!'

'On those roads it certainly does,' Annis said feelingly. Travellers on the Skipton and Starbeck roads often had the bruises to prove it for days afterwards. Starbeck was set high on the Yorkshire moors and many of the roads were poor and badly kept. Annis thought it unlikely that Ingram's tollbooths would improve matters. Doubtless the money would go directly into his pockets.

She sighed and lay back in the water, following Sibella's lead and closing her eyes. Now that she was becoming more accustomed to it, the spa water was actually very relaxing. She was starting to feel sleepy and content, a world away from Ingram and his veiled threats and the problems at Starbeck and the provocative dilemma of Adam Ashwick. She really should not have entertained his proposals of courtship for a second, but he was strangely difficult to resist—and devilishly attractive...

Sibella yawned. 'Are you glad to be rid of your charges, Annis?'

'Oh, prodigiously! Though Sir Robert Crossley paid well, it was nowhere near enough to compensate for the wilfulness of his odious niece! If Fanny Crossley does not run away before the wedding, I shall be most surprised!'

'The other girl was a sweet child,' Sibella said, 'and perhaps Miss Crossley was unhappy, Annis. Unhappiness can make people very bad-tempered. I remember Mama was a martyr to the gout and it made her very cross indeed.'

'You always look for the best in everyone, Sib,' Annis

said affectionately. 'I do believe you might even excuse Mr Ingram if you tried!'

'That reminds me—I saw Charles at luncheon,' Sibella said. Her tone had changed and Annis knew her well enough to guess what was coming. 'He told me that you and he are at daggers' drawn. Oh, Annis, I do so hate it when you are at odds!'

Annis hated it as well. She was fiercely fond of her cousins, particularly as they had made her welcome when her husband had died and she had returned home to Yorkshire. The Lafoys had held land in the Yorkshire Dales for centuries, but their estate had dwindled to nothing in the previous generation. Charles and Sibella's father had been the spendthrift squire who had lost their small patrimony, necessitating Charles to learn a profession and Sibella to marry. Annis's father was the younger son, a sea captain who had bought the small estate of Starbeck for when he retired from his travels—except that he had died before this had happened. Annis, the only child, had vague memories of flying visits to Starbeck during his time ashore, but the rest of the time was a blur of lodgings in Southampton and Plymouth, school in Bath, a passage to India and the final brief, blazing summer in Bermuda. Annis's mother had died there, shortly after her father had been lost at sea.

'I am sorry, Sib,' Annis said sincerely. 'I know that you feel it keenly when Charles and I quarrel and I hate it too. I know that he has a living to make, but I cannot stomach him working for Samuel Ingram. The man is nothing more than a ruthless bully!'

Sibella's pretty face crinkled up with distress. Annis seldom criticised Charles to his sister for she knew it was not fair. In Harrogate Sibella was protected from the rumbling discontent that dominated village life and so was unaware that the name of Ingram was fast becoming a curse in the hamlets that surrounded Starbeck.

'I am sure Mr Ingram cannot be all bad,' Sibella said unhappily. 'I hear dreadful things about him, but surely they are exaggerated. I know that he wishes to buy Starbeck, Annis, but he is offering a good price—'

'Oh, let us not speak of that!' Annis said hastily. 'It will only put me out of humour and I did so want to enjoy this afternoon. I deserve it!'

Sibella was still frowning. 'Yes, but speaking of Mr Ingram, Charles told me at luncheon that there has been more trouble at Linforth. Apparently there was a riot in the village last night, and one of Mr Ingram's barns was looted and burned. Charles was very angry, but I always think that the villagers must be so poor they cannot help themselves.'

Annis sighed ruefully. 'Dearest Sib, you know as well as I that rioting is a capital offence and cannot be condoned.'

'I know.' Sibella sighed. 'But when one is so poor, Annis...'

'Yes,' Annis said. 'I know. I believe it must be intensely difficult. And it is not as though they do not have provocation. I heard that Ingram evicted some of the villagers last week because he wanted a higher rent for their cottages. They had nowhere else to go and one woman went into labour prematurely and lost her baby as a result...' Annis winced. 'No, I cannot blame anyone who rebels against him.'

'Charles also said that he thought some of the local gentry might be stirring up trouble,' Sibella said. 'Apparently the leader of the rioters spoke like a gentleman and rode a bay horse. Ingram has offered a reward for information.' She turned her head to look at Annis. 'Who do you think it could be, Annis? Is it not intriguing?'

'Fascinating,' Annis said. She was disconcerted to find herself remembering that Adam Ashwick had a bay horse in his stables. 'There are not many men who fit the bill.'

'No.' Sibella looked thoughtful. 'There is Sir Everard Doble—'

'A ridiculous idea!' Annis laughed. 'As well suspect a tailor's dummy!'

'Well, then, how about Tom Shepard?'

'Perhaps...' Annis frowned. There had been a bay stallion in the stable at Starbeck as well. 'There is Mr Benson...'

'But he works for Ingram!'

'So does Charles, so I suppose they are both out of the running.' Annis sighed. 'I always believe that it is the most unlikely candidate in these cases.'

'Lord Ashwick?'

'Close. I suspect his brother. You mark my words, Sib, the Honourable Mr Edward Ashwick will prove the culprit!'

Sibella gave a gurgle of laughter. 'Oh, Annis, you are dreadful, blaming the rector! He is such a nice man as well.'

'So? I do not see why that disqualifies him. Indeed, I admire anyone who has the audacity to stand up to Ingram, capital offence or no!'

'Oh, well...' Sibella smiled '...we shall see, for I am afraid he is bound to be caught. Why, someone will turn him in for a reward of one hundred pounds.'

'Do not be so sure,' Annis said. She was remembering the scene at the tollhouse. 'Whoever is leading the rebels, the villagers will see him as one of their own. They will not turn coat, Sib.'

'Oh, well,' Sibella said again, 'let us speak of something more cheerful, Annis. Let us talk about you! Why do you not marry again and settle down?'

Annis laughed. 'You never give up trying, do you, Sib!'

'I should think not. I am very happy...' Sibella smiled blissfully '...and I think that you could be too!'

Annis shook her head. 'I cannot imagine it,' she said. 'You were fortunate in your choice, Sib, but I could not consent to remarry simply to secure my future. That was how I made such a disastrous mistake in the first place! No, give me my independence any day.'

Annis could see that Sibella was looking distressed again, as she did when anything did not quite fit with her own, ordered view of life. Sibella would no more wish to be independent than she would walk naked down Park Street, and she was not comfortable with those whose way of life was less conventional than her own. Annis reflected that her cousin had been lucky. Though she had been penniless, her beauty and sweet nature had attracted a gentleman of modest means who truly loved her.

Annis's life had not been so smooth. Her peripatetic childhood had been most stimulating, but it had ended in a dreadful fashion when her father was lost at sea and her mother died soon after, leaving Annis's whole world crashing about her when she was only seventeen. She had grasped the marriage to John Wycherley without thinking, needing only a little certainty at a terrible time. It was later that she had discovered that her security was bought at a heavy price.

'One day you may meet a man who pleases you,' Sibella said hopefully, her face clearing. 'Perhaps we shall even find you a husband in Harrogate this summer! There are plenty of the fashionable crowd up from London.'

I have met a man who pleases me, Annis thought involuntarily, the image of Adam Ashwick rising unbidden in her mind, *but I have no intention of risking everything because of it!*

She did not express her thoughts and gave her cousin a smile instead, knowing that Sibella was happy now as she contemplated a conventional match for her. Her cousin had tried to marry her off plenty of times before. Unfortunately her judgement was not always sound. The last potential husband, an army colonel on furlough, had later been cashiered for stealing supplies and selling them on.

'I fear you would find it a tall order catching a husband for me,' she said, stretching out in the bath. 'Not only do I have no fortune, but I am not even passably good looking. Though I can scarce complain, I suppose, having made myself look an old frump for the past five years! No, Sibella, I am well and truly at my last prayers now and I am content for it to be so.'

Her damp hair was clinging to her cheeks now with a mixture of condensation and perspiration, but it did not feel too unpleasant. The warmth of the water had seeped into her bones, making her body feel soft and pliant.

Sibella snorted. 'That was not what I had heard. I heard a certain rumour that Lord Ashwick was most attentive to you, Annis. Indeed, it must be so, for did he not dance with you at the ball at the Dragon? I hear he never dances.'

'If it comes to that,' Annis said, 'neither do I.'

'Well, then!' Sibella's blue eyes sparkled. 'Do you like him?'

Annis considered the option of escaping Sibella's questions

by submerging herself under the spa waters and rejected it ruefully. She would surely die of the smell.

'Yes... I suppose I do.'

'I knew it!' Sibella clapped her hands and set up a tidal wave. 'You must like him very much to admit to even a small partiality. So...' She paused invitingly.

Annis grimaced. 'Do not ask me, Sib. You know that it only makes you unhappy when I do not agree with you that marriage is the universal panacea.'

For once, Sibella did not argue. 'You mean...because of John? But, Annis, not all men are so domineering—'

'I know!' Annis said hastily. 'I am sure David is a paragon of male perfection. It is simply that I cannot risk such a thing again, Sib. Oh...' she threw her cousin an appealing look '...if you knew how repressive it was, not to be allowed out of the house except when John decreed, to be told how to dress, what to read, who to see! Having gained my freedom, how may I ever trust myself to a man again? I think I would run mad if I married again only to find myself so constrained!' She put her hands up to her face briefly. 'I swear, Sib, that I thought my head would burst with the misery and frustration of it all. I actually prayed for John to die and free me, and how dreadful and desperate is that?'

Sibella's face was sad. 'I do understand, Annis. I know you were ill with the wretchedness of it all. Yet that does not mean that all men are the same. I am persuaded that when you fall in love you will trust the man enough to take that risk. One day you will surprise yourself.'

'And surprise you, I'll warrant!'

'No.' Sibella shook her head. 'I shall not be surprised in the least.'

Annis lay back and closed her eyes again. She had been tempted to take a risk with Adam Ashwick, more tempted than she had ever been in her life before, but when pressed she had chosen the familiar ground and opted for safety. She would never know what might have happened had she taken a different course.

There was a splash as Sibella sat up, sloshing much of the precious sulphur water on to the floor. Annis hoped that Mr Thackwray's decorative plaster ceilings were not suffering. Sibella secured the towel about her.

'I am going to rest for a little now before we go to take a beaker of water at the well. You should rest as well, you know, Annis. The water will have extracted the impurities from your body and you should give it chance to recover.'

'Excellent. My nose in particular needs to recuperate.'

Sibella frowned. 'I do not believe that you take this seriously, Annis.'

'I am sorry.' Annis tried to look suitably repentant.

'There is a chamber through there where you may lie down for a few minutes—' Sibella pointed to one of the doorways that led off the main room '—and I shall be in there.' She pointed to the opposite door. 'The attendant has taken your clothing through and left you some blankets to wrap yourself. Try to rest, Annis! You are always so *active*; I am sure that it must be exhausting for you!'

Annis smiled wryly as she eased herself out of the cooling bath ten minutes later. Sibella did a fine line in indolence, but she had never had that habit. Despite the relaxation of the bath, she felt alert and awake, disinclined to take the rest that Sibella had recommended. She decided to dress immediately and take a pot of tea downstairs in Mr Thackwray's excellent drawing room, whilst she waited for her cousin to come down.

She wrapped herself in a large towel, which was scratchy and none too clean. Annis looked at it doubtfully, wondering if Mr Thackwray had them washed between clients. Really, one way and another, this spa bathing seemed positively dangerous to the health.

She opened the door to the bedchamber and looked around for her clothes. The bed was hidden discreetly behind a screen, but Annis spotted her underclothing and her gown hanging on a hook by the fireplace. She knew that the attendant would return to help her dress, but she had no inclination to lie around in a damp blanket; besides, she was not a fine lady who could not dress without the help of her maid. She dried herself briskly, dressed equally so, and checked her appearance in the spotted mirror. Not bad. She just needed to pin up her hair, secure her bonnet over her blonde tresses and then she would be ready to face the world again.

A sound rather like a sigh stopped her in her tracks. Annis froze. When she had first walked over to the mirror she had been intent on her own reflection and had therefore not noticed the rest of the room. Now she realised that the angle of the mirror gave a good view of the foot of the bed, and the foot of something—or someone—else. A bare foot. She walked to the bottom of the bed. And stopped dead.

Adam Ashwick was lying there. He was deeply asleep. He was also naked. Or at least, Annis assumed that he was, for one of Mr Thackwray's scratchy blankets was slung low across his hips and thighs, leaving the rest of him gloriously visible in all his hard, muscular perfection. Annis's gaze trav-

elled from his feet up the full length of him, pausing briefly
on the tumbled blanket, dwelling considerably longer on the
broad, naked chest and moving up the strong brown column
of his throat to his face. The dishevelled dark hair fell across
his brow and sleep had softened the hard lines of cheek and
jaw. His eyelashes were so long and thick that they gave him
an oddly vulnerable look, like a child asleep. Annis swallowed hard. Her chest felt tight, as though she had a chill.
But it was not cold that was causing her to shiver, nor was it
the effects of Mr Thackwray's spa bathing.

'Lord Ashwick!'

Adam opened his eyes and stared at her in bemusement.
Then he blinked and started to sit up. His blanket slipped
lower. Annis tried not to look and found herself staring at
his thighs before she hastily averted her gaze. The hot colour rushed into her face.

'Annis?' Adam's voice sounded blurred with sleep. His
eyes half-opened and his gaze drifted over her thoughtfully,
and seemed to linger on the strands of blonde hair about her
face. Annis saw a light come into his eyes and thought he was
going to smile, but his expression changed, became concentrated. He took her wrist in a negligent grip and pulled her
closer to him. Annis's other hand came to rest on his chest
and lingered there on the hard warmth of his skin.

'Well, well, sweetheart! What a pleasant surprise this is!'

Adam let go of her wrist and put out a hand and brushed
the wisps of fair hair back from Annis's face. His fingers
were gentle against her cheek, his expression intent. Annis
stared down at him, light-headed and confused. Adam took
her chin in his hand and, very gently, drew her face down to

his. Not that Annis was resisting. She felt so shaky that she almost tumbled on top of him.

When their lips met, the kiss was light but achingly sweet, drawing Annis deeper into the sensual web that clouded her mind. Her body, already soft and pliant from the spa bathing, grew warm and responsive. She felt Adam's hand at the neck of her gown, his fingers brushing the sensitive skin in the hollow of throat and undoing the tiny buttons one by one. Her lips parted on a gasp of mingled shock and pleasure, but Adam merely angled his head to take advantage and deepen the kiss, touching his tongue to hers. Annis's senses spun. She wanted to sink down onto the softness of the bed, taking him with her all the way. She wanted... Adam's hand slipped inside her bodice to stroke her breast with gentle fingers and the shock finally sent her tumbling beside him on to the bed.

It also appeared to wake Adam from what had evidently been a delightful dream. His black brows snapped together and he frowned at her in a wholly intimidating manner. Annis scrambled to her feet. She looked around, saw another connecting door open and leading to another bathroom, and felt her heart sink. No doubt it was easily done when the hotel was full, but she did so wish that Mr Thackwray had thought to lock some of the connecting doors.

Adam secured the blanket more firmly about his waist, swung his legs over the side of the bed and stood up.

Annis quailed. She had not thought him to be so tall or so intimidating. Nor did she recall him being quite so overpoweringly masculine, but then they had only met previously when he had all his clothes on, which was quite different from being confronted by an angry man who was almost

naked. A man who had been kissing her with such passion…
She tried to gather her scattered thoughts.

'I do beg your pardon, my lord. I believe one of us must
be in the wrong room…'

It sounded ridiculous, as though she was apologising for
stepping on his foot during a dance. Unsurprisingly, Adam
ignored her feeble apology. He took a step towards her, his
grey eyes narrowing ominously.

'Lady Wycherley, what the devil do you think that you
are about?'

Annis glared at him. 'What am I about? One might ask
what you are about, my lord! You were the one who kissed
me, and—' She broke off, blushing.

'And?' Adam raised a brow. Despite his lack of clothes
he looked infuriatingly confident, even rather pleased with
himself. 'Does this "and" have something to do with your
gown? It is still unbuttoned.'

Annis looked down. It was true that the row of tiny mother-
of-pearl buttons was still unfastened and the bodice was gaping in a way that gave Adam a clear view of the curve of her
breast. And Adam was evidently enjoying that view. His appreciative gaze did not falter.

Annis opened her mouth to give him a scathing set-down,
her shaking fingers clutching for the buttons at the same time.
Before she could say a word, the bathing attendant appeared,
carrying a huge pile of towels. The girl screamed loudly at
the sight of them, dropped the pile and scrabbled desperately
on the floor whilst seemingly unable to tear her gaze away.

'Oh, ma'am, oh, sir… I do beg your pardon.'

'There has been a misunderstanding,' Annis began a little
desperately. 'I think—'

'What the deuce is going on?' Mr Thackwray, florid and panting, barged through from the bathroom. He viewed the embarrassed maid and his gaze turned to Annis and Adam. His brows shot up into his hair as he saw Annis still scrambling for those last, telltale buttons.

'My lord!' he began uncertainly, caution warring with a certain man-of-the-world bonhomie in his face as he took in the situation.

'A mix-up over rooms, Thackwray, that is all,' Adam said laconically. 'If you would be so good as to escort Lady Wycherley out and close the door—'

But it was too late. Sibella, swathed in a vast bath sheet, erupted out of the next bedchamber at the same time that other guests, drawn by the maid's shrill scream, pressed curiously through the bathroom and milled in the doorway.

'Oh, good God,' Annis said faintly.

She felt rather than saw Adam's gaze rest on her face in quick appraisal. He touched her arm. 'I will square everything with Thackwray and his guests,' he said, in an undertone. 'Go back with your cousin and I will come to see you as soon as I am able.'

Annis turned her puzzled hazel gaze on him. 'My lord? I am not sure that I perfectly comprehend—'

'I am sure you do, Lady Wycherley,' Adam said, with grim amusement. 'As a chaperon you must have a perfect grasp of social conventions, so you will understand when I say that you have managed to compromise me most thoroughly!'

Adam watched as Sibella shepherded her cousin away protectively. There was a slightly stunned look on Annis's face, as though recent events had moved a little too quickly for her. Adam smiled to himself. He had been awake for a considerable time before Annis had discovered him and had thoroughly enjoyed watching her reflection in the mirror as she dressed. It had been utterly ungentlemanly of him not to alert her to his presence, and the sight of her voluptuous nakedness had done nothing to calm the urgent desire that possessed him whenever he met her. When she had come over to the bed, the impulse to pretend that he was asleep had been too strong to resist, and what had occurred afterwards had been even sweeter. It had strengthened his resolve to claim her for his own.

And now she had played directly into his hands. Adam allowed a small smile to curl his mouth. Annis Wycherley was thoroughly compromised and would have to accept his suit. Adam knew that he was in a fair way to being deeply in love with his delectable Lady Wycherley. He admired her gallantry of spirit as much as he wanted her. She was bright and courageous and kind. He did not intend to let her go.

Adam smiled as he reached for his clothes. It was time to press his advantage.

By the time that they had reached the neat town house in Knaresborough Square, Sibella was almost recovered from the shock, but still inclined to lament what had happened.

'How excessively unfortunate! It was all Mr Thackwray's fault as well, for all that he tried to shift the blame wherever he could. How they could have made such a mix up with the bedrooms defies understanding. Really, it is too vexing!' Sibella wrung her hands and fixed her cousin with a gloomy gaze. 'Everyone will talk, you know, Annis. There are some vicious gossip-mongers who frequent the spa for that precise purpose!'

Annis unpinned her bonnet and handed it to the maid with a word of thanks. She took Sibella's cloak and gloves, passed them over too and ushered her cousin into the parlour. During the drive home she had had ample time to think about what had happened between herself and Adam Ashwick, and to decide that to play the situation down was the only course of action. It had mainly been her own fault, for staring at Adam like a startled débutante, then compounding her folly by kissing him. Annis fiercely dismissed this as an aberration, and one she was determined to forget.

'Come, I am sure it will not be so bad!' she said now. 'I am sure that Lord Ashwick will be able to sort matters out with Mr Thackwray and his guests. Everyone knows that it was simply a confusion over rooms. Soon it will all be forgotten.'

Sibella settled into an armchair with a heavy sigh. 'I wish I had your faith! Thackwray does not possess an ounce of discretion, and who can speak for his assortment of guests? The story will be all over Harrogate by tonight, you mark my words! What are we going to do?'

'Order some tea for a start,' Annis said, moving to the fireplace and pulling the bell for the maid. 'Tea is always reviving to the spirits.'

'I will concede that, of course, but I meant what are we to do about the scandal?'

Annis waited while the maid came in with the tea tray, then poured cups for them both before resting her chin on her hand. 'Nothing, dearest Sib. Lord Ashwick and I are agreed that it was merely an unfortunate mistake. It need not concern anyone else.'

'If you believe that then you are naïve,' Sibella snapped, with more acidity than was her custom. 'The scandalmongers will have it that you are having a liaison with Lord Ashwick. How does that idea suit you?'

Annis raised her cup and took a sip of the tea. It was hot, strong and just what she needed. 'I have thought about it and I confess that I do not wish for an *affaire* with Lord Ashwick.'

Sibella gave her a sharp look. 'I do not believe that you take this seriously enough, Annis! Think of the gossip—a tryst in the bath chamber, with Lord Ashwick in a state of undress—why, it is a gift for the gossips and if you try to explain it away you will cause even more scandal!'

Annis sighed. 'I must admit that the whole thing does smell a little dubious—rather like the bathing room!'

Sibella frowned. 'Annis, pray be serious! Your lamentable sense of humour!'

'I am sorry.' Annis sobered at the sight of her cousin's genuine concern. 'I know you think that I possess a levity most unsuitable in an orphan.'

'Yes, well...' Sibella's pretty face was creased with distress. 'Do you not understand, Annis? You are ruined!'

Annis put her cup down with a little click of annoyance. 'Sibella, I believe that you are making far too much of this. It was mortifying, but scarcely damaging.'

'Truly? You consider it only embarrassing? And you standing there with your gown undone?' Sibella jumped to her feet and paced across to the window. 'I believe... I do believe... that Lord Ashwick must marry you, Annis.'

Annis, who had been about to pour herself another cup of tea, put the pot down with a sigh of exasperation.

'Oh, no! Now you do go too far, Sibella!'

'Not so!' Sibella was twisting her fingers together in distress. She took a turn towards the fireplace, and then strode back towards the window again. 'It is the only solution. Lord Ashwick has compromised you. I believe that he must do the right thing.'

'Oh, pish and tish, Sibella!' Annis took a deep breath to hold her temper. 'If you take that line, then *I* compromised *him*! I was the one who walked into his bedchamber when he was in a state of undress! However, I will not press him to marry me as a result. Indeed, if such a suggestion were mooted seriously, I would have to decline the match. Now, will you sit down, if you please, so that we may talk about this sensibly? Your pacing is making me quite dizzy.'

They stared at one another. Annis was determined, but Sibella could be obstinate when her temper was roused. She subsided on to the window seat, but did not abandon her point.

'I am persuaded that Lord Ashwick is a gentleman and as such the thought must have occurred to him as well...' Her gaze sharpened on Annis's face. 'Annis? Did he mention any such thing?'

Annis hesitated, torn. 'He said something to the effect that I...that we were compromised and that he would square the matter with the Thackwray and come and see me, but—'

'You see!' Sibella said triumphantly. 'Ashwick has a proper feeling even if you do not, Annis! He will call to pay his addresses, you mark my words.'

'Then I shall not receive him,' Annis snapped, losing her temper. 'This whole matter is so unnecessary, Sib. If people are foolish enough to talk, then let them! I shall not regard it. I certainly shall not accept a proposal of marriage on the basis of a misunderstanding!'

'Have you considered, then, the effect this will have on

your business?' Sibella viewed her cousin with weary patience. 'What will happen, Annis, if rumour of this afternoon's débâcle gets abroad? You will never gain any further employment. Your future will be ruined!'

This time Annis was silent. In the embarrassment of her encounter with Adam she had all but forgotten her earlier worries about Samuel Ingram and his odious threats. Yet now she could see that Sibella was quite right; this was a gift for Ingram and if he chose to encourage the gossip it could be devastating. She would be branded an unfit chaperon and would never gain any employment again.

She stared at Sibella, torn between a wish to deny the possibility and an impotent anger that such a thing might happen to her. Yet a cold fear was stealing about her heart, a belief that Sibella might be right and that everything she had worked for might be about to be lost.

'I cannot believe that any of this will happen—' she started to say, but even she could hear the note of desperation in her voice.

There was a knock at the door. Sibella jumped up and peered through the window. 'I do believe that Lord Ashwick is here. You may argue the toss with him instead of with me, coz, for, unless I miss my guess, you are about to receive an offer of marriage!'

Chapter Nine

'Lord Ashwick, ma'am.' The little housemaid, thoroughly overawed, opened the drawing-room door and dropped a flustered curtsy.

Annis watched as Adam came forward to greet Sibella. Now clad somewhat more formally than before, in pale fawn buckskins, a coat of green superfine and highly polished Hessians, he looked formidable. Her heart missed a beat.

'Mrs Granger...' The charm was very much to the fore as Adam bowed over Sibella's hand, 'I hope that I find you well. Pray do not concern yourself over the scene you witnessed just now. I am persuaded that your cousin and I may put all to rights.'

Sibella blushed and smiled. Annis watched cynically. Having been on the receiving end of Adam's charm, she knew it took a stern heart to resist him. Nor was his charm superficial, like that of most gentlemen she had met. There was real warmth there to which people responded naturally, in the way that Sibella was responding now. Annis felt cold and unhappy.

She was going to need to be very strong to resist Adam's proposals, plus the entreaties of Sibella and the promptings of her own common sense. Although a concern for her future was uppermost in her mind, she was determined not to accept Adam simply to escape from a difficult situation.

His gaze fell on her and Annis saw his expression harden slightly. She raised her chin and met his eyes with a level stare of her own.

'Lady Wycherley.' Adam bowed punctiliously. 'How do you do, ma'am.'

'Well!' Sibella said, with arch brightness. 'I shall leave the two of you alone! Just ring the bell if you require tea…or anything…' She hesitated for a moment, cast Annis a look and made a fluttering gesture with her hands. 'Very well, then…'

She went out and there was a long and slightly awkward silence. Annis was determined not to break it. Adam crossed to the fireplace and stood leaning one arm along the mantelpiece. He turned towards her.

'It seems that we find ourselves in a very awkward situation, Lady Wycherley.' He looked at her thoughtfully. 'The question is, what is to be done about it?'

Annis took a quick breath. 'I am sorry that my actions in not checking the room should have placed us in this position, my lord—'

Adam made a slight gesture. 'Do not apologise, ma'am. It was nobody's fault but that old fool, Thackwray, directing me to the wrong chamber. A mistake easily made in a busy hotel, but one I cannot help wishing had not happened.'

Annis felt a little relieved. 'I am glad that at least you do not think I had contrived the situation to entrap you,' she said. 'It would be the very last thing that I would do.'

Adam's lips quirked into a rueful smile. 'Having shown such a disinclination for my company, Lady Wycherley, I can well believe that!'

Annis blushed. 'Then there need be no difficulty,' she said swiftly. 'It is nothing more than a misunderstanding, my lord, and one that will be quickly forgotten. When you arrived I was telling my cousin that we need not regard it. Whilst the matter is unfortunate, I doubt that it will give rise to much gossip.'

Adam raised one black brow. 'You are misguided, ma'am—or an eternal optimist. I can assure you that when I left the Crown the speculation was already widespread.'

Annis's heart sank. 'Oh, but surely... How foolish!'

'Foolish or not, there is much conjecture about our relationship.' He looked at her. 'Think about it! I was wearing nothing but a blanket, and you...' he appraised her thoughtfully '...you had your hair down and your gown partly undone, you looked slightly flustered—and very pretty. Besides, there is some truth in the gossip, is there not? I had just kissed you, and...' Adam grinned. 'Well... I cannot pretend to forget what happened between us, and everyone saw ample proof that it *had* happened...'

Annis felt more than slightly flustered now. The memory of his hard, lithe body barely concealed by the blanket was disturbing, as was the reminder of his kisses and caresses.

'I suppose...put like that it does seem a great deal worse.'

Adam gestured her to a chair. 'Will you take a seat and hear me out, ma'am?'

Annis sat down reluctantly.

'In such cases as these I believe it is always the lady whose reputation suffers most,' Adam said slowly. 'As a chaperon to young ladies, Lady Wycherley, I am sure that you see the truth of what I am saying. Rumours about your virtue, even unfounded rumours, can be most destructive.'

Annis pressed her hands together in her lap. She was a little surprised to find that she felt very nervous beneath that cool grey gaze.

'I concede the truth of what you are saying in general terms,' she said, 'but I cannot accept that it applies to my case. I am older and...' her voice faltered and she forced it on '...I have been married. The rules that apply to widows are far different from those that relate to young, unmarried girls.'

Adam inclined his head. Annis did not think that he seemed particularly impressed by her point of view.

'I admit that the rules are different,' he said, 'but the gossip seldom is.' His eyes narrowed. 'I assume that you have a care for your good name, ma'am?'

'Of course.' Annis found she could not meet his gaze. 'Of course I care for my good reputation, but—'

'There is no but.' The incisive tone in Adam's voice silenced her. 'You have taken that good name for granted until now, I dare say, Lady Wycherley, as is your right as a virtuous widow. Now, through no fault of your own, your reputation is questioned. You are considered of shady virtue, perhaps... A widow prepared to indulge in a love affair. People will view you differently because of what happened today. It is inevitable.'

'It is unfair!' Annis could not help herself. 'Why should I suffer censure for something that I have not done?'

A shadow of a smile touched Adam's mouth. 'Dear me, ma'am, do you expect life to be fair? I had not have thought to find that a lady of your mature years would still have any illusions!'

The comment stung Annis. Her hazel eyes flashed.

'I do expect people to think well of me, unless they have a *genuine* reason to think the opposite!'

'Yes indeed.' Adam bowed slightly. 'I am sure that anyone who does know you, ma'am, could not believe anything bad of you. It is of the others that we speak—the people who do not know you, yet are still prepared to rip your reputation to shreds. Besides…' he sighed '…there is some basis for the gossip. I cannot forget that I had been kissing you and it was my fault that your gown was in disarray—'

Annis held up her hand. 'Please! Can we not consider that as an aberration and simply forget it?'

Adam laughed. 'No, I do not think so. It was a mistake that occurs quite frequently, is it not? That should tell you something, Lady Wycherley, although it may be a message that you do not wish to hear.'

Annis sighed. She knew that he was correct. Correct about her reactions to him, correct about the gossips and correct in saying that her reputation was tarnished.

A picture of Samuel Ingram came, unbidden, into Annis's mind. He knew her and he would take every opportunity to blacken her name. This piece of bad luck was a gift for him. Even so… She strengthened her resolve. She would not accept Adam just for the protection of his name and could not compromise her independence over a foolish mistake.

Adam straightened up. 'Annis…' His use of her name, the tone of tender reproach, brought a lump to her throat. 'We have spoken of your honour, Annis, but you must give some consideration to mine. What sort of ramshackle fellow would

I appear if I left you to deal with this scandal alone? Come, let us cease this fencing. I would deem it an honour if you were to accept my hand in marriage.'

Annis stood up and moved over to the window. Somehow the conversation had moved to a new level of intimacy with his proposal—and his use of her name.

'I had not thought that you wished to marry again, my lord,' she said. 'You told me yourself that you were sincerely in love with your wife, and I understood that you had no wish to remarry after her death.'

'I was, and I did not. Circumstances alter cases and I would like to marry you.'

'It is most chivalrous of you.'

'Thank you. Your answer?'

Annis turned and met his eyes very straight. 'I am grateful for your generosity, my lord—'

'But you are going to refuse me.' Adam came across to stand before her. 'I do wish that you would reconsider, Annis.'

Annis did not meet his eyes. 'I cannot marry a stranger, sir.'

'We need not be strangers.' Adam took her hands. 'You know that I already I have a feeling for you that is much stronger than mere liking, Annis. And you have confessed— an attraction to me...?' There was a question in his tone.

Annis looked up and met his eyes. And blushed. She could hardly deny it after the wanton way she had responded to him in the past.

'I admit to a certain partiality...'

Adam laughed. 'Thank you for that. We have time to get to know one another better before the wedding—and after.'

Annis risked a fleeting look at his face. 'You are very kind, but I cannot.' She freed herself.

Adam's expression hardened slightly. 'You must not think of it as a betrayal of your first marriage. It may not be the same, but it need not be bad.'

'My first marriage...' For a moment the images flooded Annis's mind: losing her freedom, the stifling propriety, the dreadful sense of being trapped, day after day, without end. She shuddered.

'You are most generous, sir.' She took a deep breath. 'There are reasons why I cannot accept your proposal—matters that you do not understand...'

'Then explain them to me.' Adam walked over to the window. 'You have been open with me up until now, Annis.' His smile did strange things to Annis's already shaky composure. 'Indeed, you have said more than I could have expected. If we already have a regard for one another, where is the difficulty?'

Annis looked away from that compelling gaze. 'Please do not press me, my lord. All I can tell you is that there are reasons why I simply cannot contemplate remarriage.'

Adam sighed. 'I am not a patient man, but I am content to let it wait until we know each other a little better, if that will help you.'

'There is no time.' Annis felt a little panicky. 'If we were to marry on account of this scandal, it would have to be soon. No! It is impossible!' She wrapped her arms close about her. 'I cannot even consider it.'

There was an unhappy silence. 'I presume that you have thought about the effect that this will have on your work, Annis,' Adam said, with what seemed to Annis to be unbearable gentleness. 'It cannot have escaped you that not all guardians will be prepared to entrust their charges to a

woman about whose name some unsavoury scandal clings…
You might find that your livelihood has been utterly destroyed.'

Annis turned with an angry swish of skirts. 'I know that!
I have thought of little else! But even so, the enormity of
contracting a marriage, and under such circumstances, is
not to be borne!'

An image of Starbeck flashed across her mind, and with
it the thought of Ingram. Was everything to be set against
her? She closed her eyes for an anguished moment.

'I will leave you to consider my offer,' Adam said, 'and
will call on you in a couple of days' time to ask for your answer.'

For a moment Annis considered the cowardly way out—
to run to Starbeck and not tell him. However, she suspected
that Adam Ashwick was the sort of man who would find out
where she had gone—and come straight after her.

'I am leaving Harrogate soon.' The words came out reluctantly.

'For Starbeck. I remember you telling me.'

Annis laughed a little shakily. 'How ironic that you would
gain control of Starbeck if you marry me, my lord, and so
spite Mr Ingram. Would you go as far as marriage to gain
Starbeck?'

Adam gave her a look. It brought the hot colour up into
her face. 'My dear Lady Wycherley,' he drawled, 'I would
quite like to possess Starbeck but…' he paused '…I ache to
possess you.'

Annis drew in a short breath. Her mouth was suddenly
dry. 'My lord—'

Adam picked up her hand. 'Let me help you fight your

battles, Annis,' he said softly. 'Why must you do everything alone?'

Something caught in Annis's throat. 'I confess it is a habit
with me. I have always done so.'

'Then this time allow me to help you. You might find that
you like it.'

There was something very persuasive in his tone. They
were standing very close to one another. When he drew her
closer still she fitted perfectly into his arms; fitted against
the entire length of him. Annis's heart began to race.

'After all,' Adam continued, 'you like it when I kiss you...'

Annis quivered. 'My lord—'

Adam bent his head and proved his point. He was very
gentle, the kiss light, undemanding and exerting only the
slightest of pressure on her lips. Yet when he let her go she
could see the conflict in his eyes, the urgent need that he
was holding under absolute control. He stepped back very
deliberately.

'I will call on you soon, Annis.' He paused. 'By the way,
how long were you in the bedchamber before I awoke?'

Annis blushed. 'Only a few moments, my lord.'

'I see. I hope that you enjoyed the view.' Adam gave her
a grin and sauntered towards the door.

A sudden, shaming thought struck Annis as she remembered that she had dressed in the same room. 'My lord—' she
gave him a look of entreaty '—you were genuinely asleep,
were you not? All the time?'

Adam raised his brows. His grin became positively wicked.
'My dear Annis, I would spare you embarrassment and not
answer that question! All I can say is that you could not be
more thoroughly compromised!'

Sibella's curiosity was such that she left it a very short time indeed before poking her head around the door. Indeed, she might almost have passed Adam in the doorway.

'Well?'

Annis sat down a little heavily.

'He did ask me to marry him.'

'And?'

'I refused. But...' she saw Sibella's moue of disappointment '...I believe Lord Ashwick is not a man who will accept rejection lightly. He suggested that I give the matter thought and told me that he would call on me in a day or two to hear my answer then.' She jumped up. 'Indeed, Sibella, I am not at all sure what to do. He is...very sure of himself.'

'He is entirely charming.' Sibella gave her a little satisfied smile. 'Confess it, cousin, you like him more than a little, do you not?'

'I do.' Annis gave her a troubled look. 'But, Sib, you know that I could not bear to be married again—'

'Oh, stuff!' Sibella dismissed Annis's scruples with a wave of her hand. 'I know you did not have a happy experience of marriage, but that need not be a barrier.'

'I dislike the restrictive nature of married life.'

'But being married to Lord Ashwick would not in any way be like being married to John Wycherley!' Sibella finished triumphantly. 'Indeed, Annis...' her smile became dreamy '...I think that it might be positively exciting!'

Annis looked alarmed. 'You mean, in a physical sense? I think that you might be correct, but—'

'There is no need to be alarmed.' Sibella's smile vanished. 'If you explain to him about John—'

'I cannot explain anything so intimate! I do not know

him well enough for that.' Annis's desperate gaze sought her cousin's. 'It will be difficult enough to explain why I was so unhappy and why I cling to my liberty. How can I possibly broach the topic of my first marriage being unconsummated?'

Sibella sighed. 'I understand your feelings, Annis, but maybe you will find that when you know Lord Ashwick a little better you will have no difficulty in discussing the matter. On the other hand...' she smiled slightly '...perhaps it would be better *not* to tell him. By the time he finds out he will not be in any position to stop and question you, believe me!'

Annis stared at her for a moment, then turned her face away. 'Sib, I am afraid.'

Sibella crossed over to her and sat down. She put her hand over Annis's cold one.

'Trust him,' she urged. 'You already find Lord Ashwick very attractive, Annis, and that is a good start. You already *like* him, and that is even better.'

Annis looked unhappy. 'I suppose so. I do not wish to be married to him, though, particularly not like this. I...am not ready for it.'

Sibella patted her hand. 'Think about it. Give him a little time.'

'There is no time. In matters such as this I believe it is the convention to be married at once.'

'Then do not worry. I cannot believe that Lord Ashwick would behave as a callow boy and force himself on you. Besides, he has been married before.'

Annis shuddered. 'Yes, and that is another thing! He told me quite openly that he had been in love with his wife.'

'That was a long time ago. Besides, it is a good thing, for it shows he is not a man who takes marriage lightly.'

'He may want children.'

'He may indeed. You will have to speak to him about it.' Sibella stretched a hand out to the bell. 'More tea, cousin? You seem in need of it.'

Annis nodded, frowning. 'Thank you. Charles will not like it, you know, Sib.'

Sibella frowned too. 'Because Lord Ashwick is at odds with Mr Ingram?'

'Yes. They are very cool to one another. Oh, dear, this is so very difficult!'

Sibella came across to give her a hug. 'I am persuaded that Charles's first concern will be for you, Annis,' she said loyally. 'Pray do not worry about it any more.'

'I feel so strange.'

'Because you are always the chaperon and never the bride.' Sibella laughed. 'You are accustomed to having the order of things and arranging your own life, and to find yourself in a reversal of that situation is bound to be odd.'

Annis jumped up. 'I need to go for a walk to clear my head. The fresh air might help me.' She gave her cousin a spontaneous kiss. 'I will not take that tea after all, Sibella, but I will see you again soon. Thank you for listening to me.'

'You will tell me what you decide?' Sibella said anxiously. 'May I call tomorrow?'

'Of course.' Annis smiled. 'And if I am to be the next Lady Ashwick you will be the first to know.'

Annis walked until her feet ached, but although the exercise did a great deal to tire her physically it did little to settle her mental state. She could forgive herself for the mistake of walking into Adam's dressing room at the hotel, for that had in fact been Mr Thackwray's fault and was easily done. It might have helped had she not stood gaping at Adam like a green girl until the maid came in, but it was too late to regret that. Annis winced as she thought of the salacious story that was no doubt already going the rounds of the Harrogate matrons. The scandal had all the elements of a perfect piece of gossip—the spa bath, the scantily clad chaperon, the naked lord, and the audience of outraged guests... Annis sighed. She had spent the past three years chaperoning young ladies and keeping them out of scrapes, only to tumble into far worse disgrace herself.

It was late when she returned to the house in Church Row and Mrs Hardcastle was fussing.

'There you are, pet! I was growing quite worried. I sent to Mrs Granger's to see if you had decided to stay for dinner, but they said that you had left hours ago.'

'I am sorry, Hardy,' Annis said wearily. She was conscious that she looked hot and dusty and wanted no more than to take a bath. 'I think that I shall take a tray in my room, if I may, and I am not at home to visitors.'

'Mr Lafoy called already,' Mrs Hardcastle said significantly. 'He seemed quite put out to find you from home and said that he would call again later.'

'Well, I won't see him,' Annis said. She knew she sounded fretful, which was unusual for her, but the thought of receiving a lecture from Charles was too much to bear.

She slept badly and the following morning went into High Harrogate, setting off before the streets became busy. It was another hot morning with a high blue sky and normally this would have lifted Annis's spirits, but not today. She made a few purchases in the shops, went to take a glass of water at the sulphur well and walked briskly on The Stray, and when she returned home her thoughts were still as confused as they had been when she went out.

Mrs Hardcastle was hovering when she reached home, her face working like milk coming up to the boil.

'That Lady Copthorne!' she burst out, when Annis politely enquired about the reason for her agitation. 'She was here earlier, Miss Annis, asking to see you. When I told her you were out she said to tell you that she no longer wished to engage your services to chaperon her Eustacia to London in the autumn.' Mrs Hardcastle's magnificent bosom swelled indignantly. 'Said that you were scandalous and too unsuitable to care for her ewe lamb lest you lead her into trouble! Well!'

'Oh, dear,' Annis said faintly. She sat down abruptly on the chair in the hall. 'I thought something like this might happen.'

'I gave her the right about and no mistake,' Mrs Hardcastle said, with satisfaction. 'Told her you were worth a hundred of her and that Miss Eustacia was fit for Bedlam and would run off with a groom before she was nineteen.'

'Lady Copthorne certainly will not be changing her mind and re-engaging me, then,' Annis said, trying to see the humorous side.

'Ho! I should hope not!'

As Annis toiled up the stairs she reflected that it was only what she had expected. Harrogate was a small community and, like many other small towns, it loved scandal. She had provided the gossip and now her character was in shreds. No doubt Samuel Ingram had assiduously fanned the flames.

It left her with the difficulty of what to do in the future, however. If she did not accept Adam Ashwick's proposal, the chance to re-establish herself as a chaperon looked slim indeed. Similarly she would be given short shrift if she offered herself as a governess or schoolteacher and at present she could not think of an alternative. In a thoroughly bad mood she shrugged off her outdoor clothing and tried unsuccessfully to dismiss her worries at the same time.

The house was very quiet that evening. Annis had been intending to join Sibella and David for dinner, but had cried off at the last moment, pleading a headache. A part of her wished to see Adam and resolve the situation and a part of her shrank from it. He had not called on her and Annis understood that he was keeping his word and giving her plenty of time to come to a decision. She respected him for it, but it made it no easier to decide what to do. Whenever she thought of marriage she felt the panic rise up in her, as though the waters were closing over her head and she could not breathe. Under the circumstances it seemed foolish to condemn them both to so unhappy a match, but Annis was increasingly aware that her alternatives were limited. In fact, at the moment she had no idea of a practical alternative.

She gave the servants the evening off and sat down to a cold collation alone in the dining room. Mrs Hardcastle had put it together before going off to the threepenny seats in the theatre gallery. It was her first opportunity to see Miss Mardyn dance and she had been very excited.

Annis felt tired and gloomy and for once sitting reading alone did not seem an attractive option. Instead, she soon found herself dozing in front of the drawing-room fire. When she awoke the candles had burned down and she felt a little cold and stiff. Her book had slid off her lap and was lying on the floor. And from upstairs came the unmistakable creak of a floorboard.

At first Annis thought that Mrs Hardcastle or one of the other servants must have returned home early, but then she realised that they would have come to greet her had they done so. She waited. There was another stealthy creak. This was definitely not the mice.

Annis picked up the poker in one hand and a candlestick in the other. She crept up the stairs. The bedrooms of Miss Fanny and Miss Lucy Crossley were in darkness now, the doors closed. At the end of the corridor, next to Miss Lucy's bedroom, was the study. Annis had not used it, for she had had no time whilst the girls had been with her. Now she saw that the door was ajar and a faint light flickered beyond. There was the rustle of papers.

Annis pushed the door open and advanced, wondering at the last moment if it was not the most foolish thing she could have done. But it was too late. The figure by the desk was straightening up and turning towards her. His expression was rueful and resigned.

'I fear you have caught me red-handed, Lady Wycherley,' Adam Ashwick said.

Annis put her candlestick down on the table. Anger and disappointment were warring for mastery within her. She had been so close, she thought bitterly; so very close to trusting him completely. And now she saw what a fool she had been.

'I am not surprised to see you here, Lord Ashwick,' she said coldly. 'I suppose you are following Mr Woodhouse's advice and spying on my cousin? How did you get in, by the way?'

'Over the roof and down the ivy. It is not to be recommended.' Adam had the grace to look a little shamefaced.

'I shall not be trying it.' Annis gestured to the door. 'You may leave at once if you wish, without me calling the Watch. You may also leave behind anything that you have found.'

'I have found nothing.' Adam straightened up.

'I could have told you as much. There is nothing to interest you in the desk, Lord Ashwick. It is only a list of my engagements these six weeks past and I could have furnished you with them if you had only asked.'

Adam smiled at her. 'Thank you. As you guessed, it was your cousin, Mr Lafoy, whose movements interested me—'

'I am aware,' Annis snapped. 'It does not take a genius to work out what you are doing here, Lord Ashwick. Have you had time to search the attics? That is usually where people hide things. Or is this your first port of call?'

'I was intending to search the attic next.' Adam came forward. 'I am sorry, Annis. I did not intend to startle you.'

'You did not startle me,' Annis said cuttingly, 'only disappointed me, my lord. I had thought that you would at least have been honest with me. Skulking around here when my back is turned—'

'I had heard that you were from home. My informant told me that you were dining with the Grangers tonight.'

'Careless intelligence work, Lord Ashwick. I was invited but I did not attend. I would not expect you to make mistakes.'

'I appear to have done so this time,' Adam said, a little grimly. 'I would have told you, Annis, but I had so little time—'

'Excuses, my lord.' Annis felt the angry tears prickle her

eyes. 'When we spoke at the inn, you promised to consult me before you took any action against Charles. But you did not trust me, did you? First you make me a proposal of marriage and then you demonstrate that you do not trust me one whit! I need not look very far for the reason to refuse you.'

She saw Adam flinch. 'Annis,' he said, 'I appreciate that you are angry with me, but may we please go downstairs to discuss this and would you please put that poker down as well? You are making me nervous.'

He did not look in the least uneasy, but Annis lowered the poker anyway.

'Very well. We shall go to the drawing room. You go first, my lord.'

They descended the stairs in a wary silence.

'You were acting on Mr Woodhouse's tip off, were you not?' Annis asked, when once they were in the drawing room and the poker had been restored to its place by the fire. She watched as Adam kicked the apple logs into a fresh blaze. It seemed comfortable to have him in her drawing room, as though he was in his proper place. Which was all wrong in view of his duplicity. She hardened her heart against him.

'Woodhouse said that you should look for evidence against Charles, did he not, and though you swore to me that you would not do so, that is exactly what you are doing.' Annis shrugged wearily. 'This is not Charles's house and the only connection he has with it is that he took it for me for the season. There is nothing here for you, my lord. You will have to ask Mr Woodhouse to be more precise.'

Adam stepped closer. 'I cannot do that. Woodhouse was found head down in the chalybeate well this afternoon.'

Annis whitened. 'An accident?'

Adam looked sceptical. 'A convenient one. There were plenty of witnesses to say that he was already drunk by midday. Dead drunk.'

Annis shivered and wrapped her arms around her. 'You think that it was no coincidence.'

Adam shrugged. 'I cannot say, but it is expedient for Ingram and damned unhelpful to me.'

He came up to her. 'Annis, much as I would like to find something to Ingram's discredit, that is not what concerns me now. I am sorry that I did not speak to you first before I came here—'

'Why did you not?'

Adam shrugged uncomfortably. 'Because I knew that it would upset you that I was involving Lafoy in my investigations. I thought that you might even say that I should not look for evidence here, in which case I should not have been able to proceed.'

Annis looked at him. 'You are right. It is my house and I should have forbidden it.'

Adam sighed. 'I would have accepted that. So it was easier not to ask you.'

Annis turned away. She felt bruised and tired. 'That is no excuse.'

'No, I agree.' There was a grim set to Adam's mouth, though whether he was angry with her or with himself, and why, Annis could not be sure. 'It was very wrong of me and I understand why you are angry. Do you forgive me?'

Annis frowned. 'No, I do not think so.'

'I understand why you might not believe me, but I swear to share everything with you in future, Annis. *Everything.*'

Annis shivered at his tone. He sounded sincere, but he had

just shown her that he did not trust her. Her troubled hazel gaze sought his. Adam took a step closer.

'I am sorry,' he said again. He put his hands on her upper arms and gently rubbed. Annis felt the hairs rise along her skin and trembled with sensual awareness.

'It was an unconscionably stupid thing to do,' Adam said softly, 'and I truly regret it. It was not that I did not trust you, Annis—I would have told you if I had found anything, I swear.'

The soft stroke of his hands was terribly distracting. Annis tried to concentrate.

'I am very cross with you. And disappointed.'

'I understand.' Adam's breath stirred her hair. He slid his arms about her. 'How may I make amends, sweetheart?'

'I have no notion. Certainly not by kissing me. That would be a very easy way out of the situation.'

'I agree.' Adam sat down in one of the armchairs and very gently drew her down on to his lap. Once more he held her close, her head against his shoulder, his arms about her waist. 'If I may, I will simply hold you. That may do a little to convince you that I am sincere and not just a rake.'

'And a deceiver.'

Annis felt Adam wince. 'You are harsh, my sweet. Do you hold grudges?'

'No, I do not believe so.' It felt shockingly comforting to be in his arms. Warm, intimate, all the things that Annis had trained herself to live without. She burrowed a little closer to that warmth. 'Are you truly repentant?'

'Of course. I knew at the time that it was a foolish thing to do. That is why I was so angry with myself.' He tilted her face up to his. 'I do not want to lose your trust, Annis.'

Annis sighed. 'I think I might forgive you in a few minutes, weak as I am. But only if you promise not to do it again.'

Adam kissed the top of her head. 'I promise not to break into your house again.'

Annis dug him in the ribs. 'You know what I mean.'

'I do. I promise to tell you everything, to share everything with you and only to kiss you when you say that I might...'

Annis pulled away a little. 'That is very handsome of you, I suppose.'

'So may I?'

They stared at one another.

'You may,' Annis whispered.

She saw him smile before he bent closer, too close for her to focus. She closed her eyes. His mouth took hers softly, sweetly. His tongue touched her lower lip before sliding deeper. Annis raised one hand and touched Adam's cheek where the stubble was rough against her palm. She felt as though she was melting, slipping into pure pleasure. His body was hard against hers and she could feel the pounding of his heart against her other hand as it rested on his chest. She felt hot and dizzy, overwhelmed by sensation, confused, all common sense lost. Both her head and her heart were reeling.

Adam eased away from her for a moment.

'You said that you were disappointed in me. Am I disappointing you now, Annis?'

'That was not what I meant,' Annis whispered.

'I know. Marry me.'

He kissed her again, parting her lips, his tongue taking intimate liberties with hers again until she felt weak and clung to him. His hand was on her thigh, warm against the soft silk of her stocking. Annis's clouded mind cleared slightly. His hand was on her thigh *under* her skirts and he was stroking her skin very gently. The desire shot through her like wildfire.

'Marry me,' he said, against her ear.

Annis pulled away a little, still leaning against Adam for support. 'You should not have kissed me so much, for now I cannot think straight. I will give you my answer tomorrow, my lord.'

There was a step on the tiles of the hall and Mrs Hardcastle's voice carolled, 'Miss Annis, are you still awake? I'm back from the theatre. That Miss Mardyn—what a hussy. I thought, she's no better than she ought to be—' She pushed the door of the drawing room open. 'Why are you sitting in the dark, Miss Annis? Oh!' She jumped back.

'Good evening, Mrs Hardcastle,' Adam said, with what Annis considered remarkable aplomb. He loosened his grip on her and allowed her to get to her feet, which she did, albeit shakily. Adam stood up too and put one steadying arm about her.

'If you will excuse me, I was just leaving.'

Mrs Hardcastle gave him a thorough stare. 'That's probably for the best, my lord. Gracious, Miss Annis, entertaining gentlemen callers when you are alone in the house! Whatever next?'

'I was persuading Lady Wycherley to marry me,' Adam said shamelessly.

'I saw your means of persuasion,' Mrs Hardcastle said. 'Not that I'm sure they will work, my lord. My Miss Annis is most obstinate.'

'I should be grateful if you could prevent yourselves from discussing me as though I were not here,' Annis said, recovering herself. She held her hand out to Adam. 'Goodnight, my lord.'

Adam bowed. 'Goodnight, Lady Wycherley.'

'A dangerous gentleman,' Mrs Hardcastle opined when she had shot the bolt behind Adam. 'You make sure you marry him, Miss Annis.'

Annis gave her a startled look. 'It was not very long ago that you were warning me that handsome is as handsome does, Hardy.'

'Aye, well, I've not changed my mind on that.' Mrs Hardcastle smiled grimly. 'There's plenty of men I'd tell you not to touch with a long, sharp stick, Miss Annis, but yon gentleman is not one of them. No, you mark my words. He's a good lad. You marry him.'

'I am glad to have your blessing, Hardy,' Annis said, 'for I think that that is exactly what I shall be doing.'

'No need to sound so mealy-mouthed about it,' Mrs Hardcastle said. 'I saw the two of you just then. You were enjoying his attentions, Miss Annis, so don't pretend you weren't! Either that or you're a better actress than that Miss Mardyn will ever be. The sooner you're married the better.'

As soon as Annis entered the Promenade Rooms the following day she was aware that the buzz in the air came not from gossip about her own doings but something far more exciting.

'Have you not heard?' Sibella demanded, once greetings were exchanged. 'There was the most tremendous riot last night at Mr Ingram's estate at Linforth. The windows were smashed and the outbuildings set alight and the mob delivered a letter that said that unless Mr Ingram desisted from his money-grubbing practices they would not stop until they had burned every one of his properties to the ground.' She gave an artistic shiver. '"Look to thy soul, for we shall deal with thy body," the letter said.'

Annis raised her brows. 'How very melodramatic. How has Mr Ingram responded to this warning?'

'He has threatened to have the yeomanry called out and he has offered a reward of a thousand pounds for the capture of the rebel leader,' Sibella said. 'A thousand pounds, Annis! There's many a man would sell his own grandmother for that amount.'

'We shall see,' Annis said. She looked about. Rather than promenading, the good people of Harrogate were gathered in loquacious groups, all discussing the news of the riot. Judging by the laughter and bright-eyed excitement there were plenty who felt that Ingram was getting his comeuppance.

The door opened and Adam, Edward, Della and the Dowager Lady Ashwick all came into the long room. Annis saw Adam excuse himself from the others and quicken his step as he saw her. He came straight over to her and took her hand.

'Lady Wycherley. How are you this morning, ma'am?'

'I am very well, I thank you, sir,' Annis said, her composed tone belying the flutter of excitement his presence always stirred in her.

'Mrs Granger.' Adam smiled at Sibella, who smiled back happily. Annis reflected ruefully that it was good that at least one of her family could get on with the Ashwicks.

'We were just discussing the shocking news of the riot at Linforth,' Sibella said. 'It sounds quite dreadful!'

'Very violent,' Adam agreed. 'I believe the other topic of conversation is Mr Woodhouse's sad demise. Plenty of people are wondering if it is safe to drink the water from the chalybeate well now that it has been polluted by his body!'

Annis's reply was lost as the door opened with a crash that was loud enough to stop all conversation. Samuel Ingram entered, followed by Charles Lafoy, whom Annis thought was looking quite ill. Behind them was Mr Pullen, the magistrate. Annis saw Charles look around and saw his gaze fall on Della Tilney. He winced visibly. Annis met his gaze across the room and she gave him a puzzled, questioning look. Charles shook his head slightly.

A strange silence had fallen in the Promenade Rooms. The chatter, which had swirled up briefly after Ingram's arrival, now died down to an ominous hum before fading away altogether. The three men were walking the length of the room towards them. Edward Ashwick, his mother and sister started to draw closer too as Ingram's party made its way towards Adam.

It was evident to Annis that Charles was deeply discomfited and the fact that she and Sibella were present made matters much worse for him. She moved closer to Sibella and took her arm in a comforting grip.

'Excuse me, my lord.' The magistrate cleared his throat.

Adam looked enquiring. 'Yes, Mr Pullen, what can I do for you?' His gaze moved on to Ingram and his expression hardened. He gave the slightest of bows. 'Mr Ingram.'

'If we might go somewhere more private, my lord?' Pullen looked quite agitated. 'Mr Ingram has laid a matter before us regarding the riot at his estate of Linforth last night and we must ask you a number of questions.'

'Ask me?' Adam raised his brows incredulously. 'Are you implying that I had something to do with the matter, Pullen?'

Mr Pullen looked increasingly unhappy. 'Privacy, Lord Ashwick. That's the thing. Surely...' he looked around '...you do not wish this crowd to be party to your business?'

Adam's jaw set. 'There is nothing for them to be party to and I have no difficulty in making that clear. I had nothing to do with the riot at Linforth last night.'

Ingram stepped forward. 'Do you own a bay stallion with a white star, my lord?'

Adam frowned. 'Yes, I do.'

'There are witnesses who can testify that the rebel leader rode such a horse last night. That he was a man of broad stature and he spoke like a gentleman.'

Adam looked contemptuous. 'So? That could be any number of people, Ingram.'

There was a loaded silence.

Mr Pullen hopped from one foot to the other. 'Were you at Eynhallow last night, my lord?'

'I was not. I was in Harrogate.'

Pullen said eagerly, 'I am sure that this matter could be cleared up easily if there are witnesses.'

Edward Ashwick shifted uncomfortably. 'My brother had dinner with me last night.'

Ingram looked down his nose. 'At eleven of the clock, Reverend? The damage at Linforth was done late in the night. It takes no time for a man to ride from Harrogate to Linforth on a good horse...'

Once again there was a tense silence.

'My lord?' Pullen said, uncertainly.

Adam shrugged. 'I cannot help you, Pullen.'

Mr Pullen looked as though he wanted to cry. 'Then I

have no alternative but to ask you to answer further questions, my lord.'

Annis took a deep breath. She let go of Sibella's arm and stepped forward.

'Lord Ashwick was with me yesterday evening,' she said. She looked pointedly at Ingram. 'At eleven of the clock.'

A ripple went through the onlookers. Annis saw Sibella glance quickly towards her, frowning. Charles took an impulsive step forward, then checked himself. His face was stormy. Annis glanced across at Adam. He looked studiously blank.

'Lord Ashwick called in the evening, after dinner,' she continued. 'We had a glass or two of sherry and spoke for a while. He must have left at about eleven-thirty, I suppose. My housekeeper could verify the time for you, Mr Pullen.'

'I am indebted to you, madam.' Pullen looked as though he was not sure whether to be embarrassed or grateful. Annis wondered whether he had already heard the gossip about her encounter with Adam in the spa bath the previous day and was reflecting that her standing as a reputable chaperon was well and truly done for.

Adam stepped forward to her side. Annis felt his comforting presence at her shoulder although she did not turn to look at him.

'You will appreciate that I wished to keep Lady Wycherley's name out of this matter, Pullen,' Adam said. There was anger in his tone and a tenderness that made Annis tremble. 'However, as she has seen fit to disclose the truth, I can only concur. There is, after all, no law against a man having a glass of sherry with his betrothed...'

This time the gasp of surprise was even louder. Edward Ashwick was the first to pull himself together and stepped forward to clap Adam on the back. 'No, indeed. Hearty congratulations, Ash. I am glad that Lady Wycherley has accepted your suit.'

Lady Ashwick took her cue, pressing forward to kiss Annis's cheek. 'So am I, my love. I am persuaded that you are just the wife for Adam!'

After that there seemed nothing more to say as Sibella, her face breaking into a relieved smile, came up to hug Annis, and even Charles got himself in hand sufficiently to give her a peck on the cheek.

Mr Pullen, beaming with pleasure, backed off.

'Well, then... Very many congratulations my lord, my lady... Please excuse the confusion, my lord...clearly a case of mistaken identity...'

'Indeed,' Adam said. He gave Ingram a challenging stare. 'You will have to do better than that, I fear, Ingram.'

Ingram's jaw was working. 'I am sure I will do, my lord,' he ground out, turning on his heel and stalking from the room, scattering the onlookers like chaff in the wind.

Adam took Annis's arm firmly in his. 'Ladies and gentlemen, pray excuse us. I would like to take a turn about the room with my fiancée.'

There were murmurs of approval and smiles. Annis, however, was conscious only of the bruising grip of Adam's hand on her arm. He steered her away from the group and over towards the big windows where they might achieve a modicum of privacy. He was frowning hard.

'You should not have done that, Annis.'

Annis glanced at him. 'I did not wish Mr Pullen to cart you off on a trumped-up charge and it seemed you were unwilling to help yourself! Besides, it is the truth.'

'That is not the point. Your good name—'

Annis wriggled. 'My good name was compromised two days ago, my lord, when Mr Thackwray found us together in the spa room. Was that not why you proposed to me?'

Adam gave her arm a little shake. 'Yes…no! You had no need to make matters worse!'

'I do not see why you are objecting. Mrs Hardcastle can vouch that you left and she is the very acme of respectability.'

Adam sighed sharply and let her go. 'Am I to take it then that you have accepted my proposal?'

Annis felt a small pang of guilt that the matter should have been resolved in this manner. It was not how she would have chosen and somehow it seemed to set everything off on the wrong foot. 'I…yes, I thank you. Has there ever been a more public plighting of troth?'

Adam did not smile. 'You do not really wish to marry me, though, do you, Annis? You are only accepting out of necessity!'

Annis's face crumpled up with a misery that reflected the unhappiness inside. 'It is not like that, my lord. It is not that I do not wish to marry you; it is that I had not wished to marry at all—' She broke off, aware of listening ears. 'We cannot talk about this now.'

'No.' Adam glanced at his watch. 'Devil take it, I have an appointment in ten minutes that I cannot break. Do you still travel to Starbeck this afternoon?'

Annis glanced across at Charles, who was clearly only waiting for his chance to pounce on her. 'Oh, yes. I would like to get away from Harrogate for a space.'

'I hope that the house is habitable.' Adam looked irritable. 'Damn it, I do not like this, Annis. It is not wise for you to be alone at Starbeck with a rioting mob on the loose. I have a better idea.' He looked across at his mother and Edward and Della. 'Why do you not come to stay at Eynhallow for a few days? It will give us time to discuss wedding arrangements and I would feel happier to know that you are under my roof. We may ride over to Starbeck together and decide what is to be done with it.'

When apprised of the plan, Lady Ashwick seemed pleased to offer hospitality.

'Indeed, Lady Wycherley—Annis—that would be delightful. Edward, Della and I are travelling home immediately and you are welcome to ride with us, but if it suits you better to join us later...'

'I will do that, I think, ma'am,' Annis said. She was feeling a little panicky at the way in which the Ashwick family suddenly seemed to be taking charge. Her precious independence was disappearing faster than moorland mist. She felt quite hopeless—on the one hand she realised that she had no option now other than to marry Adam, and quickly. On the other, she felt trapped and afraid. She hoped that Adam could not tell how reluctant she was, but when she looked at him she saw that he was watching her and she realised that her fingers were grasping her reticule so tightly that the tortoiseshell clasp was almost bending under the pressure. She quickly loosened her grip, but she knew that he had noticed, and when she looked into his eyes all she could see was regret.

Chapter Ten

It was getting dark as Annis's coach passed the gibbet at Welford Hill and started up the steep incline out of the Washburn Valley towards Eynhallow. The countryside was bathed in the purple of twilight as the sun sank behind the hills. They were a mere fifteen miles from Harrogate and yet it was like another world. Gone were the bandbox-neat town houses and tidy streets, gone the order and comfort of civilisation. This was a landscape that could kill the unwary, with its empty hills and sudden mist rolling down from the moors. This was a countryside where men scraped a living. The contrast with the town had always fascinated Annis, especially as night closed in and the true wildness of the moors was revealed.

The trees beside the track were etched black against the paling sky and Annis, who was leaning forward to look out of the window, shivered suddenly, although the summer air had not yet lost its warmth. There was something so free about the hills, something that called to her. Her spirit wanted to be free, yet now she felt boxed in, trapped by convention and necessity. It was exactly the feeling she had had at seventeen when, having married John Wycherley out of a desperate need for security, she had found out that she had made a terrible mistake.

The coach lurched to a halt and Annis almost fell off her seat. She opened the window.

'Barney? What is the problem?'

'Fire up ahead, Lady Wycherley,' the coachman replied. 'I thought it safer to stop and find out what is happening.'

Annis craned her neck. Some fifty yards ahead there was a building on fire. All she could see was the blazing silhouette against the darkening sky. The moon had not yet risen.

'It is the tollhouse! Mr and Mrs Castle may need help! I will go and see what is happening.'

Annis grabbed the carriage pistol from its holster and jumped down, ignoring the objections of the coachman. There was a chill in the night air now and a cold breeze from the hills. It fanned the flames and they hissed and cracked, dancing wildly. As she drew closer, Annis could see that the tollhouse had been completed and what had been a fine little building of wood and stone was now crumbling to ash in the leaping flames. There was a crash as a roof spar fell and set up a shower of sparks.

Annis hesitated, for she could see that the house was beyond saving and there was no possible way that she could even get close enough to discover whether the Castles had escaped. She prayed hard and fervently that they had not been trapped inside.

Another light flared further up the road and suddenly the air was rent with shouts and the roar of flames taking hold.

There was another shout closer at hand and Annis spun round to see Barney whipping the horses up the road towards her.

'Lady Wycherley! Get in the carriage, ma'am! They are coming!'

It was too late to run and the carriage was still too far away. Annis saw the mob spill into the road, a seething mass of men, shadowy, outlined by the firelight. Some were armed with sledgehammers, others with pistols and blunderbuss. All were masked and in the firelight they looked like mummers depicting a scene from hell as they swarmed over and around the ruined building, fanning the flames, hastening the destruction.

The air sizzled with the sound of cracking timbers and flying sparks; it was alive with the shouts of the rioters and it crackled with the excitement and atavistic pleasure of the men as they went about their destructive work. Annis pressed one hand against her mouth and flattened herself against the hedge, feeling the twigs stick into her through the thickness of her cloak, trying to efface herself in the darkness. This was a very dangerous place for any witness to be, let alone a woman on her own armed only with a pistol that, suddenly, she could not remember whether she had loaded.

Not all of the rioters were on foot. As Annis watched, a rider came down the road on a skittish bay stallion. He turned the horse expertly in front of the tollgate itself, which still blocked the road in all its five-bar splendour. Annis remembered Charles saying that Samuel Ingram had been very pleased with the design and construction of his tollhouses. Some of the structures on the roads were a flimsy affair, but Ingram had had his built to last and to bring in maximum profit. Instead they had kindled rebellion.

The leader on the horse raised his voice above the sound of the wind and the flames.

'This tollgate has no right to be here, does it?'

The crowd roared its defiance. 'No!'

The leader turned his horse again as it skittered away from the flames. 'What shall we do with it?'

In reply, a man ran forward from the ragged crowd, swinging a sledgehammer. A ripple of a sigh ran through the mob as the hammer made first contact with the wood, then a shout rang out and the men were all in there, hacking, trampling, reducing the pretty little gate to a pile of matchsticks ready for the burning. Someone thrust a torch forward and the makeshift bonfire leapt into life. A cheer rang out.

The mob was on the loose now, wild, unpredictable and masterless. As the flames jumped high in the wind they illuminated the road and the bulk of the carriage some fifty yards distant. A shout went up and the crowd rushed forward.

Annis gave a little, terrified squeak. She had the shelter of the hedge and a rough stone wall, and she had the dubious protection of the pistol, but they were scant comfort if the mob were looking for scapegoats. By the light of the flames she saw Barney jump clear of the carriage and drew in a short breath of relief. She took a step back, stumbled down a small bank and felt herself pitch over and over in the hay, stopping with the wind knocked out of her.

She was in a small hollow beneath the bank and above her head the riot roared past. Someone slithered down the slope and almost stepped on her, and Annis struggled up, raising the pistol.

A hard hand closed about her wrist and a voice she knew

well said, 'At least you remembered to bring it on this occasion.'

The relief was intense. Adam's arms went about her and Annis clung to him and all she could say was, 'Thank God you are here,' over and over, until she finally turned her face into his chest and all was quiet.

'Annis? Annis, are you hurt?'

It was minutes rather than hours later, and there was a note of urgency in Adam's voice. Annis raised her head a little and blinked. The pressure of his arms about her eased slightly.

'No. I do not believe I am hurt.' Annis moved and stretched. She felt bruised and a little stiff, but otherwise uninjured.

'I must get you away from here,' Adam said. He pulled her to her feet. 'They will not harm us, but it is not good to linger.'

'Will not harm us?' Annis' voice rose incredulously. 'Adam, did you not see what was happening? That was a riot! These men are dangerous!'

'I know, love. All the same, I do not believe that we are in danger. The Washburn Men do not hurt their own.'

Annis started to brush the hay from her skirts. 'I wish I could share your confidence. And are we their own? I do not like the sound of that.'

'Most certainly we are. Anyone Washburn born and bred...' Adam let the sentence hang. 'All the same, we should not wait around. They are looking for another target. Come along.'

His hand slid down her arm, tightening about her wrist as he drew her behind him along the line of the wall, away from the road. The firelight flickered behind the hedge and the cries of the rioters faded on the wind. They walked quickly and he was sure-footed in the dark. Annis felt the waves of shock and relief flow over her. As ever, Adam's presence was comforting. Yet it was exciting as well. She was reminded of the time they had met in the garden, except this time the danger and the relief combined in a much headier brew. The feel of him beside her, the scent of him, turned her stomach into knots.

After they had gone a little way Annis was obliged to stop to shake a stone out of her shoe. She leaned one hand against the wall for support and bent down carefully to remove her pumps. Her cloak caught of the rough edges of the wall and almost pulled her off balance and she reflected ruefully that she was hardly dressed for walking on the moors. They were high up here; she could see the fields falling away into the valley below and above them crouched the dark edge of the hills. The stars were out but there was no moon, and the summer breeze nevertheless had a cold cutting edge.

'I have to hurry you—'

There was an edge of urgency to Adam's voice. He took the pump from her hand and bent down to slide it back onto her foot. For a second his hand was warm against the silkiness of her stocking and Annis almost fell over again. She heard him make a noise of mingled disgust and resignation.

'You will not get more than a hundred yards in those shoes. This will slow us up.'

'I was not dressing for a walk on the hills, my lord,' Annis said, a little tartly. 'If we could go back for the carriage—'

'Impossible.' Adam was short. 'We will find your carriage again in the daylight—if we are lucky.'

They started to move again, more slowly, more carefully. At one point Annis was obliged to accept Adam's help over a wall and took the opportunity to lean against the rough-hewn edges for a rest. She was hopelessly out of breath.

'Please…my lord…may we not rest just a little?'

Adam gave an irritable sigh. 'Very well. And you called me Adam just now. Does this mark a return to formality between us, my lady?'

'I was very discomposed just now,' Annis said. 'I said the first thing that came into my head.'

'I realise that.' There was an odd note in Adam's voice. 'You seemed very pleased to see me.'

'I was.'

'You clung to me.'

Annis drew in a sharp breath. She did not need to be reminded. It had been more than relief. It had felt right. 'That is consistent with the fact that I was pleased to see you, my lord.'

'Are you trying to imply that you would have embraced anyone who was fortunate enough to rescue you?' Adam laughed. 'I am sorry that I was obliged to grab you in the darkness for a second time, Annis. I suppose I should be grateful that this time you did no damage to me.'

'Perhaps if you did not lurk about at night you would not run that risk.' Annis paused, curious. Up until now she had had little time to think amidst the panic of flight. Now she had some questions. 'Whatever are you doing here, my lord? Surely you are not mixed up in this riot?'

'You think me a renegade and a criminal?' Adam's tone was amused. 'You have a low opinion of me, my lady.'

'You have not answered my question.'

'No. What about you, Annis? Were you there with a purpose?'

Annis frowned. 'Certainly not. Do not be ridiculous. The penalty for burning a tollhouse is death.'

'That is the penalty for being caught, certainly. But you have a grudge against Samuel Ingram—'

'And so do you—'

'So either of us could be suspects. It is not wise to travel after dark around here, Lady Wycherley. I thought that I had told you that before. We expected you at Eynhallow long before this.'

Annis looked at him closely. She could not see him clearly in the darkness but she knew him well enough by now to read every nuance of his voice.

'You are trying to distract me, Adam. I think that you had some purpose for being here tonight.'

There was a sharp silence, then Adam laughed. 'A shame that Pullen does not have you working on this case, Annis, or he would have solved it before now. How did you know that?'

'I am not sure,' Annis said cautiously. 'Something in your voice, I think. And when you first found me you came down the bank, from the direction of the road. That was why I wondered if you had been with the rioters all along. You came from the same direction as they did.'

'I was not a part of the riot.'

Annis paused. 'I believe you. But… You came to warn them, didn't you? You knew that the yeomanry were to be called out and you came to warn them that they were in danger.'

She saw Adam grin. 'How I wish you had not guessed that, Annis! Now you know far more than is good for you.'

Annis drew a deep breath. 'Then it is true?'

'It is true. Ned knew what was planned for tonight. When we were in town earlier, we heard that Ingram had called out the yeomanry. We were…anxious…that the men should not run straight into a trap. Many of them are known to us and can only do themselves and their families harm if they are caught, condemned, transported or hanged.'

Annis studied him closely. 'Then Mr Ingram was not so far from the truth. You may not be the rebel leader, but you have aided and abetted the rioters. Perhaps you even know the identity of their leader.'

Adam shook his head. 'It does not work like that. That is the beauty of their system. Because all the men are masked and messages are passed purely by word of mouth, no one knows who else is involved. I must admit to a certain curiosity, though. I would like to know the identity of the mysterious rebel leader, the man who rides a horse so conveniently like mine that I may end up hanging for him!'

Annis frowned. 'Did you see him tonight?'

'Of course. As did you, I imagine. Who do you think it is?'

Annis was silent. 'I do not know.' Even she could hear the hesitation in her tone. 'It could be you, for all your protestations of innocence. I did not see the two of you at the same time!'

Adam laughed. 'Please keep that theory to yourself. Do you suspect any other candidates?'

Annis hesitated again. 'I saw several horses stabled at Starbeck when I was there last. One was a bay with a white flash. That is all I know.'

'At Starbeck…' Adam sounded thoughtful. 'That is interesting…'

Annis clutched his arm. 'It could be a mere coincidence.'

Adam's laugh was cynical. 'I doubt it. You see how easy it is to become involved, Annis. Already you are keeping information quiet, protecting someone. Tom Shepard... Your cousin Charles... It could be either of them!'

The shock hit Annis hard. 'Charles? You think that Charles might be the leader of the rioters? No, that is impossible! Besides, you said yourself that he is hated here. As well suspect your brother Edward!'

Adam laughed. 'Ned has a different role to play.'

Annis stared. 'I did not expect to find you excusing violence, my lord.'

Adam's voice hardened. 'Generally speaking, I do not, but Ingram has caused nothing but hunger, misery and death through his cruelty. He sowed the wind and now he is reaping the whirlwind.'

He pulled her to her feet again and with a sigh Annis complied, pulling her tattered cloak about her. Adam looked behind them. 'Come into the shelter of the wood,' he said abruptly. 'They are burning the coach.'

Annis pressed a hand to her mouth. 'But Barney—the coachman! I saw him jump down, but if he has come to any harm I shall never forgive myself.'

'If he has any sense he will have run away before they arrived. I will send to look for him as soon as it is safe.' Adam urged her onwards, down a bank and into the wood. 'Besides, they will not hurt him. They are rioters, not murderers, and their argument is with Ingram, not with one of their own.'

Annis took several more steps, then stopped again. 'The horses! Surely they will not have harmed the horses!'

This time Adam laughed. 'Certainly not, my lady! These are countrymen. In a fire they would save the horses first.'

Annis sighed. They were walking along a path through the trees now and once again Adam seemed sure of his way. The bracken crackled underfoot and, every so often, thorns would catch at the trailing edges of Annis' cloak. She ruefully reflected that it would be fit for nothing in the morning. The trees grew close here, arching overhead, providing a dense canopy through which the starlight barely penetrated.

'We are almost safe at Eynhallow now,' Adam said, in an undertone. He turned to Annis and pulled her close. 'There is something I wanted to ask you, Annis. When you clung to me before—'

Annis shivered. 'Pray do not remind me, my lord. It was most improper of me.'

'Would you also say that it was improper for your body to soften against me so sweetly, as it did then—and as it is doing now?'

There was a silence beneath the trees, but for the rustle of some night creature scuttering through the undergrowth. Annis could not think of a single, helpful prevarication.

'You smell of honey and apricots and wood smoke and your skin is smoother than velvet...' Adam's tone was conversational, as though the air between them was not hot with the sparks of a different fire. His fingers moved from her wrist to touch the back of her hand in a light caress. 'I have been thinking about you ever since we parted this morning, Annis. In fact, I seem to spend the majority of my time thinking about you these days.'

Annis's breath caught in her throat. 'I do not believe that you should say such things to me, sir.'

'No? We are betrothed.'

'That may be so, but this is not the time or the place.' She cast a glance over the hill at the tollhouse fire, burning lower now. The rioters had gone and the night was still.

Adam's hand came up to cup her chin, the thumb stroking along the line of her jaw. 'You do not find danger an aphrodisiac, Annis?' His voice was a little rough. 'You do not feel the excitement like a fever in the blood?'

'I have never done so before.'

'And now?'

Annis was trembling. It would be easy—and wise—to deny it, but there was something about this man…

'I admit that something attracts me—'

His mouth took hers with unerring accuracy and without gentleness. Her lips parted instantly under the pressure. He was demanding, overpowering, and the shock and the excitement hit Annis in one irresistible blow. The blazing heat of his body, the sheer intimacy of his caresses… Annis swayed and his arms went about her tightly. When she pulled away a little, overwhelmed, one of his hands came up to cup her head, tangling in her wind-blown hair, tilting her face up to his so that he could explore her mouth again at will.

Eventually he had to let her go, for neither of them could breathe.

'If I had done that the night we first met—'

Annis's breath caught at the raw undertone to his voice. 'I would have run away from you.'

'Do you want to run now?'

'There is nowhere to run to.'

Some of the tension eased between them. She heard him

laugh. 'That is true. You will just have to trust me then. Damnation. That puts certain obligations on me.'

'Such as?'

'Such as not to seduce you.'

'What, out here?' Annis could not keep the incredulity out of her voice. Here, in the woods, with the smoke on the air and the touch of the breeze on her skin... She shook violently at the thought.

'Yes, here. I will show you one day.'

This kiss was gentle, heavy with promise. It still stole her breath. Annis sighed. She knew marriage to be a stifling trap for a woman and yet this sweet seduction told her otherwise. And tonight she did not want to be sensible.

She raised a hand and traced the lines of his face. In her mind's eye she could see his features: the thick, dark hair, the straight brows, the hard planes of his face. His cheek was a little rough. She rubbed it enquiringly.

'Annis, you are treading on dangerous ground.' Adam's voice was husky, his fingers hard about her wrist as he restrained her marauding hand. Annis drew back a little.

'I am sorry. I was curious.'

Adam turned his mouth into the palm of her hand. 'About what, Annis?'

'About what it felt like—what you felt like. I have...so little experience.'

She felt him smile against her skin. 'Is that so? Yet it is not physical intimacy that you are afraid of, is it, Annis?'

Annis stood on tiptoe to run her fingers into the tousled softness of his hair. 'No, I suppose not. I am behaving very badly, I know. I am not sure why. It has not happened to me before and it feels a little like drinking too much wine.'

Adam laughed. 'I cannot imagine you doing that either, Annis.'

'No, indeed.'

'Chaperons do not become tipsy.'

'Nor do they kiss strange gentleman in the woods at night. I cannot think what has become of me since I met you.'

His arms about her were as warm and reassuring as they were demanding. His breath tickled her ear. 'I am a bad influence on you. Plus tonight it is the effect of the release of tension. It weakens one's inhibitions and the darkness does the rest.'

'Yes, there is something unreal about this.' Annis pressed closer to him. 'There is something anonymous about the dark.'

Adam's arms tightened about her. 'You imply that I could be anyone? I am not flattered by that thought, Annis.'

Annis laughed, but part of her felt sad. 'I only meant that everything will seem different in the morning.'

'I know. I shall want to speak of wedding arrangements and you will have that hunted look in your eye that tells me you are afraid to proceed...' His lips brushed the line of her cheek, sending quivers of sensation along her nerves. 'What are you afraid of, Annis?'

Annis almost told him, but drew back at the last moment. 'I do not want to speak of it tonight,' she said in a small voice. 'It will spoil things.'

'Very well.' Adam sounded patient, almost indifferent. 'We may leave that until the morrow as well.'

Annis thought that he meant to let her go then, but instead he tightened his grip. The whole, hard length of him was pressed against her and a shiver went down her spine at the sense of delightful helplessness it engendered. She was accustomed to fending for herself. She was not accustomed to feeling so powerless, nor was she expecting it to be so enjoyable.

His mouth engulfed hers, provoking a heated pleasure. The kiss deepened, his tongue exploring, the feel and the taste of him filling her senses. He felt frighteningly familiar and deliciously tempting. Annis slid her arms about his neck and kissed him back.

Adam's hand came up to rest just beneath her breast, languidly stroking the underside, caressing gently. Annis squirmed, wanting more. Much more. Her senses were alight. When he eased the neckline of her gown down to free her breasts from the confines of the bodice, Annis gasped with mingled pleasure and relief, needing to feel his hands and his mouth against her bare skin. He stopped kissing her and slowly traced his tongue down her breast, flicking the hard, pink bud. Annis thought she would explode with passionate need. Her knees were giving way and her blood was racing. She wanted nothing other than for Adam to take her there and then, beneath the trees with the smoke on the air and the touch of the breeze on her skin.

Adam raised his head. With a deft movement he rearranged her bodice. Annis almost screamed with frustration.

'In the morning,' he said in her ear, 'pray remember that—along with all your scruples about getting married.'

He let her go, taking her hand to guide her through the wood. Annis walked by his side, scarcely noticing where she was going, aware only of the touch of his hand on hers, the ache in her body and the memory of his kiss. The twigs and bracken crunched beneath her feet and the brambles caught at her clothes, and once Adam had to stop to disentangle her, his hands lingering for a second on her waist, tightening, before he sighed and let her go. They did not speak again.

Eventually he scrambled down on to a metalled road, where a pair of iron gates led to a wide drive. The moon was rising now, clothing everything in silver.

'I do not like arriving at Eynhallow with nothing but the clothes I stand up in,' Annis said. 'It makes me feel like a beggar bride.'

Adam laughed. 'Nonsense, my love. Della will be able to lend you anything that you may need and in the morning we shall send to Harrogate for the rest of your belongings.'

They started up the drive, hand in hand.

'My lord,' Annis said, a little shyly, 'how soon did you intend for us to wed?'

'I thought very soon. As soon as the banns may be read.' He smiled at her. 'I have always been impatient to wed you, Annis, but I believe that tonight has made things worse rather than better.'

Annis hung back. 'My lord—'

'Adam. You called me Adam earlier on.'

'If you wish. Adam, physical intimacy is not a good basis for marriage. Not at all. Sometimes the reverse is true and it completely obscures the reality.' Annis hesitated. 'I do not want this to confuse me...'

'I understand.' Adam bent his head and his lips brushed hers. 'But sometimes, Annis, physical intimacy is just another, wonderful aspect of being married, along with the friendship and the shared experience.'

Annis felt a huge sadness fill her heart. 'Is that what your first marriage was like?'

'It was. And I feel sure that with you it could be the same.'

He was kissing her again, but Annis could not lose herself in the kiss as she had before. She envied him the easy intimacy he had had with Mary. She had never experienced such a love match. A part of her that she was ashamed to admit to was both jealous of his previous happiness and afraid that he would be disappointed in his second choice.

The following morning was bright and sunny once again, with the promise of heat in the air. Adam rode out early, taking no groom with him, which caused no speculation since he made a habit of riding alone. He took the track through the woods and out on to the hillside, where he allowed the bay stallion his head and galloped along one of the old drovers' tracks that criss-crossed the moor, sending the peat flying from its hooves.

Eynhallow lay below him, curled in a fold of the hills, the sight of the manor, the church and the village bringing an ache to his throat. It had stood there for time immemorial and he was only a small part of that pattern. He felt that very strongly this morning, perhaps because he had chosen to marry again and so the sense of continuity struck more strongly than usual.

When his first wife had died, he had thought that he would never want to remarry and that Edward would have to be the one to marry and to provide an heir. Then he had met Annis and, almost immediately, the decision was made. His instinct was strong; he wanted her. More than that, he wanted to marry her. He was convinced that she was the right wife for him.

Adam reined in to pause and appreciate the view. Perhaps

it had been arrogant of him, but the last thing he had expected was that he would find the lady he wished to marry only to discover that she was reluctant to marry him.

At a softly spoken word from him, the horse moved off again, trotting downhill at a more sedate pace. Adam smiled a little as he thought about Annis. Her refusal to accept his suit had been a salutary lesson. When he had first proposed, he had assumed that her reluctance to accept him stemmed from their short acquaintanceship, and that perhaps she had happy memories of her first marriage that she was afraid she would be betraying. He had been self-confident, he realised now, assuming that a penniless chaperon would be happy to accept the proposal of an eligible lord, especially given that she had been compromised. Yet Annis's reluctance had gone deeper than that. She had admitted as much, whilst refusing to confide in him. There was something that frightened her.

Adam frowned slightly. Any notion that Annis was afraid of the physical side of marriage had been banished last night, when he had held her in his arms. She might have been in-experienced, but she was neither cold nor afraid. Rather she had seemed intrigued by the possibilities of physical passion. He had been warmed to find that with many of her inhibitions gone, she had felt the same overwhelming need for him as he had for her. It was not logical, it was not even sensible, but it was there.

As for Annis's fears, Adam knew they must stem from something else, something he had yet to discover. Of one thing he was certain. He would overcome her scruples, allay them. Nothing would take Annis from him now, just as he would never surrender Eynhallow to Ingram, nor see it lost in debt. He could be very stubborn when he chose and he chose to be now.

He turned off the track on to the turnpike road and increased the pace towards the ruined tollhouse. The ruins were still smoking and made a strange sight in the bright daylight. The gate was smashed to pieces and nothing was left but a scatter of ash and debris across the road. Further down the road, the burnt-out hulk of a carriage squatted, looking like a malignant toad.

There were men already busy about the tollhouse, sizing up the damage and discussing what should be done. Adam recognised Ellis Benson and a number of men from Ingram's estate. Bad news had travelled quickly, then. No doubt Ingram himself would be here soon to assess the damage and rail against the criminals, demanding they be caught. Adam had already sent a messenger to Harrogate to acquaint Charles Lafoy with the news that his cousin was safe, even if his carriage was not. He smiled a little. He suspected that Lafoy would already be on his way.

A small crowd had gathered, as crowds do when there has been some sort of incident. There was nothing in particular to watch, but they were watching anyway. Adam recognised some of the villagers from Eynhallow and the surrounding hamlets. A few of the men were there, but it was mostly the womenfolk and children. All had identical expressions of surly blankness, leavened occasionally by unholy glee. Mr Ingram had got his come-uppance and no one was sorry.

Adam allowed his horse to idle up to the ruined tollhouse and exchanged a few, short words with Ellis Benson. The man's gaze was not friendly. Adam paused for a few words with the villagers, then turned at the sound of another horse approaching up the road. It was Edward, looking benign and vicarly, and deploring the damage in unctuous tones.

'How dreadful! How truly shocking!'

Ellis Benson turned away, scowling, and Adam brought his own mount alongside his brother.

'Doing it too brown, Ned!' he said in an undertone. 'Everyone knows that you are on the side of the rioters!'

Edward looked suitably disapproving. 'I have no idea what you can mean, Ash!'

'Indeed? Cast your mind back to last Sunday's sermon—the one about the houses of the ungodly being scattered like dust in the wind...'

A smile tugged Edward's mouth. 'That was rather a good one, wasn't it?'

'Yes, and see what it has done!'

'Benson is looking as sour as stale wine,' Edward observed.

'Can you blame him? No doubt Ingram will—for this unholy mess. Benson should have stopped it, Benson should have seen what was happening...' Adam shook his head. 'Ingram will blame everyone but himself.'

'It is fortunate, then, that he has such willing place men to shoulder the blame.'

'Benson, Lafoy...' Adam sounded thoughtful. 'He does rather surround himself with the gentry, does he not?'

'Snobbery,' Edward said comfortably. 'It makes him feel superior that he has bought them.'

'You are harsh.'

'I merely observe, Ash. What happened last night?'

The horses picked up speed away from the smouldering ruin and down the valley towards Eynhallow. They were far away enough from the crowd now not to be overheard, but Adam still glanced over his shoulder.

'It was as you suspected it would be. Roughly forty men, armed. They burned the tollhouse, then set about Lafoy's coach. It was fortunate that Lady Wycherley was clear of it by then or it would have been the devil of a job to get her out of there safely.'

Edward grimaced. 'The coachman turned up safe and sound. He's at the rectory. I told him to go straight up to the house as soon as he was ready. Lady Wycherley will be glad to know he is safe, I think. The whole experience must have shaken her quite badly.'

Adam nodded. 'She will be glad to see him.'

Edward grinned. 'Did Lady Wycherley ask you what you were doing there?'

'Yes.'

'Did you tell her?'

'Of course.'

Edward looked alarmed. 'You told her that you had gone to warn the men?'

Adam grinned. 'She guessed that I had gone out with a purpose. Annis is no fool.'

Edward frowned. 'I did not think it. But this is dangerous, Ash. She is still Lafoy's cousin, and the more she knows…'

Adam shrugged. 'Annis knows that I have an interest in seeing Ingram brought down, but then, so does she. She is not sympathetic to his cause.'

Edward sighed. 'Are we no nearer to discovering the identity of the rebel leader?'

'No. You know as much as I, Ned. He spoke like a gentleman and rode a very fine, bay horse similar to mine. Do you have any ideas who he might be?'

Edward shook his head slowly.

'What were you doing last evening?'

Edward shot his brother an appalled look. 'I?'

'Why not?' Adam quirked a brow. 'You are a gentleman—and a fine rider—and you have a grudge against Ingram as much as I do, or indeed as much as Lady Wycherley. She and I can speak for each other since we were together. But you?'

Edward goggled at him. 'You know as well as I that I do not possess a bay stallion! Damn it, Ash, surely you don't suspect your own brother?'

'Why not?' Adam said again. He saw Edward's appalled look and grinned. 'No, I do not really suspect you, Ned. All the same, it is odd. Horses are expensive. I wondered...'

'Yes?'

'If Ingram might be setting the rioters up. You know how difficult it is to prosecute the villagers, for they will not testify against each other. He might have thought that the easiest way to capture the ringleaders would be to infiltrate the gang.'

Edward frowned. 'It is a cunning plan, Ash, but I don't think the men would fall for it. They all know each other and they know who the leaders are—'

'*You* know who the leaders are!'

'Yes, some...' Edward looked uncomfortable. 'Marchant and Pierce are behind a lot of the trouble, but I know of no one with the means to keep a fine stallion.'

'Except Ingram. Could he have bought some of the men, then? Bribed them, I mean.'

'Unlikely.' Edward winced. 'They hate him like hell's pains.'

'Then there is no one else hereabouts. Ingram's estate, and Eynhallow and Starbeck are the only estates big enough to support that kind of income. Annis has seen horses stabled at Starbeck, but swears she does not know who purchased them.'

Edward whistled under his breath. 'Interesting. I had forgotten Starbeck. Ingram and Lafoy are going to hate you even more for gaining possession of it, Ash!'

'I know. There is no denying that it would be useful to control Starbeck, but I should not wish Lady Wycherley to think that that was why I wanted to marry her.'

'I thought it was because you had compromised her?'

'It is true that is why I made a formal proposal...' Adam hesitated '...yet I should not want Annis to believe that was the only reason.' He made a slight gesture. 'I am...very much attracted to her.'

Edward leant over to unlatch the gate that led into the Eynhallow deer park. 'You have known her all of two months,' he pointed out mildly.

'Sometimes it takes two days. Or two minutes.'

'I suppose so. If you are sure—'

'I am.'

'And Mary?'

Adam sighed. 'I loved Mary. But loving once does not prevent a man from loving again.'

'Have you told Lady Wycherley this?'

'Not yet. We have had little opportunity for intimate conversation since we became betrothed.' Adam frowned. 'Also there are her feelings about her first marriage to consider. I formed the strong opinion that it has set her against marriage, but I do not know why.'

Edward frowned. 'If Wycherley was the martinet we have

been told, there may be your answer. A bully, a tyrant… Your Annis will need gentle wooing.'

'Yes.' Adam smiled. He felt warm at the thought. 'That is precisely what I shall give her.'

Chapter Eleven

When Annis went into the library after breakfast, Adam was standing by the windows in a patch of sunlight. Seeing him now in the daylight, after all that had happened between them the previous night, Annis was beset by such conflicting emotions that she could barely speak. She had known that Adam could move her to a passion that she had never experienced before, but the most difficult aspect to believe was that she had been so uninhibited with him. Not since she was seventeen in Bermuda had she felt so free from inhibition. In those days her behaviour had been prompted by innocence. Last night... She blushed to think of it. Last night she had been almost overwhelmed by her desire for him. Now, in the clear light of morning, she felt utterly tongue-tied.

Adam came forward to greet her, and when he smiled Annis felt her heart trip, missing a beat. For some reason she had thought that the effect Adam had on her would be reduced in the daylight as well. That had been a mistake.

'I trust that you are feeling well this morning, Annis,'

Adam said, gesturing her to sit on a long gold sofa before the fireplace. 'I imagine that you have heard that Barney Thompson is safe? Edward said that he had sent a message over from the rectory.'

Annis nodded. 'I am greatly relieved. The loss of Charles's carriage is unfortunate, but nothing compared to any loss of life.'

'There is the loss of the horses as well.' Adam's lips twitched. 'I doubt that Lafoy will ever see them again. Or if he does, someone will swear blind that they are completely different animals from his carriage horses! I fear the events of last night have cost him dear, assuming that you were correct and he is in no way connected with the riots.'

'Have you been up to the Skipton Road this morning?' Annis enquired. It was, in part, a genuine concern for the welfare of Mr and Mrs Castle that prompted her enquiry, but it was also an attempt to avoid the conversation moving on to more personal matters.

Adam nodded. 'I have. The tollhouse is ruined, but Mr and Mrs Castle are safe. As yet no one appears to have come forward to name the suspects and...' he gave her smile '...no one was captured last night. The militia sprang their trap, but by some mischance the rioters were already apprised of their plan...'

'How lucky for them,' Annis said, smiling back. 'Of course, you know nothing of that, my lord.'

'Nothing at all. And neither do you, should your cousin ask. I imagine he will be travelling over from Harrogate at this very moment to check on your welfare.' Adam came across to sit beside her on the sofa. 'I have been speaking to Ned about the marriage banns,' he said. 'They will be read for the first time of asking tomorrow.'

A huge panic welled up in Annis. She stood up quickly and moved over to the long windows that looked out across the parkland.

'Must it be so soon?' She sounded stifled.

When she looked back at Adam, she saw that his face had set in hard lines. He too got to his feet. 'I have the strong impression that you do not wish to marry me.' His tone was clipped. 'Such unwillingness is not flattering, my sweet, particularly after your...enthusiastic response to me last night. Can it be that you are having second thoughts?'

Annis swung round to face him properly. Adam's body was tense and his expression unreadable, but there was something in his face, a tiny hint of vulnerability, that made her wonder if she had hurt him. The thought upset her. It felt like a dreadful thing to do.

She felt something snap within her. 'I told you in Harrogate that it was not that I did not want to marry you, Adam,' she said quietly. 'It is marriage itself that I have always sought to avoid. And now that I cannot avoid it, I am afraid.'

Adam did not move towards her and the light in his grey eyes was brilliant. They threw her a challenge. 'You have no cause to fear me, Annis. Surely you know that?'

Annis struggled, with herself, her thoughts and her fears. 'Marriage is too important for me to embark upon it without the expectation that it would work.' Her tone rose with feeling. 'Yet I know so little of you, of your reasons and expectations! I do not know you well at all! This attraction we have between us...this affinity...simply makes matters more difficult.'

The panic was rising in her and she tried to crush it down, seeking Adam's gaze, desperate for him to understand. 'I have told you that my first marriage was unhappy. It made me resolve never to repeat it again—'

She found she could not quite put into words her fears of being trapped once again in marriage. The horror of such a prospect was so huge that it literally closed her throat. On the one hand she knew that not all men were alike. A small part of her even whispered that Adam would never bully her or make her ill, as John Wycherley had done. Yet somehow she could not get past that mistrust and give him her heart. Not yet. It was too soon and she was too unready.

She saw the anger go out of Adam's face and the hard lines soften, and she thought that he was a better man than she deserved. Perhaps in time she would be able to explain the whole to him—but for now this was the best she could do.

He took her hands in his. 'Annis, as for my hopes and expectations, they may be summed up quite easily. I truly wish to marry you, and not just to save your reputation or put matters to right in the eyes of the world. If you consent to our marriage, we will have the time to discover more about each other and then your fears may be put to rest.'

Annis could have wept at his gentleness. She looked up at him. 'I do not know...' The words were wrenched from her. 'I am so very bad at relinquishing control...'

His eyes filled with tender laughter. 'You are bossy, my sweet. That is why you were always so good at marshalling those tiresome girls.'

'And then there is your previous marriage to Mary...' Annis's voice faltered. She did not wish to forever live in Mary Ashwick's shadow.

Adam let her go. 'One day soon I will tell you about Mary, just as you will tell me the whole about your marriage and

the reasons you are so chary to commit to another match.'
He kissed her cheek. 'Do not look so doleful, my sweet. I am
sure that everything will resolve itself in time and for now we
had better get on with this business of arranging a wedding.'

Annis did not say anything else. Adam had offered her
his understanding and his patience and she knew that he was
being generous to her. It was more than she could have expected. But as for time, that was the one thing that she did
not have.

It was a strange couple of weeks. The banns were read
for the first time that weekend and after that Annis felt that
there was no going back. Adam had intimated that he would
like to invite a few of his closest friends from London to attend the wedding service, and, although Annis was quaking
in her boots at the prospect of meeting them all, she agreed
that it was only appropriate. Her side of the church would be
sparsely populated, with only Sibella, David and their family,
Charles, Mrs Hardcastle and the Shepards attending. Lady
Ashwick had called her own dressmaker from Harrogate to
fashion Annis's trousseau and the time seemed full of fit-
tings, re-fittings and the choosing of dress materials, from
the diaphanous négligées that brought a blush to Annis's
cheek to the day dresses, walking dresses, riding habits and
all the other outfits that seemed so essential to a lady. Soon
all of Sir Robert Crossley's money had gone, but Annis was
determined not to allow Adam to pay. He had little enough
money in all conscience, and Annis was determined that she
should not be the one to push him further into debt.

Eventually, one fine afternoon, she and Adam found the
time to play truant from their duties and ride over to Star-

beck. Mrs Hardcastle had already been drafted in to wage war on the dirt and the mice and this was the first time that Adam had the opportunity to inspect the property closely.

'It is not so bad,' he said encouragingly, as together they inspected the broken window frames and peeling walls. 'Much of the damage is superficial and I am confident that we shall find a tenant once the structural improvements are made and Mrs Hardcastle has had the opportunity to clean it up.' He smiled at her. 'Or we could keep it as a love nest for when we wish to escape from Eynhallow...'

Annis blushed and smiled, but a part of her felt frightened. Starbeck had been her refuge; now that it was to go to Adam on their marriage, it felt as though she had nothing left, no place to hide. She was very quiet as they accepted a tankard each of Mrs Shepard's cider and wandered outside to drink it in the shade of the garden.

'I hear that the Pensioners were called out again last night to deal with the latest riots,' Adam said, as they walked slowly down the path into the walled garden, past Starbeck's small sulphur well and the beautiful brass sundial that Captain Lafoy had brought back from his travels. 'Apparently they were so old and out of condition that the rioters managed to overpower and disarm them! Ingram is threatening to call the regular troops next time.' He looked closely at Annis. 'You are not attending, are you, my love? I could have been speaking a different language for all the sense I am making.'

Annis sat down on a stone bench in the shade of the apple tree. There was an old summerhouse leaning against one of the walls and in front of it a pool of water supplied from the same spring as the well. The garden was very overgrown now, with roses and cornflowers and honeysuckle all tangling together in the profusion of high summer. It was warm, scented and very peaceful. She stroked the furry head of a snapdragon.

'I beg your pardon, Adam. I was thinking.'

'Of Starbeck?' Adam came to sit beside her. 'You will not be losing it, Annis.'

His quick understanding both impressed and alarmed Annis. She cast him a look under her lashes. 'No, I know. But it will not be the same.'

Adam took her hand in his. 'You are worried because you will have nowhere to run to,' he said acutely. 'Why do you think that you will want to run away, Annis?'

Annis looked at him. His gaze was very deep and dark and she felt a shiver of apprehension. She could not tell him that she could not yet trust herself to him. That would be too hurtful when he had been so patient with her. Besides, the problem was not in him, but in her. And it was not her only concern.

'I know that you were in love with Mary and I am afraid that you will be disappointed in your second choice,' she blurted out. 'I could not bear it if our marriage was a pale imitation of what went before.' She locked her shaking fingers together. 'Perhaps it is a fault in me, wishing not to be second best, but I would rather we never wed than that we be haunted by memories.'

The words were out. She waited, trembling inside, for Adam's reply.

He did not answer at once, then he stood up and moved a little away from her. 'I should like to tell you about Mary, if I may, and then you will understand me, Annis. It is very important that there is no misunderstanding.'

Annis waited.

'I ran away with Mary when she was seventeen and I was eighteen.' Adam smiled faintly. 'We knew that my father would never have approved the marriage and neither would Mary's family. Everyone said that we were too young to know our own minds and that it was a most unsuitable match.' He shrugged. 'We knew well enough what we wanted. We ran away to Gretna and our families simply had to accept what we had done. It was uncomfortable at first, but matters soon settled down.'

A butterfly settled on a flower by Annis's cheek. She stared fixedly at its jewel-bright colours.

'We were very happy for five years,' Adam said softly. 'There were no children, but we always thought that we had plenty of time. Then Mary contracted scarlet fever. Within two weeks she was dead.'

Adam got up and walked across to the sundial, resting a hand on the warm stone of the rim. 'I could not accept it at first. We had been so young and I suppose we had never been tried. Apart from our elopement, which had seemed little more than a romantic adventure, nothing had ever gone awry for us. And suddenly I was left with nothing.'

Annis did not speak. Adam's voice was expressionless, but she knew that it must be hurting him to talk about this. She wanted to touch him, to comfort him, but she did not dare to get up and go to him. He seemed far away from her, wrapped up in the grief of years, beyond her reach. She was afraid that if she went to him he would reject her.

Adam rested his booted foot on the base of the sundial and looked away across the gardens.

'Such heartache does not last forever. Inevitably the initial sharpness will ease, although one does not ever forget.' He shrugged. 'I went abroad and fought the French. I came home and—' he smiled a little '—I confess that I played the part of a rake about Town. It is perfectly possible to survive on one's own. It is simply that one feels…unfinished. The years passed and I never met a lady I wished to marry. Until now.'

He came back to the bench with a swiftness that took Annis by surprise, and took both her hands in his.

'Annis, I love you. From the very first I was attracted to you and I quickly realised that I wanted to marry you. There is nothing to say that a man cannot love—sincerely love— more than once.' He gave her a little, loving shake. 'What I felt for Mary was a boy's passion that I believe would have mellowed into something deeper with age. What I feel for you cannot be compared with that. I am a man now, not a boy of eighteen, and I feel for you everything that a man can feel.'

His arms went around her and he pulled her hard against him. Annis clung to him, her face turned against his chest, hearing the thud of his heart, breathing in the scent of him. He was offering her everything that she could ever have asked for and she could not quite believe it. In a few moments, when he felt the warmth of her tears drench his shirt, he held her a little away and scanned her face.

'Sweetheart…why are you crying?'

Annis shook her head slightly. Her heart was too full for her to speak. 'I am sorry,' she managed to say. She freed herself from his grip. 'You are so generous and I…' Her words failed. *I cannot tell you that I love you…* The words hung in the air, unspoken between them. She wanted to say them; wanted to believe them. She was so close to it…

'I suppose that I am envious,' Annis said in a moment, 'which is no very admirable thing. My own marriage was such a poor thing in comparison.'

There was such a tender light in Adam's eyes that she almost cried again. 'That need not matter one jot, Annis. It does not mean that we cannot be happy. I am confident that when you are ready, you will tell me what happened to you. In the meantime, I can wait.'

There was a week to go before the wedding. The house in Church Row had been emptied and all Annis's meagre possessions moved to Eynhallow. Mrs Hardcastle was established at Starbeck and suddenly it seemed that there was nothing for Annis to do.

'It is very odd,' she confided in Della Tilney, as they sat together in the drawing room one morning. 'I am so accustomed to being busy that I cannot settle. I feel as though I am suddenly become useless.'

Della looked up from her needlework, a light of understanding in her grey eyes.

'It is only until the wedding, Annis. At the moment you are in that state of anticipation where you are simply waiting for something to happen. Afterwards...'

'Yes?' Annis cast her needlework aside restlessly and jumped to her feet. 'Afterwards I may do what?' She spread her hands appealingly. 'It is so long since I have been a lady of leisure, Della, that I cannot remember what to do!'

Della laughed. 'Why, there are endless things for you to do, Annis! If you do not care for the usual pursuits of reading and needlework, then you may walk or go out riding, or visiting. There are plenty of good causes for you to embrace and besides…' Della cast her a smiling look '…Adam will want to monopolise you for plenty of the time!'

'He does not seem to want to do so now,' Annis said gloomily. Adam and Edward had gone out hunting that morning and she imagined that they would be away for the whole day.

Della gave her a shrewd look. 'I rather suspect that Adam finds your company too much temptation prior to the wedding,' she said, with a wicked smile. 'Last night he was watching you all the time during dinner. I asked him the same question three times and he cut me dead! He is fathoms deep in love with you, my dear!'

Annis was spared an answer by the arrival of Tranter.

'Excuse me, Lady Wycherley.' The butler bowed low. 'Mrs Hardcastle is here to see you, ma'am. She seems in some distress. I tried to encourage her to wait for you in the library, but she insisted on staying in the hall. She is out there now.'

Annis got to her feet in some surprise. The thought of Mrs Hardcastle in distress was difficult to imagine, for that redoubtable lady had been a tower of strength for years.

'Excuse me, Della,' she murmured. 'I think I had better go and investigate. In the hall, you said, Tranter?'

Mrs Hardcastle was occupying one of the hard, straight-backed chairs that stood beside the long pier glass at the bottom of the stairs. She was looking straight ahead and was clutching in her hands what looked like a piece of old sacking. When she saw Annis approach she got hastily to her feet and Annis saw that she was not so much distressed as agitated. She launched into speech at once.

'Oh, Miss Annis! I found this yesterday when I was cleaning at Starbeck and I thought I should bring it straight over to you! I've been awake all night worriting.'

Annis took her arm. 'Come into the library, Hardy. Tranter, a pot of tea, if you please.'

'Couldn't drink a drop!' Mrs Hardcastle puffed. 'I'm that distraught, Miss Annis!'

Annis urged her to a seat and Mrs Hardcastle again sat bolt upright, the piece of sacking clutched in her hands. She seemed to recall suddenly that it was there, for she held it out to Annis and said again, 'I found this yesterday, ma'am. I was cleaning the end bedroom, the one where the gable is coming down. Anyway, that's nothing to the purpose. Proper mess it was in there, with the floorboards loose and the paint peeling. I got young Tom Shepard to bring a hammer and nails to settle the floor, but before he did I just stuck my head down. Disgraceful mess there was down there, Miss Annis, with paper everywhere, and mouse droppings and this disgusting sack...' Mrs Hardcastle paused to draw breath. 'So I bundled it all up and took it down to the fire and when I was about to throw it in I suddenly saw this!'

She thrust the sack at Annis, who looked at it dubiously.

'Yes, Hardy? It is a sack.'

'Look inside, ma'am,' the housekeeper said, in tones of deep foreboding.

Annis inserted her hand into the canvas bag.

'Careful now,' Mrs Hardcastle said, reverting to her usual practical tone. 'Mind the mouse droppings!'

Annis's fingers closed on a scrap of paper that was left in a corner of the bag. It was larger than the rest and had escaped the destruction of the mice. She pulled it out.

The first thing that she saw was the image of Britannia,

then the words one thousand pounds, ripped across by sharp
little teeth. She felt a little faint.

'But this…this is one thousand pounds, Hardy!'

'You mean it was one thousand pounds, Miss Annis,' Mrs
Hardcastle corrected heavily. 'There was ever so many of
them papers as well—banknotes, I suppose they'd be—all
nibbled to destruction by those pesky mice! I've been worriting and worriting all night about what they was doing there.
Tom and me, we searched all under the floor, but there was
nothing left but shreds. So this morning I put on my bonnet and got Tom to bring me over here in the cart because I
knew you would know what to do, Miss Annis.'

Annis frowned. She had no idea what to do. Whoever had
hidden the money in the first place had clearly not banked
on Mrs Hardcastle's obsession with hygiene, and whoever
had hidden it must have gained it by criminal means. No one
could have so many banknotes sitting under the floorboards
for a legitimate purpose.

Annis got to her feet and walked across to the window,
staring out at Eynhallow's beautiful gardens bathed on the
afternoon sunlight. The sensible thing would be to wait until
Adam returned and discuss it with him, but he and Edward
had indicated that they might be away until dinner. Besides,
Annis was accustomed to taking action of her own accord
and she was feeling very restless. She rang the bell decisively.

'I think that it would be best if I came back to Starbeck
with you now, Hardy,' she said. 'I shall leave a note for Lord
Ashwick and explain where I have gone. We must instigate
a search of the house, for who knows what else may be hidden on the premises? And then we must alert the appropriate authorities, whoever they are.'

Within ten minutes the matter was settled. Tom Shepard brought the cart round to the front of the house, looking appalled when he was informed that both Annis and Della Tilney would be accompanying Mrs Hardcastle back to Starbeck. Della was there because she had insisted that it was not appropriate for Annis to go on her own.

'I never have any excitement,' she said, a twinkle in her grey eyes as she drew on her cloak and gloves and following Annis out to the cart. 'Besides, Adam will be very displeased about this, dearest Annis, so it is better that he should have two of us to vent his bad temper on. You see what a staunch sister-in-law I shall be to you! I think that we shall deal together extremely well.'

They searched all afternoon, but found no more money and ended up dusty and thirsty for their pains. Della declared that she had seldom enjoyed an afternoon more and that Mrs Hardcastle's elderflower cordial was marvellously refreshing. Mrs Hardcastle beamed.

When the time came for them to return to Eynhallow, they hit a snag. Tom Shepard refused to take them. He stood in the hall, twisting his cap in his hands and looking bashful but determined.

'Sorry, ma'am, but I can't allow it. There's word out that it's dangerous to travel tonight.'

Annis looked at him. He fidgeted and looked away, his handsome face slightly flushed but set in stubborn lines.

'Tom,' Annis said, with ominous calm, 'are you telling me that you refuse to take the cart out? Can you possibly be afraid of the Washburn Men?'

Tom's gaze jerked back to hers. She saw him smile. 'No,

ma'am. But I have my orders. It's more than my life's worth
to go against them.'

Annis looked out at the bright summer evening. The sun
was still high in the sky. 'It will take us all of an hour to get
back to Eynhallow and it will not be dark even then. I cannot see the problem.'

'Sorry, ma'am.'

There was a tense silence.

'Why do we not drive ourselves?' Della suggested. 'I am
sure that either of us could manage the cart, Annis.'

'Sorry, ma'am,' Tom said again. 'I can't let you do that.
There's pickets on all the roads already and tonight is going
to be fierce. So…you're to stay here. Master says so.'

'I would like to meet this Master of yours,' Annis muttered. 'Of all the high-handed, arrogant nonsense!'

'Yes, ma'am.' Tom grinned. He gave an awkward bow.
'Don't think to set off walking either, ma'am,' he added as
an afterthought. 'There's men on the end of the drive that
would bring you back!'

'Of all the ridiculous situations!' Annis said, after Tom
had gone out. She took an angry swish about the room. 'Here
we are marooned for the night in a scarce-habitable house,
with no food, mice in the rafters and a restless mob outside!
I am almost inclined to walk back to Eynhallow and damn
their impudence!'

'Why do you not come into the drawing room and sit
down?' Della suggested soothingly. 'I am sure that Mrs Hardcastle can scrape together something for us to eat and she
mentioned that at least two of the bedrooms are fit for human
habitation. Although, Annis…' she hesitated '…I would prefer to sit up tonight with you, if you do not object. I am un-

likely to sleep a wink, knowing that there is a rabble of rioters outside!'

In the event they dined royally by candlelight on ham, cheese, bread and apples, with some of Mrs Shepard's cider to accompany the meal. Annis had tried to persuade Mrs Hardcastle to join them, only to be put in her place by the housekeeper, who said that she had work to do turning down the beds, heating the water and warming the bricks to put in the ladies' beds. In vain did Annis and Della protest that they would not be able to sleep. Mrs Hardcastle went away muttering that she had her housekeeping duties to fulfil.

'I hope that Adam understood your message,' Della said, pouring more cider into their beakers. 'He is going to be unconscionably worried when we do not arrive back.' She looked at Annis, her grey eyes bright with mischief. 'He will be angry as well, but I am certain that you may talk him around. I believe you could wrap him about your little finger, he loves you so much!'

Annis blushed and disclaimed. 'All the same,' she said, 'I know Adam is a good man.' Her voice dropped. 'Better than I deserve.'

Della narrowed her eyes. 'Why do you say that, Annis?'

It was dark outside now. Beyond the uncurtained windows the moon was rising and the sky was black. The moon was shining through the mullions and pooling on the wooden floor. On the makeshift table the remains of the meal sat between them. The candlelight was warm and a small fire burned in the grate. Annis drank some more of her cider.

'I do not deserve Adam for I know that he loves me, yet I am unable to trust him and love him back. I *want* to love him,' she added, with a fierce vehemence, 'but my first marriage... My husband was a bully who would browbeat me into submission. Oh, not physically,' she added hastily, as she saw the shock mirrored in Della's eyes, 'but sometimes other methods are just as bad. He would lock me in my room when he went out and he would open my letters to see who was writing to me... He dominated every aspect of my life in and in the end I thought I would run quite mad, and I was so ill that I wanted to die to escape him.' She looked up. 'That is the reason I find it so difficult to trust any man again—and the reason I cannot tell Adam why I am so cool with him.'

She blushed a little, for coolness was not precisely the word to describe their relationship. Yet for all their physical intimacy, for all the delight that she took in their kisses, there was a part of her that she always held back. It was a barrier between them. She knew it and Adam knew it too.

Della was shaking her head. 'I am sure that love and trust will come in time, Annis. I think that you do love Adam. You are just afraid to let yourself give in to it.' She laughed and drained her beaker. 'Hark at me! I was hardly such a pattern card of marital bliss myself!'

There was a bitter note in her voice. 'Humphrey was a weak man and I could not give him my respect. At least you do not have that difficulty, Annis.'

'No,' Annis agreed, thinking that Adam could hardly be described as weak. She drank some more cider. It was extremely delicious. Della evidently thought so too, for she pushed her beaker across to be filled and leaned one elbow on the table. Annis's lips twitched. It was perhaps fortunate that she was no longer a chaperon, for her recent behaviour was far below the standard that was acceptable. Shamelessly

embracing a gentleman in the woods, getting tipsy on cider...
She felt warm and pleasantly at ease.

'Your cousin, Mr Lafoy,' Della said casually. 'Is he a man
a woman could respect, Annis?'

Annis hesitated. 'I used to think so. I love Charles and
Sibella dearly, for they are my only family and have always
been there for me. Yet recently Charles has changed.' She
frowned. 'It is not so much that he has fallen under the influence of Mr Ingram, but more that he seems a different character... All his good qualities have been distorted. I cannot
quite explain it.' She looked at Della, who was now pillow-
ing her head on her folded arms. Her dark hair was tumbled
about her face and there was a dreamy look in her eyes. Annis
suddenly remembered the scene in the Promenade Rooms
and the night at the theatre. The words came out before she
could stop them.

'You like Charles, do you not, Della? Like him a great
deal, I mean?'

Della raised her head and for a second Annis could see
her heart was in her eyes. 'I love Charles,' Della said slowly,
almost defiantly. 'I have loved him since before Humphrey
died. We were lovers, Annis. There! I have shocked you—'

The shock was in fact almost enough to sober Annis up.
She stared, her hazel eyes as wide as an owl. 'Della? But
how...'

The tears trembled on Della's lashes. 'It was just the once.
I do not know... It happened so slowly, yet so inexorably,
somehow. We had known each other for an age and then
I began to realise that my feeling for Charles had changed
and then, one day, I was out riding and met him here...' She
smothered a little sob. 'Humphrey was a weak man and, as

I said, I could not respect him. But that is no excuse, no excuse…' She covered her face with her hands again, but when she looked up a second later, her eyes were dry. 'So I told Charles that it must end. It had not really begun, and since then we have barely spoken.'

Annis put a hand out to her and after a moment, Della clasped it hard, before letting her go. She took another draught of the cider and gave a watery giggle.

'Oh, Annis, look at us here like two topers drowning our sorrows in drink! I declare we must be the most outrageous sight!'

Annis started to laugh too. 'Oh dear, this is all too melancholy to be true. I cannot bear it…' She dissolved into giggles and after a moment, found she could not stop. She reached for the pitcher of cider and saw that it was almost empty. 'And as if that were not the outside of enough, we have run out of drink! I must ask Mrs Hardcastle for some more…'

She lurched none too steadily to her feet, then sat down again heavily as the door opened with a crash that shook it on its hinges. Della was still laughing, her face flushed pink, her eyes bright.

Mrs Hardcastle appeared in the doorway, carrying a candle. 'Miss Annis, his lordship is here.'

Annis waved the pitcher at her. 'Hardy, we should like some more cider, if you please.'

'It is quite clear that you have had enough,' Adam said. He strode into the room and his gaze fell on Della, now almost asleep on the table. 'Both of you,' he said, 'what the devil is going on here?'

Chapter Twelve

'Oh dear,' Annis said. She blinked at him, feeling ever so slightly cast away. 'You received my message then, Adam.'

Adam gave her a look. 'I did. However, you neglected to mention that the two of you would be carousing on cider at Starbeck with a restless mob of rioters less than a mile away. What the deuce are you doing here, Annis?'

Annis went up to him and put a hand against his chest. He looked stern and unyielding, yet she could have sworn that there was a gleam of amusement in his eyes.

'I am so glad to see you,' she said conversationally.

Adam laughed. His arm went about her. 'Do not try to gammon me, Annis! When Ned and I got back we found nothing but Mama in a state of high excitement and a cock-and-bull note from you saying that you were looking for treasure at Starbeck and would be back by nightfall! Ned and I got over here as quickly as we were able.'

The door opened and Edward came in. His gaze took in

Annis, standing within the circle of Adam's arm, Della asleep on the table and the two empty beakers of cider.

'I see,' he said, with a grin.

Annis turned towards Adam. 'Tom Shepard said that the men were blockading the roads. How did the two of you get through?'

Now it was Adam's turn to grin. 'We talked our way past them.' He gave her an old-fashioned look. 'Surely you did not imagine that we would leave the two of you here unprotected but for Mrs Hardcastle? Although I concede that it would be a brave man who tried to take her on.'

'I suppose that you have come to take us back to Eynhallow.' Annis moved away and went over to take her cloak from the back of the chair. 'If we have your escort we should be quite safe.'

Adam shook his head. 'It is not safe for anyone to be out tonight. The gang are but a half-mile from here. They are tearing down the fences Ingram put up to enclose Linforth Common.'

'And the troops,' Annis said quickly. 'Have the regulars been called out?'

Adam and Edward exchanged a look. 'I heard so,' Edward said.

'And you have warned the men?'

Adam laughed. 'Annis, do not ask! Now, what is this about treasure?'

Before Annis could reply there was the sound of a horse approaching up the drive, and fast. Edward turned back into the hall for a lantern and they all hurried to the main door. The cool night air was sobering. By the light of the moon Annis saw the bay stallion with the white flash. It was carrying a double load. One man dismounted and the other slid from the saddle to crumple on the gravel sweep. Annis started forward.

'Charles!'

Her cry was echoed by another from behind them. Annis swung round to see Della hurrying down the shallow stone steps to join them on the drive.

'Charles! Are you injured?'

In the candlelight Annis saw that her face was paper white, her eyes huge.

'Devil a bit,' Charles Lafoy said cheerfully. He straightened up. 'I did not expect to see you here, Della—nor the rest of you.' He nodded to Adam. 'Servant, Ashwick. Can't talk for the time being. Can you help me?' He gestured to the prone figure, whom Annis saw was Ellis Benson. She went down on her knees beside him on the gravel.

'Is he much injured, Charles?'

'He took a bullet in the shoulder,' Charles said. 'He has lost some blood, but I think he will be fine.'

'A bullet?' Annis said.

'The troops are out,' Charles said tersely. He glanced over his shoulder at Adam. 'We are indebted to you for sending word, Ashwick.'

'Let us get him inside,' Annis said quickly, as several ideas quickly rearranged themselves in her head. 'We may talk later.'

Adam nodded. 'I'll help you carry him inside, Lafoy. Ned, could you take the horse around to the stables? Della, would you and Annis be so good as to search out some bandages and water and whatever else we might need? I do not suppose there is much here, though Mrs Hardcastle may have some ointments.' He turned back to Charles. 'Are we to expect a visit from the militia, Lafoy?'

'I hope not, but one never knows.' Charles shifted a little to support Ellis Benson's weight. 'I do not think that we were followed, but I cannot be entirely certain.'

'Then the most difficult thing to explain will be the horse. We can hide Benson and it is not surprising for you to be visiting your cousin, but it is known that I only have one bay stallion.' Adam cast Edward a glance. 'See what you can do, Ned.'

They carried Ellis Benson across the threshold and up the stairs, laying him on the bed in the first chamber they came to, which was the one Mrs Hardcastle had prepared for Della. There was a hot brick in it and the chamber was warm.

'There are no bandages,' Della whispered to Annis. 'I suggested to Mrs Hardcastle that we might tear up some sheets, but she told me it was a waste and to make do with my petticoats!'

Annis smothered a laugh. 'We may use mine too, although I think that Hardy's would be best. She wears flannel, even in summer!'

They ripped some strips off their underclothes and then Mrs Hardcastle arrived with the hot water and she and Della set to work cleaning and binding the wound to Ellis Benson's shoulder. Annis looked across at Charles and saw that he was watching Della intently as she worked. She glanced at Adam, who met her look with a faintly questioning one of his own. Annis smiled faintly and shook her head. That was another explanation that must wait until later.

Ned returned from the stables. 'All's quiet outside,' he announced. 'How goes it here?'

'He'll survive.' Mrs Hardcastle spoke briskly. 'Tough lad, is our Ellis.' She turned accusingly to Charles. 'What do you think you were doing, Master Charles, lettin' him get beat up like that?'

Charles grinned. 'Sorry, Hardy. I did my best. I brought him here to you, didn't I? I just didn't expect you to be entertaining a house party!'

'Well, give the lad some air,' Mrs Hardcastle said, steering them all towards the door. 'I'll fetch you all some tea and then I'll sit up with him.'

'I'll get the tea, Hardy,' Annis said. 'You had better stay with Mr Benson, since you seem to know exactly what is going on here!'

The housekeeper turned a little pink and looked a little shifty. 'One hears things, Miss Annis...'

Annis looked at her cousin. 'I am sure that Charles can put the rest of us in the picture,' she said pointedly.

Charles, Edward and Della went back into the drawing room whilst Annis went along to the stone-flagged kitchen. The huge copper kettle was already hissing on the fire and she made a pot of tea with quick efficiency.

'I would rather have some brandy,' Adam said, following her in, 'but I do not suppose that there is any in the house. Just cider, I suppose?'

Annis laughed. 'I assure you that I am quite sober now, my lord. Dramatic events have a habit of having that effect!'

Adam nodded. He leaned against the table and folded his arms. 'Did you know about any of this, Annis?'

Annis raised her brows. 'Which bit? That Charles and Ellis Benson were mixed up in the riots? Of course not. I thought that *you* knew!'

Adam shook his head. 'I confess that I wondered about Benson, but I had no idea about Lafoy. He has played his hand with an admirably cool nerve.' He gave her a searching look. 'Did you know about his feelings for Della? Good God, I could not believe my eyes when I saw her come flying out of the door to save him!'

Annis smiled a little. 'I knew about that five minutes before you and Edward arrived. We were sharing confidences in our cups...'

Adam's eyes narrowed. He pushed away from the table and took a step towards her. 'I see. And what were you telling Della in return, Annis?'

Annis busied herself fussing with the teapot and the cups. She leaned over the tray, allowing her hair to fall forwards to hide her face. 'I? Oh, not a great deal... She... I...'

'Yes?' Adam said. He took the tea cloth from her nerveless fingers and put it aside. 'What were you saying?'

Annis turned away. She wondered if perhaps some of the cider was still in her blood, or whether perhaps it was simply a night for taking risks.

'Della was saying that you loved me.'

'That is no great secret,' Adam said dryly. 'Go on.'

'And that she thought that I loved you too,' Annis finished in a rush. 'She thought that I was simply afraid to admit the truth.'

'Are you?' Adam said, after a pause. A hint of impatience came into his voice. 'Will you please put that teapot down and answer me, Annis?'

Annis turned and looked at him. There was an expression in his eyes that made her heart turn over. 'No,' she whispered.

She saw the hurt on his face before his expression turned studiously blank. 'I see,' he said dully.

'I am not afraid to admit it.' Even as she spoke, Annis was aware of the lie. She was afraid, very afraid. Her heart thudded and it was all that she could do to speak the words. 'I do love you, Adam. I love you very much.'

She thought later that she had never seen anyone move as quickly as Adam did then. One moment he was standing staring at her and the next she was in his arms, held closer than she had ever been before. His kiss was overwhelming, passion and tenderness rolled into one. Annis pressed closer and gave him back kiss for kiss, without restraint. After a time, she freed herself a little.

'Adam, I want to explain to you why—'

'Some other time.' Adam's voice, husky with desire, was barely recognisable. 'My darling Annis, I do not want to talk just now...'

Some unquantifiable amount of time later, Annis was aware of the kitchen door opening.

'I wondered if you needed any help—' Edward began, then stopped. 'Evidently not,' he said, and closed the door.

'I scarce know where to begin, Charles,' Annis said. A fresh pot of tea had been made and Annis, Adam, Edward, Charles and Della were seated in the drawing room. Charles and Della were holding hands. Della looked flushed and starrily happy and there was such a look of incredulous contentment about Charles that Annis could have cried. She herself was sitting close within the circle of Adam's arm in a quite improper manner, but nothing could have separated them at that moment. She could not bear to be far from his side.

'Is it you, or is it Ellis Benson, who has been leading the rioters against Mr Ingram's property?'

Charles looked relaxed and tousled in the firelight. 'It is Ellis who has been one of the leaders, although I do believe that he shares that privilege with Tom Shepard. All the rioters are masked and they take it in turns to raise the men, so it is more difficult to identify who is involved.'

Adam nodded. 'We knew about Shepard and we suspected Benson, but what about yourself, Lafoy?'

'The horse is yours, is it not, Charles?' Annis said suddenly. 'I saw it on my first visit here and I knew that the Shepards could not afford to keep a stable.'

Charles laughed. 'So you knew about that, did you? I thought you might have seen it, though Tom Shepard swore you had not.'

'I did glimpse him. A fine stallion. I had a very nasty feeling when Pullen started looking for someone who possessed such a beast.'

Charles looked shifty. 'Well, I assure you that I have not been riding him. I have had a hand in some of the planning, but the execution has been down to Ellis.'

'A difficult task,' Adam said drily, 'when trying to control an unruly mob of forty men.'

'Yes indeed.' Charles turned back to his cousin. 'Ellis has had some bad moments where your safety was concerned, Annis, not to mention my property. Since it was imperative that no one knew that I was working against Ingram, it was inevitable that I should be a target.'

Annis laughed. 'How unfortunate that your carriage should have been destroyed,' she said unsympathetically.

'Ellis was more concerned for your safety,' Charles said.

'He knew that you were not in the coach, but he did not know where you had gone. You gave him a fright that night, Annis. Until we received Ashwick's message we were scouring the countryside for you.'

Annis sighed. 'I am sorry. Though why I am apologising to a pair of law-breakers I am not certain! I am shocked, Charles. I had both you and Ellis down as Mr Ingram's most loyal supporters.'

'That was the idea,' Charles said drily. 'Do not judge Ellis too harshly, Annis. He has his reasons for what he did.'

Della spoke for the first time. 'What are his reasons, Charles?'

'He loves Venetia Ingram,' Charles said flatly. 'They care for each other. Ingram found out and made life a misery for Ellis, taunting him, tormenting him until he was nearly mad with the strain of it all. It changed him completely from being Ingram's man to being so set against him that I believe he would do almost anything to bring him down.'

There was a silence. Annis saw Della tighten her grip on Charles's hand. None of them, knowing Ingram as they did, could find it in themselves to condemn Ellis.

Annis sighed. 'What of your own motives, Charles?'

Charles shifted a little. 'I have known for a while that Ingram has been involved in some very questionable deals, but the man is as slippery as a fish and cannot be caught. I felt that he had to be stopped.'

'I see. Why not simply refuse to work with him any longer?'

Charles met her eyes very straight. 'That is not good enough, Annis. He has to be stopped.'

Annis saw Della smile, as though Charles had confirmed

something for her. She felt the same. Both of them had thought Charles a man of integrity and neither of them could understand how that fit with his work for Ingram. Now, at last, he was free to tell the truth.

Charles frowned. 'I am sorry for deceiving you, Annis, particularly over Starbeck. I wanted to help you so much— or at the least to reassure you—but too much was at stake. I almost cracked that day you came to Ingram's offices and as good as told me you would never speak to me again. Yet I could say nothing to you, for not only was it too danger- ous but I could never risk Ingram finding out what I was up to.' He looked at Adam. 'There were several occasions on which I thought you might be a useful ally too, Ashwick, but I could never risk Ingram guessing the truth. I apologise for my apparent hostility.'

Adam's arm tightened about Annis and he smiled at her. She knew that he was remembering the time she had told him how gloomy it was to be estranged from her cousin. Her heart lifted and she gave Adam a dazzling smile back.

'Perhaps there is still time for us all to unite against In- gram,' Adam said slowly.

Della yawned. She practically had her head on Charles's shoulder by now. 'Do you know anything about banknotes hidden here at Starbeck, Charles? Is that part of Mr Ingram's duplicity?'

Everyone looked at her. Annis, who had completely for- gotten about the notes in the canvas bag, jumped up. 'Oh, yes!' She turned to Adam. 'This was why we originally came to Starbeck today, my lord. Mrs Hardcastle found this when she was cleaning the house...'

She picked the remains of the canvas bag up from the side

table and held it out to him. Adam turned the bag over in his hands, studied the scrap of banknote and handed it over to Charles.

He squinted at it, then recoiled, his shock showing on his face. 'Good God! I have been looking for this everywhere!'

Now it was Annis's turn to feel shock. 'You mean that you knew? Charles—'

'I mean that I suspected that the *Northern Prince* had never gone down.' Charles looked at her. 'Did you not wonder why I was so edgy when you mentioned it the very first day you were back in Harrogate? I was afraid that you might alert Ingram's suspicions if you asked difficult questions!'

Edward, who had sat a little apart during the whole discussion, now leaned forward. 'You suspected that Ingram had saved some of the cargo from the ship, but you did not know where it was?'

'Exactly,' Charles said. 'Ellis and I looked everywhere. He certainly searched here. It was one of the reasons that we kept the house empty, Annis, for we were certain that Ingram was using it. It was conveniently isolated. Ellis will kick himself that he never found this, though.'

'I wonder why Ingram did not come back to take it,' Edward said thoughtfully. 'Or perhaps he did... If he had embezzled the cargo of the *Northern Prince* he might be helping himself to it little by little.'

'And I would guess that he wished the hue and cry to die down before he started to spend too lavishly,' Adam said. 'Is this all that there is, Annis?'

'I fear so. The mice have eaten all the rest, or shredded it into pieces so small that it cannot be identified.' Annis sighed. 'Della and I searched all day, as did Mrs Hardcastle, but all we found was a mouse nest. Whilst Ingram may not benefit from his ill-gotten gains, unfortunately we cannot pin anything on him.'

Adam picked up the scrap of bank note again. 'The Bank of England may be able to trace this note. If so, the insurers may be interested.'

'If the ship did not go down,' Annis said, 'where is it?'

Charles shook his head. 'I have spent many fruitless hours trying to discover precisely that, Annis. The *Northern Prince* sailed from Whitby and was supposedly lost shortly afterwards, but there are any number of rocky inlets where it might be possible to unload a cargo under cover of darkness and then...' Charles made a gesture '...the boat sails elsewhere. It is repainted, re-named. The ocean is a vast place and tracing one ship, proving that it has been re-named, would be a tricky business.'

'What of the crew?' Annis said, frowning. 'Surely there is someone who would give the game away?'

'Someone did,' Adam said grimly. 'Woodhouse knew what had happened, did he not? Either he knew, or he suspected. Maybe he even tried to extort money from Ingram for his silence and ended up head first down the chalybeate well for his pains!'

Charles sighed. 'The crew were hand-picked by Ingram and I imagine that they were well paid. Very well paid.'

'So Ingram pockets the insurance money and the cargo as well, and he still has a ship left at the end of it,' Adam said. 'Very neat.'

'Very risky,' Edward said. 'He pocketed your thirty thousand pounds as well, Adam. Humphrey never incurred that debt. He was cheated.'

Della raised her head. She was looking absolutely furious. 'Oh, Adam! I cannot bear it! The man gets away with all that money and we can prove nothing!'

They all looked dolefully at the scraps of mouse-eaten money.

'There is still the gold,' Charles said slowly. 'Ellis is convinced that Ingram secreted some bags of that as well. Do not forget that he was still Ingram's man at this point and was deeper in his confidence than I. The only thing he does not know is where it is hidden—or even if it is still hidden. Ingram may have spent it by now.'

'I do not think so,' Annis said thoughtfully. She turned to Adam. 'Remember what Woodhouse said, my lord. It was like a riddle and no doubt it gave Woodhouse a sense of power to taunt you so. He mentioned sunken treasure, and suggested that you look to the skies and into the depths. Supposing that the skies are Starbeck, then the sunken treasure is in the depths—at Starbeck.'

'Sunken,' Edward repeated. 'Can it be buried in the cellars, Lafoy?'

Charles shook his head. 'We have searched there. Several times.'

'Sunken, not buried,' Adam said. There was a blaze of light in his eyes. He turned to Annis. 'There is a well here at Starbeck, is there not? I saw it that day we came to inspect the property.'

'It is a natural sulphur well,' Annis confirmed. 'There are many hereabouts, as you know, my lord.'

Charles's face was a picture. 'A fine pair Ellis and I have been! Ingram hides his paper money in the house and his gold down the well right under our noses—and we cannot even find it! Of all the damned nerve!'

Annis laughed. 'We will have him yet, Charles.'

Adam stretched. 'We may check in the morning, I suppose.' He glanced at the clock. 'I do believe that it is almost the morning already.'

'Then all we have to do is think of a way to lure Ingram into giving himself away,' Annis said softly. 'Which is easier said than done, I suppose.'

There was a gleam in Adam's eye. 'I have a plan,' he said.

Some two days later, Annis and Della were both at the Starbeck once more, concealed in the summerhouse in the garden on the night that Adam intended to put his plan into action. 'I am beginning to regret this, Annis,' Della Tilney said. 'Adam and Charles both insisted that we should not stir outside the house all evening and who is to say that they were not right? We have no guarantee that Ingram will come. We might be immured in this summerhouse the whole night long and see nothing and achieve nothing but to be tired, hungry and aching! I am tempted to go back to the house.'

'Well, I am not.' Not for nothing had Annis defied Adam's instruction to stay safely indoors until the danger had passed. Starbeck was still hers, she thought fiercely, and if Ingram had been using it for his own nefarious purposes she wanted to be in at the end of it all when he was caught. She pressed closer to the summerhouse window and stared out into the starry night. Tonight there was no moon and the gardens were all in shadow.

'I am glad that you and Charles appear to have settled your differences, Della,' she said. 'I hope that the two of you will be happy.'

'There is nothing like a shock to bring one to one's senses,'

Della said. 'When I thought that Charles had been injured I could think of nothing but all the time we had wasted.' She sighed. 'I shall always feel guilty for what happened between us when Humphrey was alive, but I cannot carry that regret forever. And one has to live.' She smiled at Annis. 'It is your wedding in two days' time. Do I imagine it, or have you and Adam resolved all your differences, Annis?'

'Almost all.' Annis gave her a smile. 'I have only to explain to him the reasons why I was so reluctant in the first place. I feel I owe that to him—' She broke off. 'Della, look! Is that not a light? There, coming down the path—'

There was indeed the light from a lantern skipping down the path from the house, through the neglected topiary garden, dodging the bushes, faint but clear. The two girls pressed closer together. They watched as the figure came on, dark against the darker background, until it reached the walled garden and put its lantern down on the stones beside the well. There was the faintest creak of a chain and the splash of water.

'He is here!' Della clutched Annis. 'I did not believe that he would come.'

'Adam said that he would,' Annis whispered. 'He said that if Ingram were given a hint that his banknotes were found he would come to retrieve the rest. Charles dropped the hint. Ingram trusts him, so he did not guess that he was being tricked. That was all that was needed...'

'Look!' Della pointed. Beyond the walled garden, out on the drive, a column of light flared.

'They are coming!'

Annis was gripped by the same primitive fear that had caught her up on the night she had first witnessed the riot.

Suddenly the air seemed alive with it. Straining her ears, she heard the insistent beat of a drum on the night air. It had a ragged, savage rhythm, an undertone of violence.

The man in the garden heard it in the same instant and raised his head to sniff the air like a hunted animal. He scrambled to his feet, turning towards the gateway. There was only one way out of the walled garden and it was already too late. Already the procession was flooding through the gateway into the garden, torches blazing, and the barbaric rhythm of the drum filling the air. The light and shadow flickered over the faces of the masked men as they lined the walls.

Annis drew in a sharp breath. She could feel Della beside her, tense as a bowstring. There was something primitive here. In this seething crowd it was not possible to tell which was Charles, or Adam, or Edward or Tom Shepard. The masks were on, the tricorne hats drawn down over the eyes, the men dressed all in black tonight.

There was a clatter of hooves and the crowd parted with something like a sigh. The drumbeat died down. The magnificent bay stallion sidled almost gently up to the cowering figure by the well. The rebel leader raised his voice a little.

'I told you that we would come for you, Ingram.'

Samuel Ingram struggled to his feet and immediately two masked men came forward to take up their stance on either side of him. They did not touch him. There was no need. He was almost expiring with fear where he stood.

'Why do you not take your money?' The leader said gently. He turned the horse. 'Take it, Ingram. Pull it out of the well.'

Ingram fell to his knees, grappling feverishly with the chain of the well, half his gaze on the horse's circling hooves.

No one moved to help him. Everybody watched him. The torches flared in the breeze. The men stood like sentinels.

Eventually Ingram managed to haul up the bucket and dropped a dark, dripping canvas bag onto the grass.

'Open it,' the rebel leader said.

Ingram scrabbled at the neck of the bag. A few golden coins rolled out to lie amidst the grass and to sparkle in the torchlight. There was a rumble as the rest of the money fell out in a huge pile.

For a moment there was absolute stillness, then Ingram gave a high, keening cry of pain and loss and started to clutch hopelessly at the piles of tarnished coins. There was no gold here, only a mound of blackened metal with a greenish tinge. There was a strong smell of sulphur.

'Take your money, Ingram,' the leader said. He turned the bay stallion and Ingram flinched away from its hooves. 'Take your ill-gotten gains and run away. Spend it, Ingram! Spend all the money you have stolen from the poor and the dispossessed and the weak! Take it and run, before we come after you.'

Ingram scrabbled in the grass for the few golden coins that still sparkled there, shoving them in his pockets, staggering to his feet. The crowd parted silently for him. He cast a feverish look around, from masked face to masked face, reeling from one to the other as he tottered towards the gate. No one moved to stop him. No one moved at all.

Ingram looked back once as he reached the gateway, then took off into the night. Five long, slow seconds passed then, and with a roar, the mob suddenly poured through the gateway after him, the primeval beat of the drum in the air, the torches blazing. Ingram took to his heels and the rabble raced after him, spilling across the gardens and fields until the night was still.

Two men only remained in the walled garden. Charles Lafoy pulled off his mask, his eyes bright, laughing. Della opened the summerhouse door and tumbled out into his arms.

Annis stood waiting in the shadows, then came forward more slowly. The man on the bay stallion turned his horse unhurriedly and brought it alongside. He looked down at her for a long moment, eyes brilliant behind the mask, then, as he had done once before, he bent down and swept her up onto the saddlebow before him.

Annis turned into his arms. 'Adam,' she said, her mouth very close to his, 'swear to me that that was the first time you did that. Swear to me that you were never the rebel leader before tonight.'

She saw Adam grin, saw the blaze of triumph and satisfaction in his eyes. 'What do you think?' he said.

Chapter Thirteen

'There was gunpowder in those sacks originally,' Charles said as, later that night, they sat once again in the drawing room at Starbeck. 'Ellis told me that he had used canvas bags like that one and the one in the attic when he went hunting on the Linforth Estate. One of them must have held his bread and cheese and the other his gunpowder. An unconscionable piece of bad luck for Ingram.'

'I am no chemist,' Adam said, frowning, 'but I assume that the gunpowder and the sulphur water combined in some way to tarnish the silver—'

'Except for the coins at the very top of the bag,' Edward finished, 'which were undamaged.'

'Poor Mr Ingram,' Annis said. 'His whole ill-gotten fortune mouse-eaten and tarnished. He may be a ruthless businessman, but he is a hopeless criminal.'

There was a pause whilst they all tried to look suitably sober, then everyone burst out laughing.

'Are you certain that he got away?' Della asked. 'For all

that I detest the man, I could not bear him to be torn to pieces by the mob.'

Adam's smile faded. 'He is safe,' he said shortly. 'We chose the men carefully tonight and they had their instructions.'

'What will happen to Ingram now?' Annis asked. 'Will he be prosecuted?'

Charles nodded. 'I believe so. There is sufficient evidence from the bank note and the gold for a number of difficult questions to be asked. The insurance companies will be very interested. And the Admiralty will probably put a watch out for a ship answering the description of the *Northern Prince*. Even if Ingram escapes prosecution he is ruined. I imagine he may well run away abroad.'

'I am sure he will,' Edward said quietly. 'He is a laughing-stock. The whole of Harrogate society will dine out on this for weeks.'

Annis shivered. 'It was very humiliating for him, was it not? I confess to feeling not quite comfortable seeing a man brought so low.'

Adam's face was hard. 'Annis, even when the man was at his lowest ebb he was scrabbling in the grass for his money! That was all that mattered to him.'

'You are too forgiving, coz,' Charles agreed. 'Remember how he threatened to take Starbeck from you.' His voice was bleak. 'Think, if you will, of the people who were thrown off their land by him, the men who could no longer scrape a living, the tolls that were too high... People have almost starved and died through Ingram's greed and cruelty.' He laughed shortly. 'I thought you were remarkably measured tonight, Ashwick.'

There was a little silence.

'What of the rioting?' Annis asked. 'Do you think that that will be at an end now, Charles?'

'I imagine so. Ellis Benson stirred much of that up; now that Ingram is brought down, Ellis will be much more at peace. Besides, without Ingram to impose his harsh rents and tolls, I imagine that the unrest in the countryside will die away.'

Charles looked at Adam. 'I am sorry that you are the loser from this case, Ashwick, having paid Lord Tilney's debt to Mr Ingram. If he has embezzled money from the sinking of the *Northern Prince*, all debts must be null and void, but I doubt if you will see your money again. We will have to see what we can do.'

Adam held out his hand. 'It is enough to know that Ingram is brought down, Lafoy.' He grinned. 'Although the money would come in handy as well!'

After Mrs Hardcastle had taken Charles and Della and Edward up to their improvised bedchambers, Annis turned to Adam.

'I must go up in a minute, for I am sharing a chamber with Della and would not wish her to imagine that I am staying down here with you, Adam.' She looked dubiously at the hard couch. 'Will you be quite comfortable? I seem to remember that this sofa was lumpy even in my father's day!'

Adam sighed, rubbing his cheek against her hair. 'I have no doubt that I shall be very uncomfortable, my sweet, not least because I shall be imagining you sleeping so close by! As for Della, I hope that you find she *is* in your chamber! I should hate to have to call Lafoy out when I am starting to like him so much!'

Annis smiled. She rested her head briefly against his

shoulder. 'I am so glad, Adam. And I do believe they shall be very happy.' She yawned and stood up. 'I am for my bed. As for the proprieties, we should not worry. What could be more respectable than having a vicar in the house?'

'The rabble-rousing vicar of Eynhallow!' Adam laughed. 'Sometimes I think that Ned was born in the wrong century!'

The wedding guests arrived from London the following day and despite Annis's qualms about meeting Adam's friends, she had to admit that for the most part they seemed harmless. The Duke of Fleet was indeed so thoroughly charming that Annis could quite see why Miss Mardyn had chosen him as her protector. The Earl of Tallant, despite being one of the most handsome man that Annis had ever met, was pleasantly self-deprecating and so utterly in love with his sweet little wife that it brought an ache to Annis's throat to see them together. Only Lady Juliana Myfleet, the Earl's sister, was a different matter. She kissed Adam far too lingeringly for Annis's taste, purred that Annis had caught the man she had always wanted to marry, then went on to entertain the company with malicious observations about various mutual friends. Since Annis had never met any of these people she felt pointedly excluded and certain that Juliana was doing it on purpose. She felt herself becoming quieter as dinner wore on that night, answering only briefly the questions put to her, her insecurities threatening to come back and swamp her. After the scene with Adam in the kitchen at Starbeck she had not had the opportunity to speak with him, for first there had been the matter of trapping Ingram and then all the wedding guests had arrived, taking all Adam's time and his attention. Consequently there had been no moment for private discussion and there was still one matter left unspoken between them.

'You must not mind Juliana,' Amy Tallant said shyly that night as she accompanied Annis upstairs after dinner. 'She is not happy and so she sharpens her claws on other people. She is particularly sharp with those who have what she does not—love.'

Annis grimaced. 'Adam has intimated that she has had an unhappy past.'

Amy nodded. 'In the same way that Adam loved Mary, Juliana was sincerely in love with her first husband, but whereas Adam has found love again, we despair of Juliana ever being happy.'

When Amy had left her, Annis felt too wakeful to go to her room. Tomorrow was her wedding day and she knew that she should try to sleep, but she felt too restless. She took up her cloak, intending to go for a walk in the gardens. She knew that Adam would be busy entertaining his male guests, but she needed some reassurance, some element of him to hold to her. She went out of her bedroom and, on impulse, pushed open the door of Adam's dressing room. After a moment's hesitation, she slipped in. The clothes that Adam had been wearing before dinner had not yet been put away and, succumbing to temptation, Annis went over to the bed and picked up his jacket, slipping her arms into the sleeves. It was far too big for her. She wrapped it about her and turned her face against the collar, rubbing her cheek against the rough twill, inhaling the scent of him. It smelled of smoke and sandalwood and Adam. It turned her knees to water.

Annis closed her eyes. She loved Adam so much and she

knew she did not have to be afraid of anything. This was no marriage trap and with the right man she was as free as she chose to be. She could fly but she would never fly away, for she did not want to. Adam had taken her on trust, not forcing her to tell him what had happened to her but giving her all of the time she needed to reach the point where she would choose to trust him too.

There was a step in the doorway. Annis opened her eyes. Adam was standing there, watching her. His face was in shadow, his expression hidden. Annis suddenly realised that she was still wearing his coat. She slipped it from her shoulders and dropped it on the bed.

'I was coming to look for you,' Adam said. 'You were so quiet at dinner that I was worried about you.' His voice was a little rough. His gaze went from her to the discarded jacket and back again. 'Annis?'

'I would like to talk to you, Adam,' Annis said softly. 'May we? Not here.' She gestured around the candlelit room. 'It is a pleasant night. I should like to talk outside.'

Adam stood back wordlessly to allow her to precede him through the door. They went down the stairs in silence and out into the night. The lighted windows of Eynhallow Hall faded into the dark behind them. The stones of the carriage sweep were sharp through Annis's slippers. She crossed on to the soft grass and made for the edge of the wood, slipping under the arch of the trees and into the heart of the forest. She could hear Adam's footsteps behind her, the crack of the twigs beneath their feet, the sound of his breathing. Neither of them spoke.

Annis reached a small clearing where the moon spun patterns through the trees and turned to face him.

'That night when we were in the kitchen at Starbeck... I was going to tell you then what I had been afraid of, Adam— the reasons that I held back from marriage. I am sorry that I could not tell you before.'

'Do not be. It was not the right time.'

'And now it is? You have been very patient with me, Adam.'

She saw the shadow of his smile. 'I told you before that I was prepared to wait for what I wanted. You have not kept me waiting very long at all, Annis.'

Annis sat down on the stump of a tree.

'I never wanted to marry again. You knew that—I told you from the first. It was not because I was afraid of intimacy, or...or that I had had an unpleasant experience in the past, at least not in any physical sense.'

Adam took her hand. 'I never thought that. At least, I wondered if that was the case at first, but then I realised that you were not repulsed by my touch, nor were you afraid.' He entwined his fingers with hers.

Annis gave a shaky laugh. 'I must beg you not to touch me yet, or I shall never finish the story.'

'Very well. I can grant you a few moments at least.'

'It was another sort of intimacy I dreaded.' Annis hesitated. 'I married at seventeen, immediately after my parents died.' She sighed. 'I suppose that they had spoiled me. The time I spent in Bermuda that summer had been the best of my life. I ran wild in the sand and the sunshine, I was unsuitably tanned, and I knew I was frowned upon by the ladies who had transported English society rules out to the Indies with them, but I did not care.' She smiled at Adam. 'I was heedless and a hoyden, and then my father was killed in a naval action and my mother went into a decline and died, and the whole structure of my life came crashing down.' She looked away. 'I had not realised until then how gravely I had transgressed. The whole weight of a disapproving society seemed to be resting on me, forcing me to conform. I was left almost penniless and there were rumours... Oh, unfounded ones, of course, but the kind of gossip that circulates when a girl is different and a little wild.'

She jumped to her feet and took a few paces away.

'Sir John Wycherley offered me security. He was older and comfortably off, and he had the gallantry to offer me the protection of his name. I was in a haze of grief and loneliness; I had no money... I took the offer.'

'That is understandable. Your parents had both died and you were left with nothing.' Adam's voice was rough. 'You cannot blame yourself for such a decision, Annis.'

'Yes, but I had no notion what it would mean!' Annis turned to him. 'Oh, Adam, I was seventeen and I was trapped into a domesticity that almost swallowed me alive! I had no time to myself, no money of my own, no identity! I was Annis, Lady Wycherley, not Annis Lafoy any more, and I had to eat, sleep and behave as my husband demanded. Why, John chose my clothes and my friends and if I were to go out alone, he would demand that I account to him for every second that I spent away!' Annis put both hands up to her head. 'Worse, he would lock me up if it suited him, and dictate my every move! Before long I thought that my very identity would disappear, utterly submerged beneath the woman that Sir John Wycherley had fashioned. I felt so trapped that it made me ill.'

There was a silence.

'No wonder that you had no wish to submit yourself to a husband ever again,' Adam said quietly.

'No.' Annis swallowed hard. 'I tried to disregard my fears, but I could not quite do it. But it was marriage that I wished to avoid, Adam, never you yourself.' Annis hesitated. 'Deep down I think that I knew it would not be like being married to John. I knew that you and he were completely different people. Yet I was so afraid. I had worked so hard to achieve some freedom. That was why I could not bear to give up Starbeck even when I could not afford to keep it. That was why I found it so difficult to agree to marriage even when I had no way out.'

Adam put his arm about her and pulled her against him. 'And now?'

'Now I realise that marriage to you will not be a cage but...' Annis smiled a little tremulously '...an adventure, perhaps?'

Adam kissed her.

'I swear I shall never bully you, or tyrannise over you, or tell you what to do.' He spoke into her hair. 'I love you, Annis. I love you exactly as you are and I would never want to change you.'

Annis played with one of the buttons of his coat, suddenly shy at what she was about to say. 'Adam—'

'What is it, sweet?'

'I love you, Adam. Will you make love to me? Here, in the woods, with the smoke on the air and the touch of the breeze on my skin...'

There was a moment of absolute stillness, then Adam's grip tightened on her with bruising intensity.

'Annis, are you sure? For once I have done that I shall never let you go.'

Annis stood on tiptoe to kiss him. 'I do not want you to let me go. Please…'

The pent-up feelings between them could no longer be denied. Adam's kiss was violent in its intent and its effect, seeking, searching, demanding everything. Annis pulled away a little, tilting her head back, a hot triumph racing through her blood. The kick of excitement was like a fever.

Adam found the ribbon that tied her cloak and gave it a tug, so that it unfurled and the velvet slid to the ground in a slippery pool. The night was warm but Annis still noticed the loss. It was as though some part of her had been stripped away, some protection had gone. There was no going back.

Adam's hands were hard on her waist, holding her still as he kissed her again, his tongue tangling with hers. One of his hands came up to her breast, pulling apart the bodice of her gown, sending buttons flying. His warm fingers cupped her breast through the thin linen of her chemise and Annis crumpled to the ground. The leaves of a previous autumn and the soft, dry bracken provided a makeshift mattress, but neither of them was really noticing. All Annis was aware of was the cold breeze against her heated skin and the wood smoke in the air… She was naked to the waist and Adam had taken one nipple in his mouth, sucking, biting, teasing until she thought she would dissolve with blind need. She moaned aloud and he covered her mouth with his in a deep, possessive kiss. Her skirts were up around her waist, her legs parted, the cold night air against her skin. And then he was bending over her, his lips again roughly demanding as he spread her arms wide, entangling his fingers with hers on the bed of bracken as he slid hard and fast inside her.

There was a momentary pause—she felt it, he felt it too. Then he started to move, the sleek friction dragging a whimper from her as she felt the desire shudder through her body. So soon, so quickly. She felt herself tumble over the edge of mindless pleasure, powerless to help herself.

Some semblance of normal thought returned and she tried to pull away from him, belatedly aware, wanting to cover her nudity. But Adam was desperate too. He held her arms apart, his gaze feasting on her nakedness as she writhed with pleasure, beneath him in the moonlight. Hot and hard, the relentless rhythm would not let her go. Annis thought she would faint from the very sensation of it. Then he gave a shout that would have raised all the birds from the trees, and drove into her with all his urgent need, finally reaching his release. And Annis, astonished and bewitched at the power she had over him, felt the same sensual desire capture her again and send her spiralling down into bliss.

For a while they lay still, wrapped in the velvet cloak. Adam's arms were about her. He refused to let go. After a while he said softly, 'Why didn't you tell me?'

Annis wriggled a little. His body felt warm and hard against hers and she could not remember a time when she had felt so happy and so absolutely free.

'Tell you what? That I had never been with a man before? I did not wish you to make a fuss. You would have insisted that we be all decorous the first time, in bed...' Annis laughed and moved languidly. 'This was much better. This was what I wanted.'

'How did it happen?'

'You mean how did it *not* happen?' Annis laughed. 'My husband was not interested in women.'

'You mean—'

'I do not know if he was interested in men instead. Possibly so. At first I thought it was me.' She paused. 'Then I observed him with other ladies and realised that they did not interest him at all. In fact, I believe that he held a very low opinion of our sex. There are plenty of men who do.'

'You never wished to take a lover?'

'Never, until now.' Annis rubbed her hand along the line of his jaw. 'And now it is too late, for I am about to be married to him.'

Adam kissed her again, softly. 'Do you wish to go back inside and make love again?'

'Again?' Annis smiled, her face dreamy in the starlight, her tone bemused. 'May we?'

Adam laughed. 'Annis, you delight my soul. We may, if you wish it. I swear it will be better next time.'

'It is difficult to imagine, but if you will show me...' She caressed his cheek. 'Must we go back inside?'

'Not if you prefer it here.' Adam's voice had roughened again. He spread the cloak under them and stripped her of her remaining clothing. The moon had risen. She was edged in silver, tip-tilted breasts, smooth skin and shadows.

'Your clothes too...' She sounded dreamy.

'Of course.'

He lay beside her, half-covering her, his hands smoothing, stroking. They kissed, languid and warm where they touched. It was gentle and urgent. Annis, running her hands over the planes of his body with love and wonderment, could not quite believe that it could be true. Or that she could know such ecstasy. Adam bent his head to her breast and his fingers stroked the inside of her thigh. Annis squirmed.

'Open your eyes,' he said. 'I want to look at you.'

She looked into his face and saw all the love and desire and tenderness fused in the blazing passion in his eyes.

'I love you,' he said.

The feeling of him inside her was exquisite and she rose to meet him, dazzled by sensation, consumed with pure love. And then they slept, intertwined, Adam's head against Annis's breast, both wrapped together closer than close inside the cocoon of the velvet cloak.

Annis woke as the birds started to stir and the first light filtered down through the branches into the wild wood. She felt a little stiff and chilly, but she pressed closer to Adam for warmth and rubbed her cheek against the silky softness of his hair. He made a sleepy sound of contentment and her heart melted.

'Adam… It is the morning and we should go back to the house…'

Adam made another sleepy sound, this time of agreement. He did not move. Annis smiled a little to herself. 'Adam…'

She ventured a small caress. Adam made another sound, though this time it was more like a groan. His eyes opened. 'Sweetheart, if you do that we shall not be going anywhere.'

Annis gave him a wicked little smile. 'I fear I may have developed a…a partiality for making love in the woods…'

Adam tumbled her into his arms. 'So have I, sweetheart. So have I. It is fortunate that I own such a great tract of woodland where we may not be disturbed…'

Eventually they strolled back lazily to the house in the

morning of their wedding day. The sun was coming up and it was going to be a glorious day. Annis had her head on Adam's shoulder and his arm was close about her waist.

'Speaking of love,' she said, 'did you see how Ned was watching Lady Juliana during dinner last night? He was so distracted I thought that he would forget to eat. I do believe he has a *tendre* there, Adam.'

Adam laughed ruefully. 'Poor Ned. He has been in love with her this age, but I fear he is wasting his time there. Juliana is way beyond his star.'

'Yet she is not very happy,' Annis said presciently. 'For all her beauty and her glamour, I do believe true happiness eludes her.' She looked up at Adam's face.

'And then there is poor Ellis Benson,' Annis went on, 'languishing for love of Venetia Ingram. I wonder what will happen to her now that Ingram is disgraced?'

'Must you be so melancholy on our wedding day?' Adam grumbled. 'All this talk of unfulfilled love...' He paused, then laughed. 'Actually, my love, you have reminded me. I fear you must include Seb Fleet on your list of thwarted lovers, for he told me yesterday that Margot Mardyn has run off and left his protection.'

Annis raised her brows. 'Has she, indeed? With whom?'

Adam looked at her expectantly. Annis narrowed her eyes. 'Not Lieutenant Greaves?'

'No, no, it is more piquant than that!' Adam smiled. 'I always suspected that Margot would exchange a life on the stage for the respectability of a wedding ring if only she could find a man willing to offer one. I understand that she is the new Lady Doble.'

Annis stared. 'Lady Doble? But Sir Everard... But Fanny Crossley...'

Adam grinned. 'I told you that it was piquant! There you were, assuming that Miss Crossley was the flighty one, when in fact it was Sir Everard who made the runaway match.'

Annis pressed her hand to her mouth. 'Oh, no!' She looked at him suspiciously. 'Did you have any inkling, Adam?'

'I confess I did.' Adam laughed. 'I mentioned his name to her on the very first day we were in Harrogate, after I had rejected her advances myself!' He cast Annis a look and saw she was frowning at him fearsomely. 'I thought it would help her,' he added apologetically. 'After that, I saw them together a couple of times, but when I heard that Sir Everard was betrothed to Miss Crossley I assumed it was just an *affaire*...'

'You men are disgraceful!' Annis said.

Adam smiled. 'Sweetheart, you have nothing of which to complain. I told you that I had rejected her advances!' He drew her unyielding body closer. 'I have no interest in any woman but you, as I have just demonstrated.'

'So I should hope,' Annis said, struggling half-heartedly to be released. 'And Fanny has received her come-uppance, I suppose. It is just a shame that everyone is in love with the wrong people!'

'Not everyone.' Adam bent to kiss her.

'It is supposed to be bad luck for the bridegroom to see the bride on the night before the wedding,' Annis said.

Adam laughed. 'It is fortunate that it was dark then, for I cannot feel luckier than I do now.' He turned to smile at her. 'I hope that you will still meet me in church later, Annis?'

Annis felt a smile curve her lips. 'I shall be there.'

'That is good, for I was afraid that you might have changed

your mind. You always said that matters looked very different in the morning.'

Annis snuggled closer to him and turned to face the rising sun. 'Oh, they do, my love. They look better. In fact, they look perfect.'

They were married six hours later.

* * * * *

MILLS & BOON®

Find out more about our
latest releases, authors
and competitions.

 Like us on facebook.com/millsandboonaustralia

 Follow us on twitter.com/millsandboonaus

 Find us at millsandboon.com.au